P9-CCU-346

7th SON:
DES(C)ENT

WITHDRAWN

ALSO BY J. C. HUTCHINS

Personal Effects: Dark Art
(with Jordan Weisman)

7th SON:
DESENT

J. C. Hutchins

 St. Martin's Griffin ≈ New York

This is a work of fiction. All of the characters, organizations, and events portrayed in this novel are either products of the author's imagination or are used fictitiously.

7TH SON: DESCENT. Copyright © 2009 by J. C. Hutchins. All rights reserved. Printed in the United States of America. For information, address St. Martin's Press, 175 Fifth Avenue, New York, N.Y. 10010.

www.stmartins.com

Library of Congress Cataloging-in-Publication Data

Hutchins, J. C., 1975–
    7th son : descent / J.C. Hutchins.—1st ed.
        p. cm.
    ISBN 978-0-312-38437-1
    1. Human cloning—Fiction. 2. Assassins—Fiction. I. Title.
II. Title: Seventh son.
    PS3608.U859A615 2009
    813'.6—dc22   2009017010

First Edition: November 2009

10 9 8 7 6 5 4 3 2 1

For Eleanor
God only knows.

ACKNOWLEDGMENTS

W riting a book is a lonesome task. Delivering that book into readers' hands is not.

What you're holding is the result of hundreds of hours of effort, put forth by thousands of supremely generous and talented individuals. I've had the great pleasure to meet some of these people. Others, I never will. All deserve my sincerest gratitude.

Kristin Lindstrom, thank you for believing in this book and its author, and seeing something here that others did not. A thousand-thousand thanks go to you for your relentless support, and for representing someone who likes to color outside the lines.

Joel Gotler, you have been a tenacious advocate of my work. You've also taught me the value of good ideas. I cherish both contributions more than I can express. Thank you.

David Moldawer, I'm convinced that I wouldn't be typing these words right now were it not for your sincere belief in my work. Thank you. The beer will always be on me.

To Michael Homler, Matthew Shear, Lisa Senz, Sarah Goldstein, Katy Hershberger, Michael Storrings, Phil Pascuzzo, and the rest of the wickedly talented team at St. Martin's Press: Thank you for embracing *7th Son: Descent*, and championing it. I'm honored to be a part of the family. Your invaluable contributions and perspective made *7th Son: Descent* a better book.

Scott Sigler, you are a wily, boundlessly creative man, and your professional drive provides daily inspiration. Thank you for being a tireless advocate of my work, for our collaborations, and your advice. The world's yours. Just let me keep the 7thSonShine State.

Evo Terra, Tee Morris, and Chris Miller: Muchly gratitude to you three, who experienced *7th Son* before darned-near anyone else. Thank you for the encouragement, and for accompanying me on this wild ride.

Big thanks to my family, friends, and MotionPoint coworkers, for their cheers as I wrote *7th Son: Descent*. It made all the difference in the world.

To my many creative social media colleagues, particularly my podcasting and "podcast novelist" friends: Thank you for your dogged evangelism and support. Special thanks roll out to authors Sigler, Morris, Mark Jeffrey, Matthew Wayne Selznick, and Jack Mangan, whose stellar work in 2005 helped convince me to release my own fiction online. A special hat-tip goes out to authors Mur Lafferty and Matt Wallace, who—in addition to being unbelievably talented—are two of my best friends. You have all been both wind and anchor during this journey.

And to the tens of thousands of people worldwide who listened to *7th Son: Descent* online, evangelized it, believed in it . . . and believed in me: You, more than anyone else, made this book a reality. Your support, more than anything, convinced me the tale I was telling was worthwhile. Your e-mails, your calls, your comments, your instant messages . . . your vociferous *belief* made *7th Son: Descent* more than words on a screen, or a voice in your headphones. "Thank you" does not convey what I wish to express to you, but it is all I have.

From the bottom of my heart to the tips of my fingers, thank you.

Now, let's go tell more stories together.

E-mail J.C. at 7thSonNovel@gmail.com.

7th SON:
DESCENT

PROLOGUE

T he president of the United States is dead. He was murdered in the morning sunlight by a four-year-old boy.

It was a simple stumping rally in Kentucky, no more than a pit stop on Tobacco Road. The Bluegrass State would vote Republican in next year's election, just as it had in the past two. At least that's what President Hank "Gator" Griffin said on this crisp October morning at Bowling Green College.

His speech was a barn-raiser, a helluva thing, roiling with Bible Belt–friendly sound bites. Keep the country strong. Reelect morality. Reelect character and faith. Next November, reelect Griffin and Hale.

God bless America. Waving now, working the crowd. Pump-pump handshake. Wink. Thank you. Kiss the lady. Hold the baby. Listen to the cheers.

Listen, as they turn to screams.

It happened so quickly: a smile and nod from the four-year-old's parents, a kiss on little Jesse Fowler's cheek for the photographers, a glint of silver in the boy's hand, the president's carotid artery open at the jaw, the scarlet wound arcing across his throat like a comet. The child's face spattered in red mist, the president's mouth forming a question, the boy's tiny teeth glittering white in the camera flashbulbs, a cry from a Secret Service agent.

The president did not stagger, did not sway; he crumpled at the knees, face white as bone. His forehead split open as it struck the sidewalk. There were many screams, many arms around him. A Secret Service agent grabbed the murderous boy as he dashed between a photographer's legs. The agent lifted Jesse Fowler high, by the ankle. The boy was furious, screaming obscenities no four-year-old should know. He swung his switchblade at the agent, knocking off the man's sunglasses. He swung again. And again.

More hands around the president. More screams from the crowd. Fowler's parents rushing the agent in shock, trying to protect their son. Secret Service agents covering Griffin's body with their own, his blood seeping into their suits. A scream rising from the child as he swung upside down by his ankle.

A chopper soon descended onto the campus's common field, its downdraft ripping the GRIFFIN/HALE signs from shocked spectators' hands. The president and an army of Secret Service and medical agents arrived at the Bowling Green hospital three minutes later. But Hank "Gator" Griffin was already dead by then.

During the chaos at the college, little Jesse Fowler had been disarmed and tossed into the backseat of a police cruiser. His parents were also apprehended.

Just before the vehicle carrying the world's youngest political assassin peeled away from the scene, a photojournalist snapped a picture of the child. It would have been worthy of the Pulitzer Prize, had it been published. In the photo, Jesse Fowler's tiny blood-stained hands were pressed against the car's rear window. He gazed at a spattered GRIFFIN/HALE sign, which was reflected in the cruiser's window in one of those remarkable moments of photojournalism.

The child's bloodshot eyes were wide. He was laughing.

By noon that day, Vice President Vincent Hale had been sworn in as the leader of the world's last superpower. Secretary of State Charles Caine was appointed VP.

The child's parents, Jennifer and Jackson Fowler, were arraigned on charges of conspiring to murder the president of the United States. The small Bowling Green restaurant they owned would never open again.

Their son was placed under maximum security in an undisclosed government facility for evaluation and interrogation. A week later, a nurse and an armed guard discovered Jesse Fowler's body. The four-year-old was lying in bed, his mouth and eyes open, dead. There were no signs of self-asphyxiation. There was no overdose, no theatrical cyanide capsule, no reasonable cause of death. Just the dried remains of a nosebleed, and eyes so bloodshot the whites had gone completely red.

Jesse Fowler had said only one thing during that week of confinement and examination. A balding, bearded doctor had asked the boy if he knew what he'd done to the president.

Jesse Fowler had looked at the doctor and giggled.

"Go fuck your mother," he'd said.

ONE

S aturday sex with Sarah was the best, John Smith decided. The very best. It was long, sweaty, dirty; nipple nibbles, fingernails raking the back and chest, obscene whispers, incomplete sentences. Headboard practically banging into the neighboring apartment's living room. Open windows to let the November Miami breeze cool them—and to let the rest of the world shift uncomfortably with envy. That sort of sex.

John marveled at this as he pulled himself off her body, panting, staring up at the ceiling with an expression that was half self-satisfaction, half awe. Sarah grabbed a sheet from the floor, laughed long and loud, and rolled sideways to face him. The sheet stuck to her sweaty breasts and hips. She brushed a red curl from her face.

"Unbelievable," she said.

John gazed at the ceiling and shook his head. "I know."

"It's getting better."

He shook his head again and blinked. "I *know*."

Sarah smiled. "You should write a song about it."

"Uh, how about 'Christ Almighty, Do Me All Nighty.' "

"You could've done better than that," she snorted, and climbed out of bed. John watched Sarah's hips as she gracefully stepped through his cramped bedroom, traversing the thirtysomething's version of hopscotch: a pile of books on the floor, last night's clothes, several ratty folders filled with sheet music, an empty box of Trojans, his Gibson guitar. She was nimble and beautiful, and John wondered, not for the first time, what she saw in him.

She opened the bedroom door. John's fat, fuzzy cat scrambled past her legs and leaped onto the bed. He stomped onto John's chest and meowed, malcontent.

"Buzz off, Cat," John said.

"You need to buy him food," Sarah said, stepping into the living room on her way to the bathroom. "You said it yourself last night. And, Jesus . . . you should really clean up this place."

"Right," he called. "Wanna help?"

Sarah laughed. "Your house. Your mess. You clean it up."

"Mañana."

John reached over and plucked a lighter and crumpled pack of cigarettes from the far end of the bedside table. He shook the pack, and two bent—but, thank God, not broken—Camel Lights rattled out and into his palm. He lit one, inhaled, and gazed at the ceiling.

Cat meowed again, sounding more surly this time. John absently scratched the critter's head, regarding him with a mixture of disdain and fondness. As Sarah showered, John watched the palm trees sway outside the window, stroked Cat, and finished his smoke.

He'd already put on a T-shirt and pulled his hair into a ponytail when Sarah came back into the room.

"Where ya going, stud?"

"Nowhere. Just to the Castle," he replied, slipping on a pair of jeans. "Gotta get the cat his food, and get me some more smokes."

Sarah looked at the unlit Camel by the ashtray. "I'm out, too."

"Have that one," John said, and kissed her. "Try to live through the nasty nonmenthol flavor. I'll take the bike. Won't be long."

Outside, as he pedaled his ten-speed into the apartment complex parking lot, Sarah called down to him from the balcony. She told him to hurry. She made a joke about how red-haired maidens reward bicycle-riding knights with breakfast and "muchly" hot sex . . . particularly if they come bearing cancer sticks.

John laughed, imagining her in bed, his head between her thighs, and said he'd pedal as fast as he could.

Alleys—honest-to-goodness damp, dark, well-worn shortcut alleys—were one of the things John missed most while living in Miami. Cycling always reminded him of his childhood in the Midwest, and of bike races with neighborhood kids, up and down the alleys. Miami was a driver's city, a twentieth-century city, a pink place that had no love for kick-the-can or cobblestones. This was the land of the planned community, where "historic home" meant that the paint on a house's shutters had just dried.

As he pedaled to the Castle convenience store—*Zero Hassle at the Castle!*—John pined for alleys and shortcuts, redbrick roads that led to scrappy basketball rims and tree houses. But there was no sense begrudging it. Miami was different. Neither better nor worse, just different. And since Miami had been around a lot longer than John had, he thought it best to adapt.

Besides, Miami had palm trees. And November weather like this.

He was making a quick turn onto Flamingo, a scenic residential road that would add a few minutes to his ride—but what the hey, it was Saturday—when he spotted the white van barreling toward him.

I don't think it sees me, he thought. *If it did, it wouldn't be going so fa—*

John yanked the bike to the left, gripped both brakes, and

nearly flew over the handlebars. The van's tires screeched. John's bike swerved between two parked cars, a Lexus and a very old, very cherry Beetle, *and isn't it the damnedest things you notice at moments like this?* The bike's front wheel struck the curb. John spilled onto the sidewalk, felt the flesh tear on his palm and chin.

He heard the van's front doors open, the rear slide-door whoosh along its rail, and the click-click of expensive dress shoes. John tried to slip out from under the ten-speed, but his foot was stuck on the chain. He looked up. Three men sporting sharp suits and crew cuts surrounded him.

"You know, a little help here would—"

"Grab him," the biggest suit said, and the other two pounced. Their gloved hands locked on to John's upper arms like talons, yanking him from under the bike in one fluid motion, as if he were in some street-fighter ballet.

One of the men twisted John's left arm behind his back—*say uncle, isn't it the damnedest things you notice?*—and John howled. The other suit held John's right arm out straight, like a wing. John couldn't move. He couldn't speak. They were going to break his arm; John could feel the muscles pulling apart.

The third man, the big suit, stepped before him. The stranger had gray eyes, a flat nose, a cleft in his chin, cheekbones carved from marble. No emotion was on that face. The men stood there on the sidewalk for what felt like an excruciating eternity.

Finally, the man raised his eyebrows. "You want it to stop?"

John nodded his head furiously.

The big man inhaled and exhaled slowly. "Good. Now. You're going to take a little ride with us."

The pain in John's left arm eased a little, and he used the moment to heave his body from side to side. His outstretched arm tore away from its captor and swung outward. He screamed for help. The talon on the throbbing wrist behind his back slipped slightly. He was going to do it, going to do it, going to run, going to break—

No air. *No air.*

The leader, the one with the Superman chin, punched John in the stomach a second time. Then a third. John fell to the sidewalk, clutching his midsection, cradling it like a squirming baby. Through the haze, he saw one of the men toss the ten-speed into the back of the van. He spotted the other with a syringe, felt the bee sting of the needle, then things became pleasant, sweet, dark, darker.

He heard one last thing before he lost consciousness, the leader's voice.

"Should've come quietly, Johnny-boy."

When Michael was a child, his mother and father took him for a drive through Indiana's corn country, the place where that state's true heart would always beat. American flags, high school basketball, Old-Time Religion. Those things were in the soil of the state—no, deeper than that even, a layer of bedrock geologists could never fathom. The drive into the heartland took two hours from where they lived in Indianapolis.

Michael had been only nine at the time, but he had noticed the transformation of the horizon during that drive: the mortar and steel of city giving way to the bland homes of the suburbs. Then, with the abruptness of a beachhead, the land of station wagons and culs-de-sac relinquished control to the flat expanse of Indiana's heart. The corn. It was a sea, Michael thought back then. Bright green combines occasionally slipped through its waves like barges. And like the sea, the corn could barely be contained; it ebbed just feet from the road.

There, at a family picnic by the roadside, Michael's mother had told him that places were like people; they had personalities. More important, she said, they had emotions. Souls. Sometimes you could feel the soul of a place. Michael had munched on a peanut butter sandwich and asked her what she meant.

"Close your eyes," she said. "Listen. Just breathe and listen. Listen with your ears. What do you hear?"

Quiet, he'd said. Grasshoppers. Corn leaves slapping against each other. A bird. The wind.

"Now what do you *feel*?" she asked.

Nice. Peaceful. Love, maybe.

"Maybe that's what this place is like," his mother said. "Maybe this place is peaceful, loving. Gentle. Maybe that is this place's soul. It's important to listen to a place sometimes, to hear what it thinks. Understand?"

Michael said he did, a little. Maybe. His mother laughed and kissed him on the cheek and said that maybe he would understand when he was older. He'd finished his sandwich, took a sip of cherry Hi-C from his thermos, and went to play Frisbee with his father.

Michael had never forgotten that conversation. And while he understood its mysteries now about as much as he had then, he always made time to close his eyes and listen to a new place. It had come in handy years later when he went to Parris Island, and then to Kosovo and Afghanistan and other countries with alien names and landscapes. Those places held power over their inhabitants. That faraway day's lesson had dovetailed with what he learned in boot, and later in Force Recon training. Know the land, and you'll know the people.

Michael knew Gitmo. He'd been here for only a week, and he knew it. Gitmo was angry. Gitmo was confused. Under the Kevlar and pride and posturing, Gitmo was crying for blood. Its inhabitants were restless. It wanted to put a hurt on whoever was behind the death of the president two weeks ago.

Michael ran to appease the lion inside. He ran to clear his

head of the irrational, the emotions, the confusion and endless discussions that were unfolding at Guantánamo and, presumably, in America. He'd learned about the president's assassination a week after the rest of the civilized world. He had been on assignment, assisting CIA types in a nation where the scorpions were the size of ashtrays and the politics as volatile as nitroglycerin. Now he was back in the fold, catching up, getting informed.

Michael was into his sixth mile when a Humvee approached from behind. It pulled ahead by a few hundred yards and stopped. A full bird stepped out and waited for Michael to catch up.

Michael stopped, stood erect, and saluted. His breathing was even, but the sweat poured from his arms and face. His thirty-year-old body was a study in sculpture, loyalty, and endurance. Scars were on his arms and back. A USMC tattoo on his right biceps. Women remarked at his physique and his blue eyes, not that it mattered much to him. Men remarked at his ability to do seventy pull-ups in two minutes.

The colonel returned the salute and stepped forward.

"It's Saturday, son," the older man said. "Even God Himself rested one day of the week."

Michael half-smiled. "I expect to go to heaven, sir, and I'd like to represent our Corps in a mano a mano boxing match against the Lord God when I get there. *This* is prep."

"Blasphemous." The colonel laughed, then clapped Michael on the shoulder. They stepped over to the Humvee. The driver passed the colonel a clipboard. The old man scanned the sheet of paper.

"Says here you're to report to the airstrip in three hours. Heading to Virginia."

"Sir? I just returned from an op," Michael said. "I'm supposed to head back home to Denver. Two weeks' leave."

"I don't know anything about that." The colonel nodded at the clipboard. "This came to my office. Classified. I'm supposed to round you up personally and get you on that plane. Now I don't take a shine to running errands, Smith, particularly when they're so hush-hush I can't have one of my staff get their nails dirty for me. You're not going to give me any trouble on this, are you?"

Michael stiffened. "Of course not, sir."

"Then be there at eleven hundred, as ordered."

"Yes, sir."

As the Humvee sped away, Michael stood in the sun, still sweating. He gritted his teeth. He breathed and listened.

Gitmo was angry. Gitmo was confused. For the first time this week, Michael was glad for that. He was glad he wasn't the only one. He began to run again, this time back toward the base.

The lion inside him had many questions.

the president is alive!! this is another attempt to create pandemonium!! an elaborate hoax is being staged against the american people. as you know my source inside insists this is nothing more than an excuse to get griffin out of the public eye. blackjack and Special(k) say there is no threat to america but the president had to be removed so he can conduct talks with the true entities behind this conspiracy.

the world had to believe assassination was true so no one could suspect the real reason why griffin is gone. the grays are finally reestablishing communications and wish to discuss total social and technological integration with us!! after two years of silence they are retransmitting their signals! there is proof, the photograph below was sent from blackjack and confirmed by another source as authentic. it is an image taken from hubble of the phobosian base where the grays have been stationed for the past decade. the time is at hand! the next great age of humanity has begun!!!! kilroy2.0 was here kilroy2.0 is everywhere

```
>ATTACH graybase.jpg
>LOAD TRACKSCRAMBLER
>EXECUTE
>UPLOAD
```

Kilroy2.0 leaned back from the computer screen in satisfaction. This new message had just been posted to his Web site TheTruthExcavated.com. It was one of six sites he updated daily.

He rocked back and forth in the wooden chair, his round, bearded face ebbing in and out of the light flickering from the five computer monitors. The rest of the apartment was soaked in shadow; the afternoon sunshine warming the rest of Washington, D.C., was blocked by the sheets of aluminum foil taped to the window frames.

Sunlight was not welcome here. This was a timeless place. A temple. Kilroy2.0 was beyond time, beyond day, beyond daylight. There were no Fridays or Saturdays or Mondays. Only Nondays.

Once, long ago during his life as a civilian, Kilroy2.0 had been known by another name, a man's name, a Pedestrian's name, forgettable. It was the name of an unenlightened tourist of the world, one familiar to worker bees who did not hear the whispers in the walls. But that name, that life, that was Before. Before he had seen the Truth that was seeping through the Media's Lies. Before he had his pulpits.

Before he was here. Before he was everywhere.

Kilroy2.0 smiled in the silence, rocking, cataloging and prioritizing the next series of Web-site updates in his mind. Beneath the desk, the small fans inside his five computers whirred softly. The wooden chair creaked as he rocked. The walls did not speak, for which he was grateful. Silence was like a sand castle to him: fragile, fleeting, golden.

The pounding at the front door shattered it all.

Kilroy2.0 started, glanced across the living room. The chain locks rattled at the impact. His eyes flashed back to Monitor Three, at the miniature video screen in the corner.

The feed from the wireless webcam he'd installed in the outside hall was dead.

The pounding, again.

Kilroy2.0 stood straight up, the chair hitting the floor like a pistol shot. Hands shaking, he dashed to the windows. This was it. They'd finally found him and they'd make him vanish, take away the Word and transform him into a Pedestrian just like Before and

—can't let that happen, have to get out of here—

He ripped at the aluminum foil on the windows, gasping and squinting through the furious sunlight.

A man was out there, waiting for him on the fire escape.

Kilroy2.0 shrieked. The pounding behind him stopped . . . then the door exploded inward, nearly flying off its hinges. Kilroy2.0 whirled toward the door. The window behind him shattered. Arms reached out to him from inside, now from outside.

The voltage from the Taser stun gun surged through Kilroy2.0's body before he knew he was hit. He crashed face-first onto the hardwood floor, taking all of his 320 pounds with him. His dirty spectacles skittered across the hardwood.

One man was barking orders. Take everything with a motherboard. Monitors, too. Look for laptops, BlackBerries, cell phones. Clean it out. Cuff him up.

Kilroy2.0 heard it all, terrified, exhilarated. They dragged his limp body out of his home and down the apartment building's stairs. As they stepped out of the building and into the sunlight, a rogue thought flashed through Kilroy's mind.

He couldn't smile at the irony, but he wanted to.

kilroy2.0 was here

Hospitals may vary in shape, size, and design from the outside. They are all identical inside.

Hallway mazes, clanging doors, floors and walls colored in muted browns and blues. Hospitals are collages of impassive colors that do not offend, that make no promises.

Father Thomas walked through the halls of St. Mary's, passing door after door, trying not to focus on the smell of sterilizer and Salisbury steak that seemed to sweat from its walls. When a place deals in illness and death, those things are in the air, the walls, the beds, of that place. In his six years as a priest, Thomas had strode through many hospitals like this one. They all smelled the same to him.

He wondered, fleetingly, if doctors smelled a sameness in churches.

The call to the rectory this morning had come as neither shock nor revelation to Thomas. It was Mark McGee. Mark's father, Gavin, had requested his last rites. Thomas knew the man, liked him, admired his humor and courage—particularly during the past three years. Gavin McGee was an optimistic man. But cancer eats everything, especially optimism.

For three years, Thomas had watched his parishioner being devoured by his own mutating flesh. The cancer in Gavin McGee's lungs took great pleasure in tearing out of remission, feasting upon the good cells of a good man. Thomas believed almost everything he'd been taught in seminary about suffering, about God's mysterious role in death and diseases. Yet he silently believed that God had no role in creating a few things on this earth. Cancer was one of them. It was as if Lucifer had left a splinter of himself in the world when he had fallen long ago, a thing whose purpose was to uncreate, to unwind man's Providence and dine on its goodness. Cancer was not a bad thing that happened to

good people. It was an arrow fired from something old and unholy.

Father Thomas found Room 511 and knocked. Mark McGee
answered, shook Thomas's hand, and motioned him inside. The
priest hugged Ellen, Gavin's daughter, and said hello to her husband. He nodded quietly at their thank-yous, told them it was his
duty and his honor; Gavin McGee was his friend, a pillar, a proud
parent, a little slice of legend at St. Barnabas. They all smiled at
that, and Thomas was glad for it.

Even through the fog of painkillers, Gavin McGee recognized
Thomas almost instantly and smiled. The patient's thick silver-red
hair was nearly gone now. His once-wide shoulders sagged downward, toward Tinkertoy arms. Gavin McGee winked at Thomas,
saying it all: *I'm throwing the fight, but I'm fine with it.*

"Hello, Gavin," Thomas said.

"I know the secret now, Father," McGee said. "Realized the
place I'm heading is a helluva lot better than where I'm at."

Thomas smiled. "That's about as true as it gets."

McGee nodded toward his grown children. Nearly forty years
ago, Gavin McGee had been the topic of dinnertime conversation
here in sleepy-eyed Stanton, Oklahoma. He had taken his ex-wife
to court to claim full custody of Ellen and Mark. As a mother,
Shellie just wasn't up to snuff, he'd told the judge. Boozing, carrying on with barflies, she was no role model he wanted his children
to follow. The judge ruled in his favor, marking Gavin McGee as
the first man in Stanton ever to win such a case.

"Not a bad life, eh, Father?" McGee said.

"No, Gavin. Not a bad life. The best life."

Thomas administered the last rites. Gavin McGee renounced
his sins, asked for forgiveness, said he believed in Father, Son,
Holy Spirit, and the one Holy and Apostolic Church. McGee held

his children's hands through the sacrament, accepted the body and blood of Christ, and smiled when it was over.

In his years performing this role in dozens of rooms just like this one, Thomas often saw such dignity so close to the end. He wondered if his own parents had felt this kind of peace. Their deaths had been sudden, but surely in the divine infinite expanse of a second, they would have felt the same calm and courage as Gavin McGee. *Surely we all will,* he thought.

In St. Mary's parking lot, on the way back to his Cavalier, Father Thomas Smith was stopped by an armed man who politely asked him to join him for a ride. The green-eyed man, who sported a crew cut—clearly military—said he didn't want any trouble; he simply wanted the priest to get in the car. As a Crown Vic with tinted windows pulled up beside them, Thomas insisted he had no money, and that he was a *shodan*—a first-degree karate black belt—and could protect himself if it came to that.

Two other men stepped out of the car. They were also armed.

The leader said he didn't think it would come to that.

A bead of sweat slipped down Jay's forehead, hung on his eyebrow, then finally plunged onto his cheek. He wanted to wipe off the sweat, but couldn't. He was handcuffed and terrified.

Two strangers were in his East Village apartment, walking through his living room, scanning the myriad spines on the bookshelves, daintily picking up and examining the trinkets from faraway lands. Their white latex gloves provided a disconcerting contrast against the many dark-hued, primitive items.

A third man stood before him, above him. This man pulled a white handkerchief from his suit's breast pocket. He reached down and gently wiped the sweat from Jay's face.

Jay did not speak. He had been told not to speak unless spoken to. He abided by this rule in silent terror, watching these three puzzle over his life. One of them gazed at a photograph of Mikhail Gorbachev with interest. The man glanced at a photo of Jay standing beside Kofi Annan and harrumphed.

A half hour ago, Jay had been enjoying a sweet tea and an intense game of Tetris—his two Saturday vices, if one could call them that—when Patricia called to tell him she was running late. The subway had inexplicably stopped service for a few minutes, she'd said. This gave Jay a few more minutes of Tetris's spinning bricks before he had to run to the market on Eighth to snag the chicken breasts. Eventually, he left. He'd been gone for no more than twenty-five minutes. In that time, these three men had broken into his home and waited.

They'd descended on him like midnight predators. A chop to his shoulder. A quick shove across the room, where he fell onto the sofa. A display of gun barrels to convince him they meant business. Impassive glares from dangerous faces.

Jay Smith had quickly learned in New York that when a man with a gun asks you for your wallet, you give it to him. If he tells you to recite the Pledge of Allegiance in Swahili, you do that, too. Say nothing threatening, do nothing threatening. Find another way to burn the adrenaline, just give him the wallet and go for a long walk afterward. Process it in the to-be, not the now.

Jay glanced over the couch now, searching for the cordless phone. A wordless 911 call, a traced line, a dispatched cruiser . . . but the receiver wasn't there. They had removed it.

One of the searching men plucked a picture frame from a bookshelf and handed it to the man standing before Jay. It was a black-and-white photograph of Patricia: black hair cropped short, eyebrows arched in surprise and joy. The leader held up the photo and looked down at Jay.

"Your wife. She's about the cutest thing I've ever seen. I bet you'd do anything for her, wouldn't you?"

Jay licked the sweat from his lips and shuddered. "Yes."

"I bet the last thing she'd want to see when she came home is her husband with a bullet where his brain used to be, hmmm?"

"Yes."

"And I bet the last thing you'd want is your little Peppermint coming home and meeting us. Meeting *us*, Jay. That could be very troublesome—downright dangerous—for such a pretty lady. Isn't that right? Why, we might have to do something to those photo-taking peepers of hers, should she see us."

"How did you know—"

The man raised his 9 mm and pointed it at Jay's head. "Answer the question."

Jay shuddered again. "Right."

"I'm sorry for the theatrics, but this way is best," the man said. "It's also the most effective."

His brown eyes bored into Jay's. "So. Are you going to continue being a good boy?"

Jay nodded. One of the men lifted him off the couch and shoved him toward the front door.

Mike Smith gazed at his reflection in the men's room mirror. He smiled. He brushed his hair again. He turned his head from side to side, looking for stubble. He flared his nostrils, searching for wily nose hairs. He checked his fingernails. They probably wouldn't be on camera, *but appearances are everything and people talk.* He straightened his tie. He gargled a handful of water. Looked for stubble again. He'd be going to makeup in five minutes, so it probably didn't matter. But still.

This is my night, he thought. *The beginning of the explosion. Ten minutes on CNN. Ten minutes on* Larry King. *Larry fucking King. The book'll shoot up the lists like a Titan rocket. The networks will call. Ten minutes with King. Then twenty with Oprah. ABC will pull Barbara Wahwah out of retirement for an exclusive. And then, nirvana itself, the speaking engagements. Oh, the speaking engagements, the huddled masses, all gathered to hear the World According to Me.*

He was going to give Rochelle the biggest, wettest, sloppiest kiss for pulling this off. Shit. He was going to give Larry King the biggest, wettest, sloppiest kiss when this was all over with, just as Marlon Brando had. This was it. The beginning of the explosion.

There was a knock at the door. That cute production assistant with the ponytail and a pen behind her ear peeked into the men's room and smiled. It was probably supposed to look like a comforting smile for Mike's benefit, but the corners of her mouth telegraphed years of experience: *I know you're nervous, that's why I gave you some time in the head. But navel gazing's over, bub.*

"Mike? It's me again, Terry. We're gonna have to get you over to makeup in the next two minutes."

"Right on." Confident. Cool.

Terry was unimpressed. "Dr. Smith, I'm going to remind you that you're the first up tonight. And since this is *Larry King* Live, you'll want to be on time."

Mike nodded and gulped. He suddenly had to pee.

"Right, right. Just give me another minute, okay?"

Terry's eyes tensed for a second. "One minute."

Mike dashed over to a urinal, frantically unzipped his fly, and barely managed to aim at the basin before the piss came. He was washing his hands when the door opened again.

It was another PA, apparently. Young man, jeans, T-shirt. A security pass dangled from a band around his neck like a flimsy convention name tag. He smiled nervously—*now* that *is a bona fide, dyed-in-the-wool, can't-hide-shit-from-a-psychologist genuine smile,*

Mike thought—and walked over to the sink. The kid was holding a copy of *Hunting the Hunters*.

"Dr. Mike?"

"I'm ready," Mike said, glancing in the mirror.

"That's great. But I was hoping that before you went, you could sign my copy of your book. I loved it, especially the chapters about the Three Ring Circus killer. I have a pen."

Mike brightened. "Of course. I'm glad you liked it."

The kid placed the book on the counter. As Mike's hand reached for the hardback, he asked, "And to whom am I signing this fine piece of—"

He opened it and blinked. The pages had been cut, hollowed out. A pistol was resting inside.

In one heartbeat, the kid grabbed the gun, pressed it to the base of Mike's ear, and said, "To your biggest fan."

Saturday night was movie night at the Smith home, though Jack often thought the rigmarole of getting Kristina and Carrie bundled up, out the door, and into the Passat was a production Hollywood could make a movie of, or option at least. Getting the twins to agree on a movie at the video store was another epic; perhaps a television miniseries. *Witness the spectacle of clashing cinematic tastes! Carrie wants to see* The Lion King *for the trillionth time! Kristina demands* Pippi Longstocking, *an untried classic! Who will win? Who will decide?*

Daddy, that's who.

Tonight, the four-year-olds had been relatively peaceful in Blockbuster's family section, particularly after Daddy slyly recommended *D.A.R.Y.L.*, a "megacool" movie he'd seen when he was a boy.

Blessedly, they took the bait. They made a pit stop in the mystery section for "Mommy and Daddy's movie" and made it home with little fuss. Jack chalked it up to James Brown's "I Got You (I Feel Good)." The twins gleefully sang along. All six times.

Lisa had already called the pizza place by the time they came home. Jack got the plates ready; Lisa and the girls grabbed the juice boxes and the napkins. Lisa was asking them which flavor they wanted—"Grape!" the kids cried in unison—as Jack turned on the TV and popped in the girls' movie.

The doorbell rang. Jack grabbed a twenty from his wallet and opened the door for the pizza guy. The men exchanged the typical *heys* and *how's it goin's*. This pizza guy . . . like all pizza guys these days, it seemed . . . peered over his shoulder, curiously eyeing the living room. *Minimum-wage voyeurs*, Jack thought. But then again, there had to be *some* perk for such a thankless job.

"How much do I owe you?" Jack asked.

The stranger dropped his box, covered Jack's mouth with one hand, and yanked him outside with the other. It was quick and silent.

The girls did not watch *D.A.R.Y.L.* with Daddy that night.

TWO

John lifted his T-shirt and gazed at the reflection of his stomach in the floor-to-ceiling mirror. His midsection hurt like hell, but there were no bruises; no proof of the assault. Even his hand and chin had been had been cleaned and bandaged. His left arm still throbbed from when those suits had pulled it behind his back and nearly broken it, that game of Say Uncle on steroids.

He lowered his shirt and looked at his reflection. Shoulder-length, sandy blond hair. High cheekbones. Five feet eleven inches. Lanky. Aside from the small Band-Aids on his chin and palm, John looked the same as he did when he had kissed Sarah good-bye this morning.

John didn't know what time it was or where he was; he'd never worn a watch, and this so-called waiting room had no clocks. Just a conference table, ten posh office chairs, several plastic cups, a single drinking straw, some cans of soda—and one large, cracked mirror. The mirror, that was his work.

About an hour and a half ago, John had abruptly been pulled from unconsciousness. He was strapped to a gurney, looking up at fluorescent lights, white ceiling tiles, and bespectacled faces.

Through the haze, those faces had looked like moons. They gently commanded John to stay calm. He did, for a few seconds. Then he remembered the bicycle ride, the van . . . the man with the marble cheekbones . . . and began screaming for answers. He screamed about constitutional rights, probable cause, and arrest warrants. He pleaded and proclaimed his innocence again and again. The restraints didn't budge. Neither did these strangers.

As the moonmen pushed his gurney down a hallway, John asked questions. He pressed his body against the restraints. He craned his neck and spotted men in military fatigues with M16s trailing beside the folks with the white coats. The ceiling tiles streaked by above him. The gurney made a right, a left, a right. He wanted to know what he'd done. He wanted to know where he was. There had been a terrible mistake. A terrible, terrible mistake. After a while, the true terror took hold and he'd stopped screaming.

When the gurney finally stopped, one of the moonmen—a middle-aged doctor, presumably—bent down to whisper in John's ear. John could feel the man's beard, his mouth was so close.

"John, I want you listen to me," the man said, his voice calm. He had an under bite, which made him sound vaguely like Sean Connery. It was annoying. "My name is James DeFalco. I'm an assistant here. I'm not the man who can answer your questions; I'm not authorized to give you any information yet. But your questions will be answered soon. Soon, John. Do you understand?"

John stared at the ceiling and blinked. He said he understood.

"Good," DeFalco said. "Now, we're going to lower this gurney, remove your restraints, and help you up. We're going to walk you through this door. We're then going to close the door. There you'll wait for the answers to your questions."

Fuck this, John thought.

"Do you understand what I'm telling you, John?"

"Yes."

"Are you going to cooperate, John?"

"Yes."

The white coats lowered the gurney. Then the soldiers loosened the restraints across his chest, wrists, and legs. John didn't move until two of the grunts had slung their rifles behind their backs and grabbed his armpits to help him up.

John swiftly swung his elbow upward and connected with the nose of one of the soldiers. Blood peppered John's shirt. The soldier fell backward across the gurney. The other grunt grabbed John and slammed him, front-first, into the wall. As the white coats screamed not to hurt him, for God's sake don't hurt him, the door was yanked open and John was thrown into the waiting room. As he scrambled to get up, the dead bolt clicked home.

John had pounded on the metal door, paced the room, and finally thrown one of the office chairs into that mirror wall, praying it would shatter to reveal a roomful of clipboard-toting eggheads— and a way out. It did not shatter. The chair cracked the glass and nearly hit John as it bounced back from the impact. It was a seven-foot-tall exclamation point for his screams.

That had been an hour ago. He'd sung to himself, to keep the terror away and the questions from eating up his brain. He sang the trusty standbys: Dylan, Baez, McLachlan. He even sang some of his own songs—"Do This for Me," "Rockefeller Center," "Winter Love," "Unscrew You."

Now John was staring at himself in a splintered mirror, wondering why men in suits had beaten and sedated him, why moonmen with rifles had thrown him into a conference room, why in God's name this had happened to him.

John heard the dead bolt unlock. He turned to see a fat man with tangled hair, pop-bottle glasses, and a wild man's beard enter the room. No, not fat. Obese. Well over three hundred pounds, a boulder with legs. The newcomer immediately waddled over to one of the chairs and plopped into it. The door closed and locked. The stranger stared and smiled at the table.

John walked over and stood across from the newcomer. The man did not look up. He rocked in his chair.

"Are you the man I'm supposed to talk to?" John asked.

Silence. Rocking.

"Listen. I've got questions," John said.

The man scratched his head. He didn't look up.

John looked closely at the man. The dude was probably his age. He slouched over a great belly. He smelled. He had dandruff. A Pollock painting of food stains covered his grimy yellow T-shirt. John watched the man reach over, grab a can of Dr Pepper from the table's center, and pour the soda into a plastic cup. He snatched the drinking straw, plunked it into the liquid.

John sat down across from him. "Hey. You the guy I'm supposed to talk to, or not?"

"No." The man's voice had a disconcerting tremble; high-pitched, almost feminine.

"Did they bring you here, too?"

"Yeah." Giggle.

"Do you know why we're here?"

The stranger looked up, grinning. Behind his pop-bottle spectacles, the man's blue eyes widened until they looked as if they'd pop out of his skull.

"I know *everything*," he whispered.

John jumped back in his chair and nearly screamed.

He knew those eyes.

Ten minutes later, the priest and the marine came in; the door locked behind them. John looked wordlessly at the pair as they entered—watched in part fascination, part horror, as they gazed each at the other, at the soda-sipping lunatic, at John.

It was an exercise in contrasts. The marine was wearing BDUs. Flattop. Broad-shouldered. Chisel-chinned. The priest was slightly pudgy; his cheeks were full and shiny, his stomach pressed against his belt. His hair was combed in a style of humility or fashion cluelessness; John didn't know which.

John did know, however, that—despite the physical differences—these men were brothers. Identical twins. They were the same height. Their blue eyes worked over each other with the same expression of suspicion. Their faces were pursed in the same look of silent fear and amazement.

John also knew that despite the physical differences, the lunatic across from him was also a dead ringer for these two.

And all three of them looked like John.

The lunatic slurped the last of the Dr Pepper in his cup and smacked out a soda-commercial *ahhhh.*

The priest reached into his breast pocket with a shaking hand and pulled out a rosary. He sat down at the end of the table, in the chair closest to the cracked mirror. He ran his fingers through his hair and gawked at John in disbelief. John was certain he was returning the expression.

The feeling was unreal, like the unsettling sensation of watching yourself on video, only magnified. *Do I really look like that?* Only worse. Only this time, the video You is sitting six feet away from the real You, wearing a priest's collar, breathing the same air, probably feeling the same slippery, sick sensation in his gut.

The marine still stood near the door. His eyes flicked over the lunatic, then sized up John and the priest. Cracking his knuckles, the marine strode back to a corner of the room and leaned against the wall, watching them, saying nothing.

The priest dropped his rosary on the table. He looked at John, his hands still shaking. "Are we brothers?" His voice had a slightly nasal quality. Had his nose been broken years ago?

"I don't know." John felt sick. "I thought I was an only child."

The priest nodded. "So did I."

"Quadruplets," the fat lunatic said.

The door opened again. This time, two more men. One of them was yelling out into the hall as the door was closing, something about who he was and whom they'd have to answer to if they didn't explain everything right fucking now. He pounded on the door as it locked.

The other newcomer was almost as thin as John. He was wearing a sweatshirt and jeans; his hairline was beginning to thin. He looked very much like the priest sitting at the table—same hair, same tightly wound shoulders, probably a dozen pounds lighter than Father Whoever. The man's eyes jumped nervously from the screaming man to the rest of the room. They widened when they spotted John's face. The wide-eyed man opened his mouth to say something. John just shook his head: *Don't know what to tell you, man.*

The man who'd been pounding on the door whirled around. This one looked like a politician. Blow-dried hair, Brooks Brothers suit, starched collar, and shiny, expensive tie. Brooks Brothers looked at his fellow captives. His face went white.

"Shit the bed," he said.

And then the wide-eyed man beside him—the one who looked like the priest at the table—fainted. The politician looked down at the body, then up at John. He shrieked, whirled around, and began pounding on the door again.

Let me out let me out let me out.

The lunatic began to laugh.

John's eyes went to the priest again. Father Whoever was clutching his head in his hands. John looked past the priest, into the splintered mirror wall. *This is just like that,* he thought. Only the reflection screams because *you're* the video You not the real You and *you're* the cracked mirror, seven years of bad luck and wel-come to Wonderland, you should've come quietly, Johnny-Boy, I really need a cigarette, and this can't be happening. . . .

By the time the seventh "twin" came through the door, the group had calmed down, clammed up. No one had spoken since the unhinging twenty minutes ago. Call it sensory overload. Call it shock. Call it brains filled with too many questions to make nice-nice pleasantries like *What's your name* and *What do you do* and *Jeez you look familiar did I know you in high school.*

John gazed up at the newly arrived bearded, bespectacled, bewildered man, but didn't look closely. It didn't matter. The new-comer looked like the priest. He looked like the lunatic, the politi-cian, the fainting man, the marine.

He looks like me. Just like me.

THREE

For a moment, Kenneth Kleinman considered straightening his tie and rolling down the sleeves of his white oxford, but it was far too late for such bullshit. He looked up at General Hill's face, looked down at the soldier's spit-shined boots, and quickly pulled out the black plastic comb from his breast pocket to style what little hair he had left. He and Hill had become unlikely allies these past fifteen years, and Kleinman half-expected the general to rattle off the usual smirky insults about the old man's appearance. They didn't come.

"Are you ready?" Kleinman asked.

"Of course," the general said. The black man's voice was a stern baritone.

Kleinman stared at the closed door before them. It was curious, this anticipation churning inside him. He felt giddy, grave, and unsettled.

Kleinman turned back to the door and told Chapman, Hill's baby-faced assistant, to unlock the dead bolt. Before he did, the lieutenant unsnapped the holster strap covering the grip of his sidearm. This was procedure, Hill had explained. Nothing personal.

Chapman opened the door. He went in first. Then the general. Kleinman whispered a prayer and followed.

All seven were at the table. In all of Kleinman's eighty-three years, no experience was as exhilarating as seeing them here, together.

The marine was standing, of course. General Hill returned the salute, and the young man sat down, clasped his hands, and waited. The others' expressions were a menagerie of terror, expectation, and what appeared to be quiet gratitude. They had probably expected another one of "them" to walk through the door, Kleinman realized. The men didn't look at each other. They looked at the towering general. They looked at Chapman, who was packing acne scars and a loaded weapon. Then they looked at Kleinman.

Chapman closed the door and stood before it. Kleinman sat down at the head of the table. His sweaty palms slipped on the dark wood.

"Gentleman. My name is Dr. Kenneth Kleinman. I'm the man Dr. DeFalco told you about; I'm the head of this facility. This is Brigadier General Orlando Hill. He oversees security and operations."

The silence didn't last long.

"You are so fucking sued," one of them said. It was Dr. Mike, Kleinman noted; the well-dressed criminal profiler. The yeller-not-a-fighter. "The whole. Fucking. Lot. Of you. I want to know what the hell's going on. I want to know why a punk put a gun in my face before I was about to go on live—fucking *live*—television. I want to know who these people are." He looked around the table. "These . . . these . . ."

"*Me's.*"

Jack said that, Kleinman saw. Last to be captured. Potbelly, beard, wire rims. Father of the twins. The geneticist. If anyone here could understand and appreciate what was about to come, it would be him.

Kleinman said nothing. He had known it would be this way, known it long before he'd stepped through that goddamned door. Let them speak. Let them vent. Just let the question come, the billion-dollar question, the question that would tear the roof off this place and cannonball these men into revelation and—*if we're not careful*—revolution.

"Where are we?" That was Thomas, the priest. He clutched his rosary. The beads chittered against the wood. The man was on the verge of tears.

The one called Kilroy twirled his drinking straw, compressed its flexible neck, then pulled it taut. Compressed it again, pulled it taut. The sound unnerved the trembling man to his left. Jay. So nicknamed in college, for there were too many students with the same name in his Foreign Policy class.

Ah. And there was John. The bard, the black sheep.

"Are we brothers?" the young man asked.

Kleinman sighed. There it was. The stone had been thrown into the lake; it was time to watch the shock waves. It was far too late for apologies, for pandering.

"You're more than brothers," Kleinman said. "Much, much more."

The child had been conceived in a saucer under a microscope, observed by more than a dozen scientists who had vowed years before—under Code Phantom orders, which meant under penalty of death—that they had made peace with playing God and were fully committed to their clandestine project. The child's mother and father were nameless donors selected from a tome the size of a Chicago white pages.

His parents' heredity, genetics, education, and major life accomplishments had been summarized into ten-paragraph biog-raphies, just like those of the thousands of other unwitting participants. The father's proficiency in athletics and mathematics made him an ideal candidate for the project. The mother's bril-liance in art, biology, and language was coveted by the 7th Son team. She was also unspeakably beautiful.

On January 1, thirty years ago, their sperm and eggs were re-moved from cryostorage, thawed, and prepared for eventual arti-ficial insemination. The parents weren't invited to the conception. Security was the overwhelming factor, of course—the project was *Code Phantom* . . . beyond Top Secret, beyond Eclipse Command.

Practicality also contributed to the decision. The father had been dead since 1967; the mother was then sixty-four years old. The lab-coat folk didn't think the woman would have taken the birth in the best of spirits.

The conception was successful on the third attempt, and the zygote was implanted into a surrogate who was paid an astound-ing amount of money to not ask questions. After the child's birth, it would be given to Dania and Hugh Sheridan, scientists working on the 7th Son project. Dania was one of the head technologists; Hugh was the lone child psychologist on the 7th Son staff. They would raise the child together as planned, in the way suggested by the scientists and the cadre of child specialists (who hadn't the fog-giest to what project they were contributing when they were ques-tioned by Sheridan, Kleinman, and the rest). The goal: to make the child the most well-rounded person it could be; to encourage the youngster to excel in any hobby or academic interest it pursued, or was connived into pursuing, if need be. Love the child. Gently push the child. Introduce religion, culture, athletics, and art to the child. Let the child grow to be playful, curious, and serious.

It would need the most supportive childhood possible, after all, if it was to be destined for great things.

The Sheridans changed their last name to Smith and moved to Indianapolis, as ordered. Regular reports by the "Smiths" and the 7th Son support staff who'd also moved to Indy would keep the project's leaders at the Virginia headquarters informed of the child's progress after the birth.

That September 7, John Michael Smith was born.

A moment after John connected the dots—right after the impact of the words *John Michael Smith* was being collected and fired from his neurons—Dr. Mike attacked. The room's silence was shattered by Mike's scream. He was already climbing across the table before John realized what was happening.

Dr. Mike's hair had quickly torn free from its blow-dried style and had descended onto his brow in thick, knife-shaped shards. His eyes bulged. His knees slid and slipped on the tabletop. One of his loafer-clad feet nearly kicked John in the face. The dude was fast and frantic, and on Kleinman in seconds.

He shook the geezer, screamed this was bullshit. Somewhere, one of the seven was shouting for help, another was cackling the word "conspiracy, conspiracy" in a singsong voice, another still was shouting to stop it stop it he's trying to tell us something. At the end of the table, the priest whispered, "That's *my* name," over and over.

John sat there, disconnected, disbelieving, as if this were some improv performance in which he and these other players would smile and shake hands afterward. It felt like a dinner mystery. Yes, very much like that.

Lieutenant Chapman grabbed Dr. Mike from behind by the Brooks Brothers coat and yanked him off the table with one arm. Mike spilled to the floor, swearing and screaming. Chapman placed his .45 against the side of Mike's head and cocked the hammer.

Dr. Mike stopped in midswing and stared into Chapman's eyes. It was like hitting pause on a videotape, or watching two kids play freeze tag. Mike's mouth hung open for a moment, his fist still in midair. Chapman dug the barrel into Dr. Mike's temple—*Are we all on the same page here?* his eyes said—and Mike dropped his arm.

Chapman's gun did not budge. Kleinman was up from the table, wiping his glasses furiously. General Hill stepped between Kleinman and the derailed assailant, his shadow sweeping over Dr. Mike like a thundercloud.

"I will not tolerate that behavior," Hill said, his voice low and cold. "Not here. Not in my post. Do you understand me?"

Mike looked up and nodded. Chapman pulled the gun away and resumed his place by the door. Hill whirled around and pointed a dark finger at the rest of them. The fat lunatic stopped giggling.

"That goes for all of you. I'll say this one time. Violence will not be tolerated here, in this room, in this facility. You're wondering why you're here. You're hoping you've slid over into some *Twilight Zone* episode. You haven't. This is real, and it's only the beginning. So shut up. Listen to Dr. Kleinman."

As Kleinman stepped tentatively back toward the table, Hill cleared his throat. "And if any of you so much as daydreams about attacking this man," he said with an icy whisper, "I'll take you down myself."

The dude gargles crude oil, John thought.

Dr. Mike sullenly shuffled back to his seat, primly brushing his rumpled suit coat. Kleinman sat down and adjusted his spectacles.

"I know how all this must seem," Kleinman said, and shook his head. "But you must trust the general and me." He waved his hand across the table, from one side to the other, as if introducing two groups at a dinner party.

"John Michael Smith . . . meet John Michael Smith," he said.

At the other end of the table, the priest began to cry. "What is this all about?" Father Thomas asked.

Kleinman offered him a tired, sympathetic smile.

"It's about the greatest experiment ever conducted in the history of our species."

Hugh and Dania Sheridan, now Smith, raised the boy in Meridian-Kessler, an upper-middle-class neighborhood in Indianapolis. They followed the child-rearing plan outlined by the project leaders and encouraged Johnny Smith in every way they could.

Johnny was raised Catholic, just as his mother had been. Although Dania was an agnostic by the time she'd entered the 7th Son project and Hugh was an atheist who had suddenly found himself in a foxhole in the name of science, they created a more than convincing portrayal of the "casual Catholic" family. Dania baked cakes for the fish-fry cake wheel, Hugh helped set up booths at fund-raisers. They never pushed the Catechism down their son's throat, but simply explained the core beliefs of Christianity and told Johnny there was a God if he believed there was one. They also taught their son religious tolerance: Judaism, Buddhism, a smidgen of shamanism, atheism.

Johnny took a shine to athletics early in life, thanks to his biological father's abilities and the ordered encouragement of his adoptive parents. T-ball and YMCA soccer were early obsessions, but—as with most children raised in Indiana—basketball became the sport he enjoyed most. When Johnny was five, Hugh installed a wooden backboard on the rear side of the garage, facing the cobblestone alley. They practiced free throws before dinner, and Hugh would always place Johnny on his shoulders for a slam dunk just before they raced each other, laughing, back to the house to eat.

Thanks to Hugh's former profession as a child psychologist, the couple explained complicated matters to the boy in terms he would understand. The family went to art galleries, attended operas and plays—potentially stodgy affairs for even the most patient of adults—and made those trips exciting for the child. Paintings were like windows into the mind, they'd say. Concerts and plays were like mythical creatures that lived for only a short time, disappeared, and were reborn at the next performance. Each incarnation was a little different, and that's what made them special. *Like the phoenix?* Johnny had asked after seeing a performance of *Peter Pan*, and the parents had smiled proudly. That's right. Just like the phoenix.

He grew up listening to 33s of Mozart and 45s of the Beach Boys. Dania would sing along and play accompaniment on the grand piano in the living room. Johnny liked it best when she'd bang out the thunderous opening chords of the Fifth Symphony and then suddenly nose-dive into "Roll Over Beethoven." The connection was not lost on the boy. He laughed every time she did that. She did, too.

Finger paints gave way to watercolors; free throws to flip-wrist bank shots; trikes to bikes.

Class sizes were small at the private grade school Johnny attended, and thanks again to his biological proclivities and his parents' unwavering encouragement, he excelled in all subjects. Johnny would become bored in his classes, but he never became a behavior problem. He simply wrote stories and long-division equations to keep occupied.

He was blond, beautiful, loved by his peers and teachers. He took karate classes and piano and guitar lessons. He played forward on the A team of his middle-school basketball team. He was an altar boy at his church. He traveled with his parents to the Indiana farmlands for picnics, and to nigh-magical places during summer vacations: Niagara Falls, the Grand Canyon, even Paris and London. His parents taught him the difference between confidence and egomania.

Through it all, the 7th Son team members were notified at least once a day of the boy's progress. The Virginia team leaders gave guidance where necessary, but since they were now creating and testing the technology for the project's Beta Phase, they had entrusted much of the daily business to the Indianapolis team. Pediatricians, family friends, occasional after-school tutors, and babysitters: many were 7th Son support staff, documenting the child's progress from the outside looking in, nearly always confirming the data Dania and Hugh were sending to Virginia.

When he was twelve, Johnny received the Catholic sacrament of confirmation. After careful research, the boy selected Thomas, after St. Thomas Aquinas, the patron saint of scholars, as his confirmation name.

Johnny had no living grandparents. He was told Dania was an only child, and both sets of grandparents had died before he was born. The only family John knew of were a far-flung uncle named Karl, his father's brother, and Karl's wife, Jaclyn. John had never met them. His father had only one photograph of them, which he carried in his wallet: a tiny, out-of-focus Kodak print from the late sixties. In the picture, Karl and Jaclyn were sitting on a picnic table, laughing at the camera. Her long brown hair was blowing in the wind, forever frozen in a grainy blur. His large, dark sunglasses matched the color of his collar-length hair. Karl and Jaclyn sent postcards from wonderful places with strange names: Caracas, Panama, Newfoundland, Beijing . . . each a geography lesson waiting to be unearthed. Transfixed by such adventures, John asked what his uncle and aunt did for a living. They worked for the United Nations, Hugh explained.

John attended an exceptional public high school, excelled in his freshman honors classes, and was exposed to many of the races and religions that he'd learned about in his youth. He loved public school, loved the clashes of skin colors and lingo. He tried out for JV basketball and was accepted. Johnny also excelled in track-and-field hurdling. He fell for a girl and received his first kiss one October night at the high school's homecoming game. They dated, if after-school McDonald's shakes could be considered dating. One day, he playfully told his mother that he would marry Patty Ross. Dania told him to be careful about making such assumptions about the future. Lots of things could happen from here to there, Dania warned.

The next day, John's parents were killed in a car accident.

The family was on its way to catch an evening showing of *Robin Hood: Prince of Thieves*. Johnny would remember getting into the car, Dad turning on Lindstrom Lane, seeing the headlights rushing through the stoplight, rushing toward them . . . hearing his father slam his hand on the horn . . . the snarl of the oncoming engine . . . his mother's shrieks.

He would open his eyes two years later in a strange city and meet his aunt and uncle for the first time.

They would tell him he had spent his fifteenth and sixteenth birthdays in a coma.

The marine broke the silence:

"With all due respect, sir, I'd like to know exactly how you know the greatest-hits version of my childhood. How you know about 'Roll Over Beethoven' and—"

"Your childhood?" said Jay, the thin man who'd fainted an hour ago. His voice was incredulous. "That's *my* childhood."

The giggling lunatic smacked his fat palm against the table. "*Mine.*"

Two voices in unison, Dr. Mike, the well-dressed psychologist, and Jack, the bearded geneticist: "And mine."

John stared at them—stared at them staring at each other—and looked at Kleinman for a heartbeat, an infinity. He felt the tears well up in his eyes. Kleinman offered a gentle smile. This was a nightmare, John realized, a postcoital nap thanks to Saturday Sex with Sarah. Any second now he'd wake up, shake his head, and have a smoke, one of the last in the pack. Any second now. Anysecondnow.

He watched Thomas the priest clutch his rosary and shiver.

John wasn't waking up.

Kleinman removed his glasses and looked at the seven of them, one by one. John, the ponytailed, lanky black sheep. Michael the marine, the warrior, body-perfection personified. Kilroy2.0, the obese, bespectacled lunatic hacker. Father Thomas, a hero at his parish in Oklahoma. Jack, the pudgy, bearded geneticist. Dr. Mike, the well-coiffed criminal psychologist on the cusp of micro-celebrity. Jay, the United Nations humanitarian.

Kleinman spoke to all of them now.

"This is going to be hardest part to believe, but you must, because we don't have time for the alternative. You weren't in a car accident sixteen years ago. Johnny Smith was drugged that night. At dinner. The car wreck was a ruse to create a memory of danger, to create a 'splinter' he could come back to later in life, to examine. Something to *remember*.

"Johnny Smith's parents took him to the Indianapolis team, who in turn brought him here, to the Virginia facility."

"I don't fucking believe this," Dr. Mike said.

"Shut up," General Hill snarled.

"It sounds impossible, but John Smith's memories," Kleinman said, "all of them, every emotion he ever experienced during his first fourteen years—every fantasy, every dream, every prayer— were recorded and uploaded into the giant hypercomputer beneath this facility. There the memories of John Michael Smith were converted into electronic form, digital data stored for two years while Beta Phase began."

Dr. Mike: "What the—"

"Shut *up*," Hill said.

"With the blood samples we'd taken during those years of research, we retrieved John Smith's DNA—entire genomes, complete chromosomal strands—and cloned him," Kleinman said. "Cloned *you*. Seven times. In seven biotanks. All at the same time. During the two missing years in your memories—the two years you were told you were in a coma—we grew those seven clones to sixteen-year-old maturity using an accelerated growth process. We took those seven sons with their seven vacant minds . . . they had no life, and no life experiences to remember . . . and 'downloaded' John Smith's childhood memories into their brains.

"You see, these clones weren't just genetically identical. You were *intellectually* identical. *Emotionally* identical. You were the perfect, complete copies of John Smith 'Alpha.' The same memories, the same . . . human spirit, if you will.

"And so, each John Smith 'Beta' awoke in a city that was not Indianapolis. And each John Smith was told his parents were dead. Each of you had an Uncle Karl and Aunt Jaclyn to raise you, to physically rehabilitate you and to reintroduce you to society. We chose to blame the post-*in-virtualvitro* muscular state on atrophy caused by the coma. The ultimate goal? To have each clone go into a different career field."

The men sat in silence for a moment now, processing what they'd just heard. Finally, a question from the pudgy, bearded clone.

"Why?"

"For many reasons, Jack. As a geneticist, you can probably anticipate my answer," Kleinman said, "the most important being to ensure the cloning and memory retrieval and insertion technology worked. But many of us approached this as the ultimate nature-versus-nurture experiment."

"My parents. They're . . . they're alive?" It was Father Thomas.

"The people you *remember* as your parents, yes, they're actually alive," Kleinman said. "Your mother is alive, yes. Your father, he's here, in this facility."

The group began to unhinge again; a common growl rose from the seven as their confusion spilled forth. Chapman, who stood beside the door, instinctively placed his hand on the butt of his sidearm. Dr. Mike's voice rose above the rest. He stood up, red-faced. The spot where Chapman's pistol muzzle had dug into his temple flared like a burner on an electric stove. His blue eyes blazed.

"Out! Out! Get me the hell out of here!" Mike screamed.

"Gentlemen, please—," Kleinman began.

"Mom and Dad, here?" Father Thomas.

Giggles. Kilroy2.0.

"—the fuck *out* of here!" Dr. Mike shrieked.

General Hill took another step forward and pointed his finger at Mike. "Sit down."

"Blow me."

Hill rushed the table, but Michael stood up and stepped in front of the general. The marine's muscles flexed gracefully, his hands raised in a cartoonish *We come in peace* pose. Hill stopped and looked the young man in the eyes.

"What do you want, marine?" Hill snarled.

"I just want to know what's going on, sir." Michael's clipped, efficient tenor finally broke into a quiet desperation. "I want to know what the hell's happening here."

Hill forced a furious exhale through his nostrils and looked over at the old man. "Tell them, Kleinman."

The old man removed his glasses and tossed them on the table.

"We need you to stop him. The man you were cloned from. John Smith Alpha."

FOUR

he stars. It had been years since John had seen them so
clearly. Miami smog, Miami lights—they killed the view
of all but the strongest stars, even if you were gazing from
the beach. Only Orion seemed brave enough to cut though South
Florida's midnight haze; only Venus was vibrant enough to shimmer from the horizon. To see stars like this, you had to be far from
big-city lights. John reckoned they were probably in farm country.

He took a drag from his Camel Light. The old scientist Kleinman had given him a pack as they left the conference room three
hours ago. The others here had said they didn't mind the smoke.
He exhaled, watching the blue-gray smoke swirl out over this
strange circular room, up and up, finally dissipating against the
domed skylight above them. It was like sitting at the bottom of a
grain silo. He was encircled by eight sets of doors. One led to a
hallway. The rest, to seven small apartments. Living quarters.

He was surprised more of them weren't out here in what Kleinman called the Common Room. How could the other "Beta
clones" sleep behind those doors, behind those one-way mirrored
windows, in those small dorm rooms? How could they ignore the
funnel cloud of questions? Yes, John was exhausted, but he wasn't

ready to turn in. Would he ever be? Could you ever be, after staring into six pairs of your own eyes and hearing that your childhood was a glorified computer file, swapped from one disc to another? That you had been grown in a jar? Could you ever be, even if you didn't believe any of it?

John wasn't willing to find out just yet. Neither were Michael nor Jack, apparently. It was late, but the three of them drank coffee and sat on the circular couch in the center of the room and, like long-lost family, endured long silences with strange, strained smiles. It was early Sunday morning. Less than a day had passed since their abductions—or in the case of the marine, since reporting for duty. John now knew a little about each of them. He supposed he knew *everything* about them to a point . . . to age fourteen . . . if what Kleinman had said was true.

The conversation came in herks and jerks at first. Talking about being clones was off-limits. But John sensed a subconscious need between them to talk, to share. He likened it to the bond cigarette smokers have with each other: pariahs, relegated to puffing outside, huddled away from the office doors where clients might pass and make judgment. When you spot a kindred smoker—stranger or no—it's almost second nature to make small talk. After all, you have at least one thing in common.

And John, Jack, and Michael certainly had something in common, didn't they?

The trio broke the ice by chitchatting about what they did, and whom they loved.

Michael was a captain in the Marine Corps; he had a home in Colorado. Single, but seeing someone. When pressed, Michael revealed his lover's name: Gabriel. "You asked, I told," he said to them, smiling. "Gabe's great. I was supposed to go home and see him. He's probably worried." Both John and Jack could sympathize.

Jack was the number two guy at the Recombinant Genetics Lab at the University of Arizona. He had a wife, two kids. Twins. Sometimes irony is as delicious as a nectarine.

John told them about his life, unglamorous by comparison. No globe-trotting or gene-splicing adventures here—no government-sanctioned murder or mutated mice, for that matter. Just a thirty-year-old jack-of-all-trades who'd leaped off the college track to travel, play guitar, and try to write a decent song now and then. He'd done Nashville and some of Georgia before heading to Miami. It wasn't too late to break into show business, if that was something he wanted to pursue. It was never too late to do that. But he'd done just about everything under (and in) the sun to keep the lights on in the meantime. Worked construction, drove a cement mixer, tended bar. He was a part-time shot-pourer at a South Beach nightclub these days and spent the rest of his time pulling handyman duty at the small art gallery where he had met Sarah.

The conversation was eerie. Like reading a letter you wrote to yourself years before. Like talking to yourself in the bathroom mirror with the door closed. No. More uncanny and invasive than that. It was almost like chatting with your mind-self, that all-knowing judge/jury singularity inside your head. The You that only you know about, the You that knows all the lies you've told, all the silent good deeds you've performed. The You that rarely escapes the straitjacket of social graces, the politics of pleasantry . . . the You that is as brutally honest as it wishes to be. It has that luxury. After all, it lives in your head.

But not anymore. Now it's sipping coffee, and staring into your eyes.

"Do you really think Kleinman was telling the truth?" John asked softly. "About this, us, all of it?"

The marine took a sip of his black coffee and placed the

Styrofoam cup on the circular coffee table. *His forearms are* huge,
John thought.

"I've been thinking of a million different explanations," Michael finally said. "Identical septuplets—if there's such a thing—
separated at birth. Plastic surgery. Brainwashing. Each idea I come
up with is easier to explain than what the old man said today.
Clones? No way. I mean, no offense, but you guys look nothing
like me. Your bodies, I mean. Your complexions." Michael smiled,
and John marveled that he'd seen that smile in the mirror a million times. "I'd *never* let my body get like that."

Jack chuckled and peeked down at his potbelly. For a moment,
it was reflected in his glasses. "None taken. I've got a serious sweet
tooth."

"One side of me says this cloning thing is too far-out to be
true," Michael continued. "That what he said is all science fiction
and I shouldn't believe it. The other side of me says it's so far-out,
it *must* be true. If it weren't, why feed us such a line of convoluted
bullshit?"

"I thought the same thing," John said. Surprised, he paused
and took a drag off his smoke. "The exact same thing."

"And that's the *truly* far-out part," Michael said.

Jack frowned and rubbed his beard. "No. I can't reconcile the
information," he said, shaking his head. "I can't put it all together.
What that old man—"

"Kleinman," John said.

"Yeah. What he said is impossible. Cloning? That I can grasp. I
do that on mice; swipe and swap genes to create knockout vari-
ants. But cloning a human: that's a more complicated matter, infi-
nitely more difficult to pull off . . . and that's with *today's* technology.
But we're talking about something that supposedly happened
more than fifteen years ago. We—I mean, scientists—we were still
waxing romantic about mapping the human genome back then,

like it was a fairy tale. You know, something we'd discover while zipping around in our flying cars."

John and Michael smiled at that.

"But toss in that bit about recording human memories and growth accelerant, and you've converted me from skeptic to flat-out cynic," Jack said. "The technology doesn't exist. It doesn't. And it certainly didn't fifteen years ago."

Jack looked at John, at his long hair, slender face, and wiry arms. John felt like a suitor being once-overed by the prom date's parents.

"Something remarkable has happened to bring us here, that I'll admit," Jack said. "But there are more rational explanations than what I heard today. There are too many questions. Too many variables. Hell, you could all be actors wearing prosthetic makeup, reciting lines to make me believe I'm part of some government conspiracy."

He nodded to the double doors at the front of this circular room, the doorway that led out into the halls of 7th Son.

"I'm waiting for Allen Funt to come into this room and tell me I'm on *Candid Camera.* That's a better—and perhaps the easiest— explanation for all of this. The joke's on me."

Michael shook his head; John noticed how similar this motion was to Jack's, just seconds earlier. Monkey see, monkey do.

"Then it's on me, too, hoss," Michael said. "I'm not wearing makeup, and I'm not reading lines. Now I've seen equipment out in the field—shit, I've *used* equipment out in the field—that civil-ians never knew existed. I've worn things you'd think were brought back from the future. I can buy what the old man said; there's plenty of tech none of us'll ever know about. But I swear to God, I don't have the foggiest what's going on here."

John smirked. Michael and Jack looked at him, curious.

"You swear?" John asked.

"That's right," Michael said.

"Pinkie swear?"

Michael paused, blinking. Then they all laughed; it was good to laugh, to crack the piano-wire tension, to hush the questions rattling in their heads.

Michael picked up his mug of coffee, took a sip, and grinned. "Aw, man, that was good. Pinkie swears. Do y'all remember pinkie swears?"

Pinkie swears. John's mind raced back to cobblestone alleys and guitar lessons and Mom and Dad and—

He dropped his cigarette. "We *all* do. Don't we?"

John, Michael, and Jack sipped coffee and told stories. As an experiment. To see if what the old man said was true.

"Okay. My first memory," John began. "You'd think it would be music, if you knew me. But I remember flying, believe it or not. Flying in the arms of my father, at a park . . ."

". . . flying like a fighter plane," Michael said. "I was scared, hoss . . . I was screaming and then I wasn't . . ."

Jack: ". . . because I was intrigued, I suppose, because I was seeing the world from another vantage point, seeing possibilities swirl around me, watching my field of vision rise and expand, like climbing a hill and looking down at where I'd started . . ."

John: ". . . then I saw Mom waving from the picnic blanket, her blond hair swirling in the wind, the reds and whites of the blanket so vibrant, like Technicolor . . ."

. . . like an old John Wayne movie . . .

. . . like a high-contrast photograph, with the whites blown out and the reds dancing across the eyes . . .

and the grass, far below

green as anything; green as jade

Dad's face, looking up at me, seeing him laugh

hearing him laugh
and hearing me laugh, too.
I never forgot that.

First kiss. The chill of the fall weather, football weather, the roar of the homecoming crowd, the shared hot chocolate, Patty's mittens, my black, knit gloves with the fraying leather palms, her face near mine, her lips, soft and salty and moist, her tongue, tiny and tentative, slipping into my mouth, the holding of hands, the racing of my heart, head swimming, delirious, somehow noticing the bright purple fringe of her scarf and thinking it was all a wonderful dream

The Grand Canyon. Realizing how large it was and how small I was . . . hearing Dad say how it'd been there millions of years before me and how it'd be there long after . . . how insignificant I felt, and how I told Mom that I felt like nothing, like a grain of sand . . . she said it was okay to be humbled. She said to remember something so large was created by something as seemingly insignificant as a whisper of wind and a trickle of water . . . *over time, little things change the face of the world; little things create great things, Johnny. You may be little now, but* . . .

Never forget that.

Cornfields, combines, Frisbees, the soul of places—*Listen with your ears. What do you hear? Now what do you* feel?—the crisp ping of red dodgeballs, the squeaks of sneakers on basketball courts, the rattles of loose guitar strings and slippery plinks of misplayed piano keys.

Mom and Dad
"and kisses—"
"and headlights—"
"and screams."

John, Jack, and Michael stared at each other, stared at the pink sunlight creeping through the skylight, stared into themselves. They shared something intimate, alienating.

Memories. Every last one.

To a point. A flashpoint of bending metal and shattered glass. The old man had been right.

Dr. Mike couldn't sleep. *Wouldn't* sleep. He lay in bed, staring up at the dark ceiling, then over at the door and then to the one-way mirrored window looking out to the Common Room (he'd closed the blinds as soon as he came in here). The room's simple setup had immediately reminded him of a college dorm room: a small, connected bathroom, a bed, a chest of drawers (filled with new Tommy and Polo khakis and shirts, all his size, things he would wear—*and is it reasonable to assume the others have similar custom-picked duds? Yes, yes, it is*), wall-mounted bookshelves, a desk, a gray telephone, and a chair. Of course the phone didn't work.

But *dorm room* was a charitable description. This was a prison cell, Dr. Mike knew. He'd seen enough cells over the past two years while researching his book.

Dr. Mike kicked away the bunched bedsheets at his feet. He rubbed his temple, the bruised spot where that round-faced soldier's gun barrel had dug into his skin. Mike's mind raced over the past day's events, settling on the face of the old man . . . the old man who'd recounted Mike's childhood. *He told me I was a clone*, Mike thought, sneering. *He told me that I was grown in a lab and my parents are still alive.*

Bullshit. Parents were dead. Sixteen years gone.

Why was he here? Why was he here, really? Dr. Mike had asked the old man that. Larry fucking King, book tour, all derailed, he had pleaded. *Hunting the Hunters* would fade fast without hype—and he needed to be there for the hype.

Kleinman had shaken his head and apologized and said everything else would be explained tomorrow. In the meantime, no phone calls, no e-mails, no cell phones or text messages. Just a

promise of a tour of the facility after breakfast and many answers
about "why you are all here" and "7th Son" and "John Alpha." Big
meeting in the morning. Get some rest.

As if.

John Michael Smith, Alpha. The so-called source of some impending doom and, according to Kleinman, the source of Dr. Mike's
body and mind.

Again, bullshit. Never, ever.

Dr. Mike started, sat up. He heard something from beyond the
door, hailing from the Common Room. Laughter. Mike stood and
peeked through the closed blinds. Three of his fellow captives,
sitting on the circular couch in the center of the room. One of
them—the marine—had a Styrofoam cup in his hands. Another
was picking up a cigarette that he'd dropped on the floor. They
were getting to know each other.

A frantic thought shot through his head.

What if it was all true?

Mike began to sweat suddenly. *No. It's not.*

*But what if? Look at them. They're cut from the same cloth. They're
cut from your cloth. What if they really were clones, and there really was
a John Alpha out there . . . and what if you could help take him down?
That's what you do, isn't it? That's what you've done dozens of times.
Taken down the bad guy.*

Mike tore his fingers through his hair and sat on the bed again.
He held his head in his hands.

*You are a criminal psychologist, buddy. Wrote a book on the subject.
If this is all true, you can help get into Alpha's head. You do that, save
the day, and then they'll let you out.*

Dr. Mike placed his fingertips to his temples. He felt the bruise.
His eyes narrowed.

No. He couldn't believe it.

And he wouldn't help them. He wouldn't help them at all.

———

In his heart, Jay knew it was all true—despite the protestations of his left brain, despite the inner voice that had politely advocated and then screamed for him to employ common sense. Because what Kleinman had said made no sense at all.

And yet, in the realm of Jay's experience, it did. In his years working for the United Nations, he had traveled to hungry—and power-hungry—nations as a field agent for the OHCHR, the UN's human rights watchdog group. He had witnessed things that defied rationality: land mines in farmer's fields, runoff from biochem facilities trickling directly into water supplies, grinning despots glad-handing and denying reports that millions of their countrymen were being eaten inside out by AIDS.

When you've stared at the green teeth of an Afghan who has to eat bread made from grass *to survive, human cloning seems almost yawnworthy,* he thought.

Almost. Jay had fainted, after all. It was too much—the kidnapping, the surreal vision of six "hims" sitting around a conference-room table. That's why he'd beelined to his living quarters when Kleinman had led them to the Common Room. That's why he had shut and locked the door, drawn the blinds, and hunkered down. He needed to be alone, not bonding with the clones.

Bonding with the Clones. Sounded like a game show. *Family Feud,* eat your heart out.

Jay smiled. That's something Patricia would've laughed at. He ached for her, desperately wanted to talk to her.

Bitterness swept over him. Christ, what would he say, given the chance?

Jay sighed and stared through the darkness at the digital clock resting on the desk: 4:30 a.m. He folded his fingers together and gazed at the glint of his wedding band. He missed his wife. His East Village apartment. His job. The routine. The normalcy.

Another minute ticked away on the clock's LED.

Funny, how—in a way—the job had prepared him for this. View enough corruption and starving masses and you learn to become detached, analytical. That's the key to avoiding burnout. Empathy and impartiality are different beaches. You either wash up on one and scream like a savage or come to rest on the other, pull out your clipboard, and get to work. Information, not passion, is best used to facilitate change. The seven of them were going to be put to work somehow; that much, Jay knew. It was best if he tucked in his metaphorical shirt, put on his tie, and contributed.

Besides, when the man with the gun asks for your wallet, you give it to him.

But questions plagued Jay tonight. Big ones, about the past. If Kleinman was telling the truth, had Jay's parents taken him to art galleries because they wanted to, or because they had been *ordered* to? Where was the line? Where did parenting end and working for this experiment begin?

And after his parents' "deaths"—and his relocation to Omaha to live with the fabled Uncle Karl and Aunt Jaclyn—just how many paths of Jay's adult life had been altered (or ignored alto-gether) because of some scientists broadcasting secret messages from a bunker in Virginia? What kind of life could he have lived if he hadn't listened to his new parents?

Where would he be? What would he be? A soldier? A scientist? Jay bit his lip.

Had he even had a childhood *at all*?

He giggled in the dark. He nodded and shook his head furiously. It was wonderful: the walls spoke here, too. They instructed him. He checked under the bed, in the desk, in the drawers—even in-side the commode—for surveillance. There was none, though that didn't stop the walls from warning him that he was still being watched; that pinhead-size vidcams were installed everywhere in the room, and nano-mics were undoubtedly floating in the air and in his lungs, broadcasting everything he said, every heartbeat.

Kilroy2.0 appreciated such warnings and told the walls so. It validated his own suppositions about this place. Eyes and ears would be everywhere. The Pedestrian cogs would try to glean the secrets of his omnipresence. They would fail.

Many things had been validated this day, had they not? Kilroy2.0 preached from his Web-site pulpits, and through his myriad contacts on the Web—especially his faithful Twelve: binary_fairy, blackjack, Accidental.Rob, Special(k), switchhit, and others—he had heard rumors about accelerated growth and neural datafiles long ago. His contacts were good apostles, delivering those fleeting whispers from faraway sources. And from his pulpit, Kilroy2.0 announced his prophecies. He exposed conspiracy.

Now he *was* conspiracy.

Kilroy lay in the dark and stared at the walls—into the walls. He listened for guidance. The walls finally spoke again.

kilroy2.0 is here kilroy2.0 is everywhere, they said.

there you are, he replied.

you are no longer in the timeless place, no longer in the temple

i know, the worker bees took me

it no longer matters you are home

home?

a new home for now; there is something important listen to us

i am listening

the life of your Before has returned; the ghost of your former life it haunts you

i don't understand

it is a splinter invading your divinity it is fallible the you/notyou can destroy you

please explain
kilroy2.0 was beginning and end
was?
now you are only omega the end; your Before ghost haunts you de-
clare war
on who
on he who is you/notyou he who is not omega
alpha
yes
john alpha is the beginning
you are the end
i will end the beginning
to save yourself you must slay your self
i shall
you will help these bees, these cogs, Pedestrians; together you will
find the alpha; together you will slay him
Silence.
kilroy2.0 is here, the walls said.
Giggles in the dark.
"Kilroy2.0 is everywhere."

Father Thomas was the only one of seven to sleep that night.

He dreamed of hellfire, of burning flesh, of demons devouring legions of the damned. He saw fields of crosses, tens of thousands stretching into the crimson horizon. Christ hung from each one. The Messiahs wailed his name.

Thomas passed through crowds of stigmatic children who smeared their blood upon their faces. Fallen angels raised their charred wings to the orange sky and screamed. Thomas saw his mother and father, very much alive, fucking in the flaming blood of skinned goats.

Spikes of rock shot forth from the ground, impaling the unfortunate. All around, a symphony of screams.

Thomas wandered to the field of crosses and knelt before his Savior. He wept. The tears sizzled on the earth and evaporated.

Leave This Place, Christ commanded.

Thomas gazed upward. "Lord?"

You Do Not Belong Here.

Thomas smiled gratefully through his tears. "Can you help me, Lord? Can you deliver me to heaven?"

Never.

Thomas faltered. "Why, Lord?"

Christ smiled, his mouth slowly tugging at its sides . . . tugging apart, splitting, and becoming serpentine . . . bloodstained teeth suddenly dripping fangs . . . His crown of thorns transforming into great horns. Thomas shrieked.

You Belong In Neither Place, the thing said, and ripped its left hand free from the nail. It caressed Thomas's cheek.

"Why? Why?"

Isn't It Obvious, Fleshling? You Have No Soul.

Father Thomas awoke at daybreak, clutching his cheek and screaming.

FIVE

$\left(T\right)$ he man's shape was drenched in silhouette as he knelt in the dusty, crumbling dead end of the subterranean passage. Nearby construction-site lights blasted their heat against his back. He welcomed the warmth. For months, he'd been a bona fide mole man, a digger, supervising the highly illegal tunnel carved here, in the bedrock of one of America's largest cities . . . a tunnel quite near one of that city's most iconic boulevards.

His breaths were measured and confident. The half-face particulate mask he wore—a fancy filtration respirator that vaguely resembled the snout and jawline of *Star Wars* storm trooper—did a fine job of blocking the oppressive haze of airborne grime, permitting him to focus completely on the work before him.

His eyes zeroed in on the tangled clusters of wires ahead, his hand extended to the battered toolbox to his left. His manicured fingernails brushed against the nearby construction jackhammer instead.

The man flinched as he felt the gritty sludge of lubricant and powdered stone eke under his nails. The particle mask wheezed as he gave a half snarl, half sigh. Disgusting.

He turned his cool blue eyes away from the nest of wires, to the toolbox. He snatched up the wire cutters and brought them to the shoebox-size metal box by his knee. A dozen black metal barrels loomed behind the metal box, like an altar.

He snipped a wire. Stripped its insulation. Twisted its conductive guts with another exposed wire. A thumb's length of electrician's tape now, wrapping round and round the connection.

A smile from behind the half mask. He clicked his teeth, like a predator.

A lone red light blinked to life inside the metal box. Look at that. A cheerful Christmas light, for a very special gift.

The man closed the toolbox with a cavalier swipe of his hand—he no longer needed it, all preparations now complete—and gave it a thoughtless shove. It screeched as it slid on the gravel, finally banging against the carved wall of the tunnel. He turned his attention to the jackhammer now, and its industrial pneumatic hose.

His manicured fingers went to work, detaching the hose. He hefted it in his left hand, then stood, satisfied.

He squinted in the blaze of the construction lights, at his creation. He tugged the half mask from his face.

John Alpha grinned again, and his teeth—glowing white in contrast to his brown goatee—glittered, looking very sharp indeed.

He turned away from the dead end and dark altar, pneumatic hose still in hand, and strode down the passageway, toward the faint light ahead.

Alpha reached the tunnel's entrance, blinking at the swaying bulbs above. Still underground, but in the sloping hallway now, the hallway once used for hired help.

The portable air compressor was here, as was the silver, pistol-grip air-impact wrench. He picked up the tool, hefted it like the hand cannon it resembled, and clamped the pneumatic hose to its base. He casually flipped a switch on the compressor. It roared, alive, belching fumes into the dim hallway.

John Alpha glimpsed his reflection in the impact wrench. What a handsome devil. Smiled again.

He stepped into the hall, toward a thick door to his left. Behind him, the machine chugged on and on. The hose slithered behind him, an obedient snake attached to the wrench in his hand.

He opened the door, and his eyes, ever cool and observant, met those of his guest. His guest's eyes were suddenly wide, wild with fear. Good.

Alpha stepped inside, past the crates filled with sorrows-to-be-drowned, toward her. He paused at the center of the storage room, beside the video camera resting on a tripod. He gave his guest a wink, thrilling in the shudders it conjured. He tapped the red RE-CORD button on the camera and finally made his way to the person tied to the chair before him.

Had *he* done that? Made that face so delightfully bloodied and misshapen? He certainly had.

"Yes, yes, you've told me everything," he said casually, as if resuming a conversation. And he was; his guest had passed out from the beating hours ago. "But I haven't told *you* anything. Not yet. I thought I'd remedy that"—he nodded toward the whirring video camera—"while finishing up this little project, our collaborative piece of cinema. I have a friend who's just dying to see how it turns out. He loves these kinds of movies."

Alpha brought the pulse tool to his captive's face. The bolt socket locked to its barrel glimmered, an inch away from her chin.

Alpha pressed the trigger. The tool screamed, a sound most often heard in auto shops—*vipppppp!*—and she screamed, too, transfixed by the spinning socket, bucking her head away. The socket was a blur. He eased off the tool's trigger.

"This can take the lug nuts off a car wheel," Alpha whispered.

He lowered the air wrench to his guest's side, then stepped behind the chair, eyeing the bound hands, the fingers.

He leaned in close, his mouth hovering near her ear. "Let me share my vision with you. My plan. Pain will unite this world. There's a great deal of pain coming."

He wedged one of her fingers into the socket. And as the air wrench came alive again, and the flesh and bone were spun into slivers, and the blood sprayed against the chair, and the wall, and the floor, John Alpha never blinked. He kept cooing into that ear, low and cruel and certain, as the unholy noise filled the room.

"So. Much. Pain."

SIX

r. DeFalco, the bearded moonman who'd whispered into John's ear yesterday when John had been strapped to a gurney, escorted the visitors through the hallways of the 7th Son facility. It was just after 7:00 a.m. DeFalco politely declined to answer any questions other than "Where are we going?" That query came from the thin one who had fainted; Jay, if John recalled correctly, and "When will we talk to Kleinman?" That had been Jack, the gene splicer.

The mess hall, DeFalco replied. After breakfast, DeFalco replied. Which prompted another question: "What's for chow?" (Michael, USMC.)

The bearded, bespectacled, gibbering fat man, whom John had nicknamed the lunatic—the only one of them who had neither bathed nor put on the new government-issued casual duds they all had in their rooms—peeped a question about his computers. DeFalco said they should be installed in the Common Room later that day. John almost questioned why Kilroy2.0 had been allowed to bring his personal possessions along . . . but then reconsidered, realizing his own Gibson probably wouldn't come in handy in a national crisis.

The hallways of 7th Son were more fascinating than frightening now that John was seeing them from an upright perspective. The lighting was practical: intermittent fluorescent panels between white ceiling tiles. The walls were pale gray slabs of unpainted concrete. A small, delicately crafted mosaic, embedded in the middle of each wall, was in the shape of a horizontal double helix, forever stretching out before them on either side.

My tax dollars at work, John thought.

They walked in bleary-eyed silence. The place had a labyrinthine, institutional quality . . . a peculiar hybrid of 1950s hospital and public-school sensibility. They passed a few doorways with keypad locks, and closed doors that slid open from the middle. John saw no windows.

The mess hall was a mammoth room dominated by swooping stainless-steel columns and at least a dozen rows of tables and chairs. John smiled up at the sun—this room had a skylight, too.

They piled their cafeteria trays with scrambled eggs, sausage links, and flapjacks from a hot bar.

"Have your breakfast, gentlemen," DeFalco said, as they were sitting down at the tables. "Dr. Kleinman will be here shortly."

"When?" asked Father Thomas, his voice trembling. John thought the man still looked priestly despite the khakis and the black Izod.

"Shortly." DeFalco closed and locked the cafeteria's double doors.

John sat down next to Jack. He squinted through the sunlight glinting from the columns, then rubbed his eyes. Last night's conversation was still baking his noodle—it felt both tangible and ephemeral, like a half-remembered dream. Like headlights in fog. Shower, shave, or no, John still felt like shit.

Jack, the geneticist, looked worse. The all-nighter had done in the family man. He sleepily scratched his beard and stared down at his breakfast. They didn't speak.

Michael clomped past Father Thomas, who was sitting alone at another table. The marine tossed his tray onto the Formica and sat across from John. Michael was alert, focused. He slapped two cartons of milk on the table and frowned at the sleepyheads.

"Get the lead out, boys," he said. "Today's a working day. Today we learn everything."

"That's what I'm afraid of," Jack said.

"What's there to be afraid of?" Michael asked, then stuffed his mouth full of eggs. John was horrified and amused. The marine held his utensils as if they were drumsticks, deftly shoveling up the grub and popping it into his mouth at a breathtaking pace.

"We get our orders today, hoss," Michael said as he skewered a sausage. "We won't be sitting on our pretty fannies anymore. We'll get to *act*."

Now Dr. Mike and Jay sat down at the table. John had noticed them wandering around the room like a couple of middle-schoolers, wondering where to sit. Dr. Mike didn't look so Dapper-fucking-Dan when he was out of his business suit, John thought. Particularly with that bruise on his head.

"You know what? That's great, just great," Jack replied. He eyed the newcomers, then turned his attention back to Michael. "But I'm not like you. I didn't ask for this, and I don't want to take orders. I have a home. A life. A wife. She must out for her mind right now. And my girls . . ." He gazed around the cafeteria, sneering. "It's sick. You know what two words have been going through my head this morning? *Lab rats*. That's what I feel like. A rat in a maze."

Michael downed one of the cartons of milk, crushed it in his hand, and harrumphed.

"What?" Jack said. "You don't feel that way?"

"I don't care who you are, hoss—janitor, gene-splicer, prez of the U.S.—there's always a chain of command," Michael replied. "There's always a bigger fish. We all take orders. The only thing that makes us different is who we take orders from."

"So?"

"So you're sore because there's been a change of command."

The thin one—Jay was his name—waved his knife in protest. "Now wait a minute." He nodded to Jack. *He loves to talk with his hands*, John thought. *Just like me.* "He's right. This is different. We're talking about cloning. Identity. Have you even *thought* about what that old man said? Have you *processed* it? Have you thought about how many international laws were broken creating this place? Have you considered that I might know every single dream— every dirty little secret—you ever had till the time you were four-teen?"

Michael glanced at John and Jack. "A little."

"And?"

"And it means I know *your* dirty little secrets, bub." Michael opened another milk carton. It looked fragile in his calloused hands. He turned to Jack. "Listen. All I'm saying is you were a rat searching for your cheese long before you came here. You cut up mice and cloned them. I went where the brass told me. John here plays guitar and makes drinks for club jumpers. The only thing that's changed now is our bosses."

Jack threw his fork onto his tray. "No. That's not all. This isn't some change of job title. *Everything's* changed. When people talk about their childhoods, Michael, they talk about seeing the same movies, reading the same books . . . they might even go on about their parents and crushes. That's not what happened last night. When you, John, and I talked last night, we talked about the same experiences. *The exact same experiences.* The same memories."

"If they were even our memories to begin with," John said.

Jay groaned and crossed his thin arms. "Then it's true."

The sound of laughter made the men stop and turn their heads. It was Kilroy2.0, John saw, sitting at a faraway table. The lunatic was staring up at the skylight, then down at the walls and the floors. Kilroy2.0 laughed again—this time at the floor—and began whispering to himself.

"Does anyone know what's up with him?" Jay asked.

Dr. Mike finally spoke up. "Schizophrenic, most likely. Either that or autistic savant. He hasn't said much yet. If he's autistic, he may not say much at all. If he's a schizo—and if we get to a subject he's fixated on—we may never be able to shut him up."

"Creepsville," John said.

"Don't worry about him," the marine said, then downed his other milk. He nodded to the table where Father Thomas sat, alone. "Worry about the priest. He's the one who's fubar."

John looked over at the man. Father Thomas was resting his head on his crossed arms like a child trying to nap. He was holding his rosary.

John turned his attention back to Dr. Mike. "You a shrink?"

"Criminal psychologist," Mike sniffed. "I've done a lot of criminal profiling for the LAPD; some consulting work here and there." He raised his chin slightly. "I wrote a book recently."

The marine chuckled. "Sounds like all of you were heads of the class. Way ahead of the curve. Bet you fellas jumped a grade or two in high school and college, didn't you? Caught the eye of your teachers, were given additional responsibilities, graduated well before your buddies? Regular Doogie Howsers?"

They looked at him.

"Well, that's what happened to me." Michael's eyes were haunted for a moment. "After I got out, I mean. Yeah."

The group didn't speak, waiting for more. It didn't come. Michael blinked and brightened as he shifted gears.

"I mean, I didn't go Corps until five years ago. You don't ordinarily score captain—and earn the right to be in Force Recon—in such a short time. Especially when you get a late start like me."

Dr. Mike cleared his throat and rapped his knuckles on the table, as if calling a meeting to order. "This conversation is cute, but let me be the first to say I don't believe any of it." His eyes flitted from the others' faces to the room around them. "This is a grand delusion."

"That's what I said last night," Jack said. "Until we talked about the Grand Canyon and piano lessons and first kisses."

Jay stiffened, a forkful of food halfway to his thin, pale face. "First kisses?"

"Yeah." Jack looked at the criminal psychologist. "The memories were the same."

"I wonder about that," Dr. Mike said, smiling slightly. "I really do. I believe you *thought* you had a conversation last night in which you shared the same memories. But I think your subconscious was trying to facilitate the delusion, based on what Kleinman had said."

John plucked his pack of cigarettes from his shirt pocket, shook out a smoke, and lit it. "What do you mean?"

"All of this chitchat about similar memories and similar appearance—it was all planted by that old man," Dr. Mike said. "Do you understand how preposterous it all sounds, how irrational it is? We've been kidnapped because we look the same—and because we have the same names. That's it. John Michael Smith? Hello? An extremely common name. People have a way of finding patterns and significance where none exist."

The men watched him. Dr. Mike smiled slyly. "Kleinman and that general, they're trying to brainwash us. They're using our fear and the removal from our comfort zones to create this delusion. Marine, you know how this goes. Get a bunch of war vets in the same room and they'll start spouting specific details about battles they never witnessed. Kleinman's playing the music. You're singing along."

"You're talking about false memories," Michael said.

"To what end?" Jay asked.

"Hell if I know," Dr. Mike said, shrugging. He pointed to the lunatic across the room, then at Jay himself. "He's a schizophrenic. You're not. You're thin and don't need glasses. Jack isn't, and does. The priest's hair's thinning—just like yours—but the marine's isn't. John here plays the guitar. I haven't strummed a chord in years. Yes, there are physical similarities between us. But if we're supposed to be genetically identical *clones*, we're supposed to be the same. So why aren't we all shithouse-rat mad? Why aren't we all wearing spectacles? Why aren't we all pining for the Hair Club for Men? Think about it."

The table fell silent. John took a drag and chewed on the words. *Grand delusion.*

He looked into Dr. Mike's eyes . . . and narrowed his own.

No.

John remembered nearly screaming yesterday when he first saw Kilroy2.0's eyes, remembered how the priest had asked him if they were brothers. And nothing could downplay the impact of last night's talk with the marine and the geneticist.

And Dr. Mike himself had lost it yesterday—most notably, after Kleinman had told them their dead parents were alive.

John reached for his wallet. "I don't believe you."

Across the table, the marine cracked his knuckles. "I don't, either."

Dr. Mike raised his eyebrows. "Why not? What I said makes sense from a psychological perspective. Talk to your jarhead friend here. This is what the military calls the craft. It's textbook psyops. They're trying to reprogram us, John. Don't you see that?"

John placed the Camel in his mouth, flipped open his wallet, and fished out two wrinkled photographs. He plunked one of them into the middle of the table.

"Who are these people?" he asked, squinting through the smoke.

Dr. Mike looked at the picture. In it, a middle-aged couple smiled at the camera. The man was hugging a teenaged version of John from behind. A snowcapped mountain dominated the horizon.

"I have no idea," Mike said. "Never seen them before in my life." He looked at the four pairs of eyes scrutinizing him and raised his right hand, palm out. "Honest Injun."

"Fair enough," John said. "But you keep staying honest, Doc. As honest as I'm going to be. These are the people who raised me after my folks were killed. They're my uncle and aunt. Karl and Jaclyn Smith. Tell me something: what were the names of the people who raised you after *your* parents were killed?"

Blue anger flared in Dr. Mike's eyes. "That's none of your business."

"But it is," John said. "It's all of our business. Anyone else here raised like Kleinman said? By an Uncle Karl and Aunt Jaclyn?"

Jack nodded slowly. Jay picked up the photograph and examined it. "They don't look like my aunt and uncle. They look similar, but not identical."

"Would they have to be?" Michael the marine asked softly. "Wouldn't you just need people who *looked* like the folks in the old picture? Remember? The one Dad always carried in his wallet? The old, banged-up one he used to show us when we'd get a postcard from them? It was faded, fuzzy. Lots of wiggle room there. Jesus."

Dr. Mike slammed his hand on the table. His silverware skittered.

"This is ridiculous!" he cried. "Listen to yourselves! There is no *us*. There is no *we*. There is only me. I'm not going to sit here and allow myself to be hoodwinked like the rest of—"

John tossed the other photograph onto the table. This time, the criminal profiler gasped.

"Now who's in this picture, Doc?" John asked. "Tell me."

They all stared down at the crinkled picture in fascination, in horror. The photo was old, faded, and unmistakable.

"Who's in the picture, Mike?"

Suddenly, another photograph was tossed onto the table. It, too, was gnarled. It, too, had the identical image of smiling man, woman, and blond-haired boy. The boy in the photograph was around six years old. John looked up—behind Dr. Mike—and saw the priest standing there. His wallet was open, too.

"It's your parents," Father Thomas said. His eyes were bloodshot; dark circles hung beneath them. "Our parents. The parents of the children who never were."

Dr. Mike laughed nervously. "Believe what you want. Continue walking down this path of delusion and you'll be just like the fat man over there. You won't know what's reality and what's concoction, what's fact and what's self-deluded fiction. Human clones. Nonexistent childhoods. An alter-ego villain who's so Freudian it's laughable. I'll believe it when I see it."

At that moment, the doors of the mess hall unlocked and opened. Dr. Kleinman, General Hill, and Dr. DeFalco stepped inside.

Kleinman gave them a patient, grandfatherly smile. "Then it's high time we began the tour."

As they strode through the halls, accompanied by four armed soldiers, Kleinman explained that the oldest part of the 7th Son facility had been built in 1951. Much of Project 7th Son was underground, due to the extreme sensitivity of the experiments and the need for secrecy—not just in principle, but in practicality. If built aboveground with the same dimensions, Kleinman said, the 7th Son facility would be about as wide as a city block and taller than Chicago's Sears Tower.

John listened and accepted this with detached awe and bewilderment, that breed of belief/disbelief found almost exclusively in dreams. (*Of course Janeane Garofalo finds me witty and attractive— even though I'm wearing only a coonskin cap.*)

The only other time John could remember pondering something so incredulously credible was in high school, as he doodled rocket ships into his notebook during American-history class. That was the first time he'd truly regarded mankind's first steps on the moon as something other than past tense. Now that was a genuine miracle; human will made reality. *We went to the fucking moon, man.* Bet your ass it was one giant leap for mankind. This here was the next leap . . . off the deep end.

Kleinman continued. The complex was located about fifteen minutes south of Leesburg, Virginia—a town about thirty miles west of Washington. Much of the land in this region was owned by the federal government, Kleinman said, and was where most of the Cold War–era contingency buildings were built. The nuke-proof auxiliary White House (apparently nicknamed the Out House by insiders) was somewhere in this farm country, as were dozens of shelters for Congress-folk (Club Fed) and the Supreme Court (Judgment Stay).

They passed more silver doorways, T-junctions, and some passersby—young army folk, mostly. Hallways flowed endlessly to their right and left; that preposterous double-helix mosaic spiraled ever onward on each wall. Finally, the hallway they were following dead-ended. A small computer device sloped outward from one of the walls. Clearly, the only people who had maintained their sense of direction during the trek were the doctors, the general . . . and perhaps Michael.

Rats in a maze, John thought. *Just like Jack said.*

Kleinman approached the computer and let a device scan his eye. The dead-end wall suddenly opened like a giant mouth. Somewhere far away, John heard the machines opening the maw— a fluid, ear-piercing *reeeeeeee* that sounded almost like a dentist's drill. He shivered. The lunatic beside him giggled.

The old man turned around to face them. Any tour-guide pleasantries were now gone from his face.

"Your retina configurations have already been loaded into the security database, so you all will have access to the elevator if needed," he said, nodding back to the dark compartment now behind him. "You might want to pop your ears now, and again when we reach the destination. The ride can be unpleasant for first-timers."

Kleinman stepped into the dark room and the group followed. Thirteen men and one woman (one of the grunts was female) crowded into the tiny, dim elevator. A computer panel inside and a small light above were the only illumination. They all watched the maw close. John felt the claustrophobia seep from the metal walls. He took in air in shallow breaths—he'd hated small places ever since he was a kid (ever since that incident in the cave, *God, getting lost in the cave* . . .), and the giggling freak show beside him reeked to high heaven. General Hill's head towered well above them like the face of a dark, stone god.

"Gentlemen, what you're about to see won't be easy for you," Kleinman said.

"It's not easy right now, old man," Dr. Mike hissed, as he inched away from Kilroy2.0.

"It certainly won't be any easier in a moment. It's time you saw where you were born." Kleinman cleared his throat and looked at the ceiling. "Computer?"

"*HERE*," bleated a disembodied voice.

"Disengage locking clamps."

Ka-CHUNG. The entire elevator car quaked and bucked downward several inches. The floor suddenly felt unsteady, as if they were floating. John looked up at Hill's stony face. The general looked down at him—his mouth inched up gently. John closed his eyes.

"Computer, prepare destination," Kleinman called.

"*READY FOR DESTINATION INPUT*."

"Kleinman?" That was Jay's voice, the thin one, the one who'd fainted yesterday. His voice was high, trembling. "Where are we going?"

"The Womb."

"*ENGAGED*."

The elevator plummeted into the earth like a rocket gone bad. The walls rattled, the floor trembled beneath them. Somewhere outside this box, a loose sheet of metal fluttered against another, screeching over the roar.

Pressed against tense bodies, feeling the fillings in his teeth tremble, John heard one of himselves scream into the howling wind, into the darkness.

SEVEN

(T) hey were two thousand feet beneath the earth's surface, beneath whatever remnant of a normal life any of them had once led. Kleinman could call the elevator whatever he wanted. John called it the Bullet Train to Hell.

The elevator door opened once again, and the seven strangers spilled out into a corridor, and its comparatively fresh air. John kept his breakfast down by breathing slowly and popping his ears. Jay wasn't so lucky. He dashed several feet down the hallway before spewing his scrambled eggs and sausage across a wall.

Jay dragged the back of his hand across his chin and looked up at the group. "Sorry."

"Dig the smell," Dr. Mike said.

Dr. DeFalco laughed, a low *ho-ho*. General Hill cleared his throat, and Kleinman nodded.

"Don't worry," the old man said. "We'll call someone to clean it up. Let's go."

They walked down the corridor. The institutional look was now replaced with a subterranean feel; fewer lights, dark stone walls, and dark metal support beams. This part of the complex wasn't as well polished as the upper decks. Not many folks made it down here, John reckoned.

They then came to another large door. It was circular. Kleinman turned and took a moment to look each of the seven clones in the eyes—John, Jay, Dr. Mike, Kilroy2.0, Father Thomas, Jack, Michael. He nodded, and General Hill approached a retina scanner on the wall. Metallic bolts inside the door released, and the metal door swung outward, like that of a bank vault.

"This is where you were born," Kleinman said.

The clones hesitated.

"Go inside. See."

They stepped through the metal portal, into a circular room with walls at least forty feet high. Old gymnasium-style lights hung from the ceiling. One of them flickered, buzzing like a furious wasp.

An enormous metal contraption mounted on the ceiling hung toward the floor, dominating the center of the room. It resembled a clutching seven-fingered human hand, or an upside-down steel flower. The base attached to the ceiling was at least fifteen feet wide. John gasped. The only things he'd ever seen that closely resembled this were those gyrating, eight-armed carnival rides called the Tarantula or Spider—the ones painted black, with the red capsules that swung madly from each arm.

But this Tarantula was shimmering and inverted . . . as if it had been plucked up by a titan, spun 180 degrees on its axis, and pressed into the ceiling. On the end of each of the seven arms was a large, hollow orb, connected and locked in place by four multiknuckled steel talons. The orbs were a pale translucent green, at least eight feet in diameter. Crisscrossing clusters of hoses and cables snaked down from the ceiling to the seven arms, then into the spheres. Seven computer consoles—each armed with four boxy monitors and keyboards—curved around the perimeter of the Tarantula.

"Jesus Christ," Jay said.

John looked numbly at Jay, then at the others. Father Thomas stared at the machine, awestruck. Jack and Dr. Mike stood side by side, mirroring each other's horrified expressions. Michael's mouth was frozen in a nervous smile, as if his expectations had suddenly derailed. Kilroy2.0 gazed at the Tarantula with wonder, childlike.

"This floor is called the Womb, but this is only one facet of it: the cloning chamber," Kleinman said from behind them. The old man nodded to the Tarantula. "This is where, sixteen years ago, we transferred the seven samples of cloned tissue from the original John Michael Smith—John Alpha. The spheres you see were filled with a nutrient-rich facsimile of embryonic fluid and a growth-acceleration compound."

Cloning chambers, John thought. *Jesus, look at them.*

"A cell sample was placed in each," Kleinman continued. "It was here where you were all born, in body. You were grown to midteen maturity in just two years."

Above them, the rogue light buzzed maniacally. John's mind buzzed right along with it. He looked at the mammoth device suspended from the ceiling. Tarantula. Spider. Step right up. What had he been expecting to see here? Not this.

Kleinman, from far away: . . . *spheres coated inside with a conductive substance that assisted in bioelectric delivery for accelerated growth . . .*

This. This made it more than a midnight, caffeinated conversation. This made it more than identical faces, identical eyes, identical photographs on cafeteria tables.

. . . *see the small speaker in each, which we used to replicate the sounds of the in utero experience . . .*

This made it real.

This was real.

Real.

An explosive bang started John from his thoughts. He looked over his shoulder, across the room. A door—a nearly seamless part of this room's curved wall just seconds ago—had propelled itself upward into a slot in the doorframe. Kleinman stepped inside and beckoned them all to enter, like a fun-house barker. John fought the cold, oily fear squirming in his stomach.

John walked—it was more like sleepwalking—toward the doorway. He didn't want to go inside. This was enough. He didn't want to see.

He couldn't not see.

He moaned as he stepped past the others and saw what was inside this smaller room. His focus was not on the wall of computer screens and keyboards, or the black, spiral staircase descending into the floor, or the anaconda cables that slithered from the walls to a looming metal cabinet with wink-wink lights.

It was the plane of seven square, metal doors in the wall facing him. Shimmering stainless steel, about four feet from the floor. Each door sported an old-time refrigerator handle, cocked on the side. They gleamed like knives in the fluorescent light.

He knew what kind of doors those were. Morgue cold drawer doors. With a number—1 to 7—stenciled on each.

Kleinman stepped over to one of the doors and yanked its silver handle, popping it open. The old man tugged on something inside, and out rolled a metal slab.

"What the hell?" Jack muttered.

The slab's reflection glowed in Kleinman's trifocals, a silver rectangle grinning at the seven visitors.

"This is where you were truly born. Born, in mind," the old man said. "Despite its appearance, this compartment brings life. More significantly, it *records* life."

John's mind formed the question, but it was Michael who asked it.

Better start getting used to that, Johnny-Boy.

"What're you talking about?" the marine asked. "That's a dead man's bed."

"What you see here is not as important as what you don't see," Kleinman said. "Inside this compartment are the sophisticated devices and sensors that record human memory. Behind this wall resides the computer system that can 'upload' and 'download' a lifetime of human memories in just seconds."

Michael shook his head, confused. *He doesn't get it,* John thought. *Ha. We don't get it.*

"Think of the human brain as a computer disk," Kleinman said. "This"—he pointed inside the dark hole—"is the disk drive. When you were removed from your cloning chambers, we placed each of you inside this. We then downloaded the memories of John Alpha . . . the memories we'd recorded from his mind just after the car accident when he was fourteen . . . into your brains."

"When *we* were fourteen," Dr. Mike insisted quietly.

"No," Kleinman said. "You were never fourteen."

Mike stood there, his mouth hanging open as if someone had given it a good yank.

Kilroy2.0 began to laugh, an effeminate hee-hee that made John jump. Gooseflesh rushed over his arms.

"We're *computers!*" the lunatic cried abruptly. "Computers! Data! One-oh-oh-one-one-one-oh-one-ohhhhh—"

"Shut that crazy fucker up," Dr. Mike snarled.

The fool kept going, like a busted Bag of Laughs toy. Incensed, Dr. Mike dashed over to Kilroy2.0 and grabbed the fat man's shirt, shaking him, stretching the yellow fabric in his clenched fists, tearing it.

"SHUT UP! SHUT YOUR FUCKING MOUTH! Not real, none of it's—"

"Hee-heeeeeee! One-oh-one-oh-oh-one!"

Two soldiers descended upon them, yanking Dr. Mike from the madman. Mike still clawed at Kilroy2.0 from behind the soldier. John found himself thinking this was all quite like an episode of *The Jerry Springer Show.*

"Keep them separated," General Hill commanded. He glared at Mike. "I've had enough of your bullshit."

Dr. DeFalco stepped between them and said, "In a way, Kilroy2.0 is right. Human memory can be stored as digital information. The MemR/I chamber can read memories stored in the brain, translate it into binary code, and transfer it to a . . . ah . . . a 'hard drive.' "

"Which in turn can be translated and downloaded into another human brain," Kleinman said.

Jack took his gaze away from the glimmering morgue table and looked at the old man.

"You cloned *memory.* How."

It wasn't a question. It was a demand. As punctuation, Jack removed his wire rims and glared at Kleinman.

"Human genetic cloning is possible, Jack. You know that," Kleinman replied. "Any geneticist worth his salt these days knows that. But this is different. What if I told you that a person—you, me, anyone—could remember everything they had ever experienced? Not just the milestones. Not just the so-called important things. I mean everything. Anything."

"Impossible," interjected Michael, the marine. "I don't care how well trained somebody is. We forget."

Kleinman raised a professorial finger. "Do we? Do we really?" He gave a knowing smile, one John wasn't entirely comfortable with. "Michael, surely you've had a long-lost memory rush into your mind that felt so fresh, so real—so *important*, even—that you marveled at how you'd ever forgotten it in the first place. A childhood teacher's name. A debt. A phone number, an address."

A line of concentration formed on Michael's brow, identical to the one above Jack's eyes, John noticed.

"Of course you have," Kleinman said, his grin wider now. He winked. "Right now, you're probably recollecting some of the memories you'd once remembered after *forgetting* them."

Michael smiled slightly.

"That's good," Kleinman said, nodding. "So imagine if your brain could not only recall all of the things you remember—and the things you remembered after 'forgetting' them—but *all of the things you may never, ever remember*. Imagine if the brain stored every moment of your life—dreams, conscious and unconscious memory—for just such an occurrence: for the possibility of future recollection. Not short- or long-term memory. All-term memory."

"That'd be one helluva noggin," Michael said.

"Indeed it is."

Jack shook his head. "That doesn't answer my question, Kleinman. How?"

Kleinman stepped over to Jack. "Genetics is your science. You know that DNA is absolute: a blueprint of the body, plans for a skyscraper that—given the correct circumstances—will be built, live, and thrive. DNA defines the appearance of a person, genetic predispositions, potential physical ailments, perhaps even behavior. DNA is what it is. It cannot be undone."

"Crude, but accurate," Jack replied.

Kleinman smiled again.

"The human memory works the same way, only in reverse," the old man said. "The quadrillions of stimuli we encounter every day pass through the hippocampus, the brain's gatekeeper for future memories. Those memories are then stored in the mind for future reference, predispositions, and behavior. Now, neurologists say the most important stimuli we receive are saved in various regions of the brain by creating 'highways' of neural connections. The unimportant stuff is stored for a while and then discarded as irrelevant, they say. Forgotten. The blueprint is drawn—and the skyscraper built—as life unfolds. Memory, like life, is truly a work in progress.

"But the unused hallways and floors of your neural skyscraper . . . those supposedly unimportant stimuli . . . are never truly discarded, Jack. They, along with every other sliver of stimuli you've ever ingested—even your internal thoughts and emotions—still reside in the gatekeeper. The hippocampus. The hippocampus remembers everything even if you never do. It's like a recording. More important, the hippocampus facilitates a critical function in recollection. Its special breed of memory—a type of neuroelectric 'flash' memory—exists so that important and long-forgotten irrelevant information can be accessed and remembered in picoseconds. What is memory if not a neural blast from the past?

"Like DNA, this breed of memory cannot be undone," Kleinman continued. "It's always there, like the foundations of a skyscraper, like hiss in a tape recording, just waiting for the right circumstance to be remembered: a whiff of perfume, a song, a visual stimulus. Every creature with a complex, hippocampus-based brain has this 'memory DNA.' We here call it Memory Totality."

John's gaze numbly followed Kleinman's hand as it waved back to the dark hole in the wall.

"In there," Kleinman said, "is a machine that is not unlike an EEG. We call it the MemR/I—Memory Retrieval/Installation—chamber."

Mem-ree, John thought. *Got it.*

"By attaching electrodes to a person's head," the old man continued, "the device scans the electrical waves of a living brain and searches for the hippocampus's unique Memory Totality brain wave; this tape hiss. It's well below other brain waves, a subliminal, working wave that is active every moment we live. It's more than that, Jack. It *is* memory in its entirety. Do you understand?"

Jack scratched his beard and nodded his head slowly.

John found his mouth saying the sentence before he could stop himself: "So the contraption in there reads the hippocampus wave and records it."

"Yes," Kleinman said. "It's indecipherable to us, of course. Gibberish. Brainspeak. We could never analyze it the way we can conventional data, like the contents of a spreadsheet file. But the computer system behind this wall does the work of—"

"—translating the gibberish into binary code," John said.

"That's right. This is critical during the 'upload,' the Memory Totality recording process. It also translates the code back into brainspeak as it's downloaded into another mind."

"How do you *know* all this?" Jay asked. "How did you know how to do . . . all of this?"

"Brilliant thinkers." Kleinman gazed into space for a moment. His voice became soft, distracted. John noticed the old man's hands tremble. "Brilliant, brilliant thinkers."

The seven stood in silence, staring into the dark square, into the place where their memories—their history—were installed into fresh brains like computer software. *The history of a stranger, the history of me,* John thought. *We weren't fourteen. We were never fourteen. Someone else was. Someone else who looks like us. No—we look like him. John Alpha. Heeee. Mad, mad fun. We're number 10010101.*

"So where do the recorded memories go?" Father Thomas asked. He looked just as numb as John felt.

"I'll show you," Kleinman said.

EIGHT

he group descended the spiral staircase at the far end of the cramped room—this one undoubtedly leading to another circle of hell, John thought—and stepped into a corridor with a second theatrically large door.

"The impetus for Project 7th Son began just after the Second World War," John heard Kleinman say. "The project's creators envisioned the overall design of this facility during that time, based on the projected needs of the program, and the technologies that would inevitably come. This was, of course, before microprocessors began to revolutionize the way we store computer information. Even when we built this MemR/I Array Vault in the 1980s, we weren't sure how much hard-disk space we would need to store a Memory Totality—an entire human memory. One might say we overprojected, though I insist we defaulted on the side of safety. Better to have too much hard-drive capacity than not enough."

Kleinman pressed a series of switches on the metal panel next to the door, and it opened with a groan of pressing pistons and spinning gears. The door slid into the ceiling. John and the rest of the clones—*yes, it's safe to call us clones now, send in the clones*—stepped through the door, onto a metal catwalk.

The MemR/I Array was gargantuan, at least the length and width of three football fields, dimly lit by more buzzing fluorescent lights. The catwalk upon which they stood hovered above clusters of curved, densely packed, ten-foot-tall, black metal containers. Each container was C-shaped, and the width of a minivan. The air was filled with a deep, throbbing hum and the chilly whoosh of air conditioners. There were hundreds of these black containers. Hundreds, all aligned in barely touching semicircular patterns, rows of giant C's, obsidian chain mail extending to the horizon.

Jay turned to Kleinman. "Are those hard drives?"

Kleinman nodded. "That's the best term for them. They're more complex than any computer storage medium you're familiar with. Hard drives, yes."

Jay pointed to a cluster of whirring black containers beneath them. "How many?"

"Two thousand," Kleinman said, his voice grave.

"Never seen anything like this," Kilroy2.0 said. Beside him, John flinched; it was the first normal thing the freak show had said. "They look like Crays. Old-school. Way back."

Kleinman's assistant nodded, smiling. "They are and they aren't," Dr. DeFalco said. "We used the brilliant horseshoe design of the Cray-1 supercomputer as inspiration and added our own modifications to fit the needs of the system. These custom-built 'quasi-Crays' weren't manufactured for number crunching and high-speed processing, as the original Cray-1s were. These are used purely for data storage. Connected, the Q-Crays behave as a massive hypercomputer. It's rock solid, cooled by an elaborate system beneath this level. The MemR/I Array has never been switched off, has never been rebooted—and it never crashes."

"Electricity bills must be through the roof," Dr. Mike murmured.

John raised his hand; this was like a school lesson, after all. "Why would it matter? Why would it matter if you switched it off?"

Kleinman's eyes crinkled behind his trifocals. "For the same reason why you can never switch off your brain without disastrous results. If there were ever an interruption in power—a glitch, a crash—it would damage the data stored inside these Q-Crays. You're gazing at the mechanical equivalent of a hippocampus, John. Memories. A computer crash would be the equivalent of blunt trauma, complete with ensuing brain damage and memory loss."

Kilroy2.0 nodded out into the humming horizon. "How much storage capacity? Just how much data can you store here?"

"The entire MemR/I Array can store one exabyte of digital information—that's one quintillion bytes, millions of times more data than personal computers can store," Kleinman said. "Of course, if we'd known about DNACs back then, our physical storage needs would have been much, much smaller."

"Dee-what?" Michael asked.

Kilroy2.0 opened his mouth to speak again.

"Forget it," General Hill said. "If you're going to tell them, hacker, do it later. We've already spent too much time here."

The lunatic closed his mouth, then stuck out his tongue when the general looked away.

"The consciousness of John Alpha—each of you—is stored in these machines, from birth to the age of fourteen," Kleinman said. "Since it's digital information, there's no degradation of the data. We could upload them into another mind even now, if we chose to. The memories would be just as fresh—just as real—to the recipient of those memories as it was for each of you sixteen years ago."

"Would be disconcerting, done today," Kilroy2.0 murmured. "Walking anachronism. Heh."

"It's remarkable," Dr. DeFalco said.

"Remarkable," the hacker repeated.

"Is it alive?" Father Thomas asked. The others turned to face him. "Are the memories, you know, *aware*? That they're imprisoned?"

DeFalco served up another low Santa Claus *ho-ho*. "Does a word-processing file know it's a 'prisoner' in a personal computer?" the bearded doctor asked. "Of course not. It merely *is*. The data is static; information is neither being added to nor subtracted from it. It's software that can be transferred again and again. No change. No sentience."

"But what about the soul?" Thomas asked. "You've incarcerated a person's s—"

"Enough," Hill said.

John felt sick again. The hum of the hard-drive containers was boring into his mind. More John Smiths could be born here. More.

He blinked himself away from the dark army of hard drives and cleared his throat. "You said you 'overestimated' when you built this place. What's that mean?"

"Indeed I did," Kleinman said. "We overprojected the storage needs for our Memory Totality recording system. After we stored the digital information from John Alpha's brain, we learned the hypercomputer here could store at least three other complete human memories. It was an exciting discovery."

"Exciting?" a voice snapped. John turned. It was Jack, the geneticist. Jack's face was turning scarlet beneath his beard. He clutched the catwalk guardrail, knuckles glaring white against the black metal. "Did you record any more memories? Did you clone anyone else, you son of a bitch? Did you play God with anyone other than me? Us?"

Kleinman stepped back, startled. One of the soldiers clomped forward, his bootheels ringing out into the void, but Jack raised his hands in surrender.

"No," Kleinman said. "Of course not. We haven't touched the MemR/I Array since . . . since we cloned you. Since John Alpha."

The old man removed his glasses and rubbed his eyes. "Alpha," he muttered. He glanced at General Hill. "It's time to brief them."

NINE

T he colossal thirty-inch flat-screen monitor glowed bright in the domed room's darkness. Data cascaded across on-screen windows; video flickered from numerous Web sites. Kilroy2.0—the drooling, walking insane asylum that he was— might appreciate the scene, were he here.

But "here" was hundreds of miles away from the 7th Son facility . . . and while Special(k) was familiar indeed with the notorious cyberprophet, "here" was the very last place he'd want Kilroy2.0 to be.

It's poor manners to invite the man whose doom you're planning into your home, you see.

Special(k) snatched the warm can of Red Bull from his work-station and guzzled its contents. He grimaced. The stuff tasted like horse piss, but it kept his twentysomething body running, *brain petrol*, he called it, and when you live the hacker life and follow the prophet's mad online rantings, you must embrace the caffeinated lifestyle.

He chucked the empty can over his shoulder, and it clatter-clanged against the grated floor. The noise echoed in the cavern-ous, windowless room. Special(k) turned his attention to the video streaming on the LCD, and his eyes went hungry and half-lidded again, drinking up the writhing bodies, the improbable positions. God yes, he could believe this was art.

He leaned closer, craving to see it all, and hear more of the moans and primal cries. The homemade footage glowed against his pale face, accentuating his sharp features, a beaklike nose. He felt himself grow hard again and smiled.

On-screen, the man moaned as he lay in a bed, spent. A woman knelt nearby, her impossibly long tongue extended at the thing in her hand. She gave it a long lick.

Then she plunged the knife into the man's chest a fourth time. Then a fifth. More blood sprayed across the once-white sheets. She laughed and looked at the screen now, at the video camera recording from some hidden locale, and licked the knife again, sliding its bloody hilt between her breasts, apparently delighting in the mayhem she'd created.

Special(k) certainly was. He marveled, unblinking. You can find anything on the Internet if you look hard enough. Photos. Movies. Subcultures and communities. And people who will do things for money. Not *fake* things such as you see at multiplex. Real things, with real blood.

Special(k) nearly purred as his eyes flitted to another window. Then another. They weren't all snuff films, though those were his favorites. Reality TV, each your heart out. (And Special(k) had seen *that* video, too, yes, he had. He'd paid a great deal of money to obtain it.)

God bless America, the land of opportunity . . . and the desperate, and depraved.

He was edging—it was exquisite, delicious, prolonging the orgasm—when the phone rang. The caller ID forced it all from his mind.

"What does the prophet say?" John Alpha's voice said on the line.

"The prophet says nothing," Special(k) replied, as he minimized the on-screen windows. "We are apparently a go. His 'radio silence' implies that he no longer has a keyboard with which to type."

"So they have him."

The hacker nodded. "Absolutely safe to assume that, yes. I know him better than you do these days."

This was true. Years ago, Special(k) had come into the good graces of the messianic mad hacker and had scored membership in the cyberprophet's instant-messaging broadcasts. He later became a trusted ally, a priceless thing in conspiracy-theorist circles. Special(k) had been spying on the mad prophet—and scoping his system—ever since.

"He spews his conspiracies from various sites all day long," the younger man continued. "If you're a true believer, you know where to go, where to look. He hasn't made a peep since yesterday. The faithful are screaming for him, concerned."

"Tremendous," Alpha said. "Ticktock clockwork. I appreciate the update. I'll want more."

Special(k)'s eyes gazed at the bar of minimized content on his monitor. He licked his lips. "I want more, as well."

Alpha chuckled. "Hungry soldier." Special(k) heard the *chk!* of a cigarette lighter. "Texting you a link to the newest video right now. Quite a performance. That's the last one."

The hacker held his breath. "Did you go all the way?"

Alpha inhaled a drag and whispered, "Nuh-uh," as he exhaled. "My friend, when we're through, the words *going all the way* will be redefined. We must be patient."

Special(k)'s instant-messenger program gave a beep. He piloted

the mouse to the application and clicked the video link Alpha had
sent. He clicked play.

The air wrench was loud in the little room. But it wasn't as
loud as the screams.

"Enjoy," John Alpha said. "And do watch for the prophet when
he finally emerges. You must be there to cheer. And . . . to steer."

Yes, Special(k) thought as he watched the horror on-screen.
Yes. Yes. Oh, God, yes.

TEN

T hey were packing into the express elevator once more, and John felt as if he and his six brethren were preschoolers, learning the ABC's all over again. It was as if the reality they knew were merely the skin of an apple that was being peeled away, exposing possibilities and technologies that weren't just science fiction, but science fact. John wondered if something was rotten at this new reality's core.

The elevator's silver doors closed, and the computer's metallic voice said, *"READY FOR DESTINATION INPUT."*

"Ops," Hill said, and they were off again. This time, up.

The trip lasted only seconds—Ops was probably only a few floors up from Cloneville, certainly still far from the surface. The doors slid open and the group was greeted by several men and women in white lab coats. Most of them were over fifty—the oldest of them, a woman, appeared to be Kleinman's age. Accompanying these strangers was a black-haired fellow dressed in military garb. A Ben Affleck look-alike, this man looked as if he'd just squirted out of officers' training school.

The introductions came in a blur—Dr. Zimmerman, Drs. Welliver, Buchanan, Edenfield—and these strangers were grinning at them intently, hungrily, as if this were a cocktail party and the seven were fashionably late celebrity guests. Strangely, a few somehow seemed familiar to John; faces he couldn't quite place. Hands were shaken vigorously. The young man's name was Durbin.

Two of the four soldiers packing M16s stepped back into the elevator and were fired off to wherever Hill had ordered them; John hoped it was the moon. This new group of hawks and gladhanding whitecoats walked down a hall to a closed doorway. The double doors were marked OPERATIONS COMMAND: AUTHORIZED PERSONNEL ONLY.

Inside, the walls were alive with video screens. The entire wall at the front of the room was made of huge televisions, each tuned to a different news channel. The oil fields in Iraq were ablaze again, reducing production to a trickle, CNN was reporting; the White House's campaign strategy, in light of President Griffin's assassination, was being analyzed by CNBC; another demonstration-turned-riot in Los Angeles, fueled by the recent wave of power outages, courtesy of FOX News. John tore his eyes away from the televisions to take in the rest.

A steel-gray lectern stood before the screens. A mammoth mahogany conference table dominated the center of the room; each of the twenty chair settings had a laptop computer resting before them. Dominating the rear of the room was a raised control platform—filled with flat-panel computer monitors and countless keyboards. Two soldiers sat back there, gazing into the screens. Dim, moody light pooled from small ceiling spotlights.

A lone man sat near the head of the mahogany table, mashing a smoldering cigarette butt into a glass ashtray. His shoulders were slumped; he seemed somehow defeated. He paid no attention to the entourage bustling into the room, seating themselves in the well-worn chairs. John looked at him.

And then John *looked* at him.

The five-o'clock shadow was unfamiliar, an amalgam of silver and fading brown—and the man's hair was thinning and in desperate need of trimming. But the face behind the thick-framed glasses *was* familiar: pale, haggard, sinking inward with age . . . but the chin was still strong, the cheekbones still high, the perpetual crinkles in the forehead still there. The old man was withered, weathered, and more frail than John could ever remember.

But John could still remember. So it was true. All of it.

"Dad." He couldn't stop—didn't want to stop—the tears welling up in his eyes. *"Dad."*

The man once named Hugh Smith—now named Hugh Sheridan once more—looked up from the flickering embers in the ashtray. "Don't call me that," he said.

They stared at him, fourteen eyes into two, dumbfounded. Their father looked back with an expression of crumpled pity. No warmth, as there had once been . . . no shoulder-riding slam-dunk smile . . . no prideful flush of the cheeks. Just deep sadness.

The priest rushed toward his father, warbling a mishmash of words. John heard "Thank God," "alive," and "see you." As Father Thomas drew near, the old man bolted out of his chair—it rolled on its casters, thumping against the wall—and backed away, his hands extended. One of Sheridan's hands was waving Thomas away, as if a fly were buzzing near his head. *Shoo, shoo.*

"Don't," their father said.

Thomas stopped and cocked his head slightly to the side. "I don't understand."

Their father's eyes pleaded with him, then with the rest of them. "Stay away from me. Just for now. It's too much. Understand what I'm saying"—*"understand what I'm saying," he used to say that when he was upset at me,* John thought, *and I bet we're all thinking that right now*—"and stay away."

Kleinman came in from the doorway, pushed through the seven sons, raised his palms to Hugh Sheridan, and shook his head.

"Not like this, Hugh. Not now. Of all the times to do this, not now."

"You shut your mouth," Sheridan snapped. He turned back to Thomas, his eyebrows arching, pained. "Just please—don't touch me. I need time."

Dr. Mike stepped forward, gently pushing Kleinman aside. General Hill rose from his seat at the other end of the table, but Kleinman waved him down with a fluttering hand.

"Why not?" Dr. Mike said. "Why wouldn't a father want to hug his son?"

Sheridan's eyes crinkled, his lips pulled back into a sad smile— a smile John remembered from long ago, the *Dear child* smile, the sympathetic expression Dad gave when John had done something stupid, such as when he was four and fractured his arm after leaping off the bed like Superman; or a year later, when he tried to pet Mrs. Dixon's cat and scored a scratch on the face for his efforts. It was the eyes and smile that said, *Dear child—oh, how little of this world you understand . . . oh, how much you will learn . . . oh, how I love you.*

And John suddenly understood.

Hugh Sheridan explained quietly, patiently, "Because I'm not your father. I was never your father."

"The hell you weren't," Michael said from behind John.

"Marine!" barked General Hill.

Kleinman wormed his way in front of Dr. Mike again. He extended his arms between Mike and Sheridan like a boxing referee. "This isn't the time or place for your belated indignation, Hugh."

Sheridan's voice was acidic. "I told you to shut your face. It's what they *remember*. It's what we planted in their heads, fresh from the Womb, like good little God-playing stooges. Charlatans. Me, you, them"—he jabbed a finger at the lab coats still standing near the doorway—"and that goddamned—"

"Be *quiet*," Kleinman said.

"What is this?" Again, from behind John. It was the shrill voice of Jay. "What are you talking about, Dad?"

Sheridan looked at him. "I'm sorry. I don't know which one you are. But I'm *not* your father. You're not my son. You are a Beta, a clone. I never had contact with you, with any of you. You're remembering things from before. Before *you*. Before you were ever born."

Sheridan's gray eyes flitted to each of them. John's guts squirmed when that sincere gaze shot into him. *So that's the way it is*, he thought. *That's the way it was. He's right. He's not my father. John Alpha is my father. And my mother. And my brother.*

"I didn't raise any of you," Sheridan repeated. His arms sagged, then fell limp to his sides. "I didn't. You think I did. It's what you remember." He shuffled over to his chair and plopped down, tired, drained. "It's what you remember. It's sick." He placed his face into his shaking hands.

A moment passed. Kleinman nervously told the seven clones and the scientists to take their seats at the mahogany table. The clones dominated an entire half of the table. In this strange lighting—and the eerie glow from the laptop computer screens before them—they looked more alike than ever.

General Hill stepped over to the silver lectern at the front of the room and cleared his throat. "We're here to talk about John Alpha, and why we think he assassinated the president."

General Hill's body loomed over the lectern, his back straight. The twin stars on each shoulder, the cluster of insignia on his dark green lapel—even those goddamned brass buttons—glinted in the overhead light. He looked like a warrior whose time had come,

John reckoned; a hawk, born for combat, a black dragon mystically contained in human form. He was at least six foot five. His eyes were the color of coal.

From his seat, John could just barely see the top edge of an opened laptop computer on the lectern, facing the general. Its screen glowed upward, underlighting Hill's dark face. John's mind suddenly flashed to Camp Champion, where he *(they) (Alpha)* had spent a month of his *(their) (Alpha's)* fifth-grade summer vacation. He and his campmates had fished, fired arrows from bows, and sat around campfires. That's where they passed a flashlight from cabinmate to cabinmate, telling scary stories *(Bloody Mary Bloody Mary Bloody Mary)*, the pale light shaking under their faces, casting wily shadows on their cheeks and foreheads. Those same shadows were on General Hill's face now. The televisions behind him continued to shimmer with commercials and CNN reports. *He's our camp counselor,* John thought. *And he's about to tell us a very, very scary story. I can feel it.*

John wondered if the others could feel it, too.

"This briefing is being held at the request of Dr. Kleinman and myself, mainly for the benefit of the seven latest members of Project 7th Son," Hill said. "Most, if not all, of the other members present already know this information either through reading the project's archives or by stories that are retold, thanks to . . . ah . . . institutional memory. For those who are new to our procedures"—he nodded to the clones, then to Durbin, the spit-shined military newbie—"let it be known that this briefing has Code Phantom security clearance. The contents of this briefing are protected under Code Phantom classification guidelines detailed by the United States and the United Nations, as created in 1948 specifically for the 7th Son project. The president himself doesn't have access to this.

"Any leak of information from this briefing will be considered an act of treason by all United Nations member countries, as specified during the creation of Code Phantom. The source of the leak will be terminated with neither hearing nor trial."

Hill looked at the clones intently.

"Loose lips sink ships, gentlemen. This conversation never happened."

Across the table, Hugh Sheridan harrumphed and sparked another cigarette.

The First Amendment and my right to a fair trial just vanished, John thought. *This just gets worse and worse.* He looked at his brothers, most of whom appeared to be similarly haunted by this realization. Particularly Jay.

"I'll deliver a concise account of the events relating to John Alpha's twelve-year involvement with Project 7th Son," Hill said, "and then let intel specialist Durbin relate more recent developments that we feel have a direct connection to him."

Hill looked down to his laptop and pressed a key. The televisions behind him suddenly went dead, then flicked alive together, each one displaying a rectangular chunk of a now wall-size image. The giant screen read, BRIEFING ON ALPHA HISTORY/ ACTIVITY. Beneath that, a computer-animated logo of Project 7th Son danced in place: a large numeral 7 rotating on its axis—now a 7, now an upside-down *L*, now a 7 again—with a halo of seven smaller 7s circling around it, as if in worship. Finally, beneath that, in bright red letters: [CODE PHANTOM].

The same image flickered onto the laptop computers before them. John stared at the animated logo. It was hypnotizing. 7. Upside-down *L*. 7 again. Round and round the little 7s danced. He reached out and touched the screen, its LCD colors swirling beneath his fingertip.

"On October fourteenth, sixteen years ago, the Beta Phase of Project 7th Son officially commenced with the fabrication of the car accident in Indianapolis," Hill said. "John Michael Smith Alpha, while sedated, was transported to this facility. His Memory Totality was scanned and uploaded in the MemR/I chamber at approximately two a.m. the following morning. When John Alpha was revived, he was greeted by his 'parents'—Hugh and Dania Sheridan."

The laptop screens suddenly flickered again and displayed a black-and-white photograph of a hospital room. The shot was taken from high above the three figures in the photo, undoubtedly from a security camera. In the picture, John saw his mother and father as he remembered them in his youth—younger, in their late forties—sitting on the edges of a hospital bed. A boy with brown-blond hair was covered in its white sheets. It was John.

But it's not, he thought. *It's* him.

The photo was grainy, but the boy's face was clearly visible. John's mother was reaching out, as if she was about to caress the child's face.

The photograph suddenly came to life, into video footage. John jerked backward, surprised. One of the other clones uttered, "The *fuck*?"

"*—am I, Mom?*" the boy on the screen said. The words boomed from speakers above the conference table. "*I thought you were hurt.*"

"*No, Johnny,*" Mom/Dania said, stroking his cheek. "*We're fine. You're fine, too.*"

"*Hey, buddy,*" Dad/Hugh said. "*Good to see you're up.*"

"Christ on a crutch," the marine, Michael, said.

"*—coming toward us. I heard you scream, Mom,*" the boy continued.

"*It was pretend, Johnny. It was kinda like a practical joke—*"

Eerie. What was unfolding on-screen had never happened to John. A similar yet frighteningly different experience happened to him with Uncle Karl and Aunt Jaclyn when he had awoken from his "coma" at the age of sixteen . . . which was his first *true* memory, when John really thought about it.

(So don't think about it.)

But what was unfolding on-screen had never happened to any of the others sitting here, either. This was new. This was where the memories diverged. This little boy had never lost his parents. This little boy was just fine. This was the beginning of the life none of them ever had. A flare of jealousy, bitter and bright, filled John for a moment.

The video image winked away and was replaced by those damned dancing sevens.

"John Alpha was told the truth about the 7th Son project not long afterward," Hill said. "The significance of the experiment's Beta stage was not just to create the, ah, you seven here. It was also to incorporate John Alpha into the program. First to live with his parents here in the facility, then soon after to work as an assistant—and eventually as one of the project leaders. It was a plan that Alpha readily embraced."

Why would they do that to him? John wondered. *Why would they want him to be a part of this?*

"Alpha was present through all of the prime stages of Beta Phase," Hill continued. "When he wasn't being schooled by Kleinman and other 7th Son staffers, he was in the Womb, watching you seven grow in your capsules."

Another video clip winked on the videowall, this one in color and shaky from a camcorder. It had no audio. It showed Alpha, still fourteen or so, in the Womb cloning chamber. The inverted Tarantula loomed in the background. John could make out shapes in those pale green orbs, humanoid things floating in liquid, curled in fetal positions. Scientists sat at the curved computer banks, staring intently at the flickering monitors. John Alpha was laughing with an elderly, bald man who looked well past his seventies. An old scar arced down the right side of this stranger's face like a gnarled riverbed. John was certain the geezer was blind in that eye. The boy's lips were moving, saying something to the old man. They laughed. The geezer ruffled the boy's hair with a shaking hand. The image froze again.

"Alpha was brilliant for his age," Hill said. "He had many questions. He took keen interest in befriending and learning as much as he could from Frank Berman, the creator of the program. That's him there. Alpha was quite—"

Suddenly, Hugh Sheridan slapped his hand on the mahogany table, startling them all. "Don't get revisionist now, you sonuvabitch!" he screamed, waving his cigarette. "You know that wasn't—"

Kleinman bolted out of his own chair. "I told you to be *quiet*!" he screamed. "You brought this on yourself, Hugh. Hill! Get him out my sight!"

General Hill barked an order and the two remaining soldiers who had been standing by the doorway clomped across the room, grabbed Sheridan, and yanked him out of his chair. Sheridan struggled against them as they dragged him out of the Ops Command room. "Tell them the truth, you sons of bitches!" he cried. "The truth! *Truuuu—*"

The double doors slammed shut. The silence was charged, tense, suffocating.

Jack raised his hand. "Just what in the hell was that all about?"

Kleinman sat down and leaned forward. "General Hill, a moment please." He gazed at the clones. "Hugh Sheridan was one of the last of the old guard to leave 7th Son. Three years ago. Personal reasons."

"Just how personal is 'personal'?" Jay asked.

Kleinman shook his head and sighed. "It was a culmination of

things. Hugh spent his entire career here—just over thirty years—
working in the shadow of Frank Berman, the creator of 7th Son.
He was jealous of Berman; jealous of his talents, his brilliance, his
vision. 'Personality conflicts' doesn't do their relationship justice.
And then there were the problems with Dania. They eventually
divorced. That was five years ago."

"But they were happy," Father Thomas said. His face looked
like a Greek tragedy mask. The man's expression would've been
comical, had it not been so genuine.

"They were different people in the end," Kleinman said. "After
the divorce, the acrimony between Hugh and Berman intensified.
Even after Berman died here four years ago, Hugh was still trying
to undermine his legacy. As you could see, he still is, apparently.
From what I understand, he's been trying to drink himself to
death ever since."

"If Dad was such a problem, why is he here?" asked Jack.

"In the end, 7th Son—and you seven—wouldn't be what it is
without Hugh's involvement. He's here out of respect for the years
of service he'd given the program. We wanted him safe."

Now John asked, "From what?"

Kleinman glanced at Hill, nodded, then looked at the clones.
"Let's finish the briefing."

From behind the silver lectern, General Hill exhaled and resumed, "As I was saying, Alpha befriended Frank Berman and
became a resourceful, responsible, and creative understudy. As
your bodies grew in the Womb, John Alpha learned as much as
he could about the cloning and MemR/I procedures. He was there
when the team finally removed your grown bodies from your capsules and was there when they downloaded his own fourteen-year-
old psyche into your vacant brains. As a matter of fact, it was John
Alpha who took the most active role in screening the candidates

who would become your new foster parents, your respective Aunt Jaclyns and Uncle Karls. He said he wanted you all to be in good hands. He said he was proud of his children."

John stared at the boy frozen on the computer screen before him. *If what Kleinman just said was true, you had a choice,* he wondered. *How could you participate? Why did you participate?*

"As you were dispersed with your respective foster parents to your new cities, the 7th Son team's role diminished. The goal of the program was now to observe your behaviors. Alpha assisted with that, as well. In fact, hundreds of government field agents have monitored your actions for the past decade and a half and reported back to 7th Son. Not that they knew who you were, much less who they were reporting to."

Kilroy2.0 grinned. The eyes behind his thick eyeglasses were wild and triumphant. "Eyes, spooks, everywhere."

General Hill continued. "Ten years after your 'births,' when Alpha was twenty-six years old, he disappeared from the 7th Son facility. Gone. Vanished. The team had no idea where he went. We discovered that our airtight security system—cameras, pass-code doors, computer-monitored security systems—had been deactivated in certain passageways of the complex. Somehow switched off from inside the complex, by Alpha. At the time, I'd been with 7th Son for eleven years. I knew that system inside and out. Even now, I don't know how he did it. Alpha left no explanation, no trace. We didn't know he was gone until the following morning. By then, he had closed a considerable savings account he'd created years ago and vanished."

He took the money and ran, John mused. *Hoo-hoo-hoo.*

"A nationwide manhunt began. Two weeks later, Alpha's body was discovered in Lake Huron by several fishermen. The body was bloated, a mess. The top of his head had been blown off by a high-caliber pistol. John Alpha had apparently committed suicide."

Silence.

Michael raised his hand. "How did you know it was him, sir? With all that knowledge about the program, maybe—"

"Cloned himself? We thought about that at the time," Kleinman said. "But the kind of technology we use here takes decades to develop and build, not weeks. We suspected he might have murdered one of you, but your foster parents—and our field 'spooks,' as Kilroy calls them—didn't report any abnormalities. The body was brought here. During our autopsy, we found that the body's blood type and genetic code were identical to Alpha's. More important, we also confirmed his identity by the small tattoo in his ear."

"Tattoo?" Dr. Mike scoffed, crossing his arms. "De plane! De plane!"

Kilroy2.0 giggled.

"The microtattoo was like the identity measure we embedded in each of you," Hill said, ignoring them. "It was on the other side of the tragus—the little nub on the ear's exterior that protects the inner ear. When the team removed you from your cloning capsules, you each received a tiny tattoo before you received the MemR/I download. It was used to distinguish you as Betas. We embedded a similar tattoo in Alpha's ear just after the supposed car accident, when he was fourteen, while he was still sedated."

The videowall flickered again. On it now was a black-and-white close-up of human skin. Pores were the size of manholes; short hairs loomed like beanstalks. A symbol, in black, was in the center of the image. It looked more logo than letter, but its shape was unmistakable: a highly stylized A.

John reached up to his ear, gently sticking his index finger inside and rubbing the interior of that little nub. He felt nothing strange. When he spotted a few of the other clones doing the same thing—Kilroy2.0 was digging in both ears with particular relish—he removed his finger, embarrassed.

Now Kleinman spoke up. "In the end, that was all the proof we needed for our autopsy. John Alpha had never been told about that tattoo, just as you never knew about yours until this moment. That was the proof we needed. Alpha was dead. The manhunt was over. Life at 7th Son—and *your* lives—went on."

"I don't understand, sir," Michael said, addressing General Hill. "You're telling us that John Alpha committed suicide. But you also told us that he's behind the president's murder."

"That's right, Captain," Hill replied. "That changed three weeks ago, a week before President Griffin was killed. One of our retired memory specialists was kidnapped from her home in Potomac, Maryland."

The giant *A* on the screen behind him dissolved and was replaced with another photograph. This one was in vivid color. It was a bathroom mirror, cracked down the center, with one word written upon it in red lipstick. The word glowed on-screen, written in slashing letters, the handiwork of a madman.

ALIVE.

The first letter in this word matched the design of the tattoo *A* the men had seen seconds earlier.

The hairs on the back of John's neck prickled. His eyes began to water. The image vanished from the screen.

"But our suspicions were confirmed last week," Hill said, "when we accessed certain images over the intel community's computer intranet. They were photographs from the autopsy of Jesse Fowler, the four-year-old Kentucky boy who assassinated President Griffin. The doctors cut up that kid, looking for any reasonable answer for his behavior and mysterious death. They found nothing. We found everything."

The screen winked to life again, filled with another color photograph, similar to the one they'd seen no more than a minute ago. There, the manhole cover pores. And there. The *A* logo, again.

John felt as if he were going to throw up.

"He sent you a message," Dr. Mike said. His voice was knowing, confident.

Kleinman nodded. "In more ways than one. The memory specialist he abducted weeks ago was a message, too. She was one of the most brilliant and beloved members of this staff."

Father Thomas looked away from the videowall, blinking. "Who was it?" he whispered.

"Dania Sheridan," Kleinman said. "Your mother."

ELEVEN

s the clones reacted to this information in an explosion of discontent and confusion, Special Intelligence Officer Robert Durbin walked over, a tablet PC in hand, and replaced General Hill behind the lectern. John looked up and gazed at the twentysomething standing there: his slick black hair, his dimpled chin, his streamlined jawbone. It was absurd. This kid knew more about their lives than they did.

The giggles tickled inside John's churning stomach—*it's too much*, he thought, *I'm a pinball machine on tilt, a one-armed bandit on payout, I've hit my three 7s, that's it for the day*—and he felt a quivering grin tugging at the sides of his mouth. He bit the tip of his tongue to suppress it. No. What they'd heard so far wasn't too much. What they'd heard, apparently, wasn't enough.

John pinched his tongue with his front teeth again and looked at the Affleck wannabe in the black jacket. Durbin cleared his throat nervously; the glowing screen of the tablet PC resting on the lectern made him look pale, ill. He tapped a button on the computer, and the monstrous color photograph of Jesse Fowler's ear canal—and that giant *A*—winked into nothingness behind him.

"Before I brief you on the abduction of Dania Sheridan, it may be in your best interest to hear some information about the early days of Project 7th Son," Durbin said.

He glanced over to General Hill, who nodded. Durbin stepped away from the lectern, computer in hand, and walked to the Ops center's double doors.

"Please, come with me. We're heading to the Lock Box."

As the group followed Durbin down the hallway, making a left here, a right there, John glanced at the other clones. Most of them—with the glaring exception of Michael and Kilroy2.0—appeared as distraught as he felt. It was as if they'd all eaten the bad oysters at the party and were starting to taste the bile gushing into their mouths.

"As Dr. Kleinman may have mentioned to you, Project 7th Son was given the green light long before the cloning and MemR/I technologies were perfected," Durbin said, as he strode. He occasionally glanced at the notes on his tablet's screen. "Project leaders had a specific timeline in which to complete the hardware and software, and a specific launch date: anytime before John Alpha's fourteenth birthday."

Why fourteen? John wondered. He glanced at Dr. Kleinman, who was walking beside him, and went to ask the question. Durbin interrupted him.

"The theoreticals behind human cloning came early. The realization of that technology evolved over more than thirty years, based mostly on the research Dr. Berman had conducted in the 1940s, prior to the project's creation."

"Hey, Kleinman, I've never heard of a Dr. Frank Berman," Jack called. He and Kilroy2.0, the tubbiest of the Beta clones, were finding it difficult to keep up with Durbin's pace. With the spectacles and facial hair, the duo looked like a weight-loss program in process. "If he's God's gift to genetics, why haven't I come across his name?"

"Another time, Jack," Kleinman said.

John looked back at Jack and saw that the geneticist's eyes were squinting, full of questions . . . and full of something that John thought was most certainly disgust.

"No," Jack replied. Beside him, Kilroy gave an exasperated huff. "Now. Tell us now. I'm getting tired of the shell game. I'm sick of this 'sit back and listen but don't ask questions' routine. Who's Berman?"

"Later," Kleinman said. Suddenly, John realized, the old man didn't look like a kind grandfather anymore. He just looked old. And cold.

"*Hey!*" Jack cried. The group stopped. Jack stood in the hall, arms crossed, his face turning red. "*Now.*"

General Hill brushed past the clones, clomping toward Jack. "Should I have you confined to your quarters?"

Jack glared at the soldier. "You don't frighten me."

Hill tensed, but only for a moment. He pressed his lips together into a sarcastic half smile. The stars on his shoulders shimmered. "Maybe not. But what you're about to hear most definitely *will*. Get something straight, Jack Smith. You're not in your ivory tower anymore, splicing genes for alumni donations. You're a ghost. A vapor. You're in my world. And right now, the only way to get out is to do what you're told. So I'm going to politely ask you to let Officer Durbin conduct his briefing."

Hill's smile broadened.

"Know this," he said, eyes glimmering. "I won't ask twice."

Kilroy2.0 nudged Jack with his elbow. The hacker's blue eyes flashed at Jack's—*Let it go.* Jack's identical blue eyes screamed a second's worth of protest, then relented. He turned back to the general. Jack nodded his concession; Hill returned it with a nod of his own.

"Later, Jack," Kleinman said. He nodded to the metal door directly ahead. Durbin was there, tapping a password into the nearby keypad. The doors screeched open.

"For God's sake, later," Kleinman whispered. "After."

John was unsure of what a room called the Lock Box could be—
and what's with all the "room naming" around here? he wondered. *Are
7th Son bathrooms called "peristalsis conclusion chambers"?*—but the
answer surprised him as they entered.

This was where Code Phantom technology went to die.

The Lock Box was a storage facility, a metal-ensconced warehouse filled with rows of crates, and dust-covered machinery. John,
who suspected he was about as far removed from "normal life" as
it got, could now only compare these moments to fictional and
fantastical ones. Frames of reference were akimbo. This room, for
instance, was all very end-of-*Raiders of the Lost Ark.*

They passed a crate with the words PAN TROGLODYTES: GENE stenciled on its side. Beneath this was the numeral 1. Other crates like
this each featured the same mysterious words, but with different
numerals. There were dozens of these.

"Chimpanzees," Kleinman explained to John, his voice low, as
they walked. "Some of our very first Beta clones. We preserved the
bodies for later study. That was a long time ago."

"You harvested their genes?" John asked, nodding to the word.

"Heavens, no." Kleinman grinned. "That was his name."

Durbin spoke up, his voice ringing throughout the warehouse.
"As I said, 7th Son's biological cloning technologies—obviously far
ahead of anything academia or private industry was pioneering at
the time—came to fruition in the late 1970s," he said, still ushering
them farther into the Lock Box. "But the recording and storage of a
human memory was much more complicated."

The group, intent on hearing the intelligence officer, passed
still more boxes and antiquated equipment. Most of this gear wasn't
worth examining, John agreed; he was certain the contents of this
crate had a world-rending discovery inside, or that boxy computer
terminal was instrumental in the research of whatthehellever, but

there was no time for such minutiae—and besides, these secrets were safely enclosed in mundane, vanilla boxes. The kind designed to not attract attention.

They turned a corner, and Durbin resolutely beckoned them onward, past an opaque-tarp-covered obsidian machine about the size of an office desk. John slowed his pace, curious. Soon the others (even Jack and Kilroy2.0) had passed.

The machine whirred softly, still powered by the facility. Another sound—a gentle thrum that sounded more organic than mechanical—purred from beneath the tarp.

"According to the project's archives," he heard Durbin say, "the team encountered several technological dead ends while trying to realize the downloading of memories into a host brain . . ."

John stepped to the machine and gently gripped the thick plastic covering it. He lifted it, careful not to rustle the tarp too loudly, and peered inside.

A face stared back at him.

John nearly screamed. It was the face of something impossibly small, yet absolutely human. Surrounded by milky orange liquid, inside a softball-size glass sphere—*roses in a bowl, my God, it's roses in a bowl, put it on your grandma's coffee table and stare, a fucking* person *in a bowl*—was an unborn child, its froglike face tranquil, eyes closed. The liquid swirled around the fetus in sync to the machine's gentle thrum.

John's eyes glanced to the sphere's left, then right. Four others were here, each in its own capsule.

"There were seven at first," Kleinman said, as he shuffled beside John. His voice was low, reverant. "But three died. This was two decades ago, in the fall. We buried them in the woods not far from the facility."

"What . . . what . . . are—?"

"Clones," Kleinman whispered. "Clones of an Alpha, just like you."

"Clones of John Alpha."

"A 'Jane Alpha,' actually. The 'Alpha-Alpha,' as it were. There was a time during the course of this experiment when we thought we'd perfected the MemR/I Memory Totality upload/download procedure on humans. This was well after our experiments with Gene, of course, but years before the 'birth' of you and your brothers. In preparation for the breakthrough, we began to create clones of our first Alpha subject, a female."

"You raised a *different* Alpha at first? Raised by whom?"

"Hugh and Dania Sheridan, of course. They were a bit older than most parents with children your age, if you'll recall. Well, John Alpha's age, actually."

John couldn't look away from the faces in the spheres. The machine whirred on. "And what happened here?"

"We manufactured the car accident, just as we did with your progenitor," Kleinman said. "Sedated Jane—"

"Jane Michelle Smith."

"Indeed, and attempted to record her memories. Unlike your procedure, we'd chosen to begin the cloning process before Jane's 'accident.' Hence, these Betas."

John shuddered. "But something went wrong."

"Yes."

"And you couldn't download the memories into the children's brains."

"Correct."

"And so you kept these brainless clones alive. Extracted them from the Womb, but couldn't bring yourself to study them like you did Gene the Wonder Chimp."

"Of course not. We're not monsters."

John looked into Kleinman's eyes. "And what happened to Jane Smith? Is she still alive?"

The doctor did not blink. "Presumably. She woke from her coma as a ward of the state. The window for optimal LTP execution had concluded. We had one opportunity. We failed. We have not followed her progess since."

"Right," John said, his voice emotionless, stoned. "You're not monsters. Excuse me while I get the hell away from you, you terrifying bastard."

John trotted back to the group, desperate to be far from the machine and the mad doctor who'd created it. The other Beta clones stood around a peculiar contraption, listening to Durbin's speech.

Again, since John's frame of reference was now leaving the solar system, he gazed at the device and thought immediately of the laboratory from a *Frankenstein* movie. It was small—six soda-can-size, black cylinders, bolted together, with electrical wires crisscrossing its surface. Atop these cylinders was a tiny metal plate, no bigger than a deck of playing cards.

The metal plate was a bed. A tiny bed. With tiny leather restraints hailing from the "floor"—the top of the wire-wrapped canisters.

"Huh" was all John could muster.

"... as I mentioned, most of these dead ends regarding the upload and download of memories were, hah, forgettable," Durbin was saying. "Outright failures. But one of them must be mentioned here. We think John Alpha may have recently exploited it."

Durbin tapped a section of his tablet PC's screen, and it displayed a new page. John found himself suddenly, desperately, craving a cigarette.

"The first upload/download of a Memory Totality occurred in 1982, on a laboratory mouse," Durbin explained, staring down at his notes. He nodded to the device before them. John imagined the animal bound to this tiny bed. "Its memories were uploaded, encoded as binary code, and stored in a portion of one of the lab's Q-Cray hard drives, just as planned. Success. Until."

The clones looked at one another, their eyes wary.

"Until what?" asked Michael, the marine.

Durbin shifted from foot to foot, suddenly nervous. "Until the scientists observed the animal after the procedure. The MemR/I process did something more than just record the memories. It created an electrical . . . ah. An electrical kickback, for lack of a better term."

John felt a bead of sweat slip down the nape of his neck. "What does that mean?" he heard himself ask.

"It, ah . . ." Durbin swiped a hand across his forehead. "The hardware apparently sent an electric shock wave through the animal's brain nanoseconds after the Memory Totality upload was complete. The recording was successful, but in the process there was an anomaly. A bioelectric hiccup. Feedback. It, ah, it erased the mouse's memories in its brain."

Erased? John thought.

"Erased?"

Yeah, what he said—whoever the hell that was.

"Complete neural erasure," Durbin said. "Immediate catatonia. The brain tissue appeared to be healthy, but . . . nothing. No brain activity. No memories. Nothing was left. It was a vacuum."

John placed his hands over his face. *Too much. Too much.* He closed his eyes. He felt his calloused fingertips tremor against his eyebrows.

To his left, a grim chuckle. It was Michael. "A neutron bomb for the brain," the marine said.

"I don't get it," Jack said.

"Neutron bombs were the big military R-and-D project of the late 1950s," Michael said, glancing at General Hill for approval. He got it. "Basically, the blast destroys organic material but leaves buildings, roads, and vehicles intact. Whoever survived could march in and literally claim the spoils of war."

Dr. Mike: "And your point is?"

"My point, Doc, is this hiccup thing zapped the software, but kept the hard drive," Michael said. "The lights are on, but nobody's home. Right, Durbin?"

The younger man nodded. "The team soon recognized what had happened—the Memory Totality had been successfully uploaded, but something had gone wrong. The intent of recording Memory Totality was never to excavate and *remove* memories from the brain; it was simply supposed to *copy* them. According to the archived report, the team chose to reverse the data on the spot. They chose to download those copied memories back into the mouse's mind."

"Why?" Father Thomas.

"To bring Algernon back from the vegetable patch," John replied.

God, that little bed. The chimps. The first Betas. The Womb. The field of supercomputers. He felt faint.

Durbin cleared his throat and tapped his screen. "Ironically, the download was completely successful. The mouse regained consciousness. Dr. Berman, Dr. Kleinman, and the other team leaders knew something had gone wrong with the upload process, but according to the report, they also believed they had discovered a temporary solution: simply download a copy of the Memory Totality back into the traumatized brain, to 'restart' the animal's consciousness. The animal would be fine."

"But we were wrong." Another voice. Kleinman's. "Let's head back. You'll want to be sitting for what's to come."

"What a fucking shock," John heard himself say.

The group returned to the Ops center, and the clones resumed their spots around the mahogany table. Durbin stood behind the lectern once more, though the facility's leader currently had the floor.

"The download didn't take," Kleinman finally explained. "The animal was fine for a few hours, and then it died suddenly. Quite suddenly. Our dissection of the brain revealed a kind of neural atrophy. Swift, catastrophic . . . neurons collapsing in on each other, brain tissue all but rotting inside the skull. It was as if the brain had been overloaded in some way, blown like a fuse."

Kinda like me right now, John thought.

"We deduced, after further experimentation, that it wasn't our uploading that had caused the trauma," Kleinman continued. "And it wasn't the downloading procedure, either. It was that unintentional blast of bioelectric feedback that occurred immediately after the recording process. It was like a neural lightning storm, screaming across the mouse's brain. It left a characteristic microscopic damage signature."

"Poor Algernon," Kilroy2.0 said.

"At first, the mouse's neurons appeared to be undamaged," Kleinman said. "But they were. Their 'run time' was diminished by a thousandfold, maybe more. When we decided to download those memories back into the mouse's brain, we didn't know the brain would later break down from the shock wave's trauma.

"I'm sure you want to know what this has to do with Dania Sheridan, your mother. Here it is. Dania was the memory specialist who identified the source of that shock wave. While her official role at this point in the project was to raise John Alpha in Indianapolis, she analyzed the dissection and hardware report data and pinpointed the cause. She also put us on the path to solving the problem. She was brilliant. It took some time, but we were able to adjust our technology to prevent other cases of this accidental memory erasure.

"But it was Dania who first suggested that our tragic misstep could have other applications. Military applications, to be frank. It was Dania who realized that the shock-wave pulse could be easily replicated and used again and again. She called the phenomenon a NEPTH-charge. Neuro Erasure Pulse Technology Hardware. We deliberately ignored her enthusiasm for the discovery; our goal was to perfect the Memory Totality upload/download process for 7th Son. But when she retired from 7th Son five years ago, Dania began pursuing the study of this technology and its uses for the Department of Defense. She's apparently made significant breakthroughs and improvements, if you could call them that. Make no mistake: NEPTH-charge decimates a human mind. It erases a person's Memory Totality."

"Why would that be useful?" Jay asked.

Kleinman's eyebrows peered over his trifocals in that grandfatherly manner that John greatly mistrusted. "To replace it with a completely different human Memory Totality, of course. Even if the brain would fall apart weeks later. John Alpha likely kidnapped Dania to obtain the secrets of NEPTH-charge."

The clones sat in silence, pondering what they'd just heard.

"Mind control," Michael said finally.

"Oh, no, Captain," Kleinman said, turning to the marine. "No. Mind control is warping another's preexisting will. There is no will after a NEPTH-charge; there is only vacancy. This is body control. Think of it as taking a videotape filled with your favorite television shows—one that you've clearly labeled, of course—and then magnetizing it, erasing it. Now you decide to tape new shows, completely different footage. On the outside, the videocassette looks the same. Same label, same handwriting . . . but now there is very different content lurking inside. Do you understand how useful this technology could be to a terrorist?"

John looked at Kleinman—then at the clones. Suddenly . . .

Holy
. . . the pieces . . .
motherfucking
. . . fell together.
shit.
"Jesse Fowler," he said. "The kid. Alpha nabbed the kid. He—"
"—tore the kid's mind to pieces and put new memories inside," Father Thomas said, nodding slowly. "A new program, like he said. With new instructions. To kill President Griffin."

"Christ Almighty," Jack said. He looked up at Durbin, who was still standing behind the lectern like a Hall of Presidents mannequin. "Is that right? Is that *true*?"

Durbin nodded again. "That's what we suspect. As Kleinman said, the NEPTH-charge leaves a damage signature. We found evidence of that damage in the Fowler boy's autopsy images. Fowler's sudden death also matches the NEPTH-charge MO: the child was placed under maximum security in Camp N— . . . ah, an undisclosed facility after the assassination. He was under twenty-four/seven surveillance. He died within a week. Complete neural shutdown."

"Just like the mouse," Kilroy2.0 said.

Dr. Mike rolled his eyes. "It sounds like all this blah-blah talkie-talk is leading up to something," he said, smirking. "So is that the punch line? That John Alpha has NEPTH-charge technology and used it on a kid to kill the president?"

Durbin shook his head. "There's more. If Alpha's alive and has NEPTH-charge technology, this might not be the punch line. It might be the setup for something bigger. Imagine being able to erase a man's memories with a few electrodes to the head and the press of a button. Imagine being able to erase an entire *family's* memories. Or a neighborhood's. Get the picture?"

"Not with all your elliptical bullshit," Dr. Mike said.

From the table, General Hill cleared his throat. "You're not putting the pieces together, son. NEPTH-charge isn't the only technology Alpha has. He must have MemR/I recording capability as well. What good is erasing a man's mind if you have nothing with which to replace it? He had to put *something* in the Fowler boy's brain. Maybe it was Alpha's own Memory Totality that was planted in the kid's mind. Maybe it was someone else's, an accomplice's. We don't know. And we don't know how he acquired these secrets. Either Alpha stole the secrets of NEPTH-charge and the MemR/I system from our data archives before he escaped, or he learned about Dania's NEPTH research for the DoD. You want it straight? Here it is: A kid with an *A* tattooed in his ear killed the president, and the woman who knows the most about NEPTH-charge has been kidnapped. With that kind of technology at his disposal, we think Alpha's just warming up."

So government secrets aren't so secret if you're determined, and when the world thinks you're dead, John mused. *Security holes the size of the Pacific. Could it get any worse?*

"Alpha undoubtedly has cloning technology, too," Kleinman said.

Hello, other shoe.

Jack flinched; Michael let out a low whistle. "What makes you think that, hoss?"

"Isn't it obvious?" Kleinman said. "Four years ago, we found his body just weeks after he vanished from the 7th Son project. Complete with the *A* tattoo on the tragus. But the body must have been a plant—a genetically identical clone. If it weren't for the matching tattoo inside Jesse Fowler's ear, I'd think the person behind the president's death was someone else. But I'm convinced it's Alpha. And I'm convinced he's had the potential to clone humans since his escape."

"This is the part where you tell us that no organization, other than 7th Son, can clone people," Jack said.

"Not to our knowledge," Kleinman replied.

"Which means he had help from the inside," Dr. Mike said, nodding furiously. "He was using the Womb, and the hypercomputer."

General Hill frowned. "No. The Womb and the MemR/I Array are our crown jewels. We monitor keystrokes and processor activity on all the computers on the Womb level. I've checked the logs from the past twenty years. The last time anyone used the Womb computers—and cloning chambers—was sixteen years ago, when you seven were born. If Alpha cloned himself, he didn't do it here. I would've known."

"So he had help from the outside," Dr. Mike shot back. "We all took the walk down memory lane this morning. That stuff would take years to build. And it would've been done off-site."

"Alpha *is* a very clever boy," Kilroy2.0 said.

"We're looking into that," Hill said, "but the trail's cold. Remember, we didn't realize Alpha was alive until three weeks ago."

"So he faked his death by killing himself—his cloned self—to keep you guys from finding him," Michael said, his eyes wide. "So he could hide in plain sight. Plan. But plan what, exactly?"

"A conspiracy," said Father Thomas.

Kilroy2.0 nodded his head in agreement, then stuck a finger back into his ear and jiggled it.

Jay eyed Durbin.

"So a man who's supposed to be dead has the world's most dangerous toys at his disposal—no thanks to any of you," Jay said, his voice high. "But why would Alpha want to kill the president? If he already had the brain-erase technology, why did he kidnap Dani— ah, screw it. What does he want with our mother? It doesn't make sense."

"Sure it does," Dr. Mike said. "I don't know the *how* or the *why*, but I've got a good idea of the *what*. All signs point to revenge. He wants sweet, delicious revenge. Revenge on 7th Son, maybe revenge on the government. You reap what you sow."

The video screens behind Durbin suddenly flashed on again. John looked at the young man behind the lectern . . . and at the glowing screen with an image of a thin, neon-green horizontal line cutting through its center.

"We think he wants more than that, Doctor," Durbin said. "What you're about to hear was found on a USB thumbdrive at Ms. Sheridan's home. We think John Alpha wants you—*all* of you—to find him."

Durbin pressed a button on the laptop, and when John heard the noises pour from the overhead speakers, he forgot about NEPTH-charges and MemR/I chambers. His flesh began to crawl, crawl as it did around the campfire when he was a boy, crawl as it did when he had first heard that flashlight chant . . . *Bloody Mary Bloody Mary Bloody Mary.*

The green line shimmered and transformed into arcs and valleys, jagged mountaintops and abyssal trenches. The overhead speakers sang, matching the neon sound waves displayed onscreen. There were no words. Just sounds.

Deee-deee . . . deeeeeee . . . deeeeee . . . deee-deee-deee . . . deeeee . . .

"The file on the drive read, 'For the Betas,'" Durbin said.

deee-deee-deee . . .

"Sounds like Morse code," Michael said.

deeeee . . .

But not to John. John thought it sounded like the voice of a ghost.

Very much like a ghost.

TWELVE

harles Caine was surrounded by the warm comforts of the limousine, but he flipped up the collar of his overcoat as the car pulled up in front of the Washington Hospital Center. *Better to be safe than sorry,* he thought. Or sniffly. Visible weakness was a bad thing on the Hill.

Especially these days.

A Secret Service agent opened the door from outside. The brisk air rushed inside, and Caine winced. From beside him, Carl Sigler, his chief aide, barked a quick "God*damn.*"

"We're ready when you are, Mr. Vice President," the agent said.

Caine put on his smile. "Let's do it." The Chattanooga accent had mostly left his voice—thirty-three years on the Hill does that to a man—but a hint of it remained to please the folks back home. "I'll freeze my balls off if we don't."

Charles Caine, appointed vice president two weeks ago, stepped out of the car into the sunlight and into the flashbulbs, the microphones, the well-coiffed reporters with their slender faces and shark's teeth. The Pack. Pudgy men with bazooka video cameras . . . Barbie-doll Botoxed TV news reporters . . . newspapermen wearing ties (as if that disguise made them respectable).

All crying for his attention. All ambulance chasers, as far as he was concerned.

Caine smiled. And waved. And smiled.

The Pack's questions were a raucous spaghetti plate of nearly indistinguishable voices—

How are you feeling, Mr. Vice President?

Any surprises from the doctor?

Hypertension?

Any leads in the investigation?

About the Iraqi-pipeline saboteurs . . .

—that Caine pretended not to hear. He kept waving and nodding as the Secret Service agents and his aides walked up the hospital's gray steps. Caine could spin with the best of them. The message was clear: the vice president was going to a civilian hospital—not a secret facility—for his physical examination. Yes, public places were safe in this time of murder and terror.

This footage would undoubtedly be followed by clips of the press conference after his examination, the doc giving a bland synopsis of Caine's good health, then Caine delivering his sound bite: *I feel right as rain, and ready to help President Hale and this great nation in any way I can.*

Trite. Lame. Clichéd. Safe. As American as apple pie and freedom fries.

The story might not lead the national newscasts, but it'd certainly be mentioned. Face time is good time. Having the physical at a public hospital and not a military post or classified location had been Caine's idea.

Bred confidence in the system.

Secret Service agents flanked Charles Caine as he nodded hellos to the lobby security guards and strode toward the elevators. The media had been banned from the lobby, but Caine could still hear the camera shutters snapping through the scratched glass.

Sigler followed, cell phone pressed against his angular face, barking orders to a subordinate about the upcoming press conference. Sigler didn't *care* if the so-called reporter from that blog had a press pass—he wasn't in the pool, his name wasn't on this list, he wasn't cleared . . . so he wasn't getting in. It was *elementary*, Sigler said into the phone. Fucking *elementary*.

The cluster of suits worked its way to the elevator bay. Two of the elevators were already open, guarded by more Secret Service. Caine and two agents stepped inside one of the lifts; Sigler and the remaining staff went into the other. The ride to the top floor was swift and smooth.

When he stepped out of the elevator, Caine couldn't hear the army helicopter on the roof above him, but knew it was there, its blades whirring in standby mode, waiting for evac orders if necessary. When Caine had been prepped by Secret Service on the escape route this morning, he'd nodded solemnly at the news and said something that rang of authority, like "Very good" or "Excellent plan." Frankly, Caine thought it was all a little silly; he wasn't used to this presidential fuss (not that he hadn't earned it, with all the years he'd dedicated to the party and to the Hill). He'd missed plenty of his daughter's birthdays for the GOP. But for God's sake, it was just a physical.

They walked down the hall, past more agents and awestruck nurses and doctors. He smiled amiably at them. Face time was good time.

He met his physician at a doorway near the end of the hall. Dr. Jared Blackwell shook his hand.

"Good to see you, Charlie," Blackwell said, smiling. "How's the old lub-dub?"

"Well, I'm here, so I guess it's still ticking. And when I'm not in an office with bulletproof windows, I'm on that damned tread-mill. Just like you ordered."

"Good for you," the doctor said, and they entered the examination room. It was bright and spacious. The examination table was well cushioned, the cabinets made of cherrywood. Clearly, Caine wasn't the first VIP to visit here.

"You just keep doing what the sawbones tell you, and you'll get along just fine," Blackwell said, motioning for Caine to sit on the table. "Besides, you'll have fewer co-pays that way."

"Huh. Whatever happened to 'an apple a day'?"

"These days, Johnny Appleseed works for Aetna."

They laughed. Then Blackwell's expression turned serious. This was the "doctor" face. Break the ice, then down to business.

"Seriously, Charlie. How're you feeling? With what's happening out there—Griffin dead and Hale stepping up, and you being appointed—how's the body reacting? You sleeping well?"

"Jared, I'm seventy-seven," Caine shrugged. "I haven't had a good night's sleep in fifteen years. I wake up at three every morning, like clockwork, to take a piss. Sometimes twice a night. I always manage to stump a toe or bump into a wall because I won't turn on the light. Jean's a light sleeper—and a real grouch when the light comes on."

Blackwell smiled. "You didn't answer my question. Consummate politician."

Caine sighed. "How'm I feeling? I'm feeling like a big, heavy bar of gold has been chucked into my lap. I'm thrilled to have it—the position, the opportunity. The other side of me can't believe how badly my lap hurts."

"Because that's one heavy bar of gold."

"Exactly. I'm sitting in the number two spot before Griffin's blood is dry on the pavement. They needed to move fast, they wanted me to step up, I understand that. But it feels so . . . big.

That chair. That bar of gold. Christ, they're telling me about launch protocols for nukes, SDI satellites, the works."

"Heavy is the head that wears the crown."

Caine nodded. "Something like that. But it's more than that. It ain't right, Jared. Little boys want to be the president. They don't want to *kill* the president. It's a goddamned mess. I feel like the shovel crew at an elephant parade."

Caine looked from the floor to Blackwell.

"Confidentially?"

Blackwell nodded. "Of course."

"The body's pooped. The brain's working overtime. I miss spending time with Jean. I haven't had a second to spare to talk to my kids—much less my grandkids. Since the appointment, I've been surrounded by strangers who are scrambling for attention and are a little too free with their advice. Alone in a crowded room, that's how I sometimes feel."

The doctor nodded again.

"I guess what I'm trying to say is, I'm doing the best I can."

"That's all anyone asks." Blackwell placed his hand on the VP's shoulder. "Listen. This physical, it's routine. I'm no headshrinker, but it sounds like you're dealing fairly well with the life changes. Keep dealing with the stress the best you can, keep running that road to nowhere on that treadmill." Blackwell walked over to the window and closed the vertical blinds. "You know the drill. Lose the shirt. The nurse will come in and do the stuff that I got the MD to avoid doing."

The doctor raised his eyebrows.

"You're in luck, Charlie. She's young, firm, and has a chestful of personality, if you catch my drift."

Caine grinned.

"I provide only the best for our great leaders," Blackwell said, stepping into the hall. "You know our rule, of course."

"Don't shit where you eat," Caine said, nodding. "I'll behave."

At that moment, forty miles away and two thousand feet underground, Dr. Kleinman was giving a history lesson to John, Kilroy2.0, and the other Beta clones. The group was in Ops, sitting at the mahogany table. Kleinman was explaining the implications of NEPTH-charge technology, and how Dania Sheridan had taken its secrets to the Department of Defense.

Kleinman was now saying that Dania Sheridan had apparently made significant improvements to the technology since she began working for the DoD. He didn't tell the clones how significant those improvements might be.

And he certainly didn't know those improvements were now in the hands of the enemy.

When the door opened again, Charles Caine was suddenly certain he was not looking at a human being. This was an earthbound angel. A mirage, somehow given three dimensions. He had never seen a woman this . . . this . . . what? Words failed him. Exotic? No, but it was the only word his mind could conjure at the moment.

She was in her early thirties. Slender. Athletic. Her eyes were black pearls. Her skin was a creamy brown, her features certainly of Indian ancestry. She wore no makeup; it would have compromised her somehow, Caine marveled, like a colorized black-and-white film. A waterfall of black hair soaked her shoulders. Her bosom pressed against the fabric of her white uniform. A plastic name tag hung from her uniform, over her heart, its lower edge dangling just off the slope of her breast. MIRA SANJAH, RN, it read.

She stepped into the room and closed the door. Caine fought the urge to lick his lips.

"Good morning, Mr. Vice President. He was lost in her dark brown lips. "How are you feeling today?"

Better. Christ. So much better.

"I'm doing well, thank you." Caine was beginning to blush. When was the last time he'd blushed in front of a woman?

"Good to hear it."

There's the slightest hint of a British accent in there, Caine thought. *Was she born in India and raised in the UK? Or here, in the States? Where had she come from?*

Nurse Sanjah smiled again, as if she'd read his mind, and stepped over to the cherrywood cabinets. She plucked two latex gloves from a small cardboard dispenser and pulled them over her hands—an effortless, methodical act. Caine suddenly imagined her face below his navel, unhooking his belt with her teeth.

Can it. You're old enough to be her granddaddy. He shifted on the table. *Don't raise the flag here, you old sonuvabitch. Think of anything else. Anything. Football. The Titans. Jean. Think of Jean.*

The nurse turned around, holding an electronic thermometer. "I'm just going to take a few readings, Mr. Caine. We'll start with your temp, then blood pressure. We'll wrap up with something new." She smiled. "Don't worry. I won't bite."

Too bad. "Sounds good to me."

"Great. Say *ah*."

The old man opened his mouth, and she placed the thermometer under his tongue. He could smell her now, an intoxicating rush of lavender and jasmine. He saw the fuzzy blur of the thermometer sticking out of his mouth and felt like a fool.

As he sat there, the nurse went back to the cabinets and bent over to open a drawer near the floor. She pulled a black, phonebook-size metal box from the drawer and placed it atop the cabinet. The nearly featureless contraption had only a few buttons on its top. Caine spotted special ports on one side of the machine; they looked like tiny headphone jacks, the kind he'd seen on Walkman radios.

Nurse Sanjah switched on the machine and offered him another smile. Caine felt himself blushing again—*Goddammit*—and sheepishly smiling back.

She slipped the thermometer from his mouth, looked at the reading, looked at him, blinked (or was that a wink?), and said, "Normal," as if it were a white lie only they would share. Which it was, Caine suspected. *How's the old lub-dub? Oh, baby, it's doing the bebop.*

She took his blood pressure without comment, though Caine nearly sighed when her right breast slid against his biceps. Caine told himself that was an accident, told himself to think about Jean, told himself that he never shat where he ate.

The nurse took the reading and wrote it on the sheet clamped in the metal clipboard.

"Lie down," she said, and Caine did . . . knowing that if his body was going to betray him, it was now. He lay on the cushioned examining table, stole a glance down at his flat crotch—*Thank you, Lord*—then stared up at the ceiling. Caine exhaled.

Nurse Sanjah brought the small black box to the table now and placed it next to his legs. She connected thin wires to the small ports on the side of the machine and connected the wires to circular foam electrodes. Caine watched with interest. Her gloved hands were small, but completely confident.

She looked into his eyes and smiled again. "Don't worry, this is a recent addition to the physical. It's a twofer: an EEG and EKG all in one. I'll put these electrodes on your head first. They'll pick up neural information and send it to the box. Then I'll remove the electrodes and place new ones on your chest. Again, the results go into the box. Dr. Blackwell will pull the data and make a note of the results."

"I've never seen anything like it."

"State-of-the-art." Sanjah leaned over him, her hair sliding off her shoulders. "I'm going to put these on you."

He nodded and watched her tongue slip out of her mouth in concentration as she grabbed the first electrode.

My God, I need a drink, he thought.

Mira Sanjah placed six electrodes on his head: two on his forehead, two on his temples, and two near the base of his neck. Her perfume was intoxicating. She then tapped several buttons on the machine, and the device made a strange, high-pitched whine, like the sound of a charging camera flash. Caine was about to ask about that noise when the goddess gazed down at him. Her eyes were different now.

"Ready?" she asked.

Caine began to frown. *Different how?*

Her eyes were cold.

Wait. Something's wro—

Mira Sanjah pressed another button.

As Charles Caine tried to shriek, to scream for help, to breathe, to blink, to reach up and tear those electrodes from his head, a tsunami of voices, images, sounds, and emotions—none of them his, none of them his, noneofthem*his*—surged into his mind, invading, conquering, slipping across his brain like an eel, screaming over the geography of hemispheres and lobes, funneling into the place where his memories lived, his consciousness, his self, his

—soul Jesus Christ Almighty my soul somebody help me—

tearing arcs of wildfire across his mind, something crushing his singularity under its incredible weight, reshaping it into something else, something

—damned—

frozen, cryogenic, obsidian, predatory, uncompromising, unflinching, unfathomable.

Charles Caine did not see the ceiling tiles above him now. He did not see the smirking woman with the raven hair. He did not feel the spasms jigging his muscles, did not feel his fingernails digging Cheshire moon-grins into his palms, did not feel his teeth grinding against each other. He did not hear the air surging from his nostrils in sputters of guttural, manic snorespeak.

He did not see. He did not feel. He did not hear.

And yet, he did.

An iron glove was closing around Charles Caine's mind. He was reliving moments, thoughts. He could feel a shimmering, alien precision overwhelming his mind neuron by neuron

—*dancing in mother's parlor to "Chattanooga Choo Choo," doesn't Mary Jean look wonderful in her dress, Charlie, her curls bouncing with the music* THIS IS MINE NOW—

enslaving him, overtaking his thoughts, his memories

—*married the childhood sweetheart, you bet I did, and did I mention I was running for* YOU *county* ARE *com*MINE—

pushing him *inward*, pushing him *aside*, pushing him *deep*

—*ly in love with you, baby, that's wonderful news, sounds like we need a house with another roo*—

—EVERYTHING YOU ARE—

compressing them, making them

—MINE—

like files in a cabinet, like a cards in a Rolodex, like

—*Jesus Christ what's happening to me God help me God help me God help me*—

words in an open book

ALL MINE

information on a disk drive, spinning round and round and round and

—*i'm sorry Jean so sorry so so sorry I can't see*—

YOU

—God can you hear—
ME
—Lord, Holy Lord beginning—
ALPHA
—and end—
OMEGA
—I—
WE
Eeeeeeee

Me.

When Caine's body stopped its tangled marionette dance, San-jah's smirk twisted into a sneer . . . then a triumphant smile. She covered her face with a gloved hand, suppressing an outburst of laughter. Her eyes were still black ice. Killer's eyes.

The old man's eyes fluttered open. They scanned the room, the woman, cataloging what he saw. Caine lifted his hands and held them in front of his face, examining first the palms, then the with-ered backs. He lifted his head and looked down at his chest and stomach, his mouth slipping into an unconscious frown. His eyes followed the wires connected to his chest and head down to the black device near his legs. A sly grin spread across his face.

"Success," he said.

Sanjah's smile vanished. She raised her eyebrows. "Almost," she replied coolly. "Let's do it. Vermilion."

Caine nodded. "Quantum."

"Methuselah."

"Mission," he said.

Sanjah's eyes glimmered. "Propagate."

Charles Caine sat up, swung his legs over the examination ta-ble, and took in a deep breath as if it were his first. He closed his eyes and placed his hands on his face; his fingertips gently trailed down and across his nose, mouth, and cheeks. He dragged one hand down over his mouth, over his chin, and onto the small wattle beneath it. Caine's eyes opened and brightened. He flicked the flesh there with his index finger.

"So this is what being old feels like."

Sanjah snickered. "You should try being a woman." She held her hands out to either side of her breasts and moved them back and forth, comically emphasizing her bosom.

Caine surveyed the nurse's body and shook his head in appreciation. "If I had scored your gig, I never would've left the house."

"You *did* score my gig."

Caine raised an eyebrow. "So I did."

Sanjah looked at her wristwatch and sighed. "You know the plan. We have two more minutes, then I get the doctor. You saw him last. Does he suspect anything?"

Caine shook his head. "Nothing." He watched intently as Sanjah scribbled several comments, many of them *Normal*, onto the clipboard sheet. He chuckled. "I think he wants to fuck you."

Sanjah's nose crinkled in disgust. She reached into her pocket and pulled out a test tube. She removed its rubber cap. "So give me the run-through. What do you know?"

Caine closed his eyes again. The surface of his eyelids rose and fell as the orbs behind them rushed side to side, like a sleeper's in REM sleep. He opened them. The pale flesh above his cheeks crinkled into well-worn laugh lines.

"Everything," he said. "I know *everything*. His daughters' birthdays. His Social Security number. Emergency bunker locations. Access codes to the intranetwork. His favorite movies—all John Wayne. Every dirty little secret. Names of his wife's pets. Pet names for his wife."

Caine gazed down at his right thigh and rubbed it absently.

"Jesus. I can remember when he was shot in Okinawa. I can *feel* it."

Sanjah shook her head. "Later. Let him stay near the surface. It's better that way; takes care of most of the unconscious stuff. Body language, signature sayings, accents, that sort of thing. If there's anything I've learned over the past three days, it's this: Don't *try* to be the host. Just let it flow. Caine's in there. Pillage when no one's around."

"Got it."

"Hold still now."

Mira Sanjah reached out and plucked a strand of gray hair from Caine's scalp. She slipped it into the test tube, then replaced the rubber cap.

"Thank God you only need one. I don't have many to spare."

Sanjah glanced at her watch again. "So, quick. Do the FBI, CIA, NSA, know anything about us?"

Caine closed his eyes. They rolled in their sockets like a madman's.

"No."

"Do they know anything about our family reunion?"

Caine smiled. "No. The bastards are apparently keeping it quiet, running it in-house."

"So I was right," the nurse said, grinning.

"No, *I* was right."

Sanjah laughed, ripped the latex gloves from her hands, tossed them into the shimmering wastebasket. She then picked up the black device and tucked it under her arm like a textbook. "Time to go."

"You know what to do from here," Caine said. "Give my best to Devlin."

Sanjah grinned. "It's *Devlins* now. Hordes, really. It's all on schedule. Unit One is already learning how to drive the trucks, and learning to love vodka. Unit Two is freezing its balls off, while

Unit Three is having fun, fun, fun till their daddy takes their T-birds away. And speaking of daddies, I'm off to find the prodigal. I'll probably need some Devs for that."

"Make as many as you need."

"That's it, then. You know when to report, of course."

The vice president nodded. "Report." It rolled off his tongue in a romantic gush. "I can't wait to talk to myself."

Mira Sanjah walked to the door and winked at him before she opened it. "You just did."

Charles Caine grinned during Dr. Jared Blackwell's predictably bland synopsis of his health during the press conference thirty minutes later. Aside from a touch of hypertension—well within normal limits for a man of Caine's age and position, Blackwell emphasized—the man was more than fit to lead the country. The Pack voraciously gobbled every syllable . . . its flashbulbs, zoom lenses, and clown-red-lipstick smiles said as much. Caine smiled through it all, too, nodding at the appropriate moments.

When he took the lectern after Blackwell's briefing, the questions overflowed from the Pack. All of them inane.

All of them perfectly, deliciously inane.

Vice President Charles Caine answered every last one. Just before he left the stage, he delivered his sound bite that would indeed be edited into the evening's newscasts: "I feel right as rain and am ready to help President Hale and this great nation in any way I can."

As he departed, no one asked the vice president why he was waving with his left hand instead of his right, as he had done for the forty years he'd been in politics. The Pack simply didn't notice.

Which made John Alpha—who was now lurking and controlling Caine's psyche from the depths of the old man's hippocampus—smile even more.

THIRTEEN

It was good to be back in the Common Room, John thought. Not because it made the day's revelations any easier to swallow, or because he was closer to his bed, which he desperately wanted to dive into. It was good because it was the closest he could get to being outside. As John sat on the circular couch in the center of this circular room, staring up past his cigarette smoke, he could spot birds swooping across the skylight above him . . . and far, far up into the blue, misty contrails of airliners. Or fighter jets, more likely. In these parts and in these times, you could never be too sure.

After Durbin had played the audio file in the Operations room—*deee dee deee dee deeeeee*—the group had taken the express elevator up here for lunch. Warm sandwiches and cold sodas were waiting for them, but only Michael felt like eating after the ride. John had made a beeline for the couch and his smokes—*just need to sit down for a sec . . . just a sec . . . process this shit*—and the others had found some similar solace in looking up into the sky, into the great freedom above.

John exhaled and watched the smoke rise. This place they were in, it was a tomb, dangerous. He didn't trust it, and he didn't trust Kleinman, Hill, or Durbin. It was a feeling, just a feeling tugging at his brain, like a sliver of popcorn shell trapped between your teeth. It nagged, insisted.

Nearly all of the clones sat on the couch. Jay and Jack sat beside each other, conversing in conspiratorial whispers. John had no idea what they were saying, but it was clear Jack was steamed about something. John smiled at the exchange. Toss them in *Star Wars* T-shirts and they'd look like kid brothers up to no good. Now, John smiled at the irony.

Kilroy2.0, however, was not at the couch. He pored over a motley collection of computer monitors, keyboards, and CPUs humming away on a folding table placed in the far end of the room. The lunatic had nearly shrieked with joy when he'd spotted the setup. John suspected these were the computers that had been taken from Kilroy's home when the spook squad had kidnapped him. Just as they had kidnapped John. And Dr. Mike. And Father Thomas. And the rest, here on Gilligan's isle.

Kleinman was with them, sitting on a section of the couch. He appeared tired, yet wired. The constant polishing of his glasses tipped his hand. Right now, with that quiet impatience radiating from him, Kleinman reminded John of a boss he once had in Georgia a few years back—during what John now called the Road Work Years. Roy Fielder was his name. He owned Athens Rock N' Roll, a paving and cement company. No matter how early John would show up to prep the mixer, the roller, or the work site, Roy Fielder was there. First to arrive, last to leave. Fielder would pace and cross his arms, silently waiting for the crew to get that first mug-o-joe in their bellies and get to work. Roy Fielder never said a word, but his eyes implored. *There's sweat to be spilled and profits to be made.*

Restless, Kleinman clapped his hands on his knees. John took another drag and looked at the old man.

"So now we're supposed to decode the message our evil twin left for us," John said. "We find Mom and save the day."

Kleinman nodded. "Something like that."

"And you're depending on seven semi-average Joes instead of superbrilliant government folk because . . . ?"

Kleinman fidgeted with his glasses. "Twofold. The first should be obvious: secrecy. To contact outsiders about Alpha's plot, whatever it may be, would reveal the existence of 7th Son. The world doesn't know about us, Alpha, or you. I wouldn't think you'd want to share a face—much less fingerprints and DNA—with a political assassin. Every post office in America would have your mug shot on a bulletin board. Instant fugitives. And I don't think any of you are ready to out yourselves as human clones."

"Got that right." John took another drag. "But it seems short-sighted. You're taking us seven whippersnappers over whatever brainiacs the feds have at their disposal. Not to mention sheer manpower, or gunpower. Doesn't make sense."

"Don't worry about the resources," the old man replied. "General Hill can get you whatever you need. Trust me." He leaned forward, resting his elbows on his knees. "Listen. Over the past three weeks, Durbin, Hill, and our team tried to decode that Morse-code message—if it's even Morse code—and came up with file after file of gibberish. They're stumped, which makes me wonder about using government 'brainiacs.' Alpha sent two messages with this kidnapping: 'You can't decode this' and 'Get the Betas—they'll be able to do it.' The label on the CD-ROM said as much."

"And since we have the same memories as Alpha—to a certain point in his life—we're suddenly very useful," John said, and smirked. "I see what you're going for. If anyone could get into Alpha's head . . . really get into his head to stop him . . . it'd be us. Seven heads are better than one."

Kleinman smiled. "You're good."

"Better hope so."

Across from the pair, Jack and Jay concluded their mini-conference. Jack leaned forward, face flushed, and tapped his index finger on the round table. "Kleinman, we want to talk to our families. They've got to know what's going on here, where we are. Jay and me. We've gotta talk to our wives. No bullshit."

"You can't, Jack," the doctor said. "Not right now. There's too much wo—"

Now Jack's knuckles rapped on the Formica. "No, I said. No. They need to know we're okay. You've got us by the balls, but at least give us a phone call."

Across the room, Kilroy2.0 clapped his hands and gave a small hoot. The five monitors were powered up now. A small webcam rested on one of the boxy CRTs. Kilroy2.0 leaned his head over the keyboards—stacked almost atop each other, like keys on a cathedral organ—and began typing. John and the other clones stepped over to see what was happening.

"Are you up and running?" Kleinman called. He stood up, grateful to escape Jack's ire. The bearded, bespectacled clone remained on the couch, knuckles still on the table. His shoulders sagged. John felt a pang of sympathy. Hell, he'd left his girl, Sarah, on a balcony in Miami, where she'd promised sex and breakfast. It was a fucking mess, all of it.

Kilroy2.0 didn't look up, but nodded his head furiously. The monitors glowed with Web-site windows, strange programs, and streaming text, numbers and graphics. John, whose computer experience was limited to the occasional visit to the public library to buy an amp on eBay, was amazed. He'd never seen anything like this: Kilroy2.0 was like an orchestra conductor on speed, his fingers already *rak-a-tack*ing across the keyboards, his hand flipping to the computer mouse to double-click a winking icon. The computers hummed, beeped, and whirred . . . and apparently did what Kilroy2.0 told them to.

. *It's like he's come home,* John thought. *Like none of this, none of us, matter.*

"What operating system is that?" Jack asked, squinting at the screens.

"Home-brewed," the hacker muttered as he typed. "Called K2."

"Our tech team installed the audio file onto your hard disk," Kleinman called. "When you're ready, go ahead and play it."

Kilroy2.0 clicked an icon on one of the monitors, which activated the sound file. It played through the computers' attached speakers and into the circular room. No one spoke. John thought of a roomful of army telegraph operators wearing their arcane headphones, hunched over their little electric noisemakers, pumping messages to wires suspended over burning battlefields.

Dee deee . . . deee deee dee . . . dee deee . . . dee deee . . . deee dee deee dee . . . dee deee . . . Dee deee . . . deee deee dee . . . dee deee . . . dee deee . . . deee dee deee dee . . . dee deee . . . dee deee . . .

There was more, but Michael spoke up over it. "Stop playing it for a minute."

Kilroy2.0 clicked an on-screen button that resembled a STOP button on a tape player and looked up at the marine.

"Gimme a sec." Michael closed his eyes; a line of concentration formed over his eyebrows. Near him, Jay did the same. "Play it again," Michael said.

Kilroy2.0 clicked the rewind button and played the file again. It was creepy: *dee deee dee deeee,* like a message from an alien race.

The hacker stopped the message when Michael opened his eyes.

"Someone grab a piece of paper," Michael said. "It's definitely Morse code."

Nearly all of the clones had dashed back to the couches when Kleinman tore a page from a pocket notebook and waved it at them. Kilroy2.0 kept his post at the computer. They crowded around the circular table at the center of the room, peering down at the letters as Michael wrote them. Even now, John couldn't help noticing the marine's handwriting.

That's my handwriting, he thought. *Jesus Christ. His A's look like triangles. Just like mine.*

Michael had written three rows of capital letters; the first two had six letters . . . the last, seven letters.

AGAACA

AGAACA

AGAACAA

Dr. Mike snorted. "What up, *Da Vinci Code?*"

"What does it mean?" Father Thomas asked, shaking his head.

"No idea," Michael said. "I didn't edit for content."

"Are you sure you translated it correctly?" Kleinman asked.

"Yeah, he did," Jay said. "It's the real deal."

Dr. Mike looked at him suspiciously.

"I had to learn this stuff to work in the field for the UN," Jay said. "When you're in the middle of the mountains of Pakistan and the satphone's on the fritz, you gotta communicate. It's usually reserved for emergencies."

"Well, this is an emergency," Dr. Mike said, and picked up the piece of paper. "But I'm with the priest. *Agaa-caa?* What in the hell is that supposed to mean?"

"That's basically what Durbin's team said," Kleinman replied. "They decoded the same letters, have been puzzling over it since."

The clones stood in silence, staring down at the letters written in Michael's handwriting—in their handwriting. They glanced at one another, that same worried expression pinching their faces.

And here we are, together at the starting gate, John thought. *That's what we're all thinking. If we get this ball rolling now, we're admitting some truths, aren't we? We're admitting that we* believe. *That it's all true. Can I trust these me's? Can I trust them like I trust myself?*

Then, as Jay began to speak, the moment passed. John's mind flitted to cigarette smokers, instant conversation. A freak is not a freak if *all* are freaks, Frank Zappa once said. Too true. The seven were in for a penny, in for a pound.

"*Agaa-caa.* Is it an acronym?" Jay glanced at the marine for a reply. "Maybe for a company or an agency?"

Michael shook his head. "Doesn't look like it. Even if you say them phonetically: 'Alpha, Golf, Alpha, Alpha, Charlie, Alpha.' That's no code I'm familiar with. It could be some kind of instruction or command—like some kind of GPS coordinates for latitude or longitude—but we don't have any kind of context. If it's an answer, we don't have the question. If it's the lock, we don't have a key. There's plenty of *Alphas* in there, for what it's worth." He shrugged. "I just don't know how much it's worth."

"Me neither," Dr. Mike said, clearly intrigued now. "Maybe it's not an acronym. Maybe it's a . . . ah, shit. What're those words you rearrange to make other words?"

"A palindrome?" Father Thomas said.

"Anagram," Kilroy2.0 said, still staring at his computer screen. The others looked at him in that strange amalgam of morbid curiosity and amazement. *The oracle speaks and the faithful listen,* John mused. Then the lunatic added, "Anagrams are your best friends in online Scrabble."

"Swell," Dr. Mike said. "Anagram. Is it one of those?"

They looked over the letters.

"Cagaaa? Aaacag?"

"Those aren't words," Jack replied.

"I'm just trying to help," Thomas muttered.

The clones continued to look at the slip of paper.

"CA. GA. Those could be abbreviations for states," Michael said. "California and Georgia."

"Yeah, but what about the other two A's?" Dr. Mike flashed a brilliant smile. "Is John Alpha telling us that he's in a twelve-step program?"

"Be serious, Doc," Michael said.

"I'm just sayin'. Maybe it's a cry for help."

"Hush," Jack said, and squatted down. His knees popped, two little thundercracks. "Of course," he said, tapping the letters with his index finger. "These are code letters for nucleotides. Nucleotides are the building blocks of DNA."

Dr. Mike grinned. "Now we're getting somewhere. The twisted fuck. Appropriate message for a bunch of clones."

Jack picked up the paper and held it. It quivered slightly in his hand. Across the room, Kilroy2.0 was already finger-pecking on his keyboards.

"So what do those letters mean?" Father Thomas asked. "Does it spell out a gene or something?"

The geneticist shook his head. "It's not that easy. Nucleotides are like little biological code words. They talk to cells. Depending on the code word, which is defined by the order of the nucleotides, the cells produce special proteins. That's how traits are passed from parent to child . . . or clone to clone. It's all about A's, T's, G's and C's."

"Mendel and his peas," John said.

"And Q's," Dr. Mike said. "I'll get the Cliff's Notes later. So what's the problem?"

Jack sighed. "Instructions for protein manufacture are composed of hundreds of nucleotides, not six or seven. This might be a part of a protein code, but it's certainly not—" Suddenly, Jack stood and whirled around. He looked at Kilroy2.0, then pointed at the computer screens. "Hey. Where can you go with those?"

Kilroy2.0 grinned. "Anywhere."

"Good. Do a search. Genetic databases. For *AGAACA.*"

Kilroy leaned over the keyboards. His fingers *tak-tacked.* John heard the distinctive double-click of the computer mouse.

"Working," Kilroy2.0 said. Dr. Mike rolled his eyes. John watched lists of data simultaneously stream across the five monitors. The mouse clicks almost became a cadence.

"Numerous hits," Kilroy2.0 said. "It's part of a wheat genome. It's also part of a sequence for an anticoagulant. Also found in some mouse and rat hormone receptors."

Michael frowned. "Okay. So what do wheat, rat hormones, and blood clotters have in common?"

Silence.

John stared at the letters. Stared past the letters.

AGAACA. AGAACAA.

"Nucleotides may not be the answer," Jack said. "If this is only part of a genetic sequence, we'll never know what Alpha's trying to tell us."

"We didn't play the entire message," Thomas said. "Maybe if we transcribed the whole thing . . ."

John continued to stare. *AGAACA. AGAACAA.*

A-G-A-A-C-A.

Of course, you bastard. Of course.

"Yeah," John said. His voice was calm, transfixed. "Play back the whole thing. Write it down. And, ah . . ."

He glanced up at the others, embarrassed.

"Somebody get me a guitar."

John realized his request was ridiculous: *Get me a guitar.* Here. In a "Code Phantom"–protected cloning facility, whatever the hell that meant.

But Kleinman had nodded and hustled out of the room. In Kleinman's absence, Kilroy2.0 replayed the entire message while Michael and Jay collaborated on the decoding. They were wrapping up when Kleinman burst back into the Common Room with General Hill not far behind. Hill's eyes were chilly.

But the soldier was also carrying an acoustic-guitar case. John stifled a laugh. *This, this . . . force of nature . . . is an axeman? What's he play? "The Army Goes Rolling Along"?*

Hill's eyes narrowed; he was looking at John as if he were reading the young man's mind.

"I'm sorry," John said, suppressing a giggle. "It's just . . ."

Hill brushed past Kleinman, strode over, and placed the guitar case on the round table. He fired a smirk in John's direction and opened the case.

The clone's eyes widened. The wood was spruce—Sitka spruce, the best around. It was deep brown on the edges, slipping into a warm gold in the center. The headstock read C. F. MARTIN & CO., and just below that was a pearlized logo of a rat and the letters G.O.W.R. The gold tuning pegs glimmered in the skylight sunlight.

"It's a Martin," John whispered. His eyes flitted from the six-string to the general, then back again. Glittering letters were inlaid on the fingerboard. When read vertically, they spelled *skiffle.*

John closed his mouth, then said, "*You* own a Martin?"

"Limited edition," Hill said.

"Yeah, I know," John marveled. "A Lonnie Donegan Brazilian. They only made seventy-five of these." He couldn't pull his eyes away from it. A Martin. He'd only strummed them in guitar shops, and then only for a minute; he'd always been too broke to afford to break one. John whistled a note of amazement. "Motherfucker. This put you back, what? Seven gees?"

"Almost nine."

Jack gasped. "Nine *thousand* dollars? For a guitar?"

"A limited-edition Lonnie Donegan," John marveled. "It's beautiful. Beautiful." He reached for the guitar. Before he lifted it out of the case, he looked at General Hill. "I'll be careful."

"I know you will."

John sat down on the couch and propped the Martin on his knee. It felt nice in his hands; it felt *right*, if that made sense. John strummed a first-position E chord and grinned. The guitar was perfectly tuned, and the sound was warm, rich, aural butterscotch. He looked down at the piece of paper on the table, read the first three lines, and began plucking the strings with his fingertips.

A-G-A-A-C-A. A-G-A-A-C-A. A-G-A-A-C-A-A.

"Huh," John said. "Does that sound familiar to any of you?"

"Negatory," Dr. Mike said.

John played it again, looked at the others for any recognition. "I don't have the foggiest, either."

He played the notes again. And again.

Nothing.

"What if you were to play them differently?" Jack offered, leaning back against the couch cushions. "I don't mean in a different order. I mean to a different beat. You just played them straight through. *Bam-bam-bam-bam-bam-bam.* Play it differently: *Bam-bam-bam . . . bam-bam . . . bam-bam,* or something like that. Catch my drift?"

"I do." Stupid. What John had just done was not really different from replaying the monotone Morse code. "Stagger the beats so they might actually sound like music."

"Like emphasizing the correct syllable in a word," Michael said.

John tried again, playing the first line as Jack had suggested: A-G, A-A, C-A.

Now *that* sounded familiar. John looked at his brothers and saw hints of recognition on a few of their faces—Michael and Father Thomas, most notably.

Something was there. "Do you feel it?" John asked them. "It's there. Tickling my brain."

"Yeah," Michael said. "Sounds sinister. Play it again."

John's fingers moved up and down the neck of the Martin as he played the notes again with the same rhythm. It *did* sound sinister; the tune was almost like a dirge—repetitive, starting in a neutral A, then dipping into a dark G, then back to A . . . up to a bittersweet C, and back to A again.

As John finished, Jack closed his eyes and softly hummed the tune over and over. Father Thomas was staring at the ceiling, nodding his head slightly to the humming—then he was nodding at something else. Nodding and grinning.

John played the six notes and listened.

"'Mr. Mo-jo ri-sin',' " the priest sang along. "'Mr. Mo-jo ri-sin'.' "

"That's the Doors," Michael said.

"Yes," John said. "That's 'L.A. Woman.' "

FOURTEEN

ohn looked at the rest of the letters written on the piece of paper and began to play them. They came easily, now that he had a pattern to work from. The first wave of notes were indeed the droning bridge from "L.A. Woman": "Mr. Mojo risin' . . ." The next transcribed lines (A-A-A-A-G-A-G-C-G-A-A) were the chorus of the song: "L.A. woman, Sunday afternoon." As John plucked the strings, Father Thomas sang that, too. Funny. The priest hadn't struck John as a Lizard King fan.

John was getting into the rhythm of the song when the last line threw him. Only three letters in the last line of the transcript—C, C, and E—were notes. The rest of them . . . who knew?

"This last bit isn't music," John said. "Take a look."

The clones gathered round the table and gazed at raw Morse code Jay had scribbled onto the paper, then to Michael's translation below it:

-.-.-.-.- -.-. . . . -.. .. . .

CCXCVIIEIII

"Those are Roman numerals," Father Thomas said quickly. "At least almost all of them are."

Jay picked up the slip of paper. "He's right." The UN specialist frowned, then tapped at the last letter of the writing. "But *E* isn't a Roman numeral; at least, I don't think so."

"It's not," Father Thomas said. "Does that mean that none of these letters are supposed to be Roman numerals?"

"One step at a time, hoss," Michael said. "Let's test the theory before we throw it out. Aside from the *E*, what's this thing say? Kilroy, can you deliver?"

"Yes," Kilroy2.0 said, and typed on his keyboards. A new window popped onto the computer screen; just one of at least a dozen. "With the exception of the *E*—which doesn't translate into a Roman numeral—the number reads 297 and then 3."

Sighing, Jack plopped down on the couch beside John, who had to quickly move the Martin so it wouldn't be bumped. "Christ. This guy doesn't give us a break, does he?"

"You gotta sing for your supper around here," Michael said. "No pun intended, John."

John smiled slightly, placing the guitar back in the case.

"Okay. Let's think about this," Dr. Mike said. The profiler began to pace. "The song is 'L.A. Woman.' It's written by the Doors. Mr. Mojo's risin' and all that. And now, 297, the letter *E* and 3. So. What do they all have in common? What's the link?"

"The words *L.A. Woman* have seven letters," Father Thomas said. "Seven letters, seven clones, 7th Son." Then, as if he needed to explain: "Just a thought. I'm a crossword junkie."

"Not bad," Jay said. "Sevens. We should write that down."

He then looked over at Kleinman, who, along with General Hill, was standing away from the group, silently watching them work. Kleinman winked and tossed Jay his pocket notebook. Jay caught it with one hand, then knelt by the table and began writing.

John spoke up. "Well, we could take the anagram approach. I mention it because there's some lore out there about the lyric 'Mr. Mojo risin'.' They say it's an anagram for 'Jim Morrison.' It's true, by the way."

"No shit," Michael said.

"Not a pebble."

" 'L.A. Woman' anagrams into 'AWOL Man,' " Kilroy2.0 said.

"That's sounds appropriate," Michael said. "Alpha ran like hell from this place."

The hacker raised a finger. "It also anagrams into 'anal mow.' " John laughed.

"Okay. So maybe it anagrams into a clue," Dr. Mike said, waving his hand distractedly, "and maybe it doesn't. Big picture first. The title. 'L.A. Woman' is significant. My gut's telling me whatever Alpha is saying has something to do with Los Angeles. Here's a happy coincidence: L.A. is my stomping ground. It's where I live."

They considered this for a moment, as Jay scribbled his notes onto the notepad.

"You know, that might be important in itself," Father Thomas said. "I mean, Alpha *deliberately* left the Morse-code file for us, even labeled it for us. He knew it'd take someone who understood Morse code to spell out the letters—and a musician to play those letters, right? And the Roman numerals. It's like he's baiting us. It's as if he knows—"

"—that what *we* know will unlock the clue," Michael said. "Sonuvabitch. No wonder Durbin's boys couldn't get this far. It's written solely for us. The general said we've been tailed our whole lives, and that intel came back to 7th Son. Alpha saw that data while he was still here. He knows us. Knows where we live. Knows our strengths."

"But we don't know what any of this *means*," Jay said, putting down his pen. "These last numbers: 297, *E*, 3. Are we supposed to multiply them? Divide them? Are they map coordinates, like Michael said? Pages in a book? A zip code? We'll be here for days trying to figure out what they're supposed to mean."

"You're missing the point," Dr. Mike said, shaking his head. "The priest is right."

"The priest has a name."

"Sorry, Thomas. But you're right: the knowledge we've all used to get to this point has come pretty naturally to us. And Michael's right, too: he's playing on our talents. We couldn't decipher the message separately, sure, but together, we've been able to piece it together with minimal brainpower."

"You call this minimal?" Jack said.

Dr. Mike chuckled. "You should see me on a tough profiling case. I get the worst fucking migraines; shit keeps me up at night. The point is, these clues—all of them, including the Roman numerals—have certainly not been Advil-worthy. The answers have come naturally. This bit with the numbers is the same way. Don't misunderstand. Alpha's smart, probably smarter than us. That's bad for the long run. But right now, it's good. He's guiding us; baiting us, just like Thomas said. I'm sure of it. We just have to make the connections."

John looked back down at the sheet of paper. *It's just like the music notes. It's all right there, if you look for it:*

-.-. -.-. -..- -.-. . . . . - .. ..

CCXCVIIEIII

297, then E, *then 3. What does the* E *mean? Where in the hell is the* E *in this thing, anyway?*

"Hey, Michael," John said. "Which one of these doohickeys in the Morse code is the *E*?"

"Our myster-*E*," Kilroy2.0 said.

The marine plucked the pen from the table and circled a single character, near the end of the code. "There it is, hoss."

John looked at the paper. "It looks like a period. You're telling me that a single dot is an E in Morse code?"

"Yeah," Jay and Michael said simultaneously. They looked at each other and smiled slightly; their mouths crooked up at the right, their dimples appearing in their cheeks at the same time. John shook his head. *"Uncanny" doesn't even begin to describe it,* he thought.

He was about to say as much when Dr. Mike scooped up the paper and looked at it. His eyes were wide, wild. "What if it *were* a period?"

"What do you mean?" Father Thomas said.

"The *E,* damn it. What if the *E* were just a dot, like John said? A period? What if it weren't supposed to be translated into Morse code?" Dr. Mike crunched the paper in his fist as he paced. He dropped the wad onto the table. "What if it were a decimal point?"

"Then it'd read 297.3," Jack said. "Does that mean anything to you?"

Dr. Mike nodded. "Yeah. I think it does. Kilroy, find me an online copy of the *DSM.* You know what that is?"

The hacker flinched. A look of horror slipped over his face for an instant. Then he blinked and nodded.

"I bet you do," Dr. Mike said. "I don't care if you have to hack, slash, or burn your way through the whole Net to find it. Just find it, Kilroy."

The lunatic began typing.

John leaned forward. "What's this all about, Doc?"

Mike looked up at John. "We were right. About Alpha. About the clues playing to our strengths. This one's right up my alley."

———

It didn't take long for Kilroy2.0 to access an online version of the *Diagnostic and Statistical Manual of Mental Disorders*, probably because he did indeed hack, slash, and burn his way through the Internet. He hijacked the identity of at least one psychiatrist (using the doctor's so-called secure information including Social Security number, address, and credit-card numbers) to get the information. For shits and giggles, Kilroy2.0 also ordered a two-year subscription of *Penthouse Letters* for their unwitting benefactor, one Dr. Robert Riehl of Toledo, Ohio. It was apparently the least Kilroy2.0 could do to thank Dr. Riehl for the kind and selfless loan of his identity.

General Hill and Dr. Kleinman had discovered an uncontrollable urge to discuss something at the far end of the room during these transactions. Their backs were turned through the whole thing. John grinned at that. There it was again. Don't ask, don't tell. Out of sight, out of mind.

Kilroy2.0 loaded and launched something called a trackscrambler before he logged on to the American Psychiatric Association's secure *DSM* subsite with the stolen ID and password. Kilroy2.0 typed "297.3" in the search field and retrieved one hit.

Dr. Mike was right. It was a psychiatric diagnosis.

"Shared psychotic disorder," Michael read aloud, from over Kilroy2.0's shoulder. The marine didn't seem to register the lunatic's ripe aroma or was charitably ignoring it. "It's a delusion shared between two or more people, usually created by an 'inducer' who's already suffering from a psychotic disorder." He turned to Dr. Mike. "I need a little dose of English over here. The shrinkspeak ain't cutting it."

Dr. Mike stood up from his seat on the couch. "I know this disorder. I studied it in grad school."

"I wonder if Alpha knew that," Jack said.

Jay and Thomas looked at each other, their faces grim.

"I think we know the answer to that," Dr. Mike said. "Shared psychotic disorder is a kind of small-scale 'cult of personality.'"

"Living Colour," John murmured. "Killer song."

"Yeah," Father Thomas said, from beside him. "Whatever happened to them?"

John nearly laughed out loud. "You're full of surprises, Father."

"We're basically talking about a close relationship between two people," Dr. Mike continued, "in which one of them is full shit-bird crazy and the other is highly suggestible but relatively healthy, from a mental perspective. The suggestible person begins believing whatever delusions the psychotic is spouting and also becomes shit-bird crazy in the process. I read about one case in which these two lovers believed, with every shred of their psyches, that the FBI was watching them through their home computer screen.

"Often the delusions are filled with persecution," Dr. Mike continued. "But there are cases in which the couple—or groups of people, this is how cults get started, you know—embrace a more, ah, *liberated* lifestyle due to the delusions."

"Kinky sex? That what we're talking 'bout here, Doc?" Michael asked.

"Oh, for heaven's sake," Thomas said.

"Sometimes," Dr. Mike said. "Think of it more in terms of people doing things they normally wouldn't do, society be damned. Bonnie and Clyde are classic examples. Back in the day, people in my field used to call this condition all kinds of different things: psychic infection, double insanity, contagious insanity. The French had a term for it."

"Yeah, it's here," Michael said, staring at the screen. *"Folie à deux."*

"'Madness between two,'" Jay whispered.

"That's right," Dr. Mike said. *"Folie à d—"*

He stopped in midsentence . . . then literally slapped his hand against his forehead. Kilroy2.0 shrieked a laugh.

"Motherfucker!" Dr. Mike cried. "You *wily motherfucker!*"

"What is it, Doc?" Michael said.

"It's a place." Dr. Mike waved his arms like a tent revival preacher. "A nightclub in Los Angeles. That's what it was called. Folie à Deux."

Michael clapped Kilroy2.0 on the shoulder. "Kilroy, pull up the L.A.-area business listings, yellow pages, newspapers, maps, whatever you can."

Kilroy2.0 nodded, grinning like the mad genius he undoubtedly was, and began typing furiously on the keyboards.

The marine turned to Dr. Mike and smiled. "We're going club-hopping."

FIFTEEN

I t was a good thing Douglas Devlin could read Cyrillic. *Da.* A very good thing indeed . . . if only to appreciate the irony stenciled on the tin sign before him.

He stood outside in the Russian darkness, watching his breath condense in the air, his exhale made visible by the few outdoor lights here at the Tatishchevo garrison. The Volga River was about sixty miles away, but the frigid wind hailing from the water made the snowy air brittle even here. And for those who hadn't grown up in such an environment as Devlin had, almost unbearable.

He looked at the sign again—the rusted thing mounted on the exterior of one of the nine 120-foot-long rectangular garages out here in the steppes of Russia—and chuckled. His gloved hands fished into his combat-jacket pockets, searching for those god-damned cigarettes. The sign was barely legible from the rust, and from the thick layer of small, black, circular smudges covering most of the letters. It read, in Russian:

ABSOLUTELY NO
Unauthorized Personnel Allowed On Premises!

ABSOLUTELY NO
Smoking!

Devlin found the crumpled pack of Primas in his breast pocket (the Primas in the camouflage-patterned box, no less—Kovalenko had apparently been a proud SMF man) and shook out one of the filterless cigs. He lit it with Kovalenko's very American silver Zippo. His hands were shaking slightly. Devlin knew it wasn't the cold. After two and a half weeks, this body was finally beginning to betray him.

The cigarette tasted wonderful and awful. He took another deep drag and mashed the glowing cigarette out on the sign, just like the hundreds of soldiers who had come before him. Governments can never regulate some things for long. Smokers, for instance. And unauthorized personnel. Devlin was both.

He grinned cynically; at least he thought it was cynically. Devlin had learned from his brethren that Kovalenko had the face of a child.

Like many things in his life, Devlin owed his fluency in Russian to the Farm . . . Camp Swampy . . . spook school . . . Langley . . . whatever the hell the fresh-faced trainees were calling CIA headquarters these days. But Langley was where he'd learned to speak and read the stuff back in '83, and right now Doug Devlin was glad he had worked there and been educated in All Things Soviet. And All Things Murder. And All Things Bang and Burn. And intel. And weapons.

Devlin coughed and listened to the sound echo throughout the garrison. Those goddamned Primas.

He hated this body. Hated its sagging flesh, the addictions to smokes and booze, the dulled reactions, the rattling cough. Most of his brethren here at Tatishchevo hated their bodies, too. "Russians don't take care of themselves," one of them had said, just

hours after Colonel Bogdanov had briefed the entire military
compound on its new mission. "Well, if your world sucked as bad
as theirs does," Devlin had replied, "you'd drink and smoke yourself to death, too."

That was two weeks ago, a literal lifetime ago. But Devlin's
path to this moment, this cigarette, had begun long before that.

By 1992, the CIA had realized it didn't need such a large army of
agents who were trained in All Things Soviet. The world was
changing. Almost all of the Company's intel gurus and satellite
spy experts—the people who had, in the past decade, managed
to point-and-click their way up the food chain of agency
importance—were allowed to stay in the family, keep their assign-
ments, and remain watchful over the Russians and their newfound democracy. But most of the field agents—the ones trained
for stealth, demolition, and wetwork in the Soviet Union and the
Eastern Bloc countries—found themselves holding pink slips.

Some of them blamed the new doves in the White House. Others blamed the fallout from the early-nineties recession. Doug
Devlin didn't blame those things. Devlin had suddenly found
himself reassigned from his realm of expertise (All Things Soviet)
to "babysitting" jobs in the Middle East (pulling glorified body-
guard duty for rising stars in the Saudi Arabian and Kuwaiti governments). He blamed this on something that was overpowering,
yet elusive.

The way governments conducted business was shifting. Evolv-
ing. It seemed that most of the world simply didn't have a place for
folks like Doug Devlin anymore: folks who lived to kill. The de-
mocracies seemed to grow out of it, as if they were adolescents finally deciding to put away their dolls once and for all. Shutting
them away from the world, only pulling them up occasionally to
reminisce about years past.

Devlin didn't enjoy being a relic, and he certainly didn't enjoy babysitting a bunch of fucking towelheads who, in a twist of divine irony, had been destined to hold America by the balls ever since Henry Ford built the Model T. So Devlin got out of the business. He worked in the revered private sector as a consultant for about six months. The desks and meetings drove him crazy.

In 1993, Doug Devlin vanished and became a contract killer. It was what he lived to do, after all.

Devlin didn't care who, what company, or which government requested his services. His loyalty to Langley and the great You-Ess-of-Ay had become null when they gave him his reassignment. He was hired by Russian gangsters to kill the leaders of rival mobs. He worked for tongs, the Yakuza, the Taliban. Once, he completed two contracts—one on an Israeli military commander and the other on a Palestinian mullah—in the same day.

By '97, he was killing or kidnapping Americans exclusively. Vacationing CEOs, mostly. Some of the best rogue hunters from Camp Swampy chased him around the globe. Devlin was careful. There were a few close calls, messy ones. But Devlin always managed to slip away, like a passing nightmare, like a shadow that moves with its own mind.

The assassination of the American ambassador to Turkey several years ago had finally done him in. Devlin thought he'd successfully disabled the embassy's closed-circuit surveillance system. He was nabbed on the way out, after he'd done the job. Goddamn Kurds and their unreliable information. He'd never work for them again. Literally.

Since he had been captured by U.S. marine embassy security, and not the spooks who were assigned to liquidate him, he was arrested. The capture, extradition to America, and trial were spectacles that Devlin appreciated. He spilled his guts to a shrink for shits and giggles, just to watch the soft-palmed bookworm squirm. He was sentenced to death by lethal injection.

Devlin didn't play the plea-bargain game, didn't fight the inevitable with appeal after appeal. He was sure the U.S. government was thrilled by that. He was incarcerated in the Ormerod Maximum Security Federal Penitentiary in Texas, due to be stuck by the needle in three months. Devlin didn't really feel like dying, but he wasn't going to fight it either.

All in all, it had been a good ride. Devlin had worked hard, become damned good at what he did. And he had been caught fair and square.

But something shifted during his days on the Row. As the time ticked by, he was no longer resigned to his future. If he *could* get out of this miserable fucking shithole, he'd show them just how damned good he was. In fact, Devlin realized he'd sell his soul to get out and show them, to show them all.

That was the day when the prison guard with the black box showed up at his cell.

Devlin blinked away the memories. He gazed down and watched the cigarette tremble, out here in the chill of the Tatishchevo November night. It had been less than fifteen minutes since he'd lit the last one and mooshed it against the rusted NO SMOKING sign.

Kovalenko's habit. It nagged at Devlin's mind like a hungry rat, made his tongue feel thick and itchy in his head. This inherited addiction aggravated him. He intellectually understood that the craving was just as much a part of Kovalenko as the silver wedding band on his right hand. But that knowledge didn't change that Devlin felt imprisoned by it.

Is this what a cocaine baby feels when it emerges from the womb? Devlin had wondered, not long after his "awakening" two and a half weeks ago. *This inhuman, irrational need for just a taste of that golden thing, just a little to beat off the monkey on his back? Just a little? Just one more smoke? I bet it is.*

The cigarette quivered in his hand, and Devlin took another drag. His time was almost up. The tremors were getting worse. It made him think about the last moments he could remember before he woke up here, in Tatishchevo, in a stranger's body.

Two thousand four. The Row. The guard. The week before he was destined to die.

Devlin had sized up the prison guard standing just beyond those steel bars back then, knew he could kill the man in less than a second if he wished. He asked the CO just what the fuck he was looking at. Devlin noted the black box in the man's hand; it was about the size of a fat laptop computer.

The guard had said nothing. Instead he passed a slip of folded yellow paper through the bars and held it between his right index and middle fingers, as if it were a $100 bill being passed between john and whore. Devlin thought about breaking the correction officer's wrist—*Goddamn, did they realize just how soft they were? All of them? All the sheep, so close to the wolf?*—but took the slip of paper instead.

He read the note. It was as if the devil himself had answered those midnight whispers. The words "death of the body, but not of the mind" were used in the letter. So were "recording the totality of your memories" and "kill and kill and kill." A deal was in the letter, of course—"under my employment for the rest of your life"—and the three words that made Devlin immediately consent to the terms.

Free. Immortal. Revenge.

He'd taken the black box from the guard—who had, he would learn much later, been paid handsomely to present this "gift"—

and connected the electrodes to his head, as instructed. He closed his eyes, pressed the red UPLOAD button . . .

. . . and awoke here, in Tatishchevo, looking at the world through another man's eyes. Only hours later at the briefing in the mess hall, after the entire forty-odd complement of the garrison had been switched, had the truth been explained to the newly formed army of Devlins. They received this information from the Russian colonel named Bogdanov. Colonel Bogdanov stood at the head of the steel tables, a sea of Slavic NEPTH-charged faces staring back at him, and filled in the blanks.

On that death-row day years back, the memories of Doug Devlin had been recorded into an extremely sophisticated piece of machinery. Devlin had opened his eyes after the transfer, removed the electrodes from his head, and passed the computer back to the prison guard. Every memory he had ever had—up to the point when he'd pressed the red UPLOAD button—had been copied into the guts inside the black machine. Doug Devlin still breathed, still lived, and still *thought* after the transfer. He was still on the Row in Texas. But now, thanks to the contents of that note, he also lived on in stasis, locked away in that little black box.

Later that day, the prison guard returned the computer to its owner and received the other half of his $2 million payoff. And a week after that, Douglas Devlin was strapped onto a prison medical bed. The needle that would carry the sodium Pentothal, Pavulon, and hellfire potassium chloride was inserted into a vein in his left arm.

The warden asked Devlin if he had any last words. Devlin replied that he did. He gazed at the journalists, corrections officers, and other witnesses who were staring back through the one-way mirror glass and smiled at them.

"Go fuck your mother," Doug Devlin had said. All of the Devlins assembled in the Russian mess hall had laughed at that. He had died at 5:01, just in time for the television reporters to file their stories for the six-o'clock news.

Then two and a half weeks ago, Devlin's mysterious savior—a man who called himself Alpha—had come to the Tatishchevo garrison, where the nine MAZ vehicles with their nine payloads had been parked in their nine garages. Alpha was disguised as Defense Minister Boris Savin. The narrating colonel didn't explain the bizarre circumstances of the disguise, and none of the soldiers asked. Alpha had brought that familiar black device with him. According to *Pravda*, Defense Minister Savin was checking up on the weapons mounted on the MAZes. Unofficially, he was there to revive Douglas Devlin many times over.

During his one-day stay, Defense Minister Savin, or Savin-Alpha, if you wanted to get technical about it, launched a plague that would eventually erase the memories of every Tatishchevo-garrison soldier and replace those memories with something much worse. It started with Colonel Bogdanov. Savin-Alpha met privately with the man, beat him, connected him to the black computer, and blasted the memories right out of Bogdanov's hippocampus. Savin-Alpha then completed the NEPTH-charge process by downloading the data contents of the black box—Douglas Devlin's Memory Totality—into the colonel's brain.

When Colonel Bogdanov opened his eyes, Doug Devlin's soul stared from them. Then, after Savin-Alpha left the military base, Bogdanov, now piloted by Doug Devlin's mind, announced immediate one-on-one performance reviews with every soldier stationed at the Tatishchevo garrison. Of course, Bogdanov-Devlin NEPTH-charged each of them. And he downloaded the contents of the special computer into the soldiers' vacant brains, as well.

Three hours later, the neural contents of the entire garrison had been rebuilt in the image of one man. Doug Devlin. And for the past two and a half weeks, forty-odd Devlins had inhabited this military post in mind, if not body.

He and the others here at the Tatishchevo garrison had since been gazing into the base's radar screens and computer monitors, pinging the Russian Terminator satellite system circling miles above them, taking note of American spy satellite telemetries and reprogramming missile coordinates. They also took turns test-driving the fleet of MAZ transports on the roads (and across the hilly off-roads) of Saratov province. The eighty-five-foot-long, sixteen-wheeled MAZes, which required four crew members to operate in combat, were surprisingly easy to drive. Each pair of wheels turned independently of each other, making the MAZes' turns tighter than Devlin had expected.

Those first few days were eerie, but the Devlin soldiers soon got along just fine. They shared identical war stories and reminisced in their newly borrowed bodies.

It brought splendid new meaning to the phrase *soul mates.*

In the case of the Devlin standing outside here in the Russian night, smoking a Prima and watching his hand tremble, his consciousness had been downloaded into a MAZ driver/engineer once named Pytor Kovalenko.

The experience was troubling; Devlin had immediately thought of shamans who enter a trance and become possessed by an entity from another where, a spirit, a *geist,* an *erosi,* demon, angel, invader. This is the view from the other side of the television. This is what the invader sees. In Devlin's case, it was through a pair of spectacles (the lack of peripheral vision was unnerving; how could people *wear* these things?), staring down at a flabby body pressing against Russian SMF-issued fatigues.

At first, Kovalenko's hands had unsettled Devlin the most.

Devlin didn't realize just how accustomed he'd become to the sight of his own hands, if only on a subconscious level. Yet here he was, flexing a strange set of calloused digits, perusing alien road maps on the palms. And the ring, on the right hand. For the first minutes after his awakening, Devlin had wanted to scream. After all, the last thing he could remember was placing electrodes to his head in a cell at the Ormerod Penitentiary.

It wasn't long after Colonel Bogdanov's explanation in the mess hall and briefing on their new mission that the peculiarities of living in Kovalenko's body began to truly reveal themselves. There was the inherited cigarette addiction, which Devlin—a non-smoker in his previous life—despised. Kovalenko was out of shape, pudgy, soft. This body wheezed like an old fume-farting Plymouth. And Kovalenko was a big eater, bigger than Devlin had been, at least. Devlin had to feed this body more than he was mentally accustomed to, lest Kovalenko's rumbling stomach keep him up at night.

For the first few days, Devlin had revisited his adolescence, peering at himself in bathroom mirrors, taking note of the strange new body. The constellation of moles and freckles on his chest. The strange wrinkles, the pronounced nose, the round, boyish face.

But these weren't the only things Devlin had inherited. Kovalenko had a wife and a child; their photographs were placed on the small chest at the foot of Kovalenko's bunk. Mysteries lived inside that chest: a rusted pocketknife, photographs taken in Moscow of Kovalenko with friends, a bottle of sand, a dried wildflower.

Devlin wondered about these people, these objects.

But Devlin had made a deal with the devil, so he never wondered for long. None of the Devlins here at the Russian Missile Forces' Tatishchevo Mobile Nuclear Missile Garrison did.

Besides, as Colonel Bogdanov explained, Kovalenko-Devlin and everyone else at the Tatishchevo garrison were just leasing these shells for a short time. Three weeks is as long as a human brain can live after it's been NEPTH-charged, Bogdanov explained. The body goes tits up after that; cataclysmic brain failure.

Three weeks to live. Beggars couldn't be choosers. And when you're born to kill—and you've become a glorified assassin-in-the-box—three weeks is all you need. There's no time for responsibilities, remorse. Only time for the job. So wreak as much havoc as you can until then. Smoke 'em if you got 'em.

So Doug Devlin did. And Doug Devlin would. They all would. The Topol-M long-range intercontinental ballistic missiles resting on the backs of the nine MAZ transport/launchers would see to that.

Revenge, Devlin thought as he took one last puff on his second Prima and mashed it out on the tin Cyrillic sign. He walked back to the garrison's main base, exhaling and grinning, blissfully ignoring the tremors in his hands.

SIXTEEN

The *stelth, krak,* and hack programs running under the hoods of Kilroy2.0's computers had done their jobs. Within thirty minutes of solving John Alpha's Morse-coded "clue," the clones had the information they needed about the now-defunct Folie à Deux nightclub: architectural blueprints, electrical-wiring schematics, police reports and newspaper articles associated with the club, bios on the owner . . . even the price list for drinks.

"This was one freak show of a club," Michael said, staring at one of the computer monitors. "Talk about sharing a mass delusion and saying 'screw it' to society. It really does live up to the name."

The marine wasn't wrong about that, John thought. Folie à Deux was one of those nightclubs you might hear about, but could never find on a map—much less find your way inside. According to one archived *L.A. Weekly Scene* feature article, it didn't have an exterior sign advertising its existence. Above the front doors, a simple stuttering neon sign in the shape of a downward arrow read YOU ARE HERE.

Reserved for the hypercool and hyperrich, Folie à Deux had apparently been the top dog in L.A.'s club scene. Thanks to payoffs to cops and councilmen, debauchery is mostly overlooked in places like this, John knew. And according to the news archives Kilroy2.0 had accessed, debauchery of the drug-dealing variety had apparently been big at Folie à Deux.

"Take a look at this statue," Michael said, pressing his finger against Kilroy2.0's computer monitor. The lunatic grunted his disapproval at the smudge. On the screen was a *Times* photograph, shot from a low angle, of Andrew P. Spencer, the club's flamboyantly vain owner, standing before Folie à Deux's centerpiece: a thirty-foot-tall, gleaming aluminum sculpture. The photo was shot at a low angle, but the form was unmistakable: a man and a woman in an orgiastic embrace. In the photo, sunlight glinted off its stylized curves from a skylight above.

John took a good look at the metal sculpture. It was as if the two abstract bodies were rising from a churning waterspout of mercury, twin folds of liquid gushing upward, forming the upper torsos of human shapes. The statue had cost a half million dollars to design and build, Spencer had said in the article.

Not that Andrew P. Spencer was saying much of anything these days. Folie à Deux had closed shop for good last year, after the LAPD and FBI kicked down the doors and scored the largest ecstasy bust in U.S. history. Spencer blew his brains out with a .22 before he went to trial, and two months later the city auctioned off the club and its contents to the highest bidder.

According to Los Angeles County property records, it had all gone to one buyer. Kilroy2.0 cheerfully pointed out that the buyer's name—Hess Venton—was an anagram for *Seventh Son*.

"Where did Alpha get the money to buy this place?" Jack asked, as he stared at the photo of the sculpture.

"That's an excellent question," Father Thomas said. "Maybe it's the same people who set him up with the ability to clone, NEPTH-charge, and then kill the president."

Dr. Mike sat on the circular couch, gazing at the club floor plans that Kilroy2.0 had printed from the supposedly secure Los Angeles County architectural database. He chewed absently on a Bic ballpoint. His fingers traced over the expertly drawn electrical lines, air ducts, and stairwells.

"Michael's right," Dr. Mike said, spitting out the pen. He tapped the papers. "This *is* one freak show of a club. This used to be a movie theater. High ceiling. We're talking fifty feet. It has a second level, a series of wide catwalks, accessible from three stairways." He pointed at the blueprint. "The second level's also where the übercool did their thing in VIP. Looks like the old movie-house balcony was renovated into one giant glass-encased room. The whole catwalk system sprouts out from the balcony and goes around the perimeter of the club. It's like an observation deck."

Michael turned from the computer screens and stepped over to the circular table. He gazed down at the blueprints, then looked up at Dr. Kleinman and General Hill, who were still standing away from the group watching intently, and then back to the clones.

"If we go in there, a second floor ain't gonna be good," Michael said. "That's where Alpha'll put the shooters. The catwalks provide plenty of coverage for snipers. If we come in from the front, the shooters can get us from their positions in the rear. We come in from one of the side doors, snipers on the front-end catwalks can get us."

"Whoa, whoa. What do you mean *snipers*?" Jack asked.

Jay, who was standing next to Jack, piped up. "And what do you mean *if we go in there*?"

"Well, *someone's* got to go in the club," Michael said. "This is the X on the treasure map—where we'll find either Mom or Alpha, or both."

"Wait a minute," Jack said as he nervously scratched his beard. "You're honestly thinking of going there?"

Dr. Mike looked up at the geneticist. "Michael's right. We can't *not* go. The riddle was written for us and the riddle says to go to L.A. This is a rescue mission. It's all about finding Mom. We're saving her . . . if she's still alive, that is . . . and hopefully taking out Alpha in the process. If the place is empty, then we look for more clues. Either way, we'll know more there than we will sitting here."

"But isn't that just the slightest bit cavalier?" Jay asked. "The message, the code, the song, the club. It looks like a big worm on a hook to me. You said it yourself: Alpha knew we would solve the puzzle. That means he knows we're on our way. It's a trap. We should get Hill here to send someone else."

The room fell silent. Even Kilroy2.0 had turned from his screens to listen in.

John glanced over to Kleinman and Hill and saw them eyeing each other.

Dr. Mike broke the silence. "Then don't go. But I am. I know that town. I've worked with the LAPD. I can handle a gun. And I don't want that psycho to kill my mother. This might be our only chance."

"I can understand if you all don't want to go; you got no training," the marine added. "Most of us here don't, so most of us shouldn't go. But someone has to. Dr. Mike wants to—it's his town. I *have* to. I've been trained for this. And if the 7th Son folks want to keep this as quiet as they've kept the rest of their operation, some of the troops stationed here will have to go, too."

Michael turned to General Hill. "Am I right?"

"If there's going to be an operation, I'd want our security team to handle as much as they can," Hill replied. "They've signed their Code Phantom NDAs. They won't talk, Michael."

"Everyone talks," a voice muttered.

"Those are UN press-leaking delegates you're talking about, Jay. Not these men." Hill looked Michael in the eyes. "They're rock solid, marine. I'd bet my life on it."

And here we go, John thought, and felt gravity loosen its grip on his stomach. He was feeling sick again, as if he'd just stepped out of that damnable elevator. *This is where it truly begins. It's rotten. The whole thing's rotten. There's got to be a better way.*

But as he watched Michael and Hill speaking to each other in that arcane militaryspeak he'd only heard in Schwarzenegger movies, John realized there wasn't a better way—at least, not for them. Michael and Dr. Mike were going to L.A. to fight what they thought was the good fight. And with Mom's life hanging in the balance, who could blame them?

But still. There's got to be a better way. John looked over at Kilroy2.0, the resident madman. John stared at the floor and thought of the secrets beneath them, buried under six decades and two thousand feet. The technology down there. The people down there. An idea began to flourish in John's mind. He nodded to himself and filed it away. He'd share it when Kleinman and Hill were gone.

Minutes later, Michael and Hill wrapped up their plans for the 7th Son soldiers who would go on the cross-country trek.

"Fair enough," Hill said. "I'll assemble some of my best and make calls to get the equipment you need." He stepped past John and strode out the door.

Kleinman still stood near the doorway. "We're evacuating nonessential 7th Son personnel in the next few hours," the old man announced. "DeFalco and the other scientists, they're going. As is our support staff: tech, administrative. Only the security team, Hill, and I will remain."

"I volunteer for nonessential personnel duty," Dr. Mike said.

"I wish it were that simple." Kleinman's voice was cordial enough, but his face was covered with worry. *No. More than that,* John thought. *He looks like a heartsick parent.*

Kleinman walked out of the room, leaving them alone.

Dr. Mike turned back to the floor plans of Folie à Deux. "Now that we've secured the supporting cast, does anybody have any ideas on how we're gonna get in? Michael says if we show our faces anywhere near the dance floor on the ground level, we'll get 'em shot off by catwalk snipers. I believe it. But these blueprints say there aren't any outside doors leading to the second floor. Just interior stairwells leading to the catwalk level. Not even a second-level fire escape."

John leaned forward and looked at the blueprints. "Well, the building did used to be a movie house. Except for the balcony—which has been renovated into a VIP room—there *was* no second floor. So why would there be a fire escape?"

"Astute," Kilroy2.0 said.

Dr. Mike picked up the Bic and drew three large circles on the floor plans. "There are more entrances than the front and rear doors, of course. At the base of all three catwalk stairwells are emergency exits. Naturally, they're on the ground floor . . . and they lead out into the parking lot, alley, wherever. Problem is, we go in through one of those doors, and those second-floor shooters can nail us from the top of the stairs."

"So you're saying we can't get in," Jay said.

"And the naysayer chimes in," Dr. Mike snapped, rolling his eyes. "It's clear you're not going. Since when is *we* a part of *your* vocabulary?"

Jay opened his mouth to snap a reply, but Michael cut him off. "Can it, both of you. There's no safe way in."

"What about the sewers?" John asked. "Is there some way to get into the basement from the sewers?"

"Well, there's the rub." Dr. Mike drummed his fingers on the round table. "There *is* a basement level, and there *is* a floor grate in the storage room—probably to deal with any basement flooding. But it's nowhere near the size of a person, not even a kid. Which brings us back to the doors."

"'Mr. Mojo risin'...'" Kilroy2.0 sang.

Dr. Mike glared at the lunatic for a moment, then turned back to the blueprints. "All the entrances are on level one. Level two has no entry points that I can see. And since this was once a movie theater, it has no original windows, either. Brilliant place for a club, really. So we're stuck with going in on the ground floor, and taking our chances."

"Unacceptable. People are going to get killed that way," Michael said. "Maybe not me, or you—but someone on the rescue team is coming back here in a body bag if we do it that way."

Dr. Mike threw his pen on the table, disgusted.

"It can't be our only option," Michael said coolly.

"Wait a minute," a voice called. "I know how to go in."

It was Thomas. He was staring at Kilroy2.0's computer monitors.

"How's that?" Jack asked.

The priest raised an index finger and pressed it against the screen, at the same digital image that Michael had noticed just minutes ago: the photograph of Folie à Deux's statue. The thirty-foot aluminum sculpture towered upward, glinting ... and there, at the top of the frame, was the answer. The skylight.

"Be the archangel," Father Thomas said. "Come in from above."

"I'll be damned," Michael said, grinning.

"Aren't we all," the priest whispered.

It was settled quickly after that, thanks to Michael's Force Recon training and his easier-said-than-done delivery of the attack plan. The rescue team would leave in a few hours, fly cross-country, and take the Folie à Deux nightclub just after sunset. The team, comprising about a dozen men, would be divided into three groups. One would stake out the skylight, drawing the fire of snipers that were likely to be stationed on the second level. With the snipers focused on the diversion, the other teams would simultaneously enter through the front and side entrances. The objective was straightforward: rescue Dania Sheridan, if she was there. If the team could kill or capture John Alpha in the process . . . well, that was fine, too.

"I understand why you're anticipating conflict," Jack said, after Michael recited his plan. "You're being realistic, looking at the evidence, and are planning for the worst-case scenario. But what makes you think that John Alpha is going to have gunmen there in the first place, much less Mom? I mean, is it ridiculous to assume that he might just want to talk?"

"Right," Jay said from beside him, his voice eager. "Talk."

Michael smiled slightly; he had a look on his face that said, *This is amateur hour, but they don't know any better.*

"Scientists talk," the marine said. "UN field agents talk. Presidential assassins don't talk, fellas. This guy kidnapped our mother and literally left a neon arrow pointing at his lair. What do you think he wants? A little teatime with the carbon copies? He's the enemy and he wants us dead, Jack. Deader than disco."

Despite the tension, John smiled to himself. *Deader than disco.* I *say that.*

"But how do you know that?" Jay asked. "Don't look at me that way. I'm not trying to be a jerk, and I'm not trying to gum up your plan. I'm just trying to figure out why you think he can't be reasoned with."

Dr. Mike stood and stepped over to the two doubters. In this little family, that's what Jack and Jay were, John reckoned. The Doubters.

"I know John Alpha is a part of you, Jay . . . and he's a part of me," Dr. Mike said. "Hell, we wouldn't be standing here having this conversation if it weren't for his blood and his memories. I haven't had time to wrap my brain around that yet, and frankly, I don't want to. But you probably think he reasons the same way you do because the way you reason is based on the way *he* once reasoned. Does that make sense? You, me—all of us—used to think the same way. Back when we—I'm sorry—*he* was a child. But something went wrong with John Alpha. Something went bad. What he's done so far . . . and I'm willing to bet we don't know the half of it . . . tells us that."

"He NEPTH-charged a kid to kill the president," Father Thomas said quietly. "And took the time to tattoo a little *A* in the kid's ear in the name of the chase. What kind of a man does that?"

Jack and Jay stood in place, saying nothing.

Michael clapped his hands. "So we've got to settle on who's going on this trip and who isn't. Now you all know that I'm going, and you know that I'm going to be calling the shots. It's that simple. But this is strictly voluntary for the rest of you. As far as I'm concerned, if you don't want to get shot at, don't go. Can't say I blame you. There's no obligation, understand?"

The six clones nodded.

"You know I'm in," Dr. Mike said. Michael nodded. Dr. Mike looked at Jay.

Jay shook his head. "I've ducked my fair share of guerrilla gunfire, but I'm not a soldier. I just can't."

"No shame in it," Michael said.

"You have to understand something." Jack squirmed in his seat. "Until yesterday, I thought I was, heh, normal. Plugging away at the white-collar gig. I've got a wife. More important, two kids. Sorry."

"Padre, what about you?"

The priest held his breath for a moment, percolating. Finally, he said, "Mom's been dead for sixteen years. To be the first one of us to see her again . . . well, that would be incredible, wouldn't it?" Thomas crossed his arms, frowning. "But how has John Alpha been able to do these things? Who's he working for, or with? Why did he want the president dead, and why has he gone to all the trouble of baiting us?"

"Conspiracy," Kilroy2.0 whispered.

"My thoughts exactly," the priest said. "I have no faith in our keepers, or anything else about this—Alpha, NEPTH-charges, 7th Son. It's all so murky. Alpha's plan is bigger than a reunion at an abandoned nightclub, it must be. And I think the history of this place"—Thomas jabbed an index finger at the floor—"is *much* bigger than we've been told. I want to see Mom, but I want to find the answers to those questions even more."

He nodded to Kilroy2.0. "And we've got the mad hacker here who can help us do that."

The lunatic giggled.

Michael looked over at Kilroy2.0. "So how 'bout it, Mad Hacker? You staying, or going?"

"Mad Hacker's staying here."

"Fine," Dr. Mike said. "And you, John?"

Father Thomas had practically read John's mind; that had been *his* plan. But with Thomas staying here . . .

"I'm going," John said.

Jay bolted from his seat. *"What?"*

"No. No. Don't be stupid," Jack said, shaking his head. "You heard what Michael said to the general. People are going to get killed, John. Michael, Dr. Mike, and the rest: They're not going to a nightclub. They're heading into hell."

John raised his chin. "I've gotta see her, man. I've gotta know."

"Then it's settled," Michael said. "Those who are staying should take Thomas's lead and find out everything they can about Alpha's operation, what he's up to. Let's see if the fucker's accidentally left a trail along the line. Meanwhile, the marine, the cop, and the bartender are heading to a nightclub."

"That sounds like the beginning of a bad joke," John said.

"Let's hope not," Dr. Mike said. "Come on. Let's find Hill and Kleinman and tell 'em what's up."

SEVENTEEN

The seven clones walked through the institutional halls of the 7th Son complex, following the double-helix mosaic on the hallway walls, walking at first, then trotting, then finally running, as if the momentum of their decisions was pushing them along. The group found the door with the retina scanner. Dr. Mike did the honors, and by God it worked, just as Kleinman had said it would. They stepped inside the express elevator, and Michael uttered the destination word: "Ops" . . . then the elevator was screaming downward again, down to where the revelations had begun mere hours ago.

They stepped out of the elevator cabin, turned the hallway corner to go into the Operations Command room, and were stopped by two young soldiers. Their sidearms weren't drawn, but both had hands near the holsters. They eyed Michael, who led the team.

"I'm sorry, sir, but you're not authorized to go in there without permission from the general," one of the soldiers said. The tag on his BDUs read MORRIS. The other solider was a private apparently named BALLANTINE.

"There's no time for this," Michael said, his eyes flitting to the soldier's shoulder, "*Sergeant* Morris, and you know it. If it weren't for us, and the machinery downstairs that made us, you wouldn't be here parroting orders. Things've changed. Clones take precedence over standing orders. You should know that."

Sergeant Morris shook his head. John saw Private Ballantine's hand jerk closer to his pistol. "Sorry, sir," Morris said. "No one gets by without permission."

Michael nodded, turned to leave, then, in an eyeblink, he reached out, snatched Private Ballantine's gun from its holster, grabbed the befuddled kid by his shirt, yanked him past Morris, and twisted his arm behind his back. Michael passed the .45 to Father Thomas, who was standing next to him. Amazingly, Thomas found himself bringing the sights of the gun up toward Sergeant Morris's chest.

The fuck is he doing? John thought. *Does he even know how to use one of those things?*

"I think Private Ballantine here is going to give us our permission," Michael said. He pulled the private's arm upward, and the young man fought back a shriek. His face was turning red. "You're willing to let us walk through those doors, aren't you, Ballantine?"

The private nodded furiously.

Sergeant Morris's Adam's apple bobbed up and down as he stared at the pistol in Thomas's hand. His eyes were wide, and his hands were shaking.

"Let us pass," Michael said. "Don't be any more stupid than you've already been. I know we're being watched right now. Hill told us all about the surveillance system. So if I were you, I'd be wondering why no one has come to your rescue. Think about it, hoss: *they're* not busting through that door because *we're* not doing anything wrong. Just let us pass so we can talk to the big man, and you can get on with watch duty."

Morris stepped aside. The clones entered, with Michael yanking Private Ballantine along in the lead.

General Hill, Dr. Kleinman, and Intelligence Officer Robert Durbin were sitting at the large mahogany table, dozens of manila folders laid out before them. Behind them, one of the wall-mounted television screens revealed that Michael had been right—Sergeant Morris's flustered face stared back at them. He was shrugging as if to say, *What could I do?* Other screens revealed hallways, the interior of the express elevator—and the layout of the clones' hastily abandoned Common Room. Staring at these screens were two soldiers, sitting in the back of the Ops room in the raised control area.

Michael released Private Ballantine. The young man offered an apologetic look to his superiors, rubbing his aching arm.

"Gentlemen," Durbin said coolly. "We've been expecting you."

"No shit," Dr. Mike said, nodding to the screens behind them. "So our room is bugged, too?"

"Of course it is," General Hill replied. "Not that we were listening. We've been pretty engrossed here."

Kilroy2.0 snorted.

"Whatever happened to a man's right to privacy?" Jack asked.

"Don't be theatrical," Hill snapped. "You've come home to roost, and you think we wouldn't monitor your conversations? It's nothing personal. Private, you're dismissed."

The young man brushed past the clones as he left. His face sported a combination of petulance and humiliation.

"Let me congratulate you, Mr. Durbin, and your whip-smart staff, on cracking John Alpha's riddle," Dr. Mike said as the private departed. "We've been doing your job since we got here. What's next, pretty boy? Are we gonna polish your Eagle Scout badge?"

The ballpoint pen in Durbin's hand nearly snapped in half.

"Stop it," Hill said. He turned to the clones. "We're presently going over the 7th Son security staff files, selecting the men who'll accompany Michael, Dr. Mike, John—and Durbin here."

"*Him?* You gotta be fucking kidding," Dr. Mike said. "They haven't cut his umbilical cord yet."

"Keep talking, civvy," Durbin seethed. "That mouth's gonna get you in trouble. I can think of a great way to wire it shut."

"*I said stop it!*" Hill screamed, slamming his hand on a nearby folder. "When this is all over, you two can go out to the playground and kick the shit out of each other, for all I care." Hill glared at Dr. Mike. "So he's younger than you and knew your life story before you did. Big fucking deal. Right now, you both—and the rest of you—will listen to me. We're picking your support team for the mission. These will be the best men our facility has. Some of them were the agents who brought you here, so if you recognize them, don't hold a grudge. We'll have the team members selected in a few hours."

"Estimated time of departure?" Michael asked.

"Sixteen hundred. Four p.m." Hill consulted his gold Baume & Mercier. "That's two hours from now. It'll give those of you who are going enough time to fine-tune your plan and brief the team traveling with you. That'll also give us enough time to bring an Osprey x-mod here to pick you up and to prep some Black Hawks and ground vehicles for use while you're in California. You'll get there fast—the x-mod is jet-powered. Brand new, no props."

"So how exactly are you going to keep this off the books?" Dr. Mike asked. "And once the bullets start flying, how are you going to keep it out of the papers?"

"Leave the fallout to me," General Hill said. "And to Code Phantom clearance."

"What *is* Code Phantom, anyway?" the profiler asked.

From beside General Hill, Durbin smirked. "Officially, Code Phantom does not exist."

Kilroy2.0 gave him a wet raspberry.

General Hill waved away the exchange. "Boys, Code Phantom is a blank check. The nearly limitless resources of the military and government are at our disposal—without any oversight whatso-ever."

The clones stared at him, stunned.

"So that's how you got those spooks to watch us over the years," John finally said. "They're the dogs. You're Pavlov's bell."

Hill smirked. "That's one way to put it. For most people in the military and intel community, Code Phantom is an urban legend. When you get the call, you drop your shit, you pull rank, you fall off the face of the earth. It supersedes any standing orders. Code Phantom orders are untraceable, written in invisible ink. It was very useful in the early days of this project, when we needed re-sources and manpower. Now it'll come in handy to get you where you need to be. You might consider this an improper use of the authority—and you'd be right."

"But it's for a good cause," Jack said. "To cover your ass."

"The world isn't ready for you," Kleinman said, glaring over his trifocals. "Or for 7th Son."

"I think the world is less ready for John Alpha," Jack replied.

"The only 7th Son team members who have Code Phantom access these days are Kleinman and myself," General Hill said. "It'll get to you to California. It'll cover up any incident you may encounter. The president himself doesn't have such privilege."

"My God," Father Thomas said.

Hill raised his eyebrows. "Precisely."

"So when do we arrive in L.A.?" Michael asked.

"If the Osprey pilots redline it, seven p.m., local time," Hill said. "It'll already be dark."

Kleinman cleared his throat. "For now, gentlemen, it's a case of hurry up and wait. I suggest you all make some time to relax. Maybe call your families, or friends."

"Uh . . . you're serious?" Jack said.

"Of course," Kleinman said. "Considering what you've been through—and how we brought you here—there are some worried family members and lovers out there." The old man glanced at Dr. Mike. "And probably some irked publicists, too."

"Larry fucking King," Dr. Mike moaned. He closed his eyes. "Rochelle's going to kill me."

Father Thomas stepped forward. "What do we tell them?" He looked at Hill, then Kleinman. "What *can* we tell them?"

"I want to say, 'Use your best judgment,' but I'm afraid it's not that simple," Kleinman said. "I've discussed this with General Hill. He feels this is a security risk, but I've convinced him to let each of you make one phone call. There are conditions. You get fifteen minutes each. No exceptions. Of course, you cannot tell who you're calling where you are or why you're here. Anything resembling details about Project 7th Son are strictly forbidden. If you fail to adhere to these rules, the line goes dead."

"Let me guess," Jay said, his eyes flitting to the wall-mounted monitors. "You'll be listening."

"Affirmative," Hill said.

"We should get going," Michael said, turning to the doors.

"Be careful what you say in your phone calls," Kleinman called to them. "And be careful in California."

EIGHTEEN

J ack's hand trembled as he picked up the gray telephone resting on the desk in his living quarters. Lisa would be worried—no, terrified was more like it. And Kristina and Carrie . . . Jesus. He was supposed to watch a movie with them last night. *D.A.R.Y.L.*, about the man-built boy with the programmed memories. Irony has a way of kicking you when you're down, doesn't it?

Jack pulled his leather wallet out of his pants pocket and unfolded it. There they were. His girls. Lisa, Kristina, and Carrie, smiling from a photograph. Taken a year ago, at a picnic in Linnell Park.

What could they be thinking right now? That he'd run away? That he'd been abducted? That he didn't love them? Jack shook his head. The call would just spawn more questions for Lisa . . . more worries. This thing—this experience, this adventure, mission, whatever it was—was going to hurt the family, Jack could feel it. More pieces to mend when he came home.

He lifted the receiver, held it to his ear. Jack scratched at his beard, that nervous tic of his. *What will you tell her? The truth? Lies? Something in between?*

He dialed their home number in Tucson. The phone on the other end rang once; just once.

"Hello?" It was Olivia, his wife's sister. Lisa must have called in the family for support. Jack couldn't blame her.

"Olivia, it's Jack."

"My God," she nearly shrieked. "Where are you, Jack? Lisa has been out of her mind!"

Jack could her his wife in the background—*Is that Jack? Give me the phone*—and then she was on with him, talking to him, saying his name over and over. Her voice was raw, like shattered glass.

"Lisa, honey. It's me." Jack looked down. There she was, in the photograph, smiling. Here she was crying. "I'm okay."

"Jack? Thank God, oh, *thank God*. Where are you, Jack? Where have you been?"

"I can't tell you." He stared at her smiling face in the photo. "I'm sorry. I can't. But it's . . . it's important, Lisa. More important than you'll ever know. Sweetie, understand me: I'm safe, I'm okay. I'll be home as soon as I can."

"What does that *mean*?" Lisa said, her voice sharpening. "You can't tell me where you are? Why not?"

Jack cringed. "I just can't. It's complicated."

"Does this have something to do with your research at the university, with the rats? Is it that protester kid, Kalajian?"

Oh, if only the stakes were so pedestrian, Jack thought. *I'd take a paint-bucket-wielding activist zealot any day over this. I'd rather be red than dead.*

"No, baby. That's ancient history. This has nothing to do with that." *Oh, but it does . . . it has everything to do with clones and rats. See, I'm a cloned rat, and me and my newfound brothers are trying to navigate the labyrinth. We're looking for Patient Zero.* "It's something else. Something important. Listen to me: I *can't* tell you. I want to, but I can't."

"What does that mean?"

"It means I love you, Lisa. I love you and the girls more than anything. And it means that, no matter what happens, I'll always love you. I just have to take care of some business with these people, and then I'll be home."

Lisa was silent for a long time.

"And when will that be?" she asked finally. Her voice was flattening, dissolving. She was shutting down, the way she did when they fought. Lisa didn't yell or scream when she was pissed . . . she went antarctic, the impassive observer, a scientist peering through a microscope.

"Please, Lisa. Please understand. This is out of my control. I want to tell you. I didn't volunteer for—"

A click came over the phone line, and for a heartbeat Jack thought they (whoever *they* were) had disconnected the call. But there Lisa was again, on the line, crying quietly. *That was a warning,* Jack thought. *Message received.*

"Baby, I love you," he said. "Just remember that. No matter how long I'm gone . . . no matter if I can't call you again for a while . . . know that I love you and the girls more than anything else in this world."

"You're in trouble."

Jack gazed down at the photo and rubbed his finger across Lisa's face. The photo blurred before him. He fought back the tears.

"Yeah, in a way," Jack said. "Are the girls there?"

She called for Kristina and Carrie. There was Olivia's frantic voice—*Where is he? He won't tell you?*—then Kristina was on the line, soft and little and just about as real as it could get.

"Hi, Daddy."

"Hey, sugar puddin'. How you doin'?"

"I'm okay." God, that voice. She was the one who watched and listened and asked the right questions. Twenty years from now,

Kristina would be a scientist, a journalist, a problem solver. Jack would bet on it.

"When are you coming home?"

Jack smiled. See? So soon with the questions. "Soon, baby. Soon. Daddy just needs work with some new friends for a little while. I have a very important job to do."

"What kind of job?"

Jack thought for a moment. "A special job. So special I can't even tell Mommy about it."

"It's a secret." Pause. "You have a secret science experiment."

"Kinda." *Try dead-on, kiddo.*

"Can you tell me *anything* about it?"

Jack looked at Kristina and Carrie in the photograph. "Only that you and your sister would get a big kick out of it. But I'm okay, sweetie. I'm just fine. And I'll be home as soon as I can, okay?"

"I believe you." Another pause. "Hurry, Daddy. We miss you."

God, that voice. His own voice was shaking now. "I miss you, too. And I love you. Is your sister there?"

A second later, Carrie was with him.

"Hey, Daddy!"

"Hey, you. How's my princess?"

"Fine. How're you?"

Miserable. Afraid. Questioning my place in the universe and busy missing the hell out of you, little one.

"I'm doing fine, just fine."

"Daddy? When are we going to watch the *D.A.R.L.* movie?"

"Oh, honey."

That's when Jack began to cry.

As he listened to the phone on the other end ring and ring, Dr. Mike stared at the walls of his quarters and considered the thoughts he'd had in this room last night (*or was it this morning?*

It's blurring together . . . goddamn sleep deprivation): screw this place; he would be no help to these people. No help at all.

That anger had come before Dr. Mike had seen his father—his dead father—this morning. Before he'd seen the man pulled out of Ops by armed men. Before he'd seen the room with the metallic, multi-armed monstrosity that had birthed him and the others. Before he'd seen the awesome field of ten-foot-tall Q-Cray hard drives whirring away two thousand feet beneath the earth.

Somewhere between last night and this afternoon, Dr. Mike had begun to believe that this was all real, all true. Talk about making a one-eighty. And now he was actually helping his captors. Dr. J. "Mike" Smith, criminal profiler, was assisting the men who'd put a gun to his head and walked him out of the most significant moment of his life. His appearance on *Larry King Live* would have made him, legitimized the book and started the word-of-mouth publicity blitz.

And yet, sitting in this cramped dorm room, Dr. Mike realized he didn't really care. If a third of what he'd learned in the past half day was true, then he hadn't just stumbled upon the best-kept secret of his life—he'd stumbled upon the best-kept secret in the history of the world. And more significant: the secret of perfecting human cloning (and, God help us, memory duplication) was apparently in the hands of John Alpha. And he had a chance to stop the sicko. What a book *that* would make.

The phone on the other end of the line rang again. And again.

I know you're there, Rochelle. Pick up.

Dr. Mike knew that she was going to be disappointed and angry—after all, at this stage in his career, you don't strut onto *Larry* fucking *King* without cashing in plenty of favors. And that's what Rochelle Romero had done to get Mike, her darling new author, on *Live*. He had told her she wasn't going to regret this . . . that his book, *Hunting the Hunters: Inside the Minds of a City's Most*

Notorious Killers, was going to bottle-rocket up the sales charts . . . and that he owed her big-time. Rochelle had smiled in her office and said just three words in that slippery Colombian accent of hers: *That's right, kiddo.*

And then Dr. Mike had gone MIA last night, right there in the studio bathroom. Put his photo on a milk carton. Call David Copperfield. He had vanished, and he'd blown it. It'd been out of his hands, but he'd blown it. Rochelle had every reason to be angry and disappointed.

But when Rochelle picked up on the other end and heard his voice, Dr. Mike realized Rochelle wasn't angry. She was *thermonuclear.*

"Just *who* in the *flame*-ing *fuck* do you think you are?" she screamed. Mike recoiled from the receiver as if he'd been burned. He imagined Rochelle in her smoke-filled office, cordless phone pinched between shoulder and chin, scrambling to find her cigs.

Rochelle was still screaming. "*Pendejo!* And just what in the *fuck* do you think *I* am?" She must've popped a smoke in her mouth; her words were slurring now. "A *door*mat? A *dish* towel? A fucking flushable tampon? *Do you realize what you've done?*"

"Rochelle, listen, I'm sorry," Dr. Mike said, wincing. *Are those my balls I feel, kissing the base of my throat? Oh, yes, indeed.* "But something—"

"Something? Oh, merciful Lord!"

"That's ri—"

"Something made you screw over your publicist, screw over your book, and screw over CNN!" she bellowed. "Something? *Something?* What could this 'something' have possibly been?"

Click-click went her Bic. Click-click went Dr. Mike's mind.

"Someone, ah, escorted me out of the building. Just before I was supposed to go to makeup."

"Someone?" But it sounded more like *sumwum;* one side of her mouth was still clamped down on that cigarette. "Who?"

"I'm not allowed to tell you. And if I could, you wouldn't believe me."

"I already don't believe you. Who?"

"Some of my biggest fans, apparently. I can't say any more about it."

"The *fuck* you can't!" Rochelle roared, her rage hissing down the line. Mike elected to change tactics, go suave.

"Listen, Rochelle, you *know* me. Dependable. Ambitious. Manic, sure, but smart. Smart enough to know that you don't walk out of CNN's L.A. studios without a damned good reason. I know how important this was to you. But I think you know just how important this was to *me*. I wouldn't leave that building unless I had to. That's all I can say."

She was silent for a moment. Mike could hear the *mmmp* of Rochelle taking a drag.

"Shit. You're up to your eyeballs in it, aren't you?"

"Of course not," Mike said, faking a laugh. "Oh, nothing that preposterous. I'm in the hands of capable people. Very good at what they do. Very interested in me, and *my work*."

Silence.

"I was calling to tell you that I'm okay. That I'm okay, and that I'm sorry something came up last night. You're the bee's knees, Rochelle. I can't tell you how much I wanted to do the show. Are you getting an idea of why I couldn't make it?"

"A vague one."

"Listen, just get on the phone and tell my buddies at the department that I'm just fine. A lot of them knew I was going to be on last night, you know . . . they'll probably want to know why I was a no-show."

"Yes." You'd have thought she had swallowed a handful of Valium, by the sound of her voice. "Is there anyone in particular you want me to call?"

Oh, that's the question, isn't it? Now's the time to drop a hint about where you are, Mike . . . and that you're going to be cruising into town tonight. Or now's the time to do what you've been told and keep your mouth shut.

He heard Rochelle exhale a lungful of smoke. She was waiting.

What's it going to be?

"Mike? You still there?"

Ride the wave. Stop trying to steer and ride the wave. See where it takes you.

"Forget it," Dr. Mike said.

"You sure?"

Dr. Mike closed his eyes and shook his head. "Listen, Rochelle. I have to go now. I know what you did to get that interview. I'm really sorry, old girl."

"I believe you."

"Good. I'll see you soon."

"I'll say a prayer, Mike."

"I'm an atheist, Rochelle."

"All the more reason," she said, and hung up.

Kilroy2.0 sat at his desk, the telephone cord curled around his index finger. He looked up at the walls . . . into the walls . . . and waited for them to speak. The day had gone well, so far. The Conspiracy was deepening, as was his messianic role in it. The clones—the cogs, the Pedestrians—could do nothing without his assistance, it seemed. The vortex of digital information was something only Kilroy2.0 could tame.

All according to plan.

The walls had spoken the truth last night. He was the beginning and the end. The prophet. Kilroy2.0 closed his eyes and silently called to the ghosts in the walls.

The walls had many things to say, many instructions to deliver. To Kilroy, the conversation lasted hours. According to the glowing numerals on the desk clock, the conversation lasted three minutes.

Kilroy2.0 unraveled the cord from his finger and picked up the telephone receiver. He dialed the pager number from memory, pressed #, then four numbers: 4-3-5-7.

H-E-L-P.

He hung up and began to smile.

Patricia was calmer than Jay had thought she'd be—but then again, she had always been the stronger one in the marriage. He was the restless one, the worried one, the spouse who gloomed-and-doomed his way through tax forms, credit-card payments, and insurance policies. Jay had never considered just *why* he was the way he was—why he had such little faith in the juggernaut he called the system. The thing most everyone else called life. Often, he perceived the world in terms of equity and fairness; mostly, in how unequal and unfair the whole damned thing seemed to be. Jay suspected this cynicism had something to do with his human rights work: Go to enough developing nations and you'll see what inequity is all about. You'll breathe it in the air. You'll taste it in the water.

However—in light of the revelations over the past day—Jay had found himself wondering more and more about his worldview. His newfound brothers had attitudes completely different from his own. These were the people he could've been, perhaps: warrior, artist, scientist, priest. These were the people he was not, for reasons that seemed to be beyond him.

It's like those comic books I used to read in high school, he had thought earlier today, while watching the group solve John Al-pha's riddle. *Those heroes were always traveling to parallel worlds, where life on Earth had evolved differently from our own . . . where history took a left instead of a right, and everything was different there. That's what staring at my Bizarro brothers is like. Staring into the eyes of a Mirror Universe me, seeing the person I could've been. Or could be.*

Maybe. If I weren't so weak.

That's why Patricia was the stronger one in the marriage. That's why she was much calmer than he'd thought she'd be. And that's why it was so good—so goddamned good—to hear her voice.

"I saw the chicken in the freezer," she was saying. "I thought you'd been called in. You didn't leave a message on the fridge."

Jay could clearly visualize the dry-erase board on the refrigerator, the white field filled with hazy ghosts of messages they had written and erased over the years: *Call Filipe—urgent . . . Don't forget the chicken . . . Deposit freelance check . . . Order more b/w film . . . Meeting with Prada on Tues.* Suddenly, Jay wanted to cry.

"I'm sorry about that," he said. "I didn't have the time."

No, I had a piece of duct tape over my mouth and a gun to my head. And when the mugger asks you for your wallet, you give it to him, and in the end isn't that my problem?

"So, was it work?" Her voice was as soft and certain as the day they had met, all those years ago.

"Work? Yeah—but not the kind I'm used to. Government work, not UN-related. Listen to me, Patty. Listen to me well. You know I like to kid, but not this time. I'm in trouble. I think you may be, too."

"What do you mean?" Still calm. A little hesitant, but calm.

Well, honey, I'm locked in a gulag with six men who all remember their first kiss at the freshman homecoming game with "Peppermint" Patty Ross of the pixie haircut and the purple scarf and I want to scream, baby, just scream, because that's you that they remember kissing, that's you *in their memories. And I want to scream because it was never me who kissed you; another boy who called himself Johnny did that, a boy who's grown up to be a very, very dangerous man. And the only thing that's keeping me from unhinging is the fact that I was the only one of us lucky enough to find you again. By chance in Rockefeller Center, after all those years.*

"I got a little information from the folks who I'm working with, baby," Jay said. "Uh, they said my life was in danger. I can't say more . . . but if I knew that if I was in danger, I figured you would be, too."

Patricia was quiet. Then: "You're kidding."

"I'm not, Peppermint. I said I wasn't."

The pause must've lasted only a second, maybe two. To Jay, it was much longer. He wanted to say—to scream—so many things into the phone. But *they* were listening. *They* were waiting. *They* were everywhere . . . and had been everywhere, all these years. The UN analyst had been analyzed, for a decade and a half. And if they'd been watching all those years, who's to say that Alpha hadn't been watching, too?

"So what do you want me to do?" she asked.

"Catch a flight to your dad's in Indy. Tonight."

"I have a project that's due, Jay," she said, impatient. "I can't just pick up and leave."

"Pack the laptop." Desperation was starting to seep into his voice, just as it was seeping into the sweat trickling down the bridge of his nose. Alpha could know where they lived. And if he knew she was alone . . .

"You're freelance, baby. Edit the photos from the road. File from your pop's house. *Harper's* won't know the difference."

"They'll call."

"And they'll call your cell." He could imagine Alpha's face now, a grinning parody of his own, opening the door to their East

Village apartment, shrieking, *Honey, I'm home*, and grabbing Patricia in the kitchen, mashing her face against the dry-erase board on the refrigerator, its blue ink rubbing into her bruised face—

Jesus Christ. Keep it together. Oh, Jesus Christ.

"Patricia, please. Just do this."

"Jay, what's going on? Just where are you?"

He wiped the sweat from his forehead. *He knew where my mother lived. Kidnapped her.*

"Can't tell you that." The fear was becoming harder to contain. It was a school of piranha eating at his guts. "I want to, but I can't. It's a . . . it's a security thing."

"A security thing? You want me to leave, and you can't tell me where you're calling from?"

Another voice, a voice that sounded like his own, but not, not at all: *I'm going to take her back, Jay. Take her back and break her face and break her pretty little green eyes and fuck her and HONEY I'M HOME*

"Just do it!" Jay screamed. "Don't trust anyone! Just get out! Get out before he finds you! Before Alpha—"

He heard Patricia start to ask a question . . .

. . . and the line went dead.

Jay screamed again, pounded his fist against the desk.

Goddamnit, Patty. Just go. Please go.

He had to stop that bastard. Even if it killed him.

Michael dialed his home number in Denver. Unless Gabe was at church—and since it was pushing noon mountain standard time, that was a possibility—he should be home to take the call. Michael hoped he was. He owed Gabe an explanation . . . after all, Michael was supposed to be en route to Denver right now. He had earned the break. He deserved it. They deserved it.

"Hello?" It was Gabriel's voice, deep and dusty.

"Hey, you," Michael said, smiling faintly. "It's me."

"Mike." Michael could hear the smile through the phone. "Are you here already? You were supposed to call before the flight."

Michael winced. If anyone had been watching him and Jack two rooms down as he spoke to his wife, they would have sworn their expressions were identical. Which, of course, they were.

"I'm sorry, Gabe. Something's come up."

Here it comes.

"What's come up?" Gabriel's voice was already cooling.

"Got nailed for TAD yesterday. It was the same old, same old. Pack your shit, head for the plane, report for duty, do not pass Go, do not collect two hundred dollars."

"Damn it, Mike." Michael could feel the hurt in Gabe's voice. "I thought we had two weeks. Now how much do we have? One?"

"Probably none. This one's big, Gabe. You know the rule; can't tell you about it. But it's big."

Michael heard a sigh. "How many times has this happened? How many times have you've gotten orders like this? I couldn't tell you because I've lost count."

I've lost count, too. Too many. Far too many.

"I'm sorry, Gabe. I really am. It's the job. I'm not a supermarket clerk who can pitch a fit when he gets called in—"

"Yeah, I know: 'The world doesn't revolve around my schedule, hoss, my schedule revolves around the world.'" Gabe's impression of Michael's voice was cruel, but uncanny. "I've lost count of how many times I've heard that, too. You know, Michael, someday you're going to come home from one of your little adventures, and I'm not going to be here."

"I said I was sorry." Gabe was right. They knew this conversation by rote. "I don't know what else to say."

"Say you'll come home today. I'm tired of living on the back burner, Michael. I'm tired of feeling like we're dancing on thin ice.

No. I know exactly what you should say. Say you and me can live like normal people, and not like fair-weather lovers who hook up whenever it's convenient."

"You know that's not how I feel."

Gabe, bitterly: "Then prove it."

Michael paused, searching for the words. "I'll prove it when I come home. It'll be soon, I hope. It's just this thing I'm doing right now, it's more important than I can ever say. Think big picture, Gabriel. Think as big as it gets. My country needs me for something that's *as big as it gets*. I can't say no. And even if could"— Michael's mind flashed to the rest of the clones, who'd been brought here at gunpoint—"I don't think it would matter. I'm locked in, Gabe. I'm sorry, but I can't say anything else about it. And I'm sorry I can't be there with you."

He heard Gabriel sigh. "I'm tired of losing count, Mike."

"You don't understand, Gabe."

"I'll never understand."

"I love you."

Another sigh. "I love you, too," Gabe said. "So when, then?"

"That's what I'm trying to tell you. It might not happen. Like I said, this is as big as it gets."

Silence. Then: "Don't you bullshit me."

Michael shook his head. "I never bullshit, Gabe. You know that."

Another silence. Finally: "It doesn't seem real."

Michael lowered his eyes to the floor. He envisioned the rooms more than quarter mile down, the rooms with the metal beasts that had birthed him. The scientists here had made the unreal real.

"Tell me about it," Michael said. "But it's as real as it gets."

"So what do we do?"

Michael shrugged. "We say we love each other more than the

world. We say it like it's the last time we'll say it. We pray that we'll
say it again, next time face-to-face."

"Amen to that."

"And a fuckin' A to boot."

Somehow, that cracked them up. Their laughter took the edge
off, and Michael was grateful for it.

"My boyfriend, the poet," Gabriel said.

"My boyfriend, the critic."

They smiled together in silence.

"I have to go," Michael said. "So give me a message, Gabriel."

"Go cast the dragon into the abyss like you always do. And be
sure to find your way home."

They laughed again and said they loved each other more than
the world.

Which, of course, they did.

Father Thomas didn't know what he'd say when the people on the
other end picked up.

This particular fact didn't seem to surprise him; Father Thomas
had been, for the most part, at an utter loss for words since yesterday. The rules had changed. Heck, the rules had been tossed into
the Cuisinart and frappéed. Hit escape velocity hours ago. Ground
control to Major Tom and all that other happy horseshit.

Father Thomas whispered a prayer of forgiveness (he rarely
swore, even to himself) . . . then clenched his teeth. Prayers were
moot now, weren't they? A praying clone. Wasn't that like dialing
911 on a broken telephone?

Father Thomas chuckled grimly and jabbed the buttons.

*Want to talk about the mystery of faith? Talk to a priest. About the
existence of God? Ditto. That's what we're there for. Arbiters of dogma,
Catechism, and goodwill. Your priest's the shepherd. The guru in a*

Roman collar. The man who's got a line to the Big Guy, Forever and Ever, Amen.

Adultery, addiction, cheating on your tax forms: now those are dilemmas, very human dilemmas, and there are moral and spiritual compasses for such matters. But to learn that you're a walking abomination . . . that you weren't born, but *built* . . . whom do you talk to about that?

Abomination. That's how Thomas had been seeing himself for the past day. No more human than the plastic he was now pressing. Manufactured. Spawn of cellular wizardry. A thing whose past was a mirage. A thing who, as the dream Christ had uttered last night, had no Providence. No soul.

It wasn't that Thomas had stopped believing in God. No. He had realized that God had stopped believing in *him*—and worse, had *never* believed in him. How could God believe in a thing He did not create? Thomas had not been conceived and born through holy Providence. Thomas had been spliced and grown in a bubble filled with growth accelerant. The life he lived afterward had been steered by liars.

Most damning: the life he remembered up to year fourteen was someone else's. Even his soul had been manufactured. How could a thing God did not create have a soul?

The phone on the other end began to ring. Thomas closed his eyes. He was no shepherd. He wasn't even a sheep. He was a breathing blasphemy, a bona fide nowhere man. A man with no soul doesn't go to heaven when he dies, but he doesn't go to hell, either. A man with no soul would not even be welcome in Limbo. No such place would accept a man who cannot fulfill the basic requirement for admission.

Such a man is . . . untethered, he thought.

The phone continued to ring. Thomas barely heard it.

An atheist's death, is that what awaits me? Where is the justice in that? I know who would have the answers. A priest.

Thomas chuckled again. He was losing his mind, probably.

The phone on the line rang again and again. Finally, a recording took the call. Thomas wasn't surprised by that, either.

"Hello. You've reached the home of Karl and Jaclyn Smith," the machine said. "We're not home right now, so leave a message and the time you called, and we'll get back with you as soon as we can. Thanks, and God bless."

That's rich.

Beeeeeep.

"It's me," he found himself saying. His hand slid across the table and grasped his rosary. These were his worry beads now. "I've come to back to my birthplace. I know everything. I know that the people who I remember calling mother and father are still alive. And I know that you two guided my life, under orders from this place. And only now do I suspect that I'm calling a special number, the exclusive 'Aunt and Uncle' line—a phone line created and answered only to maintain a ruse. You're probably already tucked away in a bunker, safe from the hell spawn this project created."

The tape rolled on, listening. Thomas held up the rosary and watched the crucifix sway back and forth in his hand.

"I don't know what's going to drive me mad first: the fact that I am what I am . . . or that my life had been all but plotted before I was even 'born.' Just how many of the decisions I've made over the years are *mine*? How many times did you slip a philosophy or religious book into my hands, to show your 'support' of the interest I had fleetingly taken? And was that interest sparked by my will or by yours? It was so long ago. Those things you don't really remember, do you? 'When you're too young to count, it's tough to keep score.' Isn't that what you once said, Karl? Huh. I wonder what your real name is."

Thomas let the rosary slip through his fingers. It bothered him to hold it. It bothered him to not hold it.

Through the window, Thomas spotted the marine, who was stepping into the Common Room from his quarters. His face was flushed; perhaps Michael had been crying.

"I'm staying here, you know," Thomas said into the phone. "I must. Must search for the truth, for understanding and answers—just as I always have. And maybe I can find something that'll bring some spiritual peace to these six, these brothers of mine. That's ironic and hypocritical, I know that. Don't you think I know that? But this is what I know, it's what I've lived. I can't let it go completely. Not yet."

No, not yet, he thought. *There's plenty to look into. Why did they pull Dad out of the Ops room this morning? What was he saying? What are these people hiding from us? Where did they get the money for this place? And what about—*

He picked up the rosary again.

"I don't know if you'll ever get this message. And I don't know if you'll ever see me again. But I wanted you to know that I forgive you, Jaclyn. I forgive you, Karl. And I wanted you to know that I'll pray that God has mercy on you. I don't know how much weight a soulless man's prayers have in the eyes of the Lord. Probably none. But I've been thinking about you two, and what role you've played in all this. I imagine you'll need all the forgiveness and prayers you can get.

"Besides," Father Thomas added, smiling bitterly, "I'm a priest. I'm doing what I was bred to do."

He placed the receiver back on the cradle and gazed at Christ's face glimmering from the rosary.

Isn't It Obvious, Fleshling? You Have No Soul.
It was cold in here. So cold.

One Day. One day is all it takes. One day to take a man's life and toss it upside down, back and forth, bash it against the rocks like a suitcase in those Samsonite commercials. Today was that One Day, John was the suitcase. General Hill, Dr. Kleinman, and their merry band of gun-toters and gene-splicers were the eight-hundred-pound gorillas.

John felt banged up and broken, both physically and mentally. He'd talked with the marine and Jack throughout last night and was suffering from a serious case of the nods because of it. There was good news, John supposed: yesterday's cuts and bruises on his hand and face were mending well, and the muscles in his left arm, which had been twisted with playground-bully perfection by one of the government spooks, only throbbed from far away. The body was putting itself back together.

But the mind. Ah. That was a different matter altogether.

Suddenly a record deal and tour seem like lame-ass life goals, John thought. *Now it's piecing together a puzzle that was my mystery life . . . and finding Mom again, if she's still alive. God,* could *she still be alive?*

John shook his head. Enough. He pulled the rubber band from his ponytail and let the hair hang down over his shoulders and face. He rubbed his temples and scratched his fingernails through his hair, feeling its weight between his fingers.

Keep the questions at bay, bub. File them away for later, for when you get there. Focus on the call to Sarah. Sarah of the amazing Saturday sex. Sarah, fair woman whom I left waiting for menthol cigarettes and staring down a grumpy, hungry cat. Lucy, I got some 'splaining to do.

John knew she wouldn't be at the gallery; last summer, Sarah had somehow finagled her way out of working Sundays. She wouldn't be at his place—at least, John didn't think she would. The only creature who could take full-time living in that grimy breadbox was Cat . . . and he was one surly fucker. *Ring her cell phone. And remember that someone else is listening to your conversation.*

He dialed. Sarah picked up on the third ring.

"Don't be mad."

"Holy shit," Sarah said. "Where in the hell did you go yesterday? And you'd better not go all 'I needed a walkabout' on me, or I'm hanging up right now."

John laughed. He couldn't help it. *Sarah, God bless you. I think I'm in love with you, girl. Not that I can tell you that just yet.*

"Nothing like that," he replied. "I promise."

"Do you know how many people I've called, John? Do you know how many of our friends have been looking for you?"

My, my. She rounded up a posse. You might be in love with me, too. And you're probably just as scared to say it as I am.

"Call off the search, darlin'. I'm okay. I'm rattled, but okay. It's been an interesting day and a half."

"People don't just *vanish*."

John's eyes flitted as he searched for the right words—and through his room's window, he spotted Father Thomas slipping out of his quarters and into the Common Room. Most of the others were out there now.

"I ran into some old friends." He noticed Jack and then Dr. Mike, standing on opposite sides of the circular room. They weren't aware of it, but both were scratching their heads with the same hand (the right) on the same place (just above the right ear). *Mimes have nothing on these guys.* "We go way back, me and these dudes," John said, staring. "These are serious Old Guard folk. From before the fall of the Berlin Wall and all that."

"Very funny," Sarah snapped—which snapped John out of his

stare. "So you're on your way to get cat food, you bump into old buddies on the way, and you don't even call to say 'Don't let the door hit your ass on the way out' much less 'Buy your own god-damn cigarettes'? And what's this old-buddy business? You didn't grow up in Miami. You're from Indiana."

Crap. You never were a good liar, Johnny-boy.

He hesitated.

Go on. Dig that hole a little deeper.

"Well, that's the part that'll blow your mind."

"I'll bet. Save it. I thought we had something really good going on here, John. Open and communicative, if you get my hint. So, you want to tell me what's really happening? You know, you're lucky I picked up in the first place. The caller ID on my phone's displaying some funky number."

They're scrambling the line, probably. Making it untraceable.

"What's really happening," John said, mystified. "I'm not in town, Sarah. Nowhere close. And I don't know when I'll be back."

"Jesus Christ."

"This has nothing to do with you, with us. We're good, Sarah. We're better than good—or at least we were. It's just that some-thing from my past kind of popped out of nowhere yesterday, and I've been playing catch-up ever since. This is the first chance I've had to call you, swear to God."

"Right. So this is when you tell me you're married."

"God, no!"

"You're wanted."

"I don't think so."

"You're two-timing me."

"Sarah! No, no. It's nothing like that! It's something, uh"—*Someone's listening in, Johnny-boy. Remember that*—"something I never knew about my past made itself, ah, *manifest*. No one could've seen this coming, least of all me."

"Fuck me running. You're gay."

"Sarah, enough!" John cried. "It has something to do with my parents, okay? Something important."

There was a click on the line. Then silence.

She's hung up on me.

But she hadn't. She'd just been taken aback, apparently. "Your parents? But they're dead."

"Right."

Another click. *That's not her phone. That's something else.*

"What's going on, John?"

"I can't tell you right now," he said hastily. "In fact, I think I should get off the phone."

"But why? *Why?*"

"I can't tell you why. And I can't tell you when I can call you again. But I'm all right, Sarah. I just got to do this thing and then I'll come home with a whole goddamn carton of Newports, I promise."

"I'm scared, John. Why can't you tell me what's going on?"

"It's the rules," he replied simply. "I've got it bad for you, Sarah. I don't want this to hurt us any more than it has. I'm yours, Sarah. Remember that. I'm yours . . . and I'll be yours when I come home, if you'll have me."

She was silent for a moment, then said, "I'll keep you for now. But don't be too long."

"Thank you."

John closed his eyes. There wasn't anything else to say—and there was a whole new world's worth to say. Sometimes One Day does that to people.

"Just one more thing," John said.

"Anything."

"Could you, ah, adopt Cat for the time being? You know, feed him, pet him, and call him George? Just for a little while."

Sarah laughed. "You've become quite the high-maintenance beau in the past twenty-four hours. It doesn't become you."

"Sorry. I just don't want the critter going hungry."

"You'll be back to take him?"

"I promise."

"Then it's a deal."

John smiled. He loved her. He sure did.

"You take care," he said.

"Take some of that advice yourself."

John thought of the group that was coming together outside in the Common Room. Things were going to get a lot more complicated in a few hours. People were going to get hurt. He could feel it.

"I will," he said, and hung up.

"I will."

NINETEEN

he *Bucky Lastard* shuddered as it tore through sky and cloud, lurching in the turbulence, jostling and unnerving the fifteen inhabitants of its steel belly. The V-22-X Osprey pilot was under orders to redline it the whole trip from Virginia to California, and to forget the flight—and its passengers—as soon as it was completed.

Pilot Les Orchard had voiced no objections when he'd received this proclamation an hour ago, standing before Brigadier General Orlando Hill on the off-the-map airstrip twelve miles west of the 7th Son complex. On the tarmac, Hill had invoked Code Phantom secrecy, and the pilot had flown enough off-the-books flights to know the rules. Ask no questions, and fly hard.

The men inside the highly modified V-22-X's passenger/cargo bay did not know Les Orchard, but they knew he was redlining it. The aircraft—equipped with experimental VTOL jet engines—heaved and trembled under these conditions, rattling unsecured equipment crates off their pallets and across the payload floor. The men would get up, stagger and sway their way to the boxes to secure them. They gripped the walls as they scrambled back to their seats.

Few of them spoke; it was difficult to hear over the roar of the *Bucky Lastard*'s triple-timing-it engines. There wasn't much to say, actually. Before they'd left an hour ago, Michael had briefed the eleven 7th Son guards recruited for the mission—more than half of the facility's security staff. They appeared to be competent men, trustworthy. Word of this little soirée could never leave the fold. The men understood that. The men also understood quadruple combat pay, which General Hill had promised them.

The mission was dangerous, more cavalier than any official mission would be, and bordered on suicide. Armed with only scraps of information about the building—and absolutely no recon data or human intelligence—they were to invade Folie à Deux after nightfall. The recruits had asked questions, of course. Was the target inside the building? Michael told them that they didn't know. What resistance could they expect inside? They didn't know. The unanswered (and unasked) questions hung in the air during that briefing. Why were they conducting the mission at all, considering the catalog of risks?

Because this target must be eliminated, Hill had told them. *He's rabid. Lost his mind. Has access to technology that'll tear this planet apart, if people find out about it. You're going to make sure they don't.*

But you don't go into the doghouse when the dog's got rabies, one of the soldiers had said.

Tonight you do, Hill had replied. That comment had frightened them the most.

So, other than the roar of the V-22-X's engines and the constant unnerving rattle of metal on metal, the personnel bay of the *Bucky Lastard* was quiet. Michael, John, Dr. Mike, and Robert Durbin sat among the 7th Son soldiers, strapped into their stiff-backed seats.

John, who'd never enjoyed flying, clutched his knees. Dr. Mike clenched his eyes shut. Only Durbin and Michael seemed unaffected by the conditions. John had glanced at the marine's face during the worst of the turbulence and saw that Michael's chiseled jaw never moved, the expression in his eyes never wavered. The man was a silent storm of focus and discipline.

The soldier sitting across from John screamed a "Hey!" John barely heard it over the rattling metal around him. He looked up and saw one of the men who'd thrown him into that that grinning white cargo van yesterday morning. John wanted to ignore the man . . . then he remembered what Hill had said in the Ops room: *Don't hold a grudge.*

"Yeah?" John cried over the din.

"You're the one from Miami, aren't you?" the soldier hollered. The tag on his BDUs read JELEN.

A few of the other soldiers looked over in interest.

"That's right."

"You really drop out of college to become a musician?" Jelen asked. Above the din, the kid's voice was high and loud, a squeaky door hinge. "We read your file before we picked you up. Said you were a dropout."

"You didn't 'pick me up,' " John yelled back. "You kidnapped me."

"So are you that guy or not?"

Now Dr. Mike and Michael were looking at John. The plane cleaved its way through another cloud, heaving them in their seats. John wanted to puke.

"I am," he said finally.

"Kind of a waste if you ask me," the soldier said. "You got a big thing like 7th Son under your skin, and you spend your time with, what, open-mic nights? I bet you even got a demo tape."

A few of the soldiers whooped. John wasn't sure why. Jelen seemed proud to have brought up the subject.

"This may not make sense to you," John said, "but I didn't

want to take orders for the rest of my life. Didn't want to salute to anyone, didn't want to work in a cube farm, or whatever. I just wanted to be, well, me. I hit the road, didn't look back."

"Makes sense to me," Michael the marine said. A few of the soldiers sitting near him glanced over. "Gotta find yourself if you want to fight the good fight."

"Oh, honestly," Dr. Mike piped up. "Dollars to doughnuts, you're living paycheck to paycheck, John. Probably not even. What's marching to the beat of your own drum got you, other than calluses?"

John looked up from the floor into Dr. Mike's smiling eyes. "I'd rather drink my crappy light beer and strum my chords and live my very 'live and let live' life than be a cynical cocksucker like you. My checks might bounce, but at least I can sleep at night."

Even more of the men "hoo-ahhed" at that.

"Touché," Dr. Mike said, and saluted.

The *Bucky Lastard* flew westward, ever onward.

Dr. Mike, Michael, and John had left the 7th Son compound an hour ago, and despite having known them for just over a day, Father Thomas missed them. Their absence ate at his mind, as did the silence they had left behind.

Not until they were gone did Thomas realize just what a guiding force Michael and Dr. Mike had been, here in their little clique. Michael drew plans, cut through the group's stammering confusion, and pushed people from being talkers to doers. Dr. Mike was selfish and standoffish, but blessed with an ability to glean meaning from the puzzle John Alpha had created. Those two were the closest thing to leaders this motley crew had. And now they were heading off into the literal sunset to be the cavalry.

And John? Honestly, Thomas didn't know what to make of him. A sliver of the priest was suspicious of the ponytailed musician. John was charismatic in an unapologetically unpolished way; Thomas's parish at St. Barnabas back in Stanton had more than its share of such folk. The man was sincere enough. But heading to West Hollywood like some righteous knight . . .

No, that wasn't it. Like a *rogue.*

If there were rules in this world—and despite Father Thomas's personal crisis, he still believed *that*—John didn't seem to be the kind of man who liked following them. There were leaders of others, such as Thomas. There were followers. Then there were the few who led themselves, others (and followers) be damned. Masterless, that was John.

Thomas smirked. It wasn't suspicion he was feeling. It was envy. Here Thomas was, in his room, hungry to hide from the past twenty-four hours. There John was, soaring off to his destiny.

And this was the closest thing Thomas could get to hiding, lying here on the bed of his living quarters. The remaining four clones—Jay, Jack, Kilroy2.0, and himself—had agreed to rest before embarking on their own little adventure: trying to piece together what conspiracy, if any, John Alpha was concocting. If the L.A. shebang ended with the rescue of Dania Sheridan and the capture (or death) of John Alpha, so be it. But Thomas didn't think it would be that easy. Spills rarely clean up quickly in real life. You always need more paper towels than they use in the commercial.

He stared up at the ceiling, then at the red LED numbers on the clock. Five o'clock. He was exhausted, but he couldn't sleep. Yes, the absence of—what would you call them? Friends? Newfound family?—was to blame. But only partly. Thomas's stomach churned. He wanted to pray, relentlessly so. His soul wanted to process the past day's events. His mind craved being out there, in the Common Room, watching Kilroy2.0 hunt-and-peck his way across those keyboards and into answers.

What do you want, John Alpha? Why are you doing what you're do-
ing? I can understand why you escaped this place—to fake your death so
the 7th Son surveillance squad would leave you in peace. But why this?
Why kill the president? Why rape a child's mind to do it? And why kidnap
Mom and then leave bread crumbs to find her? Just what are you up to?

Thomas shuddered. He didn't know. So far, none of them did.
Dr. Mike had mentioned good old-fashioned revenge as motive,
and Thomas could buy that. But revenge couldn't possibly be the
only thing at work here. From what Thomas understood, Alpha
was smarter than that.

Thomas rolled his body so he couldn't see the clock. He closed
his eyes. He tried to shut out the questions. He wanted to sleep.
Just a few minutes of sleep. Just a few minutes from all this. *Rock*
of ages, cleft for me. Let me hide myself in thee.

He was actually grateful when the knock came. Jack was waiting for him at the door. He looked the way Thomas felt.

"Couldn't sleep, either?" Thomas asked.

"Riiiight," Jack said, skeptically peering over his spectacles.
"Kilroy's got his computers fired up. Looks like the freakin' Batcave out here."

Thomas took a deep breath. "Let's get to it, then."

The four clones sat on the circular couch in the Common Room,
waiting for someone to speak first. Kilroy2.0's eyes bounced from
face to face, then to the notebook and pen lying on the round table before them. Jack sighed and leaned back against the cushions. Jay gazed up at the waning evening sunlight. His knee
bounced up and down as if charged by an electric current.

It's still downright spooky to look at them, Thomas thought. *My*
eyes, my ears, my nose, my hands. There are differences; enough to keep
me (us?) from going crazy, I think.

It was true. Kilroy2.0 was bye-bye upstairs, slovenly, shaggy, and obese. Jack's beard obfuscated his round cheeks; he sported a potbelly from too many dates with the Dolly Madison machine at the genetics lab; his hair was straight from the School of the Conservative Comb-Over. Jay was truly a dead ringer for Thomas (the same comb-over, the same receding hairline), but thinner and downright sickly in appearance—his face was thin, with cheekbones that looked as if they were about to pop through his skin. Thomas reckoned Jay was one of those folks who always looked as if they needed more sleep.

And what did they think of *him*?

Best not to go there; priests received enough uninformed, malign grief out there in the "real world" as it was. No sense in bringing that here. Thomas had enough to worry about.

"So how are we going to do this?" he asked.

Jack sat up, grunting. "That depends on what we want to accomplish. If we're trying to find what John Alpha's up to, we'll have to think like him. To do that, we're going to have to know where to look."

"I'm not sure we can do that," Jay chimed in, his face drawn down in concern. *For once, I'd like him to smile*, Thomas mused. And then, fleetingly: *Do I look that dour when I'm worried?*

"Think about it for a minute," Jay said. "You're John Alpha. You're the crown jewel in a top-secret experiment. You learn the ins and outs of the most remarkable technology on earth. You fake your death, brew up a scheme to kill the president—and it works. Then you kidnap your mother for kicks. Is it even possible to go there? To get inside that?"

Thomas tugged his rosary from his khaki slacks pocket, holding it for comfort. He shrugged.

Jay shook his head. "He's too smart."

"Maybe," Father Thomas said. "Maybe not. We did just fine with the Morse code. I'd say we knocked that out of the ballpark."

" 'L.A. Woman,' " Kilroy2.0 whispered, then giggled. "Anal mow."

"Thank you, Beavis," Jack said.

Jay rolled his eyes. "That was a game and you know it. Alpha *left* that clue for us. He knew Kleinman would bring us together to solve it. The Morse code, the music, the *DSM* diagnosis . . . he *wanted* us to solve it, Thomas. He served it on a silver platter, and now the Mikes and John are on their way into the trap."

"So what's your point?"

"That Alpha probably will be very good at stringing us along when he wants to be seen," Jay replied. "But when a man like that doesn't want to be found, consider the tracks covered. As in by-an-avalanche covered."

Jay crossed his arms and leaned back into the couch, as if there were nothing else to say.

But Lord above, there was. "I validate that," Thomas said, nodding. "But there has to be something, right? A clue. A misstep. Something we can work with."

Jack spoke up. "Again, I say, we have to know where to look. But where? L.A. may be the answer."

"Which is a trap," Kilroy2.0 said.

"We don't know that, and we can't do anything about that," Thomas said. "Those three are doing their thing. Let's do ours. So come on, fellas, what do we know about John Alpha?"

"Two things," Jay said. "Jack—"

"—and shit," Jack said, scowling.

Kilroy2.0 was the first to say it: "Seventh grade. Sam Jeter told me that joke in seventh grade."

Father Thomas shivered. *That's right. Sam Jeter. Sam Jeter knew two things: Jack and shit. And the weather was always colder than a witch's titty. What was the other thing he used to say? Right. It's either ass-whoopin's or lollipops . . .*

". . . and I'm fresh out of lollipops," Jay muttered.

Thomas clamped a hand over his mouth to stifle a shriek. Kil-roy2.0 saw this and began to titter. *This is what it's like in his world. This. The voices in your head coming from someplace other than your head. The floor just fell out of my stomach. My skin's about to crawl right off the bones. This is no good. This is*

"Too much," he heard Jack say. The color had drained from his face. "This is too damned much."

Thomas rubbed the gooseflesh on his arms. The rosary swung madly in his hand.

"Don't think about it," he said to Jack, to himself, to all of them. "Please, don't think about it. It's too soon."

"Wait." Jay picked up the pen and pad and jotted down a few words. "That *is* something we know about Alpha. We have his whole childhood at our disposal." To illustrate, he tapped the side of his head with the pen.

"Anyone here remember ever plotting to take over the world?" Jack asked.

They laughed, and like that, it had passed. Thank God.

"Good. What else do we know?" Thomas's voice was shaky, but he was eager to keep them moving away from the fear, and toward the truth—whatever it was. "His childhood is our childhood . . . and, as far as I can remember, it was on-the-surface normal as it gets. What about his time here at 7th Son? What did Hill say about that?"

"We know he's good with computers," Jack said. Kilroy2.0 har-rumphed. "Like the man said, Alpha shut down the entire security system to go AWOL."

"And we know he had access to everything in this place," Jay said as he scribbled into the pad. "He learned all about the clon-ing chambers, the MemR/I hypercomputer array, the Memory Totality upload and download process—"

"Must have had access to archived files," Kilroy2.0 said. "Maybe not Code Phantom clearance, but something. Had to know about the first experiments."

Father Thomas stiffened in his seat. *Wait a minute.*

"NEPTH-charge," he whispered. "That's how he first learned about NEPTH-charge, maybe. From the archives. The Lock Box, I bet."

They looked at him expectantly. Jay nodded slowly. "And?"

"Kleinman told us that a person doesn't live long after the NEPTH-charge process. When you erase a brain and then dump a new, ah, soul in there, you've got three weeks to live, tops."

"Sure," Jack said. "He said it leaves some kind of special tissue damage on the brain. Something telltale, like a watermark. They found it in the Fowler kid's autopsy. So?"

Thomas was up on his feet now. "So if I'm John Alpha and I have a plot that's bigger than killing the president—which we're assuming—I'll probably use that technology. We know it's useful: have a killer's brain hijack a body to do the dirty work for you. One little kid isn't going to be enough for my dastardly plan, right?"

Kilroy2.0 clapped his hands and grinned. "Do not use after March fifteenth. Please keep your proof of purchase."

"Exactly!" Thomas cried, and gave the lunatic a high five.

"What are you two talking about?"

"I'm talking about expiration dates, Jay," Thomas said. "I'm talking about disposable toadies. And I'm talking about a way to see where John Alpha's been using them."

"The bodies," Jay said, nodding. "And the watermark."

"Give the man a cigar," Father Thomas said. "Maybe we can look for cases where people died of some unknown ailment—people who seemed perfectly healthy up until their deaths. It's the closest thing we have to a paper trail."

Jack gave a low whistle. "The clue we've been waiting for." He looked admiringly at Thomas. "*What* do you do for a living?"

"I'm a priest. You know that."

"You should've been a scientist."

Thomas smiled. "There was already one in the family." He turned to Kilroy. "Fire up the Batcave, Mad Hacker. We've got some serious research ahead of us."

The first four hours were a bust.

Kilroy2.0 hacked, slashed, and giggled his way through Lexis, Associated Press, and other media-archive Web sites, unleashing some kind of home-brewed "spider" program that swept through the sites, searching for relevant obituaries. Thomas was alarmed to see that far more people in America had died of brain aneurysms over the past six months than he would've expected. And old folks passing on from strokes, they had plenty.

That, Thomas could believe. He'd prayed with many a dying elderly parishioner.

But who—if any of them—was a suspect? Take Lucas Qualls, a forty-four-year-old schoolteacher who'd had a grand mal seizure in his San Diego classroom last month. He'd bitten off half his tongue before a roomful of dazed fourth-graders and was dead before his head split open on the floor. Was he an agent of John Alpha's? What about Kimberly Fortuner, senior VP of finance at Glickman-Beecham, maker of many a fine pharmacological pick-me-up? A blood vessel in her brain had burst during her commute home from Seattle; her Saab rushed over the interstate median into oncoming traffic, causing a seven-car pileup that took four lives and four hours to clear.

Was it Oscar Flores of Brendanville, Kansas? Nora Reed of Little Rock? Jered Reynolds, lifelong Memphis resident? The Reverend Terry Bruce of Baton Rouge? Manhattan socialite Susan Zekanis?

Who knew? Who in the hell *knew*?

The second hour was spent red-flagging the more suspicious deaths, then skulking through password-protected autopsy reports locked away on law enforcement intranets. At first, Thomas, Jack, and Jay had a compelling lead: the aforementioned Reverend Terry Bruce, leader of the Redemptive Fire from Heaven Pentecostal Church (membership: twenty-eight). Tip-offs were in the newspaper obit—his behavior had become erratic during the last two weeks of his life, he was keeping odd hours and "acting like a different person," the widow Bruce had said. A meek allusion was made to an unexpected death that was "neurologically related."

They had cross-referenced the death with the coroner's report stored on the East Baton Rouge Sheriff Department's intranet server. The reality was very different from the newspaper story: Bruce had died in a local no-tell motel of a cocaine overdose while giving a reach-around to his gay lover. Thomas scratched the preacher's name off the list.

Every few minutes, one of Kilroy2.0's computers would *ping!* a compatible search result from his spider program, and the clones would dutifully peruse the story, see if it was worth cross-referencing on the Five-O's Web networks. Most times it wasn't. When it was, they found the occasional subterranean and secret tale—one Chicagoan had accidentally killed himself by overdosing on heroin that he had injected into his tear duct—but mostly the deaths were quiet and seemingly painless affairs. Death often came to people in their homes, Thomas learned. This quiet door-to-door salesman had an offer you simply couldn't refuse.

The files from which Thomas and the rest learned these things were cold, unflinching, and sterile: toxicology and autopsy reports recorded by men and women trained to keep things terse. But after two hours of this, Thomas felt filthy. Despite his love for people-watching, this was one strain of voyeurism he would never, ever revisit. Peeking in a stranger's medicine cabinet during a cocktail party is one thing. Knowing what food was in his stomach when he croaked was something else.

Kilroy2.0's computer *pinged!* again, and Thomas looked up from the empty cup he'd been staring into. He was sitting to Kilroy2.0's left; Jay sat to Kilroy's right. The obituary on the screen was about a Wichita bank owner who had popped his cogs at a cocktail party. He was a good man to the day he died, sobbed his sister. I can't believe he's gone, blah-dee-blah, yackety-shmackety— *surely I've never been this indifferent to the deaths of strangers?*

"I hate to admit it, but this is going nowhere," Thomas said, a little disgusted with himself.

From behind him, Jack said, "I agree. Another coffee?"

"Yeah."

Jack plucked the empty cup from the table and shuffled to the coffeemaker near the doorway of the Common Room.

"It made sense in my head in the beginning," Thomas said, accepting the cup a moment later. "Compare obits with autopsies, find a pattern, we're done: Professor Plum in the Study with the revolver. But this"—he waved a hand at the whirring bank of computer towers—"isn't getting the results I expected. Maybe there's a paper trail, maybe not. But it's going to take us forever to find out." He sipped the coffee and shrugged.

Jay leaned back in his seat and looked over at Thomas. "Believe me, this is how you *find* patterns. Waiting, wading. Lots of analysis. When you're finally certain, then you act."

"Is this a lot like your role at the UN?" Thomas asked.

"In some ways. I work in the Human Rights division. My team tracks human rights violations, civil rights issues, that sort of thing. We basically hold leaders responsible for the inequity that always seems to be brewing beneath the surface in most countries. We try to intervene before the pot boils over. We meet, we go over data, we travel to the country, speak to the leaders and the locals. Sometimes the OHCHR agrees with our analysis and advises the General Assembly to intervene. Sometimes it doesn't."

"Sounds interesting," Jack said.

"It can be," Jay said. "I remember my first internship out of college—a nonprofit in California that gave legal aid to migrant workers. Citizenship, fair wages, workers' rights, helping them not get gouged by the local farmers and landlords. That sort of thing. At first, the job was all stars and moonbows because it was all about *the cause*, you know? Doing the right thing, beating down the Man, a serious 'César Chávez is God' kind of vibe."

Thomas and Jack smiled.

"Three weeks later, I'm finally learning where all the proverbial light switches are . . . and I'm beginning to overhear the gossip and office politics. It was bullshit, it always is. Every organization has this stuff: the power plays, the control freaks. But in the end, it was okay because it was all about *the cause*. Idealism at its finest.

"These days, despite all the good that we do—all the good *I* do—I can't help but think the UN's cause has been mixed up with the bullshit office politics. The UN should be nimble, should react quickly to crises. It usually isn't. The cause is lost in subcommittee. At least that's how it feels sometimes."

Kilroy2.0's computer *pinged!* again. The lunatic's fingers began dancing across the keyboards. None of the others looked at the screen.

"So the UN is obsolete?" Thomas asked.

"Not at all," Jay replied. "I think the UN is the only thing keeping this planet from becoming unglued in a serious way. The

United Nations is about making the world a better place. It's about making countries responsible and accountable for their actions. It sounds pat, but I truly believe that. And when it works, it *works*. The problem isn't the charter. The problem is nearly two hundred countries pushing their own agendas in committee—or worse, being parrots for other countries' agendas. Cause versus committee. Ideology versus reality."

"You should attend a university regents' meeting sometime," Jack said. "Same shit, different setting. Pardon my French."

"Je ne prenderai pas vos mots tellement littéralement," Jay said, his accent smooth, the words easy.

"Keen," Thomas said, impressed. "How many languages can you speak?"

"Fluently? Including pig latin, nine."

"Cool," Thomas and Jack said simultaneously.

Jay grinned, then waved it off. "So anyway. Wading and waiting. That's what analysis it. Patience."

Kilroy2.0 grunted and turned his face from the glowing screens. "Foo. This isn't working. Conspiracies don't play in the sun. Spider's catching flies, but the data's no good."

Jack nodded and rubbed his beard. "That's what I was afraid of. I think we're looking for the right things. I just don't think we're looking in the right places."

"What do you mean?" Thomas asked.

"Kilroy2.0's right: conspiracies thrive under stones. The places we're looking—newspaper clippings, autopsy reports—they're too mainstream. I think Thomas's idea is sound; I just think we need to search in places a little less—"

"Pedestrian," Kilroy2.0 said.

"Exactly. Let me give you an example," Jack said. "My university calls the media when it's itching to boast about something—but only when it's ready to boast. There are many studies being conducted in my department, for instance, that we wouldn't dream of making public until we've completed the research and finalized the results. And only then if it's something significant that proves alumni dollars are being well spent."

"Talk about cause versus committee," Thomas said.

"It's a cruel world," Jack replied. "What I'm getting at is this: Perhaps there *are* reports of the phenomenon John's describing, but they're so significant—or insignificant—that there's no reason for the information to be released into the mainstream. Maybe there are people out there who are examining parts of Alpha's trail, but don't have the necessary backstory to understand its importance. Or maybe they do have the backstory, but don't want the information to get out."

Jay leaned forward and looked at the computer screens. "Universities, like yours?"

"Perhaps, but that wasn't what I was thinking," Jack said. "I was thinking more up your alley: government agencies. I'm thinking we should start with the Centers for Disease Control, see if they've found any NEPTH-charge victims." He turned to Kilroy2.0. "We need to go federal. Can you get us where we need to go?"

Kilroy2.0 grinned. "Let me call some friends," he said, already typing.

The windows filled with obits and autopsies vanished from the screens. With a few deft mouse-clicks, several smaller windows began to pop up. Thomas recognized a few of them from TV ads— three AOL chat windows flickered on-screen; MSN Messenger winked to life on another. The contact lists on each went on forever. There were also programs he didn't recognize: down_low, Cloaque, secURL. One, called BlackHat, had a grinning skull and crossbones icon in its upper left-hand corner. Still another was merely an empty window with a blinking cursor in its center. These were programs found off the beaten path. Decidedly un-Pedestrian.

Kilroy2.0 had been holding back the big guns.

This was another peek into his mind, Thomas realized, Kilroy's connection to the myriad *con-spir-a-cies* in which he undoubtedly believed. Funny. Conspiracy theories didn't seem so ludicrous anymore.

"You really know how to work these things, don't you?" Thomas said, clapping Kilroy2.0 on the shoulder.

Kilroy turned toward him and winked. "Kilroy2.0 is everywhere. *Evverry-where.*"

Thomas shuddered. Kilroy2.0 chuckled, then turned back to the computer screen.

And they entered his world.

The three clones quickly saw that Kilroy2.0 had hacked the online chat programs, so they worked together. Whatever he typed in the simple, featureless window in the center of the monitor appeared on all the other chat screens. They watched the letters simultaneously appear one by one on the baker's dozen of active software windows. Thomas felt gooseflesh ripple across his arms. *Big Brother isn't watching,* he thought. *He's broadcasting.*

On the thirteen chat programs, this message appeared:

> *Kilroy2.0 is here*

And every window suddenly sprang to life; each computer monitor swarmed by an armada of pop-up message windows, each from a unique name on Kilroy2.0's buddy lists. MSN Messenger and AOL IM chimed repeatedly, like a doorbell gone mad. BlackHat's skull icon burped robotic laughter. The prophet had come to preach to the faithful. They were all online, all flooding Kilroy2.0 with questions and riddles and praise-be-unto-hims.

cthulhu_call: Speak to us, Messiah

silent(e): i n33d ur h3lp

it's_a_wonderful_lie: Where have you been

Special(k): Tell us

wicked_lil_critta: Tell us, please

codeshaman: Where did you go?

three-five-zero-zero: Please . . .

Kilroy2.0 leaned back in his seat, a sly grin of satisfaction emerging on his lips. The computers continued to chime, the messages overran the monitors. Why. How. Is the time nigh. I have questions. I have information. Tell us where you were. Speak to us. Speak to us. Please speak to us.

The windows kept on and on—dozens now. That slippery smile never left Kilroy2.0's face.

Thomas turned to Jack and Jay and whispered, "Go tell it on the mountain." *Or under it. A whole world of them out there, just under the surface, talking their special talk. A point-and-clique.*

"Fascinating," Jack said. "How many are out there, do you think? Dozens? Hundreds?"

"Does it matter?" Jay asked. His eyes were wide; the color had drained from his face.

No, not really, Thomas's mind answered. *They're out there and they think he's some kind of cybermessiah. He preaches from nowhere—from* evvrery-where—*and they listen. Part priest, part prophet, part diety, all blasphemy . . .*

Kilroy2.0 gazed up at the clones. He waved a hand toward the monitors, toward the maelstrom of pop-up windows.

"My flock," he purred.

"You've got quite a fan club, Kilroy," Thomas said.

"Oh, yes."

"Are they all hackers, like you?" Jay's voice trembled, betraying the cool expression he was trying to maintain.

"Most," Kilroy2.0 said, turning back to the screens. His voice sounded disinterested. *You bore me, norm.*

"They read your sermons, don't they?"

Kilroy2.0 nodded at Jack's question. "They read the things you never read. My homilies about the shadows, my speeches about the squirming earthworms in our government, the transmissions from beyond, the plagues unleashed by the Adversary, the dark matter—and what it *really* is . . ."

Thomas's eyes met Jack's. The look said everything that need not be said. *Let him speak. Let's learn.*

". . . the chemtrails in the sky, the low-frequency Kokomo and Taos 'hums' in our ground, the cameras on our street corners, the radiation in the groundwater, stolen supercomputers, the eyes everywhere, watching us, always watching us, always watching us." Kilroy2.0 licked his lips, nodding. "Always. Watching. Us."

The chimes were a roomful of grandfather clocks now. The windows piled over each other, cascading like rows of solitaire cards. Kilroy squinted at the monitors.

blackjack: Please speak to us

J3nnyB3ntoBox: Are you there?

anthropohedron: speak speak speak speak speak

Kilroy2.0 began to type again.

> *It is a night of insurrection. In? SecURL. Out? Logoff.*

Almost a third of the instant message windows immediately blinked off the screen.

Kilroy2.0 tittered knowingly. "Some of them are afraid of the call to arms," he said to no one. "Most of them are not. You see the loyalty? These ones will create the force we need for storming the data beaches. Right now, they're activating their trackscramblers. They're shifting their CPUs into secURL shells. They will be our stealth fighters."

"They can't be tracked. That's what you're telling us."

"Indeed, Jay."

"What about us?" Jack asked. "Can anyone trace *our* signal?"

Kilroy2.0 sighed and ran his fingers through his greasy hair.

"Newbie," he said, exasperated. "*That* was the first thing I activated when I sat here at the workstation hours ago. Been stealing
7th Son bandwidth from the beginning. No one knows we're doing this. Not even 7th Son. The 7th Son computers monitoring us
are convinced I'm still googling every newspaper obituary published in the past year. But I've been in the slipstream of the facility's subnetwork, mooching off its *muy muy* high-speed satellite
uplink the whole time."

"What does that mean?" Thomas asked.

"It means Kilroy is transmitting to his flock from outer space,"
Jack said.

Kilroy2.0 nodded furiously. As he typed his next message, he
whispered, "Just like God."

They watched Kilroy2.0's message *rak-a-tak* to life on the
monitor.

> *I am in the hands of the Adversary. I am well, but have no time for*
explanations. Need information located on the CDC intranet. Need your
help to access it. Unleash your worms. Your swarmers. Your warez, hacks,
kraks, all the so-called "malware" the Adversary despises. Post no graffiti,
take no credit. Tonight you rise from the shadows for your prophet.

> *One goal. Deluge the network. Pummel the CDC servers. Let the*
lawkeepers gaze at your distraction. Let them wring their hands. Let
them squirm. Let them talk. Let them scheme. Be the diversion I need.

> *You are many, but act as one. For two hours, the Network will be*
yours. Be the ghosts in their machines. Be the poltergeists in their attics,
the chaos they fear above all. And then disappear. I will do the rest.

> *This, I ask of you. Comply?*

Kilroy2.0 executed a key combination on his keyboard, and
the message was zipped to the chat programs. A second passed.

Jay gasped. At least seventy new message windows flashed on
the screen at the same time. The chimes and BlackHat's skull
laughter sang through the computers' speakers.

"Is this really happening?" Thomas whispered.

Jack nodded at the screens. "There's your answer."

Oh, yes. Message received. Replies posted.

They all said the same thing:

I comply

I comply

I comply

TWENTY

A. U. Rookman didn't give a piss about a great many things. Being old and rich—and let's face it, America, being *A. U. Rookman*—had its privileges. One of the great many things A. U. Rookman didn't give a piss about, for instance, was "bad" cholesterol. The bacon and egg and medium-rare-steak-extra-gravy-on-the-mashed-potatoes cholesterol. These days, doctors were waving their hands in the air about the stuff like a gaggle of Holy Rollers at a tent revival, wailing on about how you should avoid the "bad" cholesterol and eat more foods with the "good" cholesterol. A. U. Rookman didn't give a piss. The doctors were telling him to eat more fish, and Rookman didn't like fish ('cause it tasted like goddamn *fish*) so he didn't. No, sir. Give A. U. Rookman a slab of Texas longhorn any day—and don't jew him on the A.1., fuck you very much.

Bad cholesterol. This, coming from the same bunch of bookworms who'd told A. U. Rookman in the late eighties to avoid eating foods high in cholesterol, period. There was no "good" cholesterol back then, no yin to the cholesterol yang, if you wanted to get philosophical about it. Hell, when Rookman was a boy, you piled on the eggs and bacon and scarfed it down with a shit-eating grin.

And that's why Rookman still drank two raw eggs for breakfast. (He didn't give a piss about salmonella, either.) Every morning, one of the help would bring him a crystal goblet filled with the syrupy stuff, both yolks bobbing inside like great big eyes, like the snotty globs in a lava lamp. He'd scoop the goblet from the platter, raise it to the sky as if making a toast, and slurp it down in one breathless gulp. During the ever-increasing house calls in the past five years, the doctors had discovered this ritual and had given him six kinds of grief about it. He would wave the words away. For those who knew him, this was A. U. Rookman's way of saving his breath to say the words *I don't give a piss.* And in these wretched golden years, goddamnit, saving breath had become a necessity. The cancer. The old-timer's.

Rookman was turning eighty next year. He rarely looked in the mirror anymore; he hated the wraith's face that stared back. He was, according to his own harsh self-summation, a wheezing mess of a man who'd spent too much of his life spending his fortune in hazes of cigarette smoke, inebriation, and misplayed poker hands. The booze and the smokes (and the drugs for a while, we can't forget the times we hit the slopes) were his lifelong companion, the common-law wife that'd stuck by him when the times were good and bad. They'd been particularly loyal when times were bad. Now he was reaping the whirlwind, and all that bullshit about "good" cholesterol and "bad" cholesterol and healthy living didn't amount to a hill of ass-tootin' beans, if it ever had.

Not that Rookman regretted it. A. U. Rookman hadn't become *A. U. Rookman* by entertaining navel-gazing idiocies such as regret. He'd been through four divorces and had endured the headline-grabbing antics of his shitbird son Lionel, but he never

felt regret. Regret was a gutless thing, a thing that implied fallibil-
ity. And A. U. Rookman never made mistakes. Ever.

Still, as he'd felt his body wind down like a music box over
these past seven years, he *had* felt another breed of gutless emotion slip into his mind. Fear. It was going to end, it was all going to
end much sooner than later, like the unnerving off-key plinks and
plunks of that music box, an impending dirge, a death rattle,
something slowly fading from the earth . . . then gone. It was
bad—goddamned bad—and it was going to end. And he was
afraid. *Afeard,* as his daddy used to say.

Which was why he was sitting at his bedroom desk (this morning's empty goblet still resting on its edge like a trophy), staring
into this computer screen that he would have felt great satisfaction throwing through his bedroom window if he had the strength
to lift it . . . not that it would shatter the bulletproof glass. The
world of ledgers and ticker tape and typewriters had gone the way
of the dodo. A. U. Rookman couldn't keep up anymore.

But he could. He *would,* once this little under-the-table deal
was seen through. Rookman had made many of his billions in
under-the-table deals—the closed-door meetings, the surveillance
sweeps, the payoffs, the line to the White House, and, yes, the
more-than-occasional use of discreet folks who worked outside
the law. Many of those deals had taken years to finally bloom into
windfalls. But none were like this. And things were close to bloom-
ing now. Very close indeed.

He would experience a rebirth, and then he'd make a killing.

The little clock icon at the top of the computer screen chimed
4:30 p.m. That was Rookman's cue to start the videoconference.
He steered the computer mouse toward the appropriate screen
icon and launched the application. The spasms in his chest began—
not now, goddamnit, I don't give a piss about you, you fucking cocksuckers,

not now—then the rattling cough started, erupting from his throat like cannon fire. One of his hands instinctively reached for a fresh handkerchief in the small pouch on his wheelchair; the other hand clutched the oxygen mask in his lap. His body quaked as the coughs increased. He tried to keep his eyes on the screen (the video window was winking to life now), but couldn't. They snapped shut as he whooped and retched.

Breathe, you old bastard, breathe breathebreathe . . .

Finally, he spat a wad of bloody phlegm into the handkerchief and placed the mask over his mouth and nose. The canned air rushed into his lungs, and things were better. For now.

Rookman opened his eyes, wiping away the tears as he did so. He gazed at the screen.

John Alpha stared back at him. The youngster was smiling.

Then: part one.

A rumor had circulated through the press back in '94 that when a president was elected, he had to make a special phone call within three days of his acceptance speech. That call would, the rumors claimed, be to one A. U. Rookman, founder of Rookman Oil Inc. *George*, a now-defunct political magazine, had quoted an anonymous source as saying, "When a man's crazy enough to run for president, he's crazy enough to think he's the most powerful man on the planet. Once in office, he learns very quickly that he is not. That's why every president since Kennedy rings up the old man. Just to say hello, get the formal blessing. It's like the senior-class president asking the high school principal if he can pretend to be leader for a while."

The rumor wasn't true, of course. President-elects had two days to make the call, not three.

The leaders of the Free World were all meek as lambs when speaking with A. U. Rookman. Insiders called this phenomenon

Rookman's Rules. For many things, they were the only rules in town. If you knew oil and politics, you knew A. U. Rookman was the Dangerous Man, the Big Planner, the slippery Texan with an ace stashed up his sleeve, the wildcatter with whom you should never fuck.

By 1960, Rookman had made it clear that he wasn't a card-carrying member of the "big oil" industry. He *was* the big oil industry. His influence on politics could be likened to plate tectonics: patient and nearly silent, but impossible to ignore. His political strings were long and tight. For example: After the OPEC embargo of '73, Rookman had concocted an idea to ensure that he'd never again be squeezed by the towelheads. He applied political pressure from the shadows, the result being the Energy Policy and Conversation Act, which Gerald Ford made law in 1975. Under this law, the federal government could purchase and store up to 1 billion barrels of crude oil, none of which could be used unless there was another national fuel crisis. While the first 412,000 barrels purchased for this new cache were Saudi crude, Rookman Oil Inc. had provided the lion's share of the reserves since—and made tidy and quiet profits decade after decade in its name.

In the late 1970s, A. U. Rookman convinced Detroit's Big Three to play along with his quiet political push to create an apparently pro-consumer, pro-environment plan that would apply strict miles-per-gallon standards on passenger vehicles to increase fuel economy. But the scheme had a delicious loophole: sport utility vehicles could be classified in the same category as light trucks, which had much lower MPG standards. The punch line? After a decade or so in which the Big Three would focus on making more inexpensive, fuel-efficient cars (and barely break even), they would start pushing the sport-utes as the Next Big Thing. Larger, and allegedly more dependable in inclement weather, the SUVs would become the "new station wagon." By building family-oriented

SUVs on truck chassis, auto manufacturers could sidestep pesky fuel-economy standards and particularly stringent passenger-car bumper and crash regulations.

The auto manufacturers made a slaying with the much more profitable SUVs, of course. Rookman also laughed all the way to the bank. Not only had gasoline consumption increased, but one of Rookman Oil's many subsidiaries, ARX Automotive, made a windfall on the manufacturing of after-market SUV bumpers, hoses, body paints, and more. All fabricated from petrochemicals, that ever-profitable by-product of oil refinement.

In the early 1990s, Rookman had also pioneered the price-control tactic that most big oil companies now employ. Touted as a cost-saving measure for his company (and therefore consumers), Rookman made it standing policy for his facilities to produce gasoline at 90 percent of their capacities—instead of the usual 60 to 70 percent—and funnel it into the market right away. Since all efforts were going into production and distribution, Rookman Oil had only a few days' reserves at any time. This convenient lack of "rainy day" reserves drove up the price of gas. It also made the market more volatile and vulnerable to production problems, geopolitical fluctuations, and the like. This ensured higher prices. As Rookman was fond of saying to his few confidants: if a mullah in Iran flapped his gums in protest of the West, prices at the pumps in Middle America could soar. Which was the whole fucking point.

Rookman Oil Inc. was also the first oil company to employ batteries of sociologists, psychologists, and financial theorists to raise profits. With their data, Rookman quickly learned that by *lowering* production capacities in some states and hopscotching oil supplies from one U.S. region to another, he could spike prices in different parts of the country and appear blameless. By studying people's traveling habits, such as the plummet of travel after the September 11, 2001, attacks, Rookman Oil could "shrink" its oil supply, justified by the lowered overall demand, raise prices, and continue to gouge the American consumer.

Like all successful empires, Rookman's corporation extended overseas. Rookman Oil wells, offshore drilling platforms, and refineries operated in more than a dozen countries. When A. U. Rookman planned an oil pipeline through Afghanistan and its neighbors in the early 1990s, he urged the Clinton administration to open talks with the Taliban-controlled Afghani government. Those talks failed, and Rookman soon knew why: Clinton and his boys were pussies. In January 2001, Rookman convinced the Bush administration to relaunch the talks. The deal was too simple and sweet for the Taliban to ignore: if you turn over Osama bin Laden and make nice-nice with the Northern Alliance (the native guerrilla force that was taking over the northern part of the country), Rookman Oil would build the pipeline . . . and bestow the Taliban with a generous cut of the billions in annual profits. The Taliban were interested, and scheduled a meeting with American officials and Northern Alliance representatives in July of that year.

The Taliban delegation didn't show. Word quickly spread that the negotiations had dissolved because someone in the American delegation had sent a special message to the Taliban leadership: "Either accept our offer, granting you mountains of riches, or we bury you under a mountain of bombs." When the president asked Rookman if he had sent the message, the oil baron had simply shrugged. Of *course* Rookman had sent it. He wanted the Taliban to go apeshit, to create serious anti-American sentiment for the CIA to record and report . . . which could then empower the United States to take a preemptive strike against the hostile government. The administration could then install a U.S.-friendly and therefore Rookman-friendly leadership base—and pay less for the pipeline privileges.

The Taliban did go apeshit. The terrorists the Taliban were protecting flew two jets into the World Trade Center. Another into the
Pentagon. Yet another almost made its way to the White House.
Even Rookman hadn't expected that. But the U.S. military did indeed bomb Afghanistan shortly afterward, and the Taliban were
replaced with leaders who saw the infinite wisdom of a $3.5 bil-
lion Rookman Oil Inc. pipeline cutting through their land.

Rookman got his way, after all.

Naturally, Rookman also had a hand in the 2003 invasion of
Iraq. Two years previously—a few months before the Taliban talks
fell through, in fact—Rookman helped pen the *Energy Policy in the
New Century* report, which was presented to the freshly inaugu-
rated president. The document basically stated that Iraq was the
problem child of the Middle East, but it could also be the number
two oil-producing country in the world. Iraqi production was being logjammed by United Nations export sanctions. If sanctions
were lifted, the oil would flow freely. But lifting the sanctions
would allow then-leader Saddam Hussein a symbolic victory
against the West. The only way to uncork the bottleneck and save
face, the report stated, would be to take out the "destabilizing element" in the equation—Hussein. Military intervention was politely suggested. American companies could "rebuild" the country
after an invasion, the report said.

Thanks to the Rookman-spawned attacks on September 11,
the oil tycoon got his wish. After the U.S. military invaded Afghanistan, it swarmed and stormed Iraq, ousting Hussein. A U.S.-
friendly government began to run the show afterward. Hundreds
of "rebuilding" contracts were awarded, including for the construction of new oil-production facilities and oversight of older
Iraqi state-run facilities. Most of those contracts fell into the laps
of Rookman Oil Inc. and its subsidiaries . . . as Rookman had
planned all along.

Yes, indeed. Sometimes it pays to have a direct phone line to the White House.

A. U. Rookman was the man who wore blue jeans and an *I SHOT J.R.* T-shirt to President Reagan's inaugural ball. A. U. Rookman was the man who quietly convinced Washington to make Alaska's Arctic National Wildlife Refuge—ANWR—a political buzzword. A. U. Rookman was the man who founded Castle Chemicals, the number one petrochemical supply firm on the planet. He was credited with legitimizing the synthetic-fiber industry; almost every American has a shirt, dress, or suit made from Auxillium, one of the many fibers Castle Chemicals has created over the past forty years. He was also the man who slyly suggested SUVs should have MILES OF FUEL REMAINING displays mounted in their dashboard so drivers, if only subconsciously, were always thinking one thing when they piled their rug rats into the car: gas, gas, gas.

Of course, folks living in the heartland never saw that side of Rookman. Neither did the press. The media loved Rookman's flamboyance, his lavish philanthropy, his opulent weddings and destructive divorces. Reporters salivated over the bumblings and arrests of his drug-addled son. The Rookman name made good ink.

The press covered his health problems with equal relish.

Which is how a young man who called himself John Alpha came to contact A. U. Rookman with a very special business proposal.

Then: part two.

When Rookman finally went public with "havin' the cancer" and the early signs of Alzheimer's disease in 2001, it was only after the rumors of his ailing health had hopscotched from the tabloids to *The New York Times*. He didn't like the way the media were using adjectives such as *mysterious* and *frail* and—perhaps the most blasphemous of all—*diminished*. As in, *In recent months, Rookman's vitality has appeared diminished.*

That line had sent him over the edge. "They're making like I'm some faggot dyin' from the butt flu," he had screamed that day, to one of the nameless women who fetched his coffee. He would later have a vague memory of tearing up the newspaper and hurling the empty coffee mug at her. "Goddamn cancer. Goddamned oldtimer's! You want to hear what I say, toots? When in doubt, whip it out . . . and piss all over them."

He called a press conference on his front lawn that afternoon and came out of the cancer and Alzheimer's closet. Yes, he'd been diagnosed. Yes, he was considering experimental treatment. Yes, he'd consider chemo—if he had to, if he absolutely had to. Rookman used his "raising Cain" voice, full of bluster and hellfire. The reporters laughed when they were supposed to (goddamn vultures), the photographers snapped pictures when they were supposed to (they're big on hand gestures), and everyone left with their quote-hungry bellies filled. All of the Texas dailies ran the story front page, above the fold.

The nationals played it below the fold, but Rookman made 1A on every pissing one of them. *Dance for me, my little monkeys, dance.*

But only after the pack of scribblers and shooters had left his lawn had Rookman truly felt afraid. *Afeard.* That was the night he realized it was true, it was all true, no sense hiding it anymore, he had the cancer, had the oldtimer's, it was all going to end. If the rogue cells inside him didn't do it, the chemo would. And if it wasn't the chemo, it'd be the loss of his mind. And what then? What would happen to his legacy? His company? Everything he had built would collapse and burn, a funeral pyre to dishonor the recently departed.

Rookman cried that night, the first time in sixty-three years.

Helluva ride, A.U. But your time to hang up the spurs is a'comin'. You're the Titanic, ever-heading nearer my God to thee.

A few years later, his office received a FedEx addressed from one of Rookman Oil's VPs based in California. "URGENT & PER-SONAL," read the envelope inside. It was forwarded to Rookman with great speed and efficiency—no doors hit any asses on the way in or out that day—and Rookman had opened it with a cynical scowl.

The letter was not from Boyles, as the FedEx envelope had said. In fact, it was not signed at all. But there was a message, one that both infuriated and (given the past years' plague of nightmares) intrigued him.

> Mr. Rookman,
>
> You are a man of your word. So am I. You are a man of few words. As am I. I can help you, sir. I can cure your cancer and your Alzheimer's. Completely.
>
> I will not insult you by saying this solution will come quickly or cheaply. But it will come; you will experience a re-birth, and live longer than you have ever dreamed possible. You have my word.
>
> If you wish to discuss a partnership, please contact me at the Four Seasons, Beverly Hills. Ask for John M. Smith.

Rookman had nearly torn the letter to shreds. But something stopped him. Fate, perhaps. Or fear. Or hope.

He phoned the hotel that night. He spoke to John Alpha for less than a minute. Rookman met the kid the next day, listened to his proposal, downed a triple Scotch, and shook on it.

When you're the fourth-richest man in the world, you can spare a few billion dollars in the name of immortality. Not to mention a few million souls, including your own.

Now.

"A.U.," Alpha said cheerily from the computer screen. "You look well."

"Fuck you." Rookman squeezed the bloody handkerchief until he felt his fingernails dig into his palm. *Young people. Don't give a piss about their elders.* For a moment, Rookman wondered what he looked and sounded like to the youngster on the other end. A ghoul's face, probably. A Texas accent slurred behind a translucent blue death mask. *I hate talking to him. He's young, dumb, and full of cum. Thinks he's indestructible.*

"Such language." Alpha winked. "Now tell me, A.U.: what would the ever-nubile wife number five do if she heard such filth coming from that mouth of yours?"

"She does whatever the hell I tell her to," Rookman snarled. "None of your goddamned business anyway. Piss on you. I reckon you've forgotten just *who* you're talking to."

"I've forgotten no such thing. You're my Abel Magwitch."

"What?"

"My mysterious benefactor," John Alpha said. "My sugar daddy." The youngster smiled his condescending smile.

Thinks he knows everything. Well, fuck you.

"That's right. Your sugar daddy." The oxygen mask whistled gently as Rookman spoke. "Glad you said that. Reminds me of something *my* daddy once told me: never bite the hand, boy. You understand me? Never. I'm the *-er.* You're the *-ee.* Our relationship don't get much simpler than that."

Alpha cocked his head to one side, like a wife who knows his beloved is lying. "Our relationship is a little more complex than that, A.U. We're *collaborators.* Our goals are different, certainly, but we both come out winners. I need you, and you . . . well, just look at you. You most definitely need me. Perhaps an analogy your crass Texan tongue can appreciate is in order. You and I, we have a little circle jerk going here. If we both keep stroking, we'll both cross the finish line with grins on our faces. Everybody wins, A. U. You, most of all."

Rookman stared at the screen. This conversation was as familiar as the doctors' orders to lay off the bad foods. He and Alpha had danced this dance too many times over the recent years: the kid's smart mouth would send Rookman up on his high horse, then the tug-of-war over who called the shots would begin. The kid was right, of course. They both had each other by the balls . . . but Rookman would walk away from this deal with a smile on his new face, billions richer. The kid was right, all right. But he didn't have to be so goddamned *smug* about it. It was exhausting.

Rookman sighed as he thought this; the mask literally squeaked from the pressure change. "So what's your point, young man?" His voice sounded hollow, like a line of stage dialogue uttered for the umpteenth time.

"Just trying to clarify the -er/-ee dynamic," Alpha said. "Just encouraging you to think about where you want to be and who can get you there. You want this to come to pass? You want Rookman Oil to become the plaything of that freak-show board of directors when you go? You want to actually stick your willy into that *Penthouse* Pet wife of yours? I'm the one who can deliver you, A.U. I'm your knight in shining armor. That's something *you* should never forget."

Stalemate. They stared at each other for almost a minute, saying nothing. A side of Rookman enjoyed these insipid power struggles; Alpha was the only man he'd ever met that didn't back down, didn't compromise, didn't flinch when Rookman used his Texan foghorn bellow to drive home a point. Rookman appraised the slender face on the screen, its cool blue eyes, thin lips, slicked-back blonde-brown hair. The man's goatee was meticulously trimmed.

Rookman likened Alpha to a Doberman—sleek and dangerous. The ambition coursing through the kid's veins transcended anything even Rookman had dreamed of in his youth. Rookman admired it and was frightened by it.

Are you really going to tack your future onto the coattails of this lunatic?

He recalled the wraith's face staring back in the mirror, the vision of that music box winding down: *plink . . . plink . . . plunk . . .*

"Bed's made," he whispered.

The pixelated vision of Alpha raised his eyebrows. "Beg pardon?"

"I said I'm bored," Rookman snarled, straightening in his wheelchair. "Piss on it. Are we here to talk business or to see whose dick's bigger?"

"Everyone knows you've got a Louisville Slugger swinging between those legs. No contest there."

"That's more like it." Rookman felt a smile crinkle against his oxygen mask. Goddamn kid. "So. What's my horoscope?"

"I see a beautiful stranger coming to your home tomorrow, with knockers out to here." The video feed became blurry as the webcam on the kid's end tried to focus on Alpha's hands—which now appeared to hold two invisible watermelons.

Rookman cackled, his chest rattling like a jalopy.

Alpha's smile vanished. "Everything's square on your end, I trust."

"Bet your ass it is. The will's been changed. The board, even now, can't fart unless I say so. And I expect you to bring you-know-who for a little meeting tomorrow, just as planned."

Alpha nodded, then his face darkened. "Nothing can go wrong, A.U. Understand? *Nothing.* Your contact will arrive whenever she can and will take care of everything. It's not going to hurt. The rest is up to you and the unwitting—and undoubtedly unwilling—

participation of your host-to-be. This is it, old man. Tomorrow is your day. Fuck it up, and *you're* fucked. Our little scheme will be all for naught. Dig?"

Rookman nodded impatiently. He tore off the oxygen mask for emphasis. "Yes, yes. I'm not a child, you pissface."

"That much is clear."

Rookman leaned toward the computer screen. He licked his lips. "And what about our other little scheme up north? The clincher that makes you rich and me even richer?"

"Already under way."

Rookman grinned; his face was like that of a leering corpse.

Alpha smiled on the screen. "We've talked business. Now let's talk pleasure. What are your plans for tonight?"

"I've made plans with Chenille. Paint the town, live it up while there's still living to be done. I'll have ye olde Houston paparazzi snap a few with that buxom bitch by my side. Great fodder for the fallout."

"Splendid word choice," Alpha said. "Sounds delicious."

"Victory always is."

"Make a splash, A.U. Tomorrow night, you'll be a new man. And you'll soon have a new place to plant your company flag."

"Christ on a crutch. That's terrific. Just terrific."

John Alpha agreed. It was terrific. It was indeed.

TWENTY-ONE

T he *Bucky Lastard* landed at Edwards Air Force Base at 7:00 p.m. local time. Pilot Les Orchard's V-22-X Osprey had logged a six-hour flight, his personal best. Not that anyone would ever know about it. Off the books, you know. As would be the flight back. Oh, yes, they were round-tripping it. The orders from General Hill were clear: *Drop them off. Refuel. Bring them back.* Orchard and Schubert would need a little pill of the pick-me-up variety for the return jaunt.

Fatigue-management capsules. Sheeeit. The air force could call it whatever they wanted, but it was speed, plain and simple.

As Orchard and his copilot flipped rows of switches to power down the plane, Orchard watched his living cargo walk from the craft, out onto the tarmac. Fifteen men—most of them just kids from the looks of it. Several had broken into pairs, carrying the crates they'd brought with them. Orchard looked past them, toward the horizon. Two Black Hawk helicopters were waiting, their rotors spinning like impatient whirligigs, forcing the approaching men to lean into the gale as they walked closer.

"It's their world; we're just livin' in it," Orchard muttered, his hands still flipping console switches and toggles. "Chauffeurs is

all we are. A buncha Morgan Freemans driving our Miss Dai-
sys."

He glanced over to see if Schubert had caught the joke. Schubert was busy flipping his own switches and speaking to Control
via his helmet comm. Oh, well.

Orchard turned back to the windscreen. He watched the group
draw closer to the choppers and made a mental note to watch for
those three—the three who were walking ahead of the bunch—on
the return flight. Something was hinky about them. Their body
types were different—one of them was a jarhead for sure; the
other two had the soft bodies of civvies. But all three had the
same gait, the same posture, the same body language.

Separated at birth, Orchard thought, and a chill shot down his
spine. He watched the three men climb into one of the Black
Hawks and eyed them carefully as they helped the others pull the
crates on board. Huh. The three were all left-handed, to boot.

The rest of the troops climbed into the other chopper.

Weird. Weird.

John took the advice of the quiet voice in his head. He shut the
hell up and hung on. Shutting the hell up and hanging on was
fairly easy, he'd learned, ever since reality took a detour about two
days back. So sure, what the hell, let's disembark from the Plane
Ride from Hell (Tums, anyone?), walk across an airstrip (that's the
Mojave Desert to your right and we're moving, we're moving),
climb into a chopper, and take another magic-carpet ride. He'd
never flown in a helicopter before. It was just another of the week-
end's ongoing series of surreal moments, and it wouldn't be the
last . . . *so, John, just do what the bumper sticker says: Get in, shut up,
and hang on.*

He could imagine the L.A. skyline glimmering in the far south;
pinprick skyscraper lights pressing through the smog. He couldn't

see it, of course; the lush San Gabriel Mountains were blocking the view.

Los Angeles was at least another 70 miles away. Somewhere out there was Folie à Deux, and his mother and—*Mr. Mojo risin'* . . . *Mr. Mojo risin'*—John Alpha.

John watched Michael secure the large equipment crates in the Black Hawk's cargo hold. Despite his size, Michael had a catlike elegance to his stride. The marine brought a small suitcase with him into the passenger compartment and sat down on the bench facing Dr. Mike and John. Michael snaked his arms through the safety harness and clicked it home. The small suitcase—about the size of two telephone books—was at his side.

As Michael unlatched the case, the turbines above them began to increase in pitch. It was hard to think now, like putting your head against a washing machine on spin cycle. The marine didn't seem to notice.

Michael opened the container and began to speak, unperturbed by the roaring engines above them. ". . . ee airing eees or eh ishin . . ."

"What?" John screamed.

Michael looked over to Dr. Mike, who appeared equally puzzled. Michael nodded and motioned them to lean inward, closer to each other.

"I said we'll be wearing these during the mission," the marine cried, pointing down at the briefcase's contents: gadgets encased in custom-cut black foam. John nodded emphatically. Dr. Mike nodded, too, his head bobbing like a jack-in-the-box.

"We're not going to have much time for prepping when we land," Michael hollered. "What time we do have will be spent gearing up." He stopped, his eyes looking for confirmation. The clones nodded again. The engines kicked up a notch. John looked at the ceiling apprehensively, but Michael waved his hand at the musician and made an okay sign. John forced a smile.

"This is a rush job, no doubt about it," Michael said. "Now is the best time to teach you about these—"

The engines exploded into a symphonic drone, and the chopper jerked upward. John groaned as what felt like a cement block fell into the pit of his gut. Nearby, Dr. Mike instinctively clutched at the harness crossing his chest. Michael frowned and held up an index finger—*I'll finish in a minute, gotta wait for the kids to quiet down.* The helicopter pushed upward, teetering gently to the left and the right, its passengers rocking in place like Weebles wobbles. Through one of the small window ports, John could see the tarmac listing to and fro, and then downward, past the porthole. The roofs of the base's hangers passed next, then it was all dusty sky and horizon, merging together like watercolors.

The cement block stopped digging at John's gut. But he couldn't shake the sensation that he was *floating* more than *flying,* as if the chopper were a toy suspended by a giant fishing line. It wasn't a pleasant feeling.

He glanced from the porthole to the criminal profiler. Dr. Mike looked as if he were coming back from Vomitville, too. Michael, the mission-jaded marine, grinned at them.

"First time?" he cried.

John and Dr. Mike nodded.

Michael laughed. "Thought so. Don't worry. It gets easier, trust me."

Michael leaned forward again, and the other two understood the cue. Michael picked up the container and pulled out one of the gadgets, a dark gray plastic cylinder, about the size of a toilet-paper tube. He passed it to the clones. Its surface was rubberized; plastic Velcro notches covered one side. John cocked the front end of the cylinder and spotted the characteristic purplish blue glimmer of a camera lens inside. The other end of the cylinder sported a nipple-shaped rubber button and a dime-size hole.

"It's a thermal imager," Michael called over the din. "Heat-sensitive recording device. Has a couple of settings. See this?" He pointed to the plastic Velcro strap. The clones nodded. "Connects to the side of the Kevlar—your helmet. See this?" He pointed to the hole on the end of the camera. "Cable plugs into the screen you'll wear on your forearm. Hold on."

He reached into the case and presented a thin cable and an off-the-shelf digital pocket organizer. The PDA was covered in a similar rubberized case, but the shape and screen size screamed Circuit City. Adjustable straps dangled from its sides. Michael plugged one end of the cable into the PDA, the other into the back of the thermal imager. The PDA's LCD screen winked to life.

Michael pointed the camera at Dr. Mike. They watched as the image on the PDA transformed into a human-shaped blob; its chest and head were consumed in a fiery red corona; arms and legs throbbed orange and yellow. Dr. Mike raised his right arm. The thermal ghost raised its right arm. Amazed, the profiler waved his hand back and forth. The ghost waved with him, the colors slurring together on the LCD screen.

"Bitchin'," Dr. Mike said.

Michael nodded. "Here's another setting." He pressed the button on the imager and pointed the device toward the cargo hold behind him. The LCD screen was now dominated by gray and black—with shimmering violet lines crisscrossing over the dark colors. The lines looked like a road map, complete with glowing superhighways and throbbing culs-de-sac.

"Electrical system," the marine explained. "This picks up heat from the current in the wires. No electricity, no purple lines. The higher the current, the brighter the lines. Understand?"

John and Dr. Mike nodded again. Michael pressed the button and the screen now glowed in hues of bright green. He pointed the imager at various spots in the dim passenger cabin. They perfectly saw the dark corners of the compartment, all flickering in that same eerie green.

"Good ole night vision," Michael said. "This setting's sensitive to light. No light, good. Lots of light, bad. I press this button again and the imager switches off."

He did, and the PDA's screen blinked to black.

"Like I said, imager goes on your helmet," Michael continued. The helicopter suddenly lurched to the left. John shrieked; the marine didn't blink. "You slip the cable into your BDU shirt, down the shirtsleeve, comes out at the cuff. The screen goes on your forearm like this." In three taut moves, Michael strapped the PDA to his inner forearm, just above the wrist. "This design was meant to be used while holding a rifle or a pistol; you can easily get an eyeful without compromising your field of vision. Understand?"

They nodded.

The marine smiled, reached into the container, and pulled out another device. It was a black plastic earpiece with a microphone attached at its end; something very much like a wireless cellphone headset.

"Comm gear," Michael said. "We'll all be wearing these, and they'll all be locked onto the same channel. What you say, we all hear." He flipped a quick smirk in Dr. Mike's direction. "When we get into this thing, it ain't gonna be time to chitchat. I'll do most of the talking, okay?"

John watched the blood rush to Dr. Mike's face and suppressed a grin. Dr. Mike nodded. Michael placed the gear back in the box and closed it.

"I've talked to the rest of the group about this next part, they're in on it, so listen up," Michael said. "You two are civilians, but tonight, things'll be different. You're going to wear the same camo, Kevlar, and body armor we wear. You are going to have a commlink, a sidearm, explosives. Tonight, you're one of us."

"Do I have to carry a gun?" John shouted. "Never used one before. I don't know if—"

"Nope."

"What about the, uh, explosives?"

"Not if you don't want to," Michael said. "It's your life, hoss. Your choice. But both of you, make no mistake: you advance when I say, you hold back when I say. This is law. That voice you'll hear in your commlink might as well be the voice of God.

"You're not used to this—it's not a part of your life, and I understand that—but *you* had better understand where *I'm* coming from. How you come out of that nightclub . . . be it on your feet or in a body bag . . . depends on your un-fucking-compromising ability to *do as you're told*. Do you understand?"

For a second, just a second, the droning engines were the only noise in the cabin. And then:

"Yes, sir. We understand."

Dr. Mike watched his adopted hometown slip by in the Black Hawk's windows as they flew south. The sun sang its last through the right porthole, the desert lay sullen and dim through the left. Terrain quickly slipped from sand and scrub to the hard chaparral of the San Gabriel; oaks and pines emerged next. The two helicopters crossed the mountains and dipped over into the valley. Dry rocks and angry-looking trees glared from below.

Then they were screaming past the mansions on the hills, over Pasadena, past the studios in Burbank—all familiar sights for the criminal profiler—then the HOLLYWOOD sign blazing white atop Mt. Lee. Then the chopper abruptly banked east, toward downtown. Twilight had come and the freeways were already filled with the familiar molasses traffic, even on a Sunday. The US Bank Tower loomed in the distance, the lights around its circular roof glowing like a crown. The nearby Westin Bonaventure's mirrored surface glittered, an enormous stack of quarters.

The choppers cruised above the streets, the hotels, over Los Angeles City College, toward West Hollywood. It was strange seeing the city this way, Dr. Mike realized—zipping past skyscrapers, whirring above all those unsuspecting people. L.A. was filled with bad things, bad places; it didn't take long to see them when you lived in the city. You heard the screeching tires, the breaking glass, the screams of the desperate . . . and you learned to tune it out. You learned to live with the news choppers ripping through the night, the police chases on the tube, the red-white-red-white-red-white strobes of ambulance lights on street corners. Somehow you learned to ignore the elephant in the room.

West Hollywood, now. Screaming over Santa Monica Boulevard. The two choppers would be landing soon. Folie à Deux was on the southeast corner of Sunset Boulevard and Hammond Street, the heart of chic clubland, and a few miles north of their landing coordinates.

The Black Hawk banked sharply to the right, then the left, resurrecting the peptic tantrum in Dr. Mike's guts. He looked out one of the portals. They were here. The chopper was hovering over the landing coordinates. The other Black Hawk had already landed, dropped off its cargo, and was soaring off the pad, into the west. Dr. Mike watched it go, then turned his attention back to the ground. He saw the 7th Son soldiers waiting by the helipad's perimeter. Closer to the helipad's center, several men in fluttering white jackets were trying to wave away their chopper. The cinder block in Dr. Mike's belly danced as the craft began its descent.

The helipad's lights seared through the windows. Silhouettes of the furious ground crew cast shadow puppets inside the cabin.

Dr. Mike turned to Michael. The marine was already up, safety harness long gone, stepping his way to the doorhatch. He squinted through the porthole.

This is it, Dr. Mike thought. *This is* it.

Michael turned his face back to them. His mouth was turned upward in an impish grin. "Welcome to the Cedars-Sinai Medical Center." The marine threw open the door. "Do mind your step."

The marine spotted the two blameless white cargo vans at the exact GPS coordinates General Hill had assigned: in the northwest corner of Cedars-Sinai's P9 parking lot, near North San Vicente Boulevard. So far, this was going better than he'd expected. Michael feared Hill might have lost his combat talons in that decade and a half behind a 7th Son desk. Not so. The general had been sharp and contributed heavily to the strategy of this invasion/rescue timetable. And Code Phantom's power was coming in handy for resources such as these.

The lot was nearly a quarter mile from the helipad. The run was brisk. John was the last member of the team to reach the two vans; he was a sweating mess.

Forgivable. Being a civvy injected into a combat mission does that to a person.

Michael'd have to watch John during this trip. The longhair was sensible (to a point) when he mentioned he didn't want a gun or grenade for this mission. With no training, he might be a friendly-fire liability were he armed. But did the man have the steel deep inside for what was to come? Michael didn't know.

The marine clapped John on the shoulder, then pushed him past the white vans. John eyed the vehicles as he panted, then looked ahead. A pair of vans were up there (these were black with tinted windshields). Members of the 7th Son team were climbing inside them. He looked back at the closer white vans. The engines were running. The exhaust stung his nostrils as he fought to steady his breathing.

"Why . . . aren't we going . . . in those two?" he gasped.

Michael nodded at the white vans. "These guys go ahead of us. Inside are the folks who brought us the vehicles."

"Who are they?"

"Dunno. Doesn't matter. They're probably under Code Phantom orders. Hill set up the jet, the choppers, and the vans. These guys here are gonna take the heat off of us. Remember those doctors on the helipad who were trying to wave us off? They've gotta be on the phone with the cops right now. The cops are going to ask them what vehicles we dashed to. And the doctors are going to say 'two white vans.' "

"These guys are a diversion," John said. He seemed to understand. Good.

"Red herrings all the way, hoss," Michael agreed. They walked faster toward the two black 7th Son vans. "They'll get the attention of John Law and get them off our tail. It shouldn't be too hard, either."

"Why?" The 7th Son vans were closer now. Behind them, the two mystery vans roared out of the lot, tires squealing.

"Because in about a mile, they're gonna scream right by the West Hollywood Sheriff's Department. If the plan fires on all cylinders, the cops'll spot them and take chase. Once they get the attention of the Five-O, our nameless friends head east, away from West Hollywood and Folie à Deux.

"Meanwhile, we head north on San Vicente about twelve, fifteen minutes later. We'll turn off when we can and use the side streets to get to the club. Cause, effect. Problem, solution."

"Pretty clever," John said. It was becoming easier for him to breathe now.

"We'll see. Let's hurry."

By the time they'd climbed into the nearly full van (Michael in the front passenger seat, John and Dr. Mike on one of the benches in the back with the rest of the group), the police scanner beneath the dashboard was alive with reports of two white vans heading out of the Cedars-Sinai lot. Dispatch gave the order for pursuit.

"Bingo," Michael said. "We're in business."

"They'll get caught," Dr. Mike said. The air here reeked of sweat and adrenaline. "What do they do when they get caught?"

"Not our problem," said one of soldiers near him. That was Lockwood, Michael noted.

Michael nodded his agreement and placed one of the black commlinks into his ear. He turned to the driver, a fellow named Fleming. "Let's go."

Fleming dropped the gearshift into drive, and they went. So did the second van. The black duo slowly cruised through the lot and turned onto San Vicente Boulevard.

Michael turned back to face the men. "Kevlar, armor, jackets," he ordered. "Suit up. Pass two of everything up this way."

One of the men—Jelen, the dude who'd given John a hard time on the plane—flipped open a large container resting on the rear bench and began distributing bulletproof vests to the men. Michael watched Dr. Mike and John tug the vests over their heads and strap them together beneath the each armpit. The vests reminded Michael of sandwich boards. He could see John anticipated the vest to be much lighter (sorry, hoss, stopping a bullet don't come cheap), as he wrestled with the connector straps.

Next came the black combat jackets, snug around the midsection, lightweight and long-sleeved. Then the Kevlar helmets, also black. As promised, a strap of industrial-strength Velcro was placed on the right side of each. Then came the holsters, actually a waist/shoulder combo that sported a pouch for a sidearm, and a sheath for a combat knife.

Somewhere far away, the voice of Dispatch crackled on the police scanner. High-speed pursuit of the two white vans, heading east on Santa Monica. Shots fired. It was working.

Beretta M9s and ammo magazines were distributed—each man was given six magazines, thirteen rounds in each. True to his word, John declined the gun. Dr. Mike didn't, and as he loaded and switched its safety, he was clearly familiar with this pistol. Then the knives came, wicked things that snarled in the passing streetlights. Then the thermal imagers. Then the commpieces. Then the PDA wrist devices.

The soldiers were given XM8 compact-carbine automatic assault rifles, snub-nosed things with curved magazines. Neither Dr. Mike nor John received one of these. The criminal profiler was given a hand grenade, however, and a squeamish expression passed over his face as he hooked it through the loop in his chest harness as did the others.

We're all out of our comfort zones tonight, Doc, Michael thought.

The van cruised San Vicente, past the baseball diamond and tennis courts of West Hollywood Park. For a moment—just a moment—the West Hollywood Sheriff's Department building loomed on the right. No one spoke. Then they had the green light, and the vans sailed through the Santa Monica Boulevard intersection.

A left onto Cynthia Street, pass Hilldale. A right on Hammond.

Michael commanded Fleming to pull over at the corner of Hammond and Harratt. Up ahead, Michael saw the bright lights and passing cars of Sunset Boulevard. People ambled across the street. A threesome of tipsy coeds skipped on the sidewalk, arm in arm. Folie à Deux was a block away. The second van pulled up behind them.

Led by Michael, the soldiers placed their commpieces into their ears. Dr. Mike and John played catch-up.

"Comm check," Michael said. "Van One first. Smith."

"Fleming," the driver next to him said.

"Lockwood."

Down the line. "Tomasello." "Andrade." "Jelen." "Smith, John."

It was Dr. Mike's turn. "Smith," he said, then added quickly, "Uh, Doctor."

"Van Two," the marine said.

The voices came through clearly. Durbin. Weekley. Hall. Amador. Birdsey. Travieso. Rubenstein.

"Good," Michael said. "Get ready, boys. It's my voice from now on. We are go in five minutes."

The last block was driven in silence, without headlights. As they neared the club, Michael realized it was set next to another abandoned building on the property. Just beyond the club, on its east side, was a crumbling six-story, low-rent office building. Most of its windows were covered with boards plagued by dry rot.

The vans coasted into the parking lot, their engines off. Fleming quietly pulled the gearshift into park.

It was quiet. It was time.

"Ready steady," Michael said. "Three teams of five, just as planned. Don't talk unless I tell you to. Team One's with me. We head to the roof for a better look at the club's skylight. Teams Two and Three stay in the vans until I give the all clear. Then head to your positions. We're gonna keep this quiet if we can. No one's making the news and no one's making the blotter."

The marine opened his door and climbed out. The cargo door slid open. Jelen, carrying a large rucksack, stepped past the others. So did Lockwood and Tomasello. Dr. Mike and John (members of Team Three) stayed behind, peering out from the van's hold. Another soldier from the second van joined Michael's group.

The five men stepped briskly through the lot in a recon formation, toward the rear of the nightclub. The compact rifles were extensions of their arms now. They arrived at the brick wall. Michael nodded to his men, then stared up the side of the building, toward the roof.

"All right," Michael's voice said. "We're going up."

TWENTY-TWO

F ather Thomas stared at the bank of monitors before them, here in the Common Room. Eerie. Nearly a hundred members of an army were there—*in* there, *out* there—acknowledging the orders given to them by a madman.

I comply

I comply

I comply

Kilroy2.0 chuckled, looked back at his fellow clones, and waved his arms toward the screens. "I knew they'd help us. We have two hours to slip through and get the information we're looking for: your paper trail of Alpha's disposable assassins."

He whirled back to his keyboards and began launching new computer windows. He didn't miss a mouse click as he spoke.

"Under normal circumstances, this wouldn't be easy," Kilroy said. His wild eyes narrowed. He sighed, then snarled, "Fedgov sites're nearly impossible to hack—most have that so-called uncrackable Egg encryption running in their defense software."

This is the most we've ever heard him speak, Thomas realized. *Not as crazy as he'd like us to think, eh?*

"Egg is dangerous stuff, truly wicked programming," Kilroy

continued. "Malicious intent, all the way. Rusty-barbed-wire ware."

"I don't understand," Jay said.

"Of course you don't," Kilroy2.0 snorted.

"Easy, Kilroy," Jack said. "He just doesn't know." Jack turned to Jay. "Egg is the Next Big Thing in defensive software. I read about it, what, about a year ago in *Newsweek*. The feds, and presumably other governments, are clients. Lots of global retailers, too. From what I've read, it's a new breed of firewall program that protects Internet and intranet servers. Some Silicon Valley wunderkind developed the idea when she was still in middle school. That was two years ago; kid's working on a doctorate now. Can you believe it? After the company debuted—Mom's the CEO, natch—the kid placed an ad in all the major newspapers on every continent, which got a lot of attention. Kid challenged anyone—no, *every-one*—to crack Egg."

"And?"

"Nobody has."

"True, true," Kilroy said, nodding and smiling. "Gov hacks are way down since Egg. Egg finds you poking a system it's protecting? Pings you with a tracker. Most security programs end there. Not Egg. Egg hacks *you* back, roots *your* box. Commandeers privileges. Makes a backup copy of your hard drive on its end for evidence. So while you're freaking out on your end, ripping the phone line from your PC, Egg's busy doing two things: cross-reffing your name and IP profile with your street address and phone number, and calling the cops. You're on the run after that."

"Goodness," Thomas said. "Is that legal?"

"As of this January, yes." Kilroy2.0 lowered his voice, doing an uncanny imitation of a game-show host. "This piece of legislation brought to you by the War on Terror. Patriot Act Three, the excit-ing conclusion to the civil-liberties-slaying trilogy."

Rack-a-tacka. Click-click. Giggle.

Kilroy grunted. "*This* is the real war. What John Alpha's doing. Feds never had a clue."

"Did you?" Jay asked.

Kilroy stopped typing. His fingers hovered over the keyboard. The manic energy left his face for a moment. His shoulders sagged. As he spoke next, even the perpetual tremor in his voice had nearly vanished. Thomas was surprised by the sudden lucidity.

"No. Heard rumors. Early stages of cloning. Accelerated growth on mice. Information that didn't come from my Twelve. My best sources are the Twelve."

"Knights of the Round Table?" Jay asked.

"Disciples. They're my eyes and ears, my protégés. Trained them myself." Kilroy turned and gave Father Thomas a wink. The conspiratorial edge was returning now. "If information hails from them, it's gospel. But the sources for those rumors were unreliable, spotty. Usernames I'd never seen before. Couldn't trust them. Didn't give it much credence. Creedence. Heh. Now there's a bad moon a-risin'."

A conspiracy nut with quality-control standards, Thomas thought. *You just get more and more complicated, Kilroy. Whoever thought the paranoid community needed reliable sources?*

Kilroy2.0 shrugged and began typing again. "Doesn't matter now. My flock will swarm the CDC network and ring the doorbells on those servers so many times, the starched-shirt buttholes in IT won't know what to do. They won't notice us. In about ten minutes, we'll have all the distraction we need to get into the Centers for Disease Control internal government mainframe, which, by the way, is protected by Egg. We'll access stuff you'd never find on the Web."

"But you just said Egg was uncrackable," Jack said.

"It is."

Raka-taka. Click.

"So how could we possibly get past Egg to access the information in the CDC?" Jay asked.

"I said it'd be extremely difficult under normal circumstances. This isn't normal. Let's just say I have a follower in high places. A friend who owes me favors."

Kilroy nodded toward the computer screens. His fingers let loose with an explosive string of computer code, and yet another chat window popped up on the monitor. He began to type:

> *did you get my page? were you watching?*

The program chimed, and a reply immediately appeared.

binary_fairy: yes

Kilroy2.0 smiled and typed his next message.

> *can you give me a key?*

binary_fairy: things must be serious

Thomas watched Kilroy closely. The man's smile had faded into a faint frown; he was nodding slowly. Kilroy typed his message.

> *more than you know. more than i ever knew.*

And then . . . nothing.

Thomas had quickly become accustomed to the whirlwind pace at which Kilroy 2.0 and his followers could chat. Almost faster than speaking. But now there was only cybersilence. For more than a minute they watched the screen. Finally:

binary_fairy: a temporally challenged backdoor key has been made. 24 hours. it's on the way.

Kilroy clapped his hands together and laughed. "See?" he cried. "I knew she could help!"

"Who's *she*?" Jay asked.

"Oh, don't be a fool. The inventor of Egg. The wunderkind. She's given us a key to the palace, good for an entire day. We're in. Hah!"

" 'A follower in high places,' " Jack said. "You weren't kidding."

Kilroy rubbed his hands together furiously. The computer beeped. Kilroy checked his e-mail, nodded, began typing again.

> got it. *the prophet thanks you, my child*

The reply came quickly:

binary_fairy: be careful

Kilroy2.0 closed the program's window and turned to the other clones. His face was triumphant, a grin splitting his shaggy beard.

Thomas couldn't help but smile, too. *And now's a good time as any for the second half of my wily idea,* he thought.

"You guys," Thomas said, standing up from the workstation. "You guys will be all right here, right?"

"What's the matter?" Jack asked.

"Here. Okay. You guys," Thomas replied, slipping the rosary back into his pocket. "You're good to go? Using the key? Getting into the files?"

"Should be." Kilroy2.0 slouched back toward the screens, chuckling and humming to himself.

Thomas walked over to the Common Room's round table and scooped up the onyx pistol that Michael had commandeered from Private Ballantine during this afternoon's Ops standoff. Thomas had never fired a gun, but it didn't hurt to have something that went boom for the sake of intimidation. He tucked it into the waistband of his jeans.

"Good. I'm taking off for a while. Dig a little deeper about this place. Work another angle."

He stepped to the double doors that lead out into the halls, out into the 7th Son compound.

"Where are you going?"

Thomas opened the doors and looked back at Jack. "I'm paying our dad a visit."

TWENTY-THREE

ichael gave the parking lot of Folie à Deux a final once-over, looking for curious Sunset Boulevard revelers who might take offense to the four machine gun-toting soldiers standing out here by the club's rear wall. Seeing no one, he turned back to Lockwood, Jelen, Tomasello, and Hall.

The young men were terrified, Michael saw. They'd have to get over it. Like, right fucking now.

"All right," he whispered into the mic. "Prep the grappler."

Jelen removed the rucksack from his back, pulled out two metal cases, and passed them to Lockwood. Their contents were assembled in seconds: a chunky pistol the size of a flare gun; a small canister of CO2; a fist-size spool of flexsteel cable; an arrow-shaped titanium bolt that connected to the cable, then slid into the gun barrel. The men in Force Recon called the gizmo a Rorschach. Michael didn't know why.

Lockwood passed him the grappling pistol. Michael tilted his head, aiming his helmet's thermal imager at Folie à Deux's concrete wall. The PDA screen on his wrist was dark; no hues of orange or red. He switched the helmet's imager to its second setting.

No telltale bright purple lines coursing through the wiring. The building was empty, and off the power grid.

Not good. The bright glow from Sunset Boulevard's street-lights wasn't going to be much help inside. Hell, the full moon above them would provide better illumination; aside from its sky-light, Folie à Deux was a windowless box.

Michael aimed the Rorschach upward and pulled the trigger. The metal arrow plunged into the roof ledge at the top of the wall. A nearly invisible cable of flexsteel danced in the shadows for a moment, then quickly *sproinged* taut as Michael gave it a tug.

Michael turned back to the men. Good. Jelen was sealing up his rucksack; the others had already slung their XM8s across their backs. Smiling to himself, Michael ascended the wall, feeling the cable passing over his palms, never making a sound.

Seconds later, he gave a brisk gesture to the dogs ogling from below. *Get a move on, pups.*

They did. The boys appeared a smidgen rattled and exhila-rated and that was okay. They'd need that adrenaline. When the last of them stepped onto the roof, Michael spoke into his mic.

"We're in place. Teams Two and Three, take your positions and wait for my signal."

In one ear, Michael's commpiece whispered the men's grunts as they climbed out of the vans. With his other ear, he heard the faint sounds of the van doors opening, then closing. The rustle of boots and vague *clink-clink* of soldiers running with rifles. He could hear them, yes . . . but they were good.

He could imagine Dr. Mike and John in his mind's eye, run-ning alongside the others. He frowned, then grunted. Now wasn't the time to think about them, or 7th Son. He pushed the doubt away with a flick of his mental wrist.

Here we go, said the calm voice in his head, the voice that sounded just like those of the musician and the shrink and the four other clones back in Virginia. Michael smiled at the irony before he cast that aside, too.

John pressed his back against the brick wall of the nightclub. His team was on the east side of the building, just below where Michael and the rest of Team One had slid across the sky. Dr. Mike was with John. So were Durbin, Andrade, and Travieso. Andrade was crouched in front of a metal door, one of two emergency exits the clones had red-circled on the blueprints back in the 7th Son Common Room. Andrade held a lockpicking device in his hands, less than an inch from the silver dead bolt. They were waiting for the go-ahead from Michael. Team Two would be in a similar position near the other emergency exit.

The cars and pedestrians streamed by on Sunset Boulevard, less than a hundred feet away. No one noticed them in the shadows.

John fought the instinct to hum a song—one of his, "Katabatic," a ditty about staying frosty, maybe—his usual self-prescribed cure for stress-outs. But here it would likely dilute his focus, give his head a familiar blanket in which to wrap itself. He didn't want that.

He blinked away a bead of sweat and looked over at Dr. Mike. Where were the quips now? The psychologist was just as shaken and stirred as John was. And why wouldn't he be? This wasn't their world. They were not built for this.

Well, that's not exactly true, is it, Johnny-Boy? a side of himself whispered. *Good ole Mikey Marine took the road less traveled and he's built for it just fine, a real killing machine. Which means, somewhere deep down, you're a killing machine, too. Aren't you? He's dedicated his life to something, something real, something with goals. And you? Not so much, wanderer. But you come from the same killer stock—*

"Damn it, hush," John whispered.

The men around him flinched at the sound. Dr. Mike gaped at him, blazing with fear and adrenaline. John shook his head, his eyebrows raised: *I'm okay. I'm okay.*

"Cut the chatter," hissed Michael's voice over the commpiece.

John angled his head toward the side of the building, then looked at the PDA strapped to his arm. The thermal imager scanned through the wall, the PDA screen flickered black and shades of dark gray.

Nobody's home. So what were they waiting for?

A Corvette screeched past them on the Strip. The Vette's engine roared, a woman shrieked in glee, the deep bass of a Missy Elliott song thudded into the distance.

Andrade's hands trembled slightly as he held the lockpick centimeters from the door.

Durbin and Travieso exchanged fearful glances.

Dr. Mike licked his upper lip.

What's taking so long?

Only a minute and fifteen seconds had passed since they had come to the door. Time is funny that way.

Michael passed the propane glass-cutter back to Jelen, who promptly packed it into his rucksack. Lockwood and Hall gently tugged the large-handled suction cups that had been placed on the skylight glasspane, and it slipped out of its frame. Slick and as silent as oil, the work of salty pros, not FNGs. Michael nodded approvingly. When the chips are down, most any man will rise to the occasion. These fellows were no exception.

The pair placed the man-size sheet of glass to the side, then got to work on setting up the rappelling ropes. Michael peeked at his wristwatch. A minute-twenty had passed since he'd ordered the teams to get into position. Good time, given the circumstances. He scanned the interior of the club with his thermal imager again.

First the ground floor: the bar, the dance floor, the DJ booth, the thirty-foot-tall silver statue. Next, the second floor: the catwalk circling the perimeter of the club, the glass-encased VIP lair. No body-heat thermal readings. Good. Michael's PDA screen winked faint reds and oranges on the north and east sides of the club at ground level . . . but he knew those were his boys the sensor was reading. They were patiently waiting outside for the go-ahead.

Soon, gentlemen. Soon.

The ropes were ready now, and so were his four teammates. They connected their carabiners to the ropes and waited by the skylight. The fear was in their faces, pouring from their pores. Michael looked at them, and when he spoke, he knew all three teams could hear him.

"Ready steady, men. You're smarter and stronger than this. Listen to me and use your brains."

He took a deep breath. Jelen, Lockwood, Hall, and Tomasello look relieved. Good. And now—

"Go," Michael said, and jumped down, rappelling into the darkness of Folie à Deux. The soldiers followed him. "Go. Go. Go. Go."

John heard the signal and turned to watch their team's keymaster. In one fluid movement, Andrade plunged the lockpick into the door's dead bolt, twisted the device clockwise, and yanked open the door. Durbin and Travieso dashed in, their XM8 machine guns ready, their eyes flitting from the darkness of the club to the LCD screens on their wrists. John came in next, then Dr. Mike, pointing his pistol ahead. Andrade pulled up the rear.

It wasn't completely dark in Folie à Deux—the dance floor was dimly illuminated from the moonlight streaming through the skylight. John saw two members of Michael's Team One descend like spiders from the skylight and scramble into the shadows by the DJ booth. Team Two, charged with getting through the other door, was already inside. They, too, ducked into the shadows.

The building's blueprints had been accurate: by Team Three's emergency exit was a stairwell. Durbin, the team's point man, scanned the second floor with his thermal imager. They climbed the stairs to the second-floor catwalk, above the dance floor.

To the right, the catwalk arced past a row of semiprivate nooks with chairs and couches, then ended at an observation deck at the rear of the club. To the left, the path was a straight shot toward the front of the club, ending at what once was a theater balcony—now a posh VIP section. John looked past the railing in front of him and spotted an identical catwalk on the west side of the club. This second level was a like a curved racetrack, designed for watching whatever was happening below. The bartender inside him fleetingly appreciated the place. Nice digs.

Andrade and Travieso cocked their machine guns over the railing and did a visual/thermal sweep of the catwalk across the way. No thermal signatures. Durbin nodded and raised a clenched fist: *Hold this position.*

Michael's voice crackled in their ears. "Leaders, report. Team One inside, no sign of enemy."

"Team Two inside," another voice hissed through the comm. Probably Amador's. "The only thing we're reading is you guys."

"Team Three in," Durbin said. "Catwalk secured. Lotta nothin' up here."

"Quieter than we expected," Michael said. "Good. Take a look around. The building's been taken off the grid, so don't bother looking for electrical signatures. Go from thermal to night vision. Break up into teams of twos and threes."

John tapped the button on the back of his helmet camera until his PDA wristscreen showed the characteristic green hues. Durbin pointed at John and Dr. Mike and then to himself. *You and you with me*, he was saying. John nodded and stepped over toward Durbin. Dr. Mike was behind them.

They walked toward the front of the club, heading toward the VIP lounge. The team's other half stepped off in the direction of the observation deck.

Now that he could "see," John realized the club was about the size of a small warehouse, with walls that seemed to stretch upward forever. He imagined the place in its previous movie-house incarnation—hundreds of red-velvet chairs sloping downward from the lobby, a projection screen the size of a barnside, Fleischer *Superman* serials flickering on-screen.

They continued in silence toward the VIP lounge/balcony, stepping past more couches, chairs, and tables. The club's geography spread out before them in infrared green.

And there it was. John had spotted it long before now, but didn't want to look at it until they were closer: the club's testament to its name . . . the tangible realization of the Folie à Deux disorder. The silver statue.

Its aluminum surface glinted menacingly in the dim light, much of it lost in shadow. But the massive shape was unmistakable: two human forms, slipping around another in a helix, then merging into a single streamlined, churning vortex at its base. Their bodies arched toward the catwalks on either side of the club.

Durbin made a motion with his hand—*Come on!*—and John caught up with him. They stepped closer to VIP, a human fishbowl with lush curtains hanging from its ceiling.

The commlink crackled in John's ear. "Wait." The voice was panicked. "No, no, waitwait, waitasec. Something—"

Not Michael's voice. Someone from his own team? John whirled around and saw . . . what?

There. Impossible. A man flying off the catwalk, somersaulting, legs swimming back and forth in a green blur, heading for the center of the dance floor . . .

holy shit, was that Travieso?

. . . and now a shape (no, a *shade*) emerging from one of tiny nooks, planting a buck knife squarely in Andrade's Adam's apple, the blood spurting black into the air, Andrade's eyes wide and neon green with surprise . . .

it was safe up here, it was safe the imagers told everyone, itwassafe

. . . the sickening crunch of Travieso's body landing twenty-five feet below . . .

"CONTACT!" shrieked Durbin beside him. "East catwalk! North side!"

Several voices barking in John's ear now.

"Don't see—"

Michael's voice: "Quiet! Shut up, shutup—"

Andrade's death rattle crackled over the comm. The shade began striding down the catwalk, toward John.

no gun, sweet Jesus, I'm dead, no gun

"I see 'im!" someone cried. "Up on the catwalk! Shadow! Looks like a fucking shadow!"

That's when the shooting began.

TWENTY-FOUR

F ather Thomas encountered no one on his trip to the elevator. The cleaning crew and guards he'd seen this morning
were long gone. Evacuated, as Kleinman had said.

Thomas strode down the halls, passing the closed doors and
keypads, following the DNA mosaic embedded in the walls. The
tilework was a preposterous, pompous thing, but it also provided
a road map to the compound's express elevator.

He placed his eye up to the silver machine in the wall. Recall-
ing what he'd seen earlier in the day, Thomas leaned his face near
the machine. A green light blinked across his eye.

The computer gave an approving chime.

Pistons whined as the door opened once more. Thomas stepped
inside the elevator, giddy and fearful. He stood in silence for a
moment, befuddled, waiting. Finally, he remembered.

"Uh, computer?"

"HERE" came the metallic ceiling-voice.

"Yes. Yes, you are. Ah—computer, prepare destination."

"READY FOR DESTINATION INPUT."

"Level Fourteen." During this morning's tour, Kleinman had
said the living quarters were there.

"ENGAGED."

The trip wasn't as unnerving as the first two had been. The plummet downward didn't seem to take as long, either: Level Fourteen actually seemed closer to the surface than the Ops and Womb levels.

The elevator doors slid open and Thomas stepped cautiously into the hall. No one was there to stop him, beat him, cuff him, throw him back into the grand circular prison cell called the Common Room. The hallway curved off in opposite directions. He had no idea where to go. Had no room number. *Heck, I don't even know if this is where they've got him locked up.*

And Hugh Sheridan *was* locked up. Thomas was certain of that. When they were back in the Ops room and Sheridan had screamed at Kleinman, those two Jerry Springer bouncers had yanked him out of the room—metaphorically kicking and literally screaming. Hugh Sheridan knew something. Something about this place, maybe something dangerous. He'd gone postal when Kleinman started talking up that doctor—the so-called founder of 7th Son. The late great Frank Berman. *Tell them the truth,* Dad had said.

The grunts had hauled him out . . . and Kleinman had told the clones that all would be explained later. Ruse. Kleinman wouldn't make time for explanations. Thomas was realizing that he and the rest of the John Smith Betas had been brought here to unscrew John Alpha's head. Kleinman, Hill, and Durbin thought the clones could outsmart 7th Son's Frankenstein monster. End of story. Thomas and his brothers had been given the least amount of information to work with, a *Reader's Digest* version of how they came to be. Thomas couldn't see Kleinman spending hour after hour answering questions. That would take them away from the Great Villain Hunt . . . and that wasn't going to happen.

Which is why Thomas needed to see dear old Dad.

I'm not your father, he had said.

True, but we'll sweat the semantics later, Thomas thought. *So. The hall. Left or right? East or west? Bubble gum, bubble gum, in a dish, how many pieces do you wish?*

Thomas went right.

He passed door after door, all slate-gray variations of the *Star Trek* doors he'd seen up on the Common Room level. Each had a small keypad embedded next to the door. Almost all of these little keypads sported tiny metal grilles and flashing red lights. Thomas had seen enough action movies—*we all have our harmless vices, Hong Kong actioners especially*—to assume the pads were connected to intercom systems, and the doors were locked.

Most of the doors had numbers stenciled on their surfaces (14.10, 14.11, 14.12), but some had names just below the numbers.

He kept walking down the curved hallway. Past Kleinman's quarters now, Hill's, Durbin's, DeFalco's—and then Thomas knew exactly which room his father was in. A soldier was guarding the door. The name SHERIDAN was printed on the door's surface.

Thomas got a look at the soldier's face as he neared, and stopped. It was the green-eyed military man. It was the man who, just yesterday, had told Thomas he "didn't want any trouble" in St. Mary's hospital parking lot back in Stanton, Oklahoma. *The man who'd pointed a handgun at my chest.*

His own personal boogeyman, guarding the door.

Thomas felt his confidence wither, like time-lapse footage of a dying rose.

"No admittance," the soldier said. Thomas thought fleetingly of locked gates and private doors. He read the name tag on the boogeyman's chest. STONE.

How appropriate. *Thanks for the irony, Lord.*

"I have to see him," Thomas said simply. "You know that."

"You're not going to." The grunt glanced down at the gun at Thomas's waist and stiffened.

Thomas lowered his head, then looked back at Stone. "Don't worry. I won't use it. Thought it would be a good idea for, you know . . . for show. And I suppose there's no way I'm getting in. Not while you're here."

"That's right." Stone smirked. "So leave."

"I'm a black belt," Thomas said.

The soldier blinked. "So you said. And so am I. Do really you want to do this?"

Thomas smiled, shaking his head. "Kleinman and Hill. They expected me, or someone who looks just like me, to come down and try to see him. That's why *you're* here, babysitting the old man locked behind that door. My father."

"I said leave."

"I know, I know." Thomas raised both hands: *I surrender.* "But please, take a moment and try to see things through my eyes. Sympathize with me. *Empathize.* I thought he was dead. T-boned at an intersection. I've dreamed about him for the past fourteen years. I had nightmares about how he must've died—swallowing broken windshield, a headlight flying off the other car, smashing into his skull like a cannonball. But he's *alive*, brother. To me, it feels like something out of a zombie movie. And then they hauled him away and locked him up here."

Thomas looked into the soldier's eyes. "So you have to at least understand why I'm here. You have to understand why I have to try to see him. You must give me that much."

"I don't have to give you shit."

"So it's a stalemate, then."

"Guess so," Stone said.

As Father Thomas sighed and leaned against the wall on Level Fourteen, Jack, Jay, and Kilroy2.0 were observing future history being written on the screens before them. Kilroy2.0's hacker army had assaulted the Centers for Disease Control's Web site in an unprecedented coordinated attack. Every shred of bandwidth dedicated to the agency's Web site became suddenly dedicated to the onslaught of countless page hits. A mouse click in Topeka fired a thousand "pings" to the CDC Web server. Another in Des Moines fired five thousand. This created a bandwidth logjam: the server could no longer grant normal Web-surfers access to the site at all, due to to the plague attacking its system. One 404 Web-site error message became ten, then one hundred, then a thousand. It was the Internet equivalent of rush-hour gridlock.

While government information-technology brainiacs undoubtedly wrung their hands in puzzlement—after all, who slams the Centers for Disease Control?—Kilroy2.0 used binary_fairy's key to slip through the Egg security software's back door.

Kilroy2.0 pointed at the CDC home page on a far monitor. A cryptic "Host Unavailable" message was displayed where graphics and text should have been. "Superduper," he said. "Now. Our turn. The stuff we're after is too sensitive for norms and lamers. Likely stored on one of the CDC's independent computer servers."

The computer chirped an approving noise, and Kilroy slapped his hands against his knees. His massive gut quaked as he gave another high-pitched laugh.

"The data is ours for the taking! The line is scrambled and the only ones who'd notice are busy restarting the crashed-o-rific public servers." The hacker leaned even closer toward his monitors. "So let's start looking for NEPTH-charge victims."

The CDC's intranet access page was a sterling example of graphic minimalism. At the top of the window was the organization's slogan, *Safer • Healthier • People*, as was the logo of the Department of Health and Human Services. A light-blue column on the left side of the screen displayed a list of security-related text links: *NEDDS Protocol & Guidelines* . . . *X.509 Certification* . . .

IRMO Monitoring . . . Report Unauthorized External Users! The center of the page was sprinkled with links to various sections of the network. Kilroy2.0's mouse sped across the screen, left to right, as he read the links.

>*White Papers/Releases*
>*Community Bulletins—Low, Med, High*
>*Studies (Ongoing)*
>*Studies (Concluded)*
>*CDC/ATSDR Archives*
>*File a CIO Request*
>*Search DBase, MFrame, SQL*

Kilroy2.0 clicked the last link. A new page loaded, a spartan screen with a simple text-search field. Beneath the search field was a grid of clickable boxes, designed to narrow the search.

"Should we do searches based on individual obituaries, or in individual states?" Jay asked doubtfully. He took a seat next to Kilroy. "Going through those on the newswires didn't seem to work very well."

"Agreed," Jack said. He plopped down in the chair at Kilroy's left side. "Kilroy, can you do a more generalized search, based on location? Maybe instead of city- or state-based searches, we go all out with a regional search request?"

Kilroy's fingers were already skittering across the keyboards. "No. More ambitious. Nationwide search."

He typed in the search field a vague list of symptoms they'd thought a NEPTH-charge victim would experience: *neurological disorder, personality change,* etc., set the search to retrieve documents from the past six months, then clicked the SEND button. A timepiece icon flashed on screen as the network processed this.

"So what do you think's going on down there?" Jay asked.

"Clarify," Kilroy2.0 said.

"Down *there*." Jay pointed to the floor. "With Thomas and the man we think is our father."

"Preposterous," Kilroy answered. "More lies, obviously."

"That's the voice of a paranoid talking," Jack replied.

Kilroy2.0 chuckled. "Just because you're paranoid doesn't mean they're not out to hack you. People who rule do not rule by sharing all of their knowledge, Jack. They rule by sharing *selections* of knowledge. Selections that will influence those around them to pursue an agenda." The man's eyes glittered behind his pop-bottle glasses. He nodded enthusiastically to his other brother, his greasy bangs bouncing. "It's called manipulation; ask Jay here about the grinning despots he's encountered in his career. We've been given select parts of information to ensure our cooperation—but we haven't been told the truth. Surely you can know that."

"We are owed details, that I won't argue." Jack's voice was low, defensive. "I want to know, more than any of us. But it'll take time for those details to come."

"When?" Kilroy's eye flitted to the screen. The search was still running.

"Just after we finish this . . . and just before I go home to my wife and my little girls."

The computers belched a series of chimes. The three clones turned to the monitors. The intranet search was complete.

"*Mamma mia*," Jack said, gazing at the screen. "Look at all of them."

There were dozens of results, each an arcane sequence of numbers and letters. Many of the results were colored in ubiquitous hypertext-link blue. But at least ten of them were red. A menacing animated logo pulsed beside each of these file links. *CIO AUTHORIZATION REQUIRED: LEVEL 7*, they read.

"These are the ones we should look at," Jay said, as he reached forward and tapped the throbbing logos. "CIO is government-speak for Center/Institute/Office."

"What does it mean?" Jack asked. "Don't we already have authorization?"

"I'm not sure," Jay said. "This looks like another level of security in the system. Let's say there're hundreds—maybe thousands—of professionals who have access to the CDC intranet. That doesn't mean they're all allowed the same level of access." He tapped on the logo again. "This is the sensitive stuff. The stuff that Joe Professor or Joe Doctor in Nowhere, Nevada, can't get to. It's been my experience that either you have CIO authorization or you don't. Those who need access to protected files can ask for a limited pass. Their request is reviewed by whoever grants CIO authorization. We've broken into the house, but we've encountered a locked door inside."

Jack turned to Kilroy. "So can that golden ticket of yours get us into the chocolate factory?"

Kilroy steered the mouse pointer over one of the red links and clicked. A small window popped up in the center of the screen. *Checking authorization . . . ;* it read.

A moment later, a new message appeared. *Authorization approved.* The forbidden page began to load. The first several lines of the document screamed at them in twenty-point type.

Report # nu4446-ot-898vf
Security Clearance: Level 7 (upgraded from Level 2, *see related docs*)
Incident Location: Arkansas, Heber Springs
Summary: Sudden Neurological Atrophy, 10 Dead
Viral Classification (if applicable): UNKNOWN
BioSafety Level: UNKNOWN (study ongoing, *see related docs*)

"Doompadeedoo," Kilroy said.

TWENTY-FIVE

I magine two eighteen-wheelers parked side by side. Now, imbued with the power of a giant, press them toward each other, into each other. Moosh the mess downward a bit, flatten out the trailers so they're the same height as the cabs. Lay a massive cylinder atop the monstrosity—a construction-site sewer pipe, maybe—where the two trucks meet. Spray-paint the thing camo green.

That would be a layman's view of the MAZ transport-erector-launchers currently stationed at the Tatishchevo Mobile Nuclear Missile Garrison.

Like most Russian vehicles, the MAZ was an exercise in angles. The only streamlined thing on it was the missile launch canister resting atop the truck's spine. The drivers' cockpits were actually separated by the girth of the tube: a trapezoidal compartment resided on either side of the canister (whose nose hung in front of the MAZ by about six feet), each of which allowed a single man to squeeze inside and drive the behemoth. The two large windshields cursed the MAZ with the appearance of a mechanical insect.

Doug Devlin admired the vehicle here, under the sputtering lamps of the garrison's garage. He strode past one of the front tires, gave the five-footer a kick with his boot, then climbed up the metal ladder built into the side of the MAZ. Devlin opened the eight-inch-thick door and slid into the left-side cockpit. He tossed his Primas and Zippo onto the dash and kicked on the heater. He eyed the chunky high-frequency radio built into the dash, the linchpin in what would unfold hours from now.

The MAZ driver in the other cockpit had once been named Boronov. Now, like the rest of the Saratov garrison, he was a Devlin, too. Thanks to countless drills during the past two weeks, Devlin knew what his copilot was doing: Boronov-Devlin was flipping switches, tapping gauges, and twisting dials necessary for start-up. For his part, Devlin jonesed for a smoke and made sure the Kalashnikovs he'd brought aboard were loaded with full magazines. They didn't expect trouble during their first (last) mission . . . but it didn't hurt to be prepared.

Behind both of the drivers' cabins—inside the sealed targeting/launch compartment—two other Devlins sat at the ready, undoubtedly fighting the pangs of claustrophobia, staring into flickering monitors and prepping their payload through a series of keyboard taps.

Again, Doug Devlin thanked himself for learning Cyrillic. It had been more than handy during this mission. From learning the computer targeting software to decrypting the Permissive Action Links—specialized computer chips built into the missiles that prevented an unauthorized launch—to laughing at Russian TV commercials, those lessons had been damned useful.

The MAZ started up just fine, belching its dark diesel fumes into the mammoth garage. In eight other garages, eight other MAZes like this one were filled with Devlins and roaring to life. An orchestra of bodies conducted by one mind.

Devlin felt Boronov-Devlin depress the clutch, shift into gear, and gently press the gas. From somewhere behind him, the eight-

hundred-horsepower engine snarled like a tyrannosaur. The 120-
ton truck rumbled out of the garage and into the November air.
Inside the launch canister slept its payload: one RT-2PM2 Topol-M
intercontinental ballistic missile. Seventy-five feet long, six feet in
diameter. Weight: fifty-three tons. Range: six thousand five hundred miles. In flagrant violation of the U.S./Russia Strategic Arms
Reduction Treaty (a clandestine order by the Russian president
last year), each missile carried three nuclear warheads, not one.
Total yield: two thousand seven hundred kilotons.

The sun was just beginning to rise in Saratov; the fog was
burning away in the morning light. The MAZ rumbled through
the mist along with its brethren, all piloted by Doug Devlins. All
hungry to make the biggest kill in history.

Three groups of MAZes were to drive sixty miles in three separate directions (north, east, and south) and, upon arriving at the
predetermined coordinates, set up each MAZ for deploying its missiles. When it was time, they'd launch the nukes right into the history books. It would take them less than two minutes to do so.

Nine missiles. Twenty-seven warheads. Two targets.

Doug Devlin slipped on his helmet and activated its comm
unit; this would enable him to speak to the NEPTH-charged men
in the targeting compartment. "How are we doing back there?"

"Superb" came the reply. Devlin nodded. He couldn't see his
two comrades; they were separated by two feet of wires, insulation, and steel. The voice crackled in his ear again. "During the big
show, there are two seats back here with your names on 'em."

Boronov-Devlin's voice snickered into his comm line. "Don't
you mean *your* names on them?"

All four of them chuckled at that. The MAZ rolled past the garrison's electric fence, past the minefields on either side of the
road, out into the frosted countryside beyond. Eight other MAZes
followed it. Combined, the missiles would launch 24.3 megatons

of destruction—a blast hundreds of times more powerful than the weapon that had annihilated Hiroshima.

"What a lovely day for World War Three," Devlin said.

His comrades laughed and agreed.

That was the great thing about this gig. Everyone had such a wonderful sense of humor.

TWENTY-SIX

L evel Fourteen. Stalemate.

Father Thomas sighed and slid his back down the wall until his butt touched the floor. He crossed his legs. It felt good to sit like this. Not in an office chair or on a circular couch in front of a mountain of computer screens. Just here, on a concrete floor, with his back against a wall. It felt . . . appropriate.

"Mind if I just sit here for a while?"

Stone's eyes narrowed into slits. "I'm not going anywhere."

They sat and stood in silence for the next minute.

"You know, you remind me of a man I once knew," Thomas said finally. "Met him just before seminary, back in what I call my crotch-rocket days. Motorcycle, see. Fast one. Japanese."

Stone grunted. "Folks call 'em rice rockets where I'm from."

"That's kinda racist."

"Racist as hell."

Father Thomas smiled, then continued, "So, yes. This guy. He was a bouncer at this bar I used to hang out in, back in St. Louis. I'm human; this was my last hurrah before a life of the cloth. This guy? Nice guy. Big as a bear, but cool around his buddies and the regulars. But you didn't want to tick him off, you know? It's like there was an animal under his skin. A lion. He always seemed ready when a scrap went down."

Thomas exhaled. Stone looked down at him, imperious.

"Does that make sense?" Thomas asked. "When people came into the pub, this fellow knew which customers were the merry drunks and which ones were sad drunks and which ones were going be the mean drunks. He just *knew*. Like he could smell it. When you walked through that door, he knew if you were *right* or if you were *wrong*. Read people like a book, Knuckles could. I think he would have made a helluva priest, actually."

Stone harrumphed. "Knuckles."

Thomas looked up from the floor and laughed. "Ridiculous, right? But that's what everyone called him. 'Don't fuckles with Knuckles,' this one old lush used to say. Absolutely inappropriate, but that's what he said. And you'd think Knuckles wouldn't tolerate that . . . I mean, the one person you don't want to mess with is the bouncer, right? But it was okay for the geezer to rib him like that. Why? Because Knuckles knew the old lush was *right*. Not *right* as in 'correct,' but *right* as in the opposite of *wrong*. Cool, harmless. On the white side. Understand?"

Stone nodded slightly.

"That's who you remind me of, Stone. Knuckles. The man with a lion inside. The man who makes you on sight. The man who knows the difference between who's *right* and who's *wrong*."

The soldier crossed his arms. "I know what you're trying to do. Don't even think about it."

Thomas waved it away. "I'm not." He shrugged. "I am. A little. Okay, a lot. I have an agenda." He sighed. "Do you know what I am?"

"Yeah. A soulless freak."

Thomas flinched. *Yes. An untethered monstrosity,* the dark voice within him said. *A parentless, godless thing . . . no right to exis—*

Stop it. Stop listening.

"Ah . . . I think our panel of judges might accept that answer," Thomas said, recovering. "But I'm also something else, Stone. I'm just like you. I have a life and a job and bills and flaws and problems. I have baggage from my childhood—even if it wasn't *mine*, I remember it as such. The most brilliant things I've ever said I've never said, because the real zingers come hours after the cocktail party, yes? I've been a jerk. I've been a jewel. Most times I'm somewhere in between, though I do my very best to stay on the path and lead by example.

"I'm you, Stone. Just a man. Just another guy making his way in this wondrous and confusing world, dreaming secret dreams and praying they'll come true. And I've been dreaming about my dead father for *fourteen years.* I've been haunted, been lied to. What I thought was right wasn't. It was wrong. I'm going to learn to live with it. But all the questions I now have—the questions about this place and what it's really all about—they can be answered by only one person. He's six feet away from me, Stone. Just beyond that door you're guarding. Six feet, fourteen years, seven sons. Please. Don't be the man who denies me the right to ask those questions."

With a beeping sound and a gentle whoosh, the doors slid open. Thomas looked up, past Stone, into the open doorway of the living quarters.

Into the eyes of his father.

"Let him in," Hugh Sheridan said, and disappeared back into the dimness. Stone nodded.

Thomas stood up, dumbfounded. Stone hadn't opened the door. Thomas looked at the soldier, amazed. "I thought Kleinman and Hill . . ."

"Nope," Stone said. "The request came from Sheridan."

Thomas stood for a moment, his mouth open in surprise—then

he threw his head back and laughed. Of course Sheridan had wanted to keep them away. *You're not my son,* he had said. *You just think you are. It's what you remember. . . . It's too soon. Too soon.*

"Why didn't you tell me?" Thomas asked.

Stone smirked. "You didn't ask."

Thomas looked into the soldier's green eyes. "You were never going to move. No matter what I said, you were never going to let me in."

"No. And you were never going to move, either."

"No."

Stone smiled. It looked out of place, there on his face.

"So we have two things in common," Stone said. "We're both black belts, and truly stubborn bastards."

Thomas laughed again.

"That thing in Oklahoma," Stone said. "It was business, you know. Nothing personal."

The priest nodded, his smile fading. "I'm beginning to understand that more and more." He stepped into his dead father's home.

The doors whooshed shut behind him.

TWENTY-SEVEN

I n Los Angeles, Durbin was screaming. Screaming through what was left of his mouth.

Dr. Mike didn't know when it had happened, but the horror show unfolding before him didn't lie. Durbin had been shot in the face. A bullet—*just one? surely more than that, surely more*—had blasted off the man's lower jaw. Dr. Mike had seen it happen. One second, Durbin was screaming at Dr. Mike and John to run like hell for the glass-encased VIP lounge; there was cover there, tables and couches, and hurry the fuck up . . . and an eyeblink later, Durbin's entire chin had exploded in a mist of bone and blood.

It had taken another second for Durbin to realize something was wrong. That moment played out in hyper-slow-motion for Dr. Mike. Durbin's head rocked from the impact. His eyebrows rose, as if he were asking himself a question. The man had then looked into Dr. Mike's eyes . . . and the pain had taken hold.

Durbin screamed, was screaming now. Screaming without lips, without a tongue. It was a hollow, rattling noise; a monstrous, unfocused gurgle-roar.

Dr. Mike shrieked as another bullet blew out Durbin's left eye.

And then Durbin the asshole, Durbin the fuckwit, Durbin the Ben Affleck look-alike who deserved much more than this, fell to the catwalk floor and lay still.

A bullet droned past Dr. Mike's head and exploded into the wall behind him. The world quickly resumed in real time. He leaped to the floor, next to Durbin's body. It was sensory overload: the strobe light and thunderclap of automatic gunfire, the wood and steel fixtures here in Folie à Deux exploding from bullet impacts. He spotted John's face in the darkness. He was to Dr. Mike's left, also lying low, taking cover, way out of his element, trembling like a leaf in a hurricane. Dr. Mike heard the screams of other men, from below—from the ground floor. And from the commlink in his right ear, his marine clone shouting orders to the men.

"Above! Above!" Michael was screaming. "Two on the second level! Two more at the skylight!"

Dr. Mike tilted his head up toward the skylight in the center of the nightclub's ceiling. *What in the fuck is he talking about?* he thought frantically. *I don't see anyone up—*

Guttural spurts of machine-gun fire suddenly flickered through what was left of the skylight windows. Someone screamed below.

"Fuck!" a cry came from the commlink. "He got me! Can't see—"

Another explosion of gunfire sputtered from the skylight. The voice on the commlink fell silent. But Dr. Mike still couldn't *see* the person up there firing the guns.

I should at least be able to spot something *up there*, he thought frantically. *At least the blast from the gunfire should give me some kind of glimpse. But . . .*

He glanced down at the PDA strapped to his wrist. The thermal imager on his helmet was still set to night vision. He could see the ceiling and the skylight in perfect detail, painted in liquid-crystal shades of green. The screen erupted into a flash of bright green as another volley of bullets was fired from the skylight. A dark gray shape—barely visible, blending into the night sky—loomed over the window. Dr. Mike reached to the imager on his helmet and clicked the rubber button several times. The imager finally switched to body-heat mode. The shape was still dark gray.

The fuck? How can—

"They're shades," a voice whispered. Dr. Mike looked to his left. It was John. The man's eyes were wide, manic.

"Do you see them?" Dr. Mike asked. "On your screen?"

"They're shades," John hissed. "Devils. Ghosts. We're being hunted by *ghosts.*"

Dr. Mike shook his head. *Goddamn civvy's lost it.* The wall behind them exploded in puffs of plaster and wood. Splinters fell around their faces. *We can't see them, but they can see us,* he thought. *Whoever* they *are.*

One of the 7th Son soldiers on the ground level fired up at the skylight. What few panes of glass that were unbroken exploded as the bullets zipped through them . . . then the entire frame of the skylight suddenly sank inward and plummeted forty feet down, smashing spectacularly into the center of the dance floor.

"Jesus!" Dr. Mike cried.

He stared at the wreckage in the dim light from the full moon above. Parts of the metal frame flickered. Shimmered. He glanced down at the screen on his wrist. Hues of orange and yellow were popping in and out of the screen, like fireworks. Suddenly the screen revealed the glowing thermalized shape of a man. Mike looked from the LCD to the floor. A man, dressed in a skintight black suit, lay dead in the center of the crumpled skylight frame. His face was covered in a spandexlike ski mask and goggles. A box-shaped backpack smoked behind his shoulders.

"Shit, that's what I thought," said a voice over the commlink. It was the marine, Michael. "They're wearing light- and heat-protective camouflage. Vaporwear."

"How do you know?" said another voice. Maybe Lockwood's.

"Because I was one of the soldiers who test—"

But Dr. Mike didn't hear the rest of the transmission. Someone had yanked the commlink from his ear.

It was probably the same person who was now pushing a gun barrel into his cheekbone.

John tried to stop shaking, but his body had checked out, stopped listening to the commands his brain was transmitting.

Calm down. Calm down.

It wasn't helping. Just seconds ago, one of the shades—*they're men, just men; look at the dead man on the dance floor, that's what they all are, just men wearing special camouflage*—had pulled John off the floor. The man's gun dug into the side of the clone's face.

A second shade had done the same to Dr. Mike and had taken his commlink. The two clones were hauled over to what was once, in a former life, a movie-house balcony. Now it was a dusty VIP lounge, and just outside the doors of the glass-encased room, the shades shoved John and Dr. Mike toward the balcony railing.

It was strange, being handled by these things. Even here, up close, John couldn't see their faces and could barely make out their shapes. The Vaporwear really did make these men nearly invisible. A subtle distortion of the surroundings was the only giveaway. John's mind flitted briefly to *Star Trek* reruns, Romulans and cloaking devices. Vaporwear was clearly a cloaking device for a person. But nothing could hide the odor of these men—they reeked of filth and booze.

Why would soldiers smell like this? It doesn't make sen—

The shades shoved John and Dr. Mike even closer to the balcony railing. The expanse of the club lay below them, the mam-

moth silver statue glimmered directly ahead. John spotted several
bodies in the moonlight.

Christ, how many of us are left?

John felt the barrel of a pistol gnaw into the base of his skull.
One of the shades behind him screamed over the sporadic gunfire. "Anyone moves, anyone fires another shot—and they die. Anyone tries to call for backup or transportation—and they die. There
are two of us up here. There's another watching from the skylight.
The angles are covered well enough. Try anything . . . *anything* . . .
and their pretty freak faces go bye-bye."

Silence. Somewhere, a splintered chunk of metal clanged to
the floor.

From below, Michael's voice: "What do you want?"

The shade behind John laughed. "To give you a message. A message from John Alpha. But to hear it, you have to come out. And
not just you, marine. All of you. Come out. Come out!" A chuckle,
then a whisper: "Wherever you are."

John squinted past the statue, to the dance floor. Nothing.

Finally, Michael's voice boomed from the shadows. "I have
wounded down here. Some of them aren't going to make it. They
need a doctor."

"We've got one up here, faggot—though it's not the kind you
need," the shade behind John cried. The clone flinched as the gun
pressed harder into his neck. "Play cowboy, now. Round up your
tin soldiers and bring them out here in the open. We know where
you're hiding—we can see you. Can you see us? Can you see us
well enough to risk taking a shot when these freaks here are
standing so close? Come out, homo, and bring your wounded."

More silence. John felt a bead of sweat slide down his nose.

"We can't trust you," Michael called.

"Of course you can't," the first shade, who stood behind Dr.
Mike, replied. "To wit."

Dr. Mike's right biceps exploded in a shower of blood. The gunshot was almost deafening at this range.

"*FUCK!*" Dr. Mike howled. "He shot me! I'm fucking—"

"Shut up!" the shade bellowed. "Don't you fuckin' fall down, Doc. You stand right there, stand straight. Shut your face and listen. That's what you're best at, isn't it? Listening to killers? Writing about killers? Take notes, pretty boy."

Dr. Mike clutched his arm now; blood oozed between his fingers, soaking his combat jacket. He breathed heavily between clenched teeth . . . but he did not fall. And did not speak.

"Blame the cowards!" the shade cried into the darkness. John could smell the alcohol on the man's breath. It was nauseating. "Blame the gutless ones who won't do as they're told! You're good at following orders, marine, so why aren't you doing it now? I need not remind you that the next bullet is going into someone's cerebellum. And wouldn't that be a shame, all those shared childhood moments spraying onto the floor?"

In the low light streaming from the hole in the ceiling, John spotted movement from below. Michael stepped out of the shadows, from behind Folie à Deux's smashed, shattered DJ booth. He was covered in dust and grime. He held a XM8 machine gun in each hand.

"Good dog," the shade behind John said. "Drop the guns. Order the other mice to come out of their holes."

Michael tossed his weapons and made a quick motion with his hands. Slowly, the rest of the squad emerged from their positions. They, too, threw their guns to the floor. Of the eleven soldiers who had flown here with the clones, only five were now alive.

"So." Michael looked up at John, then past him. "We've made one enormous leap of faith with you punks."

Faith, John thought. *We all need a little more of that right now.*

The gun barrel dug into his neck again.

"Aw, you're all almost ready for big-boy pants," the first shade said. "So here we are. Three clones, five soldiers who have a hard-on for suicide missions, and us. Us. Three men who have your lives in our hands. Amazing, how so many can be cut down by so few."

"Picking off the enemy is much easier when you're invisible," Michael called. "Who are you people? Where'd you get that gear?"

The second shade chuckled from behind John. "When your employer has a connection with DARPA, there's plenty to borrow."

From the dance floor, Michael considered this. "DARPA. That's what I thought. The suits work a lot better than when I tested the prototypes a year ago. You know, you're giving away an awful lot—how many men you have here, where you got your duds, tidbits about who's funding you. Sloppy."

"True. But are we giving away an awful lot . . . or are we spoon-feeding you hints?" the first shade said. "Am I feebleminded, or are we playing a game? I'm mum on the subject. And speaking of Mum, let's talk about her."

"That's why we came here," Michael said.

"*Wrong*," the shade snapped. "You're here because you followed the bread crumbs. You worked from a supposition that John Alpha kidnapped your so-called mother and that you'd find her here and save her. But, as I'm sure you discussed at some point, you had no *proof* of any of those things. You made, as you just said, a leap of faith. Here's another possibility: you may be here simply because Alpha wanted an economical way to murder you. Perhaps the failure of tonight's mission isn't that *you* didn't find your mother, but that *we* didn't get to kill all seven clones at once."

"That's bullshit," Dr. Mike said from beside John. Sweat was dripping from his face. "If you wanted us dead, you could've killed us weeks ago. *Years* ago."

The first shade whipped his gun into the back of Dr. Mike's helmet. The clone nearly collapsed from the impact.

"Keep quiet!" the shade barked. "Unless you want to eat another bullet."

"No, he's right," Michael called from below. "This isn't about bringing us together to kill us all. It's about playing the game. He's testing us."

"You're smarter than you look, faggot," the second shade said.

"I'd appreciate it if you didn't call me that. That's my business, and my business ain't the business we're here to discuss. Is our mother alive?"

"She is."

"Is she in this building?"

The second shade behind John chuckled. "What's left of her, yes."

"Is John Alpha also here?" Michael asked.

"Indeed."

"Where?"

And on cue—*because it's certainly on cue,* John thought, *Michael's right, it's a game, we're just little plastic cars in Alpha's board game of Life*—a set of doors on the far end of the club swung open. The doors slammed theatrically against the walls. Out of the dimness stepped a man who looked just like John and Dr. Mike and Michael, only . . .

. . . only different.

His stride was measured. Confident. Deliberate.

The full moon shone though the wrecked remains of the skylight. The man stepped toward the center of the dance floor, now illuminated.

"Ta-daa," John Alpha said.

TWENTY-EIGHT

ack, Jay, and Kilroy2.0 read the CDC report in silence, here in the 7th Son facility's circular Common Room. The report, filed by a CDC field agent five months ago, flickered on one of the hacker's five computer monitors.

That July, the corpses of ten men had been discovered in Heber Springs, Arkansas. Two maintenance engineers at Greers Ferry Dam had spotted the bodies lying on a maintenance catwalk used by employees. How or when these strangers had invaded the premises, no one knew. Also unexplained was how the ten men had received access to the catwalk, which was mounted approximately two-thirds of the way up on the 243-foot-tall dam wall.

According to Cleburne County Sheriff investigations, whose data was included in the CDC report, nearly all of the men had been reported missing by family or friends about three weeks before the gruesome discovery at the dam. Most of the men were friends, employees at a local metal-stamping factory. Reports stated that at least four of them had exhibited erratic behavior at home before their mysterious departure. The men acted as if they were unfamiliar with their surroundings, rejected favorite meals, and ignored family members outright.

What the ten men did during their three-week "lost time" was unknown, though at least one wife assumed her husband had left town to binge, purge, and "dip his wick into some sin-den hussy." The CDC agent did not elaborate on this accusation in her report.

The ten bodies were found at various places on the catwalk. Autopsy reports revealed no toxic substances in the bodies; in all cases, blood-alcohol content was practically nonexistent. No heart failure. No strokes. No long-term diseases. They had just died sometime in the night. Were they poisoned? The test results said no.

This dearth of explanations sparked the county coroner to call the CDC field office in Dallas. The bodies were flown to Dallas for further examination. The brains of all ten men were examined . . . and that's where things got spooky. An inexplicable pattern of cell and tissue damage had devoured their brains. Nerve centers had decayed. Entire lobes had lost their solidity. Their brains had *liquefied.* No carcinogenic or foreign elements were discovered after several tests.

The CDC field agent noted in her report that this discovery could not be classified by current CDC standards. No existing virus or illness—absolutely *none*—came close to describing the condition of these men's brains. It was as if the minds had physically burned themselves out and begun to cave in on themselves. A case of, as the agent put it, "brainrot." The cause could be environmental or viral, the agent wrote.

If the deceased are victims of an as-yet-to-be-identified environmental or viral invasion, the report concluded, *the agency must consider further study of this incident and apply quarantine and outcome scenarios, if appropriate. However, this agent is reluctant to condone such an action at this time for the following reasons. (1) All ten subjects were found wearing an identical "dog tag"-style necklace featuring an unidentifiable symbol. (2) Each victim had a peculiar tattoo on the back of the neck featuring a unique letter/number combination. (3) Also found at the scene were inscriptions made on the dam wall by the men. These messages are either gibberish or in some kind of code.*

These three peculiarities may imply membership in a local club or cult, a theory which is currently supported by local law enforcement. Attempts have already been made to keep the discovery of a so-called ritual suicide out of the local newspapers for this reason. Bearing these anomalies in mind, the results of this report should be considered once the lost-time activities of the deceased can be accurately determined by local law enforcement. At present, there are too many x-factors in the case to recommend an immediate course of action.

Included in this file are photographs of the bodies at the CDC Dallas office, and at the scene of discovery.

"My God," Jay muttered. He rubbed his eyes and looked to the others. "Is this . . . is this what we're looking for?"

"Could very well be," Jack said. "The NEPTH-charge symptoms that Kleinman told us about are all here, especially what this agent calls 'brainrot.' The personality change is evident in the men, too—a possible sign that the original memories were erased, and a new identity was downloaded into the mind. That may be the clincher. What do you think, Kilroy?"

Kilroy2.0 placed his hand on the computer mouse and directed it to the bottom of the page. The pointer rested over a link that read, *Attached image 1 of 24: nu4446-ot-898vf-1.jpg.*

"I want to see these photographs," he said, and tapped the mouse button.

It was a crime-scene photo, taken from one end of the dam's sixteen-hundred-foot-long catwalk. There they were, all of the men lying on the walkway. They didn't look dead. They looked as if they were sleeping . . . except for one strange detail. Each man held a fat permanent marker in his left hand. Near the body of each man was writing on the dam wall. The photo was taken from too far away for the messages to be legible, but one thing was clear: the writing looked like the chicken scratchings of a child, or of the elderly. Jagged, ghoulish. The men had written these words as their bodies went spastic, as the brains inside their skulls were rotting. Their last words.

"What does that say?" Jay asked, pointing to the message in the foreground of the photo. " 'Yg'? 'Ygcn'?"

"Let's find out," Kilroy said, and clicked another link.

"Jesus!" Jack hissed.

They stared at the photograph, the jagged red lines slashing across the slate gray of the dam's concrete surface. It was a mad-man's signature, a killer's taunt . . . in another language.

ygcn ygclj

"What the hell?" Jay said. "That's no language I know."

Kilroy clicked more links. The images appeared, and they looked at them in horrified silence. The rest were written in that same creepy nonlanguage.

"These were written by ten different men," Jack said. His face was pale. "But look. The handwriting is identical."

"So they *were* NEPTH-charged," Kilroy said.

Jay stared at the screen. His eyes were watering. He couldn't blink. "What does it mean?" he whispered.

"It means this is bigger than we thought," Jack said. "These are messages. For us. It's another goddamned puzzle."

Hugh Sheridan's quarters smelled of cigarettes and dust. Beneath that, an underlying aroma of mothballs. The place was a base-ment studio apartment, complete with kitchenette, dining alcove, and Murphy bed. In the dimness, Father Thomas spotted a couch and two comfy chairs; Sheridan was sitting in one of these. Most of the overhead track lights were out, either switched off or filled with long-dead bulbs. A single spotlight shone uselessly into a corner.

"Can I sit down?" Thomas asked.

The shadow of his father waved an arm toward the couch. "I certainly don't expect you to stand."

Thomas sat on the far end of the couch. That musty smell was everywhere now. He squinted through the dimness at his father. Most of the man's features were lost in the shadows, but the hair seemed familiar. So did the curve of his chin, his neck. His shoulders. The silhouette of his ears, of all things. Thomas stared at him. The sensation was like finding an old photograph in a closet-shelf shoebox—that feeling of discovery, of nostalgia, bittersweet, fragile, of emotions and memories furiously whipped together by a brain surprised with such a find. It was more than looking at an old photograph, of course. But for a moment, for Thomas, that's how it felt.

He cleared his throat. His palms were sweating. He pulled the pistol from his belt and placed it on the cushion beside him. He noted Sheridan's curious glance. The priest felt a moment of regression, as if he'd just been caught with a hand in the cookie jar.

"It was just for show," he stated, embarrassed. He sighed. "Okay. I know you're not my father. I know that I only *remember* you as my father, and that those memories are someone else's. I know that. But I don't *feel* that. Not yet. There's a difference."

Hugh Sheridan nodded.

"It's hard for me to look at you . . . to hear you . . . and not associate it to a childhood with you," Thomas said. "But I'm going to try. I have—"

"I heard some of what you said through the intercom. But let me be the first to ask a question. Which number are you?"

"Number? I don't follow."

The shadow-dad changed position in the chair; he was reaching for something in his shirt pocket. Smokes. Thomas heard the characteristic tinny *chik-chik* of a disposable lighter. His father's face glowed behind the flame, an orange portrait of not *then* but *now*: bags under blue eyes, wrinkles crisscrossing over eyebrows, trenches of crow's-feet above the cheeks. Thomas felt what all estranged children feel when they see a parent after years of absence: *He looks so old. What happened while I was gone?*

Sheridan's eyes flicked up from the cigarette and gazed into Thomas's. The flame hung between them for another second, then vanished.

"I guess Kleinman didn't tell you about that," Sheridan said. "The numbers."

Thomas watched the cigarette's amber tip, transfixed. "I think there's a lot Kleinman didn't tell us."

Sheridan smiled. "I wouldn't doubt it." His voice was low, acidic. "Complicity is best given by the uninformed. You clones were given numbers when you were plucked out of those plastic wombs years ago. When the Memory Totality of John—John Alpha—was downloaded into your vacant minds, each of you was given a number . . . the number being the order in which you received the data. Numbers. Unoriginal, I know, but we were excited new parents of septuplets. I suppose if we'd cloned only four of you, we could've called you Eenie, Meenie, Miney, and Moe. But '4th Son' just doesn't have the same ring, does it?"

"Stop it," Thomas said.

Sheridan's teethed glittered. "I'm being rude, I know. What you've learned in the past two days, I've lived with for the past thirty-four years. Pardon my insensitivity. So which one are you? Are you the oldest of them—the first to receive the mind of John Smith? Or perhaps a frustrated middle child? Don't tell me who you are. Tell me *what* you are. I'll tell you your number."

"What you heard from me out there in the hall. That's . . . that's me."

"That's *who* you are. You love, you dream, you put on your pants one leg at a time just like the rest of us. Eloquent, in an endearingly naïve way. But that doesn't tell me *what* you are. To wit: you don't look like a soldier. Or a U.N. analyst."

"I get it," Thomas said, crossing his arms. "I'm the priest. Enough for you?"

"Quite." Sheridan smirked. "Johnny Five. You're alive."

Thomas blinked, not understanding.

"I'm a little surprised it would be you to come here," Sheridan said. "Fascinating. This is behavior beyond what you'd typically do. You're a rule-follower, party-line LTP." He sucked a lungful from his cigarette, then exhaled. "I thought you might be the wild child. Lucky Seven, the youngest, the black sheep. Kleinman likes him best, you know. He admires the kid's spirit."

"Black sheep."

"Of all the clones, he was the only one who completely rejected the LTP we'd assigned him. A painstakingly devised and plotted LTP, I might add. He was called the 'failed experiment.' But not by Kleinman. He told us Seven was the triumph of human cloning and MemR/I integration. Independence. Free will, if there is such a thing.

"But you, priest. You followed the LTP to the letter. It's just as well. I'm sure you're doing good things for all those true believers in the heartland."

"Stop. Please," Thomas said. "I'm not with you. What is 'LTP'?"

"Life Template Plan." Sheridan took another drag of his cigarette. He blew the smoke toward the ceiling. "Your road map. Surely you've seen the significance of *when* you were awakened from your fictitious coma, all those years ago." Thomas stared blankly at him, and Sheridan tried again. "I'm referring to your age. Sixteen. The cusp of adulthood. The time when a youngster casts an eye to the future and to career—but also a time when he is still very, ah, impressionable. Malleable. The scientists here at 7th Son built a Life Template Plan for each of you Beta clones: careers in the military, psychology, biology—"

Oh. My God.

Thomas interrupted, finishing the thought. "And our respective Uncle Karls and Aunt Jaclyns pushed us in those predestined directions. And such a well-rounded childhood would have prepared us for almost any career. I get it now. I truly get it."

It felt as if Thomas's stomach were sinking in on itself, deflating his entire body. His mind quickly flashed to fragments of his junior year in high school, after the accident. Still a new school, still a stranger in a new city. Those first few years, he had clung to whatever advice his new foster parents had given him. And why wouldn't he? In a way, he'd known them his whole life—all the postcards they'd sent from those faraway places. Uncle Karl and Aunt Jaclyn were trustworthy. They were family.

They were anything but. You learned that yesterday, Thomas. But now you realize just how badly you and the rest of the clones were hoodwinked. They preached the faith, didn't they? Karl and Jaclyn practically pushed your nose into that Catechism. Just what does that mean?

"You took advantage of us," Thomas said, his voice rising, newfound anger coursing through him. "You woke us up in new cities with new parents and terrible news. And you had already plotted out our little lives for us. What a bunch of self-righteous pricks!"

"Tut, tut, Five. We had constructed the LTPs years before you were cloned and they were for career only. We based the Life Template Plans on future-centric social studies. What 'future' careers, technologies, and political climates would be like." Sheridan grinned. "Those projections were very accurate, I might add, considering that the future is now."

Father Thomas resisted an urge to reach over and smack the man's face. It would solve nothing. He fumbled for the rosary in his pocket.

"So I was destined to become a priest, in the great and powerful plans of 7th Son."

"Indeed. You didn't go rogue, like Seven. He charted a course into the unknown, damning any guidance thrown his way. You could have been anything you wanted to be, of course. We all have that drive. But you followed the plan. In contrast, Seven had the capacity to become a nuclear physicist. It would have rounded out the team quiet nicely, don't you think?"

"Team. Kleinman didn't say anything about a team." Thomas leaned forward; the rosary beads *click-clacked*, reassuring him.

"I don't doubt that, either."

"He said we were part of a grand nature-versus-nurture experiment. He said 7th Son was designed to observe what forms our seven separate lives would take, seeing how we came from the same 'past.'"

Sheridan threw his head back and laughed. It was a wicked, rattling sound. "Sounds like soggy marketing copy, doesn't it? Heh. Proof that absolute power corrupts absolutely. He's rewriting history. Changing the past just for you, Five."

"Stop calling me that. My name's Thomas."

Sheridan laughed again. "Of course it isn't. You're *Five*. Just as the marine is *One* and the geneticist is *Four*. Do you think something as insignificant as an identity actually matters in this place? A place where a lifetime of memories can be stored as ones and zeros . . . a place where we can grow a human clone to adulthood in two years? A place where we bent the will of you and five of your brethren to embrace the livelihoods we chose for them? Do you think something as dignified as a *name* has any place here? You're even more naïve than I thought."

Thomas shook his head. *He's not making any sense.* "What does that mean?"

"It means, my dear Thomas, that 7th Son was—and still is— something much more than a glorified master's thesis about nature and nurture. It's about teams. About creating . . . no, *constructing* teams. We're going to play a little game: I start the joke, you give me the punch line. It goes like this. Clone seven different children, give them the same memories, separate them, train them in different fields of study, and then bring them back together. After an adjustment period, what do you have?"

Thomas's head was swimming. "I don't know."

"Oh, come now. Think. You're a preacher. Think about *allll* of those Christian sects out there, across the world. Each of them uses the Bible as the foundation of their faith. Don't they?"

Thomas sat in silence for a few seconds. "Yes and no."

"Explain."

"There's different translations of the Bible. Different interpretations. Nuances. Variations on a theme."

Sheridan's eyebrows raised in approval. "Precisely. Variations. The same man—in body and in childhood memory—but in seven different adult incarnations. With seven different areas of expertise, brought together for a common purpose. Follow?"

And there it was.

"You're talking about building an army," Thomas said.

TWENTY-NINE

T a-daa," John Alpha said. The words echoed in the silence of the smashed Folie à Deux nightclub.

The killer wore a black business suit, Italian. Collarless white shirt. Alpha was pale, almost sickly, his blond brown hair slicked back. He grinned past a trimmed goatee and stretched his arms outward from his side, palms facing out.

John gazed down at the villain from the club's balcony. For a moment, the man looked like a car salesman. Or a mortician.

"I honestly didn't expect to see you here," Michael the marine finally said. His voice was low and calm. "I thought you'd be the hide-in-the-bunker type. The puppetmaster who doesn't get dirt under his fingernails."

John Alpha glanced down at his manicured nails, then folded his hands together. His eyebrows raised as he smiled. "Who says I'm not? But I couldn't let my little NEPTH-charged killers have all the fun."

"Fuck you," one of the 7th Son soldiers said. Fleming. John Alpha looked up at the ceiling, bored, as if he hadn't heard. John followed the man's gaze. He was looking through the hole in the ceiling, probably at the invisible sniper still posted up there.

"My shooters," Alpha said, turning back to the group on the dance floor. "I'm actually quite proud of them. They were all a mess when I found them days ago. Homeless and hungry, each one."

One of the Vaporwear guards behind John grunted his assent. The air was thick with that rancid, boozy smell again. John held his breath.

"But with a deep-fried personality change, even human garbage can become government-trained killers," Alpha continued. "You know a little something about that, don't you, Michael?"

"Who are they?" the marine asked. "Who'd you put inside their heads?"

Alpha laughed. *That laugh sounds like mine,* John thought.

"The direct approach is dollar-store material, marine," Alpha said. "It's tired, trite, and cheap—and it certainly hasn't gotten you very far today. Find the answer for yourself, if you live through this night." Alpha paused, and grinned. "That's called foreshadowing, by the way."

"We get it," Michael replied. "So I guess it comes back to one thing. We're here."

"Yes." John Alpha looked up toward the balcony, where John and a bleeding, wheezing Dr. Mike stood. His eyes met John's, and his face blossomed into a look of delight. John shuddered; it felt as if someone had poured ice water down his spine.

"Hello, walkabouter," Alpha called. "Untrained, untested— and yet you still charge into a battle zone such as this. Can I make a confession? Can I admit that I'm unsurprised by the surprise visit? That it's yet another fine piece of free will you—"

Suddenly, Alpha took a quick step backward. "Kill him!" he cried.

A single shot rang out from above, from the sniper in the skylight. John instinctively closed his eyes. He did not see Fleming's chest explode and spatter across the wooden dance floor. He did not see Fleming's body fall to the floor. He did, however, hear the knife Fleming had been holding clatter to the ground. John opened his eyes and watched the man's blood spread from his body, oozing across the floor, slipping past the fallen blade. Fleming had apparently intended to throw it at Alpha.

"Now where were we?" John Alpha said pleasantly. "Yes, the guitarist. It's only appropriate that you're here for the sacrifice. The highly exaggerated deaths of my parents hit you hardest, didn't they, John? Aimless wanderer you are, playing hopscotch all throughout your life, anchorless, wasting the gift the man-gods at 7th Son gave you."

Alpha smiled. It was a cruel expression.

"Oh, the life—the lives—you could have lived, Beta. And yet you idly strum and smoke away your existence, so confidently living in your leashless world, inventing the rules as you go, so damned driven to be something you know not what. You disgust me. You have no shackles like the others, and yet you're damned by your own mediocrity. You're not a triumph of free will. You're imprisoned by it. What a *waste*."

John felt a tittering doubt tickle at the base of his brain, a voice that insisted Alpha was right, so very right. Had he dedicted his life to being dedicated to nothing? It felt true, horrifyingly true.

But does it matter? he thought frantically. *He's trying to break you before you can ever raise a fist to fight. Trying to . . .*

"Shut up," John said, looking down at Alpha. "I'm not the damned one. I'm not a killer."

"Nor am I. *I've* killed no one. Not even Dania Sheridan, my— our—mother." Alpha nodded and jabbed a thumb over his shoulder, toward the open double doors. "She's back there. In the cellar storeroom. The floors and walls must have shielded her thermal readings from your cute RadioShack toys. Well, that and the very special insulation I had installed. John, I haven't murdered a soul."

From beside John, Dr. Mike made a half-harrumph, half-groan. "No, you've just been the Bond villain calling the shots from the shadows," the profiler muttered. John turned to look at the man. The color was draining from Dr. Mike's face. The blood from his wound covered the entire sleeve of his jacket. Now one of the Vaporwear shades behind them was telling Dr. Mike to shut his yap . . . and John winced as Mike's head recoiled once again from a pistol-whipping. Dr. Mike swayed, then steadied himself.

And that's when John spotted the hand grenade hanging from Dr. Mike's chest holster/harness. His mind flitted to what Michael had said just minutes before—*a leap of faith*. John turned his eyes from his brother to the shimmering statue before them. He began to plan. He even whispered a prayer.

John Alpha laughed. "A Bond villain. That's nice," he called to Dr. Mike. "A compliment . . . if I thought what I was doing was evil. You see evil every day in your job, Mike. But I'm trying to save this world. Consider this: Only at the darkest hour does humanity pull itself together to become truly great. Only in times of calamity and chaos do signs of true unity and genius shine across the globe. Wars bring out the worst in mankind—but they also bring out its best."

John looked over at Dr. Mike, to the grenade strapped to his chest. *I can do this*, he thought. *It won't take much. A distraction, just a second.* He glanced behind Mike, trying to see the shade holding his brother at gunpoint. It was nearly impossible to make out exactly *where* the shade was. Whatever this Vaporwear was made of, it was doing a bang-up job—even at this close range. John squinted.

"Keep those eyes dead ahead," the shade hissed. John did as told. One fact played in his favor: he knew exactly where the second shade behind him was standing; the sour-sweet rank of booze was a dead giveaway. And John had a feeling he knew how the shade standing behind Dr. Mike did business.

Meanwhile, Alpha was saying, "Take World War Two. Axis powers decimate country after country, commit wholesale slaughter . . . and the Allies band together. Build the bomb. Win the war. Redirect the course of humanity."

Come on, come on, John thought. *Wrap it up. Make a fuckin' quip. Just give me a second. Just one measly second.*

"But we are complacent," Alpha droned, "lethargic, morbidly obese from our creature comforts. Humanity shines brightest when there is a problem to solve, but we no longer have problems. America's enemies are illiterates who live in caves and dream of suitcase bombs. There is no innovation of the human spirit. There are only sleepwalkers. I will wake them up, Mike. I suppose this would be my Bond-villain manifesto—the obligatory monologue the evil genius makes before the tide turns in favor of the heroes. What, pray tell, do you think of it?"

This is it. God, if you're up there, help us, help me . . .

Dr. Mike chuckled. "I think you're more Beale than Blofeld. You're mad. As hell."

The shade behind Dr. Mike snarled and again cracked his pistol across the back of Mike's helmet . . . just as John had hoped. Dr. Mike wasn't stoic this time—he couldn't be, not anymore— and staggered forward, toward the balcony railing. He cried out in pain.

You can't come back from this. Not ever. No takebacks.

John stepped over and steadied his brother. The shade behind him began to bark a protest, but John didn't let him finish. As he held Dr. Mike for leverage, John swung his leg backward in an improbable, ungainly arc—a downright ugly maneuver, graceless. But it worked. John's boot crashed into the shade's stomach. The

shade belched a ridiculous sound—*poooh!*—and staggered backward.

In one smooth motion, John snatched the grenade from Dr.
Mike's vest, pulled the pin, and threw it behind them. The grenade smashed through one of the glass walls of the VIP section,
leaving a hole the size of a baseball. Somewhere far away, the first
shade was beginning to shout.

"The hell?" Dr. Mike whispered.

John nodded quickly to the silver statue standing beyond the
balcony.

"We're superheroes. Time to fly." He then pushed them both
toward the waist-high railing. It wasn't much of a running start,
but it was all they had. *Just like track and field back in high school,*
John thought. *Just like the hurdles.*

They leaped over the railing, into the void, toward the shimmering statue. Behind them, all hell broke loose.

John and Mike soared through the air and slammed into the open
arms of the Folie à Deux sculpture. Both men recoiled from the
impact—the statue *gonged* its disapproval—and tumbled down the
warped helix of its silver base. As they landed, the grenade upstairs unleashed its war.

The explosion was brief, but merciless. The glass walls of the
VIP section exploded outward, flinging fire and millions of glass
shards onto the balcony. For an instant, the air was filled with
lost, glittering amber crystals . . . then they found their homes,
slicing into the walls, the balcony furniture, and the Vaporwear
shades. The blast shoved both shades forward, slamming them
into—then over—the railing. They crashed onto the dance floor
and flopped to rest like rag dolls.

Then both shades suddenly became *men* again, the technology inside their protective camouflage suits shredded by the shrapnel. Their bodies were covered in thousands of glass shards.

The diversion was more than enough for Michael and his soldiers. They dashed over to the pile of guns on the dance floor. The lone shade posted at the skylight began shooting at them. The wooden dance floor exploded upward from the gunfire. Lockwood's right calf disintegrated from a sure shot. Michael grabbed an XM8 and fired at the ceiling. Plaster snowflakes fell from above.

John Alpha scrambled back to the end of the club from where he'd emerged just minutes ago. The doors slammed shut behind him.

The sniper on the roof was going crazy now; his shooting was sloppy, unfocused. Several rounds ripped past John and Dr. Mike, who had taken cover behind the statue.

Michael sprayed more rounds toward the skylight. There was a shriek from up there . . . then silence.

Silence.

No, not quite. Police sirens were crying out in the distance now, getting closer.

"L.A.'s finest. My buddies," Dr. Mike croaked. His helmet was lost in the fall; a gash above his left eye spurted blood down his face. He looked up at John and grinned though the mess. "If we get out of here alive, I so owe you a beer."

Michael clomped up to John and Dr. Mike.

"Good work," the marine said. "Listen up. I just radioed both choppers to come and get us, emergency evac from the roof. They'll be here in about ten minutes." He nodded toward the center of the dance floor; what was left of the team was prepping the dangling rappelling ropes. He turned to Dr. Mike. "You're going up first, along with Lockwood. The rest will join you on the roof.

If Alpha's goons were telling the truth, you won't have to worry about any more shooters."

"No argument here. I'm fucking over this place."

Michael then looked at John. "Anything broken?"

John shook his head. "We have to get Mom. She's still here."

"So's John Alpha," Michael replied.

Two of the four surviving 7th Son soldiers—Rubenstein and Weekley—ran up to the clones. "The gear's ready," Rubenstein reported. Michael nodded, and the soldiers pulled Dr. Mike to his feet. Dr. Mike slung an arm over each soldier's shoulder and was dragged off toward the skylight.

Michael stared into John's eyes. He pressed a Beretta pistol into the man's hand.

"We got ten minutes to find Mom and capture Alpha," Michael said. "We're not gonna have another shot, so don't hesitate. If you have to kill him, kill him. Understand?"

"Line's already crossed," John muttered. "Can't come back, not ever. No takebacks."

Michael's expression softened for a moment. He nodded.

They ran to the rear of the club, toward the closed doors.

The doors weren't locked, as Michael had feared. In fact, they swung open easily to reveal another surprise: a long, sloping hallway with lighting—lighting that worked. Glowing bare-bulb lights swung listlessly from the ceiling by their power cables. Whatever insulation Alpha had installed to confound the team's thermal sensors had clearly done the same for the devices' electrical-sensing setting. Until now, Michael hadn't had a clue that there was working electricity in Folie à Deux.

They stepped into the hall. Michael reached up to his helmet, tapped the thermal imager's button, and looked down at the LCD screen strapped to his wrist. "Check your sensor."

John did. His display was a sputtering, pixelated mess of static and snow. He tapped the screen, perplexed.

"Whatever shielded these lights from our sensors is scrambling them now," Michael said. "Let's hope the lights stay on."

They stepped down the sloping hall, their boot soles squeaking on the green-and-white-tiled floor. Whatever überstyle of the rich and famous that had once lived on Folie à Deux's dance floor was abandoned here for practicality. The hall floor sloped steadily downward, heading underground. According to the blueprints they had examined back in Virginia, this hallway had been built for keg runners and staff. At the end of the hall would be another door, that one to the storage cellar . . . and beyond that, John Alpha and Dania Sheridan. Mom.

The swinging bulbs above created more shadow than light. The men continued down the hall, the squeaks of their boots dying down as they went. *Stay cool, salty,* Michael thought. *You've fried bigger fish than this.* He took a slow breath through his nostrils. The air was stale, musty, and there was something else. Like the smell of a construction site, of jackhammer dust.

Now their steps were producing another sound, the brittle *crunch-crunch* of treads on gravel. Michael looked to the floor. Stones and dirt covered the linoleum tiles. He glanced up to the walls. Cracks were in the plaster on the left-hand wall, jagged horizontal zigzags lancing from the shadows at the end of the hallway. The smell intensified as they skulked onward; a voice in the back of Michael's mind pined for a breathing mask.

They came to the end of the hallway. The metal storeroom door was before them. Closed. Probably locked.

But it wasn't the end of the hallway, not anymore. A jagged hole had been cut into the hallway's left wall, about six feet in diameter. A crude passageway lay beyond, carved through the building's foundations. Alpha had been busy in his new club. He'd been digging. A faint light glowed from beyond a curve deep within the passage.

Two paths. Two clones. Less than ten minutes. *Goddamnit.*

Michael turned back to John. The civilian was nodding; he'd already done the math. *He's fleet-footed. A survivor. Let's hope he stays that way.* Michael jerked his chin toward the tunnel. "I'll take this way. You take the storeroom. We meet up topside. If the choppers come and I'm not up there, don't wait for me. Get out. Tell me you understand."

John cocked the Beretta in his hand. "Yeah. I got it." Michael saw his brother was trembling. Shaking enough to notice, but not enough to count him out. Good.

"Try the door," Michael said. "I got you covered."

John reached for the doorknob. The tremor in his hand was more pronounced now.

What if it's rigged? Michael suddenly thought, watching John's hand draw closer. *We'd never know, with the sensors scrambled. What if there's a brick of C-4 just beyond that wall, and a trip cable set to spark as soon as the door opens? What if . . .*

John wrapped his hand around the knob. His hand was shaking so hard now the doorknob rattled in its metal frame. John jerked his hand back and wiped his palm across his chest.

"Nerves," he said, looking up and smiling nervously. "Just give me a—"

Suddenly, a sound from their left. From far down the tunnel. Something scraping against rock and dirt, then a hiss of pebbles spattering to the ground.

"Go, hoss," Michael said. "Go in so I can get down there."

John grabbed the doorknob, twisted it, and pushed. It swung inward on rust-coated hinges. Nothing happened. No booby trap, no shrieking John Alpha, no bouncing betty spitting fire and metal. Michael glanced into the room beyond—dark—then to the doorframe. He caught the glint of an exposed light-switch fixture just beyond, inside the room.

"Light's by the door, on the wall, to the right," Michael said as he stepped away from John. "Good luck."

Michael didn't wait for a reply. He ran into the tunnel, his machine gun pointed straight ahead.

THIRTY

A cross the country, in the Common Room, Jay tore his eyes from the monitors. "How do you know these messages are for us?" he asked, pointing to the digital photographs. "There's no way—"

Jack waved his hand impatiently, cutting off the question. He nodded to the screen.

"It fits the pattern of Alpha the puzzlemaker, doesn't it?" Jack's face was turning red. "John Alpha—or whoever he NEPTH-charged into these men's heads—is talking to *us*. Damn it!"

"It means more than that," Kilroy2.0 said quietly. Now submerged in his element, deep-diving in conspiracy, his words came out easily, measured. "These messages, whatever they mean, imply that Alpha knew we'd be looking for him—and he knew it long before we were brought together. These messages were written five months ago. That was before the president was murdered, before Dania Sheridan—Mom—was kidnapped."

Kilroy2.0 tapped the screen. "This was orchestrated." He gave a low, appreciative chuckle. "This was planned. Alpha knew we'd eventually be called to hunt him down. So he planted some evidence for us to find. This presumable puzzle. Probably the first puzzle he made . . . but not the first puzzle we would solve."

"The Morse-code bit," Jay marveled. "With the song—that was the first puzzle we encountered. But that was planted three weeks ago, when Mom was kidnapped."

"As I said," Kilroy replied. "Orchestrated."

"He's playing with us," Jack said. "He knew he'd get to play with *us*. But how?"

Kilroy2.0 offered a grim smile. "He created the game, Jack. Remember the Fowler boy? Yes? The one who killed the president? Yes? Now, remember the clue. What clue did Alpha leave that he *knew* would alert the right people that he was behind it?"

"The tattoo," Jay said, nodding. "The tattoo in the ear."

Jack scratched his beard. His eyes were wide. "Let me get this straight. Alpha deliberately puts the tattoo in the kid's ear because he knows that Kleinman—or someone else at 7th Son—will spot it and know what it means. And Alpha, in turn, also knows Kleinman will bring *us* together to stop him. So he plants these messages months before he NEPTH-charges the Fowler boy to show us how smart he is. That's what you're saying? Unbelievable."

Kilroy raised his eyebrows. His eyes turned slowly to the photos on the screens.

"Okay," Jack said, sighing. "Let's say you're right. Alpha's given us a shout-out from the past. He's telling us that he knows we're trying to find him—and the mere existence of the photos tells us he's been plotting for at least five months."

"At least," Kilroy said.

Jay leaned forward, toward the monitors. "Let's see what else we can glean from this."

They stared at the screen. It was filled with nonsense words: vowels and consonants tossed into a maddening mishmash.

Jack shook his head. "We should write these down, download them or something. We only have about an hour and a half before Kilroy's army stops clogging up the bandwidth."

Jay snatched the pen and pocket notebook from the table and began scribbling. Kilroy2.0 downloaded the pictures on the screen. He then began downloading the images of the victim's necks, and the strange letter/number combinations tattooed on them.

"One last photograph we haven't looked at," Kilroy said, circling an on-screen link with his mouse: *Attached image 24 of 24: nu4446-ot-898vf-24.jpg.* "This must be the dog-tag necklace the dead men were wearing."

"As if we didn't have enough to digest," Jack said. "Go ahead, click it."

The photograph popped up in a separate window. Just as the CDC report said, the necklace was engraved with an unidentifiable symbol. It was triangular, a vaguely satanic-looking thing, with hooked barbs curling outward from its three points.

"What in the hell is that?" Jack asked.

No one had a reply.

An army.

The words echoed in his mind as Father Thomas instinctively clutched at his rosary.

"*Army* is a strong word, Thomas." Sheridan pulled himself from the comfy chair and stood. The apartment spotlight above made him look like a wraith. "But you're partially right."

As the old man stretched and stepped around the efficiency apartment, he told Thomas to consider the possibilities of such a group of men. Their common childhood experiences would be a built-in cohesive, and they would bond more quickly than strangers in similar circumstances, thanks to those shared memories. As living "variations on a theme," their body language would be similar, as would their references and conversational shorthand. They would communicate far more effectively than a team of strangers.

These clones would react better as a unit, Sheridan said. They would be personally invested in the team, whatever the team's mission might be. And they would each bring a similar yet viably different perspective to a problem.

"I'm telling you that 7th Son was designed to build teams of men—brilliant men in their respective fields—and bring them together in times of crisis. The perfect team, unified emotionally and mentally at its core. Do you understand what I'm saying?"

Thomas fleetingly replayed the past day. He and the other Beta clones had swapped memories, stories. *We did bond*, he realized. *Tossed out details that only we/I thought we/I had. And we worked pretty well together when we cracked John Alpha's message. It works. God help me—no, God help us—it really works.*

"Yeah. I understand." Thomas placed his head between his knees. "So what are we then? Michael, John, Jack, me, and the rest of the Beta clones?"

"You're the dry run. The lab rats. The first tentative step in a long-term project exploring the viability of this, ah, *technique* of team creation. We never planned to bring you seven together— you were supposed to live out your LTPs, retire, and die, blissfully unaware that you were clones. Meanwhile, 7th Son would have a wealth of data to apply to the next stage of the project. The growth-accelerant serum, for instance, has already been improved for the next generation of clones. What we grew in years would now only take months. From what I understand, the next stage of the experiment is to begin by the end of the decade . . . with a new Alpha and new Betas. But *this* Alpha apparently had other ideas."

Thomas lifted his head. "Revenge."

"That's right. And he's invited his 'children' to stop him. Whatever he's planned, you and the rest of the Betas apparently play a
pivotal role."

Thomas shook his head. He looked down. His hands were
trembling again.

"Come on, Thomas. Walk with me. You probably need it more
than I do."

The door to Sheridan's apartment whooshed open, and Thomas
nodded to Lieutenant Stone as they stepped into the hallway.

"Where are we going?" Thomas asked.

"I haven't been here in years," Sheridan replied. "Let me follow
my bliss."

The priest nodded.

"You do have an edge," Sheridan said as they strode down the
halls of Level Fourteen. "Against Alpha, I mean. Your childhood is
his childhood and that might help. But to be honest, I'm not sure
how much. While you and the Betas woke up to your new lives all
those years ago, John Alpha lived and worked here at 7th Son. He
watched each of you. He *studied* each of you."

The man stopped now and stared into Thomas's eyes. "And he
took lessons from one of the greatest predators who has ever lived
in this century."

"I don't . . ."

Sheridan began to chuckle again as he raised his arms to the
ceiling. The old man's eyes glinted in the darkness. His voice was
cold, damned. "The great creator of this place."

The clone blinked. "Are you talking about Frank Berman?"

"That's *not* his name," Sheridan spat, lowering his arms. "That's
the name Kleinman gave you in that conference room, another
revision of 7th Son's history. Why? Probably to bluff the geneticist
and the conspiratorial hacker; they might have recognized his real

name. The man's name was Klaus Bregner. He was the lost *Teufels-Chirurg*. Do you know the phrase?"

Thomas shook his head.

"You shouldn't. Not many do, not anymore. It's German. A literal translation would be 'devil surgeon.' He was a Nazi, Thomas. A Nazi doctor."

Thomas felt his body stiffen. He hadn't heard the phrase *Nazi doctor* in a long time. That was dark stuff. Bad mojo.

"You're joking."

"Of course not," Sheridan replied. "You do know what I mean when I say 'Nazi doctor,' don't you?"

"Yeah." Thomas made an effort to catch up with Sheridan, who'd already resumed his trek. "Human experimentation in the concentration camps, right? Vivisection. Exposing Jews to everything from the plague to compression chambers. Mengele. Experiments on twins. *Marathon Man. The Boys from Bra*—" Thomas looked at Sheridan, his mouth agape. Finally: "Not really. Not for real."

"Bregner was the head of a Nazi project code-named *Doppeln*," Sheridan said. "It was composed of biologists. Germany's elite, naturally. A very small group; by Bregner's accounts, only five scientists ever contributed directly to the project. Only a precious few knew of its existence. It was clandestine and well funded. Bregner reported to Hitler himself, if that gives you an inkling of its sensitivity."

Thomas nodded.

"Do you speak German?" Sheridan asked. "No. That's the other one—the UN man, the lovebird. *Doppeln* is a verb. It means 'to double.' That was what Hitler wanted. Duplicates. Not of himself, but of the Reich's *Überkrieger*—its so-called superwarriors. The *Überkrieger* were the SS's upper crust. The elite's elite, top-drawer

men. Given what you've learned in the past two days, the goal of
the *Doppeln* project should be obvious."

Sheridan paused. He lit his cigarette and watched the smoke
tendrils float skyward. Thomas waited in silence. He was beyond
questions now.

"The Nazi doctors you've heard about . . . Josef Mengele, Clau-
berg, Oberheuser . . . they all had a tenuous connection to the
Doppeln project," Sheridan said finally. "The thanatology experiments at Auschwitz and other camps were never performed to
satisfy some professional or medical curiosity, as the world has
been told. Nor were they the inexplicable actions of men consumed by power and madness. The findings of their experiments
were compiled and forwarded in secret to Bregner and the *Doppeln*
project. It was *organized*, Thomas. All those terrible experiments
you've ever heard of were ordered from on high. The beast had a
brain. Bregner."

Sheridan turned a corner, and Thomas followed. The old man's
face was pale, haggard. His blue eyes were looking at something
far, far away. He was walking on autopilot; a kind of muscle memory, if that made sense.

"Not all of the Nazi elite escaped Germany, like Mengele," he
said, shaking his head slowly. "Most of them were captured. And
nearly all of the doctors tried at Nuremberg committed suicide,
were imprisoned, or swung from the gallows. But not Bregner. He
vanished. Rumors of his actions have made a few history books—
secrets of the Reich don't stay secret forever, after all. But Bregner,
the true mastermind behind the Nazi experiments, only scores a
sentence in most history books, if that. He's a mere footnote of a
footnote in the annals of Nazi history."

"Why?"

"Extreme secrecy or sheer disbelief, mostly. But I assume it's
something else, as well. Bregner's *Doppeln* project didn't use the

death-camp Jews as its test subjects. No, the *Doppeln* scientists ex-
perimented upon members of the very *Überkrieger* they were trying to replicate. The Reich's most cunning wolves were sacrificed
to further the Great Cause. To re-create the perfection of a brilliant Aryan, one must plumb its pure source, no? Let the Mengeles
cut open the filthy Jews and send back their reports. But only
Bregner and his conspirators would touch pure Aryan blood. That
was the logic behind the *Doppeln* experiments. And in the eyes of
the historians who might actually believe this history, Nazis cutting open Nazis isn't an atrocity. It's poetic justice. Hence, no
mention in the books.

"When the Allies took the southern-German mining town of
Merkers in 1945, they discovered enormous caches of art and
money hidden in its salt mines. They also found the country villa
which housed the *Doppeln* project. Did Kleinman mention he was
a part of that team? It's true. They captured Bregner; in fact, he
was the only *Doppeln* scientist who hadn't gobbled his cyanide
capsule when Joe came crashing through the gates. He was held in
secret for more than a year. After the Nuremberg trials were over,
his new life began. His life here in America."

Sheridan looked into Thomas's eyes again. "Have you ever
heard of something called Operation Paperclip?"

"No," Thomas whispered.

"Created by the United States government after World War
Two. From the mid-1940s to the late fifties, hundreds of former
Nazi scientists emigrated to America. Their accumulated military
and scientific knowledge was what our government craved, particularly since the Red Menace was looming on the horizon. These
Nazis were given a deal: in exchange for amnesty and the acquit-
tal of war crimes, they would divulge their wartime secrets and
help build America into a superpower. Nazis helped make our
bombs bigger, our planes faster. They got our asses into outer

space. Not many people know that former Nazis contributed to the success of the U.S. space program."

Thomas was about to admit his ignorance, too, but Sheridan absently waved his hands.

"It doesn't matter. What does matter is that Klaus Bregner was brought to this country to continue his research, albeit in a much more, ah, *supervised* setting. And thus endeth the tale of the lost *Teufels-Chirurg*—and the beginning of Project 7th Son. Bregner was never formally in charge of this experiment, and he had no official power or policy-making ability. But he was its driving force from the beginning. In exchange for his survival, Bregner lived here in the complex, a slave to the research. He was never permitted to go topside. From the time he came here until his death four years ago, Bregner never left this facility. As far as the rest of the world was concerned, he *was* dead.

"When John Alpha was brought to this facility after the fictional car accident and was explained the truth behind 7th Son, he and Bregner bonded. Despite the age difference, they became good friends. Bregner was a grandfather, a teacher. Alpha and Bregner avidly followed the progress of you Beta clones. As I said before, they studied you. When John Alpha escaped from the facility, Bregner became depressed. The more sentimental staff members here said the old man was suffering from a broken heart. Appropriately enough, Bregner committed suicide by overdosing on his heart medication just months after Alpha left. Dania and I were divorced by then, and she was long gone. But I wasn't. I was still here. The staff had always thought he was a nice man—friendly, forthcoming. But I said good riddance when I learned of his death."

"Once a Nazi, always a Nazi," Thomas said.

"My sentiments exactly. Perhaps the roots of Alpha's betrayal can be found in the lessons Bregner taught him those years ago.

I've been wondering about that lately. Old habits and old beliefs die hard, especially when there's a new generation with which to share them. Perhaps Bregner did just that. Perhaps he didn't."

Thomas nodded. They walked together, in silence.

So that begins to explain it, Thomas thought. *The roots of this place. The need for secrecy, no outside involvement. No wonder Alpha ran. No wonder he's scheming for revenge against this country, against us. He was taught by a caged animal. A caged animal teaching another caged animal how to survive.*

And what does a caged animal pine for most? To be free.

Finally, Thomas spoke.

"So tell me how Dania Sheridan fits into all this. And why John Alpha has kidnapped her."

THIRTY-ONE

ohn silently wished Michael good luck as he saw the marine dash into the void beneath Folie à Deux. Then he
reached forward, his fingers spider-crawling against the
inside wall, searching for the light switch. He felt the rough cinder-
block walls, a small metal box protruding . . . there. He snapped
the switch upward.

The cellar's fluorescent lights hummed like houseflies in a jar,
then sputtered to life. It was the storeroom, just as he remembered
from the blueprints. John held his gun outward, sweeping it left
and right as his eyes adjusted to the illumination. No one was in
here. Just an empty room filled with memories of what Folie à
Deux once was.

It was all familiar to the bartender. There, in a far corner: old
boxes, stacked nearly to the ceiling, of Grey Goose, Maker's Mark,
Absolut, Southern Comfort. Directly in front of him was the
stainless-steel door of a walk-in refrigerator. Another corner was
dedicated to mops, buckets, bags filled with sawdust. A utility dolly
lay on its side, just by the door. John could smell the ghosts of
broken liquor bottles and tapped kegs.

He holstered his pistol. *There's nothing here. That means I shouldn't be here. I should be running after Michael. Alpha's back there, in the tunnel. Mom's back there.*

Nodding to himself, John turned to leave the room. And that's when he spotted the chair. There was nothing special about it; just a dark wooden chair left leaning carelessly against the wall. But the wall just beyond the chair, that was the curious thing. A Jackson Pollock wannabe had splattered reddish brown paint all over it.

A chill snaked its way down John's back, then through his arms.

He gazed down at the floor, and at the dotted-line trail of paint drops—*blood drops*—that began from the chair resting cockeyed against the wall.

They ended at the door to the walk-in refrigerator.

"Mom?" John whispered.

Trembling, he began to walk toward the glinting steel door. He did not draw his pistol.

Michael trotted down the carved stone passageway, toward the dim light ahead, trying to keep his breathing measured, shallow. The dust and grit from the freshly cut rock was almost a mist in this cramped space; it fought into Michael's nostrils and eyes.

Alpha was back here, running from him, scrambling deeper into the rathole he'd made for himself. *Fine. Run. I'll catch you.*

The tunnel turned steadily to the left . . . then another straightaway. Michael considered the path of the tunnel against the layout of the club. *We're double-backing toward the club proper. I'm probably somewhere beneath the dance floor now. Does he have a tunnel leading out to the sewer lines beneath Sunset Boulevard? Is he going to worm out of this?*

Wait. Another smell through the fog of stone-stink. Cologne. *I'm catching up.*

The light was growing brighter as he neared the end of the

tunnel. Directly ahead now. Light shining not from above, but from nearly eye level. A construction work light. Michael stopped running and squinted through the glare. A shadow moving, up ahead. Stepping in front of the light.

The silhouette raised its hands.

"Don't shoot!" a voice cried. Panting. Panicked. Male. Alpha's voice. *My voice.*

"GET ON THE GROUND!" Michael screamed. *"DO IT NOW!"*

The shadow-Alpha shook its head. "I've got a bomb." Voice nearly tittering now. "You really don't want to—"

Bluffing.

Michael pulled the XM8's trigger. Three rounds sprayed forth, strobe-lighting the tunnel walls. The light behind John Alpha burst open in a shower of sparks and glass. Alpha was flung backward by two invisible punches and crashed onto the floor. He screamed.

The marine slung the machine gun to his back and sprinted the remaining thirty feet. He reached into a pouch on the backside of his belt and yanked out a signal flare. These flares were worthless during the mission—the need for stealth upstairs was critical, both before and after the ambush. They were for signaling the choppers.

He popped off the flare cap as he covered the last twenty feet. The tunnel exploded into a manic light show of bright crimson and dancing shadow. John Alpha lay on the floor, bleeding . . . and laughing.

"That's—that's just like you, Michael," Alpha said, grinning maniacally. His teeth were slick with blood. It looked black in the flare light. "Shoot 'em all, and let God sort 'em ou—"

He coughed a mouthful of blood onto his shirt. Michael's eyes flitted over the body: one bullet in the shoulder, one in the gut.

"Brilliant shooting," Alpha said. His body was trembling from the shock now. "Lucky, too."

Alpha pointed behind himself, to where the tunnel dead-ended. Michael followed the path with his eyes—then saw it. Saw them. Saw all of them.

Metal barrels, at least a dozen, flickering in the flare's sputtering light. Each had the same words painted on its side, in bright orange letters.

Rookman Oil Inc.—JP-8 Aircraft Fuel
CAUTION!
—EXTREMELY FLAMMABLE—

"I told you I had a bomb," Alpha whispered.

John wrapped his fingers around the refrigerator door's silver handle. It was cold. Everything was cold now. That was his mother's blood splattered against the wall. Was she dead? Didn't John Alpha say something about her being alive? Was any of it true?

He wiped the sweat from his forehead with his other hand. He just couldn't seem to let go of the handle. *She's in there. No. She isn't. It's a lie. It's—*

THUNK.

The door vibrated outward. John screamed. His eyes flashed from the handle to the dull silver surface of the door before him. His blurry reflection gawked back, wide-eyed, petrified—

THUNK.

A person was in there, wanting to get out. *I thought she was dead for more than half of my life and she's just beyond this door, a prisoner, and I'm too scared, 'cause what if it isn't, what if it's something else, something wicked, something*

THUNK.

THUNK.

John closed his eyes and yanked the handle. A blast of cold

vapor swirled around him, conjuring gooseflesh. He heard the
faraway whir of the refrigeration unit, the thud of the walk-in's
door as it slammed against the wall . . . and a voice saying nothing, just grunting, pleading, trapped inside itself.

John opened his eyes. Tears began to form.

The woman was lying on the metal floor, her hands and legs
tied together. She had been gagged; two pieces of duct tape splayed
across her mouth in an X. Dried blood covered her face, her
scalp, her shoulders. Gashes were along her bare arms. A crimson-
stained bandage covered her right hand . . . only the tips of her
thumb, ring finger, and pinkie poked through the gauze. Her long
skirt had been cut in several places, her yellow blouse was stiff
with dried blood. Some of her hair was gray, presumably her natu-
ral color. The rest was red.

Blood leaked from the soles of her bare feet. The thunks had
been her kicks against the inside of the door.

Dania Sheridan writhed on the floor. Her voice, bouncing inside her mouth, begged him to free her. John looked at her face,
her high cheekbones, her brilliant green eyes. This was not his
mother. It could not be his mother. His mother was dead. This
woman was worse than dead.

But it was. It *was*.

"Mom," he said, and rushed to her. She was nodding furiously
now, and John could see that under her duct-tape gag, Dania
Sheridan was smiling.

Michael punched John Alpha in the face a second time. Then a
third. The signal flare hissed on the ground nearby; Alpha's eyes
glittered pink in the light. He was laughing again.

"Hoo-aah, marine!" Alpha cried, spraying blood through his
teeth. "I bet this takes you back to the good old days! Before the
order crushed the chaos! Remember those days, boy?"

Alpha closed his eyes and cackled. It echoed against the walls, the floor, the barrels of jet fuel behind him. Electrical wires criss-crossed over the surfaces of the barrels of JP-8, all converging into a shoebox-size metal case resting near Alpha's body. A single red light blinked from its side like a stoplight.

"Where's the switch?" Michael demanded. He squatted next to Alpha's trembling body. He grabbed the lapels of John Alpha's suit jacket, lifted him upward, slammed him onto the ground. Alpha groaned. "I see the rig you've got here," Michael barked. *"So where's the detonator switch?!"*

Alpha's head lolled to and fro; he was trying to shake his head.

"I bet the others have no idea who you were . . . before," Alpha muttered. "But I do. I watched you from the belly of 7th Son, since the Womb. Had the *haint* all over you in the beginning, Michael. Inhuman bastard, you were."

Shut up. Shut up. I'm not—

"I'm not that man anymore and you know it," Michael snarled. There wasn't much time before the choppers arrived now. *So stop wasting time,* he thought. *Get the answers you need. Now.*

Michael hands raced over Alpha's body, through his jacket pockets, over his legs, ankles . . . nothing. No remote control device to detonate the bomb.

"You were nothing, Michael. Trash. Detritus. Deadwood."

Michael punched Alpha in the jaw. More blood sprayed into the dark. Alpha coughed and spit out a molar. It skipped across his chest and fell into the shadows.

"Careful! I need those!" Alpha cried. His voice was high, goading. A sneer curled on his lips. "A man needs his choppers, Michael. You know that. I bet this *really* takes you back. Remember the Banetti job, back when you were eighteen—or rather, when you *thought* you were eighteen? Got thirty bucks for every tooth you brought back on that job. You made almost two hundred bucks that night . . . all because the guy couldn't pay his bookie. You were the mob's whore."

That was before. Before I picked myself up. Before drill. Before Force Recon. Before my love, my improbable love, my Gabriel. That was a long, long time ago. I'm a better man now—

This is exactly what he wants. End it!

"I'm not going to ask you again," Michael said. The lion inside was ravenous. It was tired of asking questions.

Alpha lay his head against the ground. Beside him, the box's red light blinked on and off. The barrels loomed in the darkness.

"I don't have it," Alpha muttered. "Dropped the remote upstairs, when I was running away from that explosive turn of events. That John is quicker than he looks."

Michael smiled. "So am I." He punched Alpha one last time. His enemy's head rocked from the impact, and that was all. Alpha was unconscious. The perfect state, Michael reasoned, in which to be during a helicopter evac.

Michael glanced at the canisters of jet fuel, then to the wires, then to the blinking box. There's no way he could defuse the thing.

He grabbed Alpha's arms, then heaved the body over his shoulder.

"I got you, fucker," he said, and ran back toward the entrance of the tunnel.

Somewhere under all that blood was Mom. Somewhere.

Using the knife from his chest harness, John cut the ropes from Dania Sheridan's quivering wrists and ankles. He pulled the duct tape from her mouth.

Dania winced from the sting, but the movements in her eyes were measured, decisive. Under control. Whatever horrors Alpha had done to her, he hadn't slain her spirit. John could see that right away. Spend enough pouring drinks for dead-enders and you know what a crushed soul looks like. Dania Sheridan didn't have that look.

She reached up and placed her trembling hands on his face. She smiled, her swollen lips spreading across bloodstained teeth. But somewhere in that smile—and in John's memories—he saw the smile of his mother. She kissed him on the forehead.

"Which one are you?" Her voice was hoarse.

"I'm John. I'm the—"

"The musician," Dania said, nodding. "I remember you. I . . . never thought I'd ever meet you. Any of you."

And I never thought I'd see you again. And here I am, seeing you for the first time. Seeing you again.

"If we don't get out of here, I'll be the only one of us you ever meet," John said. "There are choppers coming for us. Can you stand? We have to move."

She nodded. He pulled her upward, and Dania cried out as she put her full weight on her bloodied feet.

"Sorry."

"No. I'm the one who's sorry. Thank you, John."

He shook his head—*later, let's do this later*—and guided her out of the frigid chamber, out of the storage room, into the hallway. As they limped up the incline toward the ground floor of Folie à Deux, John thought of Michael and the passageway.

Is he okay?

As John kicked open the doors at the top of the hall, he found the answer to his question: Michael was already up here.

"Careful!" Michael screamed to the pair as they emerged from the hall and stood on the dance floor. Several lit signal flares were on the floor; they hissed their red light into the gloom. John saw the limp body of Alpha lying facedown on the floor beside the marine.

As Michael stepped up to the pair, John glanced upward, at the ruined skylight hole. Two rappelling ropes still dangled from above. His eyes flitted around the club. The place was a splintered, shattered wreck . . . but something was different. The realization made him cringe: the *bodies* were missing. Bodies of the 7th Son recruits. Even the Vaporwear shades were gone. *It's a cover-up. This is the proverbial china shop* . . .

John heard the wail of police sirens—much closer now—and the roar of approaching helicopters.

. . . and the bull has a getaway car.

"There's a bomb beneath us," Michael said as he hoisted Dania Sheridan's other arm around his shoulder. "Alpha's rigged a roomful of jet fuel to a detonator. He dropped the controller switch up here, so watch your step." They moved toward the rappelling ropes.

"You believe him?" John asked.

"I searched him. And with half the LAPD heading this way, we don't have time to look for it."

"How much time?" They were at the ropes now.

"Evac ETA, three minutes." Michael waved his free arm to the soldiers who were peering through the skylight from the roof. "Everything accounted for?"

Rubenstein waved back. "Affirmative. All guns, gear, and armor were retrieved. And the KIAs. We scooped up as many shells as we could. But we've got a problem up here."

Michael grunted. "What?"

"The sniper you shot. He's still alive. Says he's got a suicide pill inside his mouth. Wants to speak to one of you."

Michael glanced to John, who appeared equally mystified, and

muttered, "What a fucking mess." Then, to Rubenstein: "Keep watching him. We'll be up soon. We've got what we came for. Drop me
two EEHs."

Two beltlike nylon harnesses fell from the sky. Michael caught
one of them before it hit the ground. He turned and for the first
time acknowledged Dania Sheridan.

"Hi, Mom." He grinned. He didn't flinch from the gore on her
face, didn't bat an eye. "Good to see you again."

Dania Sheridan smiled back weakly. "Are you Michael?"

"Yeah." He adjusted the straps on the harness. "One of the few,
the proud. We don't have time to chat, Mom. Big reunion happens
later. I'm gonna put this harness on you, then you're going up."

Dania Sheridan nodded. John stepped back as Michael slipped
the harness over her chest. "This might hurt," Michael said, and
tugged two straps dangling from her shoulders. The harness
pulled taut across her chest. Dania Sheridan winced.

Michael pulled the rappelling rope close to his mother. At the
base of the rope rested a black contraption that bore an undeni-
able resemblance to Pac-Man; the rope snaked through its pie-
wedge-shaped mouth and continued through a small hole on the
opposite end. A carabiner dangled from the device. Michael
clipped the carabiner through a metal ring on Dania Sheridan's
harness.

"The ride's quick," he said. "Just let them take care of you
when you get to the top."

"Michael. Why? Why did you come for me?"

The marine's chiseled features warmed for an instant. "It's
how you raised us, Mom."

Michael pressed the round button on the device. It whined for
a few seconds, as if something inside were whirring in a centri-
fuge, then it shot up the rope, lifting Dania Sheridan along with

it. Her body rose through forty feet of space, then stopped at the roof. Rubenstein and the remaining soldiers pulled her through the skylight. The Pac-Man device slid back down the rope.

One of the choppers was overhead now. A spotlight lanced into the club, then flitted away. The helicopter wouldn't be able to land on the roof—Folie à Deux's couldn't hold the weight—but it could hover just above it. That's what the chopper pilot was doing now. The downdraft from the rotor blades roared through the skylight, creating a gale of broken metal, glass, and wood.

The clones turned to John Alpha. "He's unconscious, so this shouldn't take long," Michael said. He picked up the second harness and slipped Alpha's arms through it. He rolled Alpha's body over to tighten the straps.

John grimaced. Alpha's face was covered in blood. His nose had been broken. His bottom lip was split. Fresh splotches of purple bruises were already appearing on his face.

Michael did this.

Alpha opened his eyes.

"You should really talk to that man on the roof, John." Alpha grinned. "I'm certain he wants to confess his sins. As does Michael. Isn't that right, Michael? You've lived a *very* sinful life."

"Shut up," Michael said. He secured the harness clasps and pulled the straps taught. Alpha howled. The marine pulled a pair of plastic flex-cuffs from one of his vest pockets and slipped them over Alpha's wrists. Michael grabbed the collar of John Alpha's suit and dragged him over to the other rappelling rope.

"He lives in sin! He *bathes* in it!" Alpha screamed as Michael connected the harness to the Pac-Man device. The downdraft was a hurricane here, blowing Alpha's once well-coiffed hair about his face. "Ask him! Ask the great archangel Michael about his lover! Ask him about Gabriel!"

Michael jabbed the device's button and John Alpha shot skyward. A moment passed, and the rope-climbing machine slid back to the floor.

John looked at Michael. Even through the whipping winds around them, Michael didn't blink. "I'm a good man."

"I know," John said.

They attached the rope-climbers to their belts and zipped upward together, to the roof, to their mother and brother.

It was a spectacle worthy of a Hollywood action picture. One Black Hawk was hovering less than ten feet above Folie à Deux's roof, its rotors spinning precariously close to the abandoned office building next to the club. Another was flying in a holding pattern, scorching a path above Sunset Boulevard. Below, on the street, police cars were screeching up to the front of the club, their alert lights casting blue- and red-colored strobes across the confused faces of pedestrians and commuters. LAPD officers were trying to block the streets and sidewalks, pressing the mass of stunned bystanders away from the scene.

Michael and John climbed onto the roof and disengaged the Pac-Man climbers. Those left of the 7th Son squadron were crouching near the skylight. Dr. Mike, Dania Sheridan, and John Alpha were with them. Beyond them was the Vaporwear sniper, lying in a pool of blood. And beyond the sniper, the hovering chopper awaited, its side cargo door open and waiting.

"The KIAs are in there," Rubenstein shouted over the din, nodding to the helicopter. "There's still room for two more. You want to take the prisoner here?"

Michael nodded. "Let's stick to the plan. Alpha and I will take this ride, but only after you all have loaded up in the other bird. Radio the chopper. Tell it to move back and hold position—then get everyone else on the second one when it moves up. This one will come back for us."

"What?" John said. "No! Go now! Take Alpha with you! We'll
be fine!"

Michael shook his head. "I'm not leaving anyone behind," he
cried. "I'm the first to go in and the last to leave: that's how it
works, and that's how I want it. My word is law, remember?" He
turned to Rubenstein. "Do it."

The soldier began barking orders into his headset. The hovering chopper rose upward, then banked away from the buildings.
The crowd below on Sunset Boulevard gaped and gasped.

"And find the police band on your radio," Michael screamed to
Rubenstein. "Tell them to pull back, pull everyone back. There's a
tanker's worth of JP-8 under the building rigged to explode."

As the second helicopter swung into position, Michael grabbed
John's shoulder and pointed to the bleeding sniper. The man's
Vaporwear face mask had been removed; he was pale, wheezing,
no longer a threat. He was young. A kid, really.

"Go on and see what he has to say," Michael said. "I'll cover
you."

Michael unholstered his Beretta and drew back the slide. John
considered this, then walked over to the sniper. He went to one
knee, struck by the killer's age. *So young. No more than seventeen.
What happened to make him homeless?* He wondered how Alpha had
found this boy and administered the NEPTH-charge. John exhaled.
*Whoever he was, he's gone now. You're not speaking to a child. You're
speaking to whoever Alpha zapped into the boy's brain. An assassin.*

"You wanted to talk to me," John said.

The sniper nodded and pulled his lips apart into a grin. A
white, triangular capsule was clenched between his front teeth.
The suicide pill.

"You don't need that. We aren't going to hurt you."

The sniper placed the tip of his tongue behind the pill and
maneuvered it over, so it was placed between his molars.

"Jesus, it's over," John said. "We can take you back alive, give you medical attention. Do you understand?"

The boy/not-boy chuckled, the pill still between his teeth. "I don't want a doctor; I'm dead already. I want you to listen. I have a message—a very important message."

John stood up.

The sniper grinned. "It's the voice of the demon. My voice. The voice of Legion, the one who was many. Don't you want to know my last words to the world?"

John took a step backward, pale. "No."

The sniper laughed, cocked his head to one side, and chomped down on the fang-shaped pill. His body jittered into immediate convulsions.

"*Go fuck your mother!*" he cried through clenched teeth. The boy/not-boy doubled over, arms slamming onto the roof, foam and spittle running from his mouth. Then it was over. John shuddered, wanting to scream.

"Come on," Michael said, gently pushing John away, toward the hovering chopper. The other 7th Son soldiers—and Dr. Mike and Dania Sheridan—were already aboard. Only Michael, John, John Alpha, and the dead sniper remained on the roof.

"Go," the marine said. "I'll take both of them on the other chopper. It's doubling back now."

John nodded numbly and ran to the helicopter. He glanced out toward Sunset Boulevard. The police cars were pulling away; cops were waving back the pedestrians, most of whom were running down the block now. The bomb report had everyone backing off.

John climbed into the Black Hawk and sat in the seat next to a bloody, beaten Dr. Mike. John looked back at Michael. He waved once. Then one of the soldiers inside slammed the cargo door shut.

"Buckle the fuck up, kemo sabe," Dr. Mike said, his voice a stoned slur. "Your in-flight drinks will be served shortly. I heartily recommend the morphine."

John nodded, but wasn't listening. He was hearing the echoing voice of the sniper.

Michael quickly conducted an inventory of the situation: The helicopter filled with survivors swooped upward and outward, then hovered several hundred yards away. It would wait there for the second chopper to pick up Michael and John Alpha on the roof, then both helicopters would arc northeast. Back toward Edwards Air Force Base. Michael peered down to the street. The once-gawking bystanders were bolting away from Folie à Deux, the cops waving them away. Good. The second chopper was moving into position now. Also good.

He turned his attention to John Alpha, who lay on the roof, grinning up at him.

"All alone again," Alpha said. "You going to pull another Rodney King while everyone's looking the other way?"

"You're getting everything you deserve." The second chopper was now hovering over the roof. Its downdraft rushed across Michael's face. He walked over to John Alpha and again grabbed the man's suit jacket, dragging him across the tar-covered roof toward the helicopter. Alpha didn't struggle.

They passed the body of the NEPTH-charged sniper.

John Alpha laughed. "He didn't make it, huh?" he screamed hysterically. "But then again, he was going to die anyway. My assassins have a very short shelf life."

Michael released Alpha's jacket; the villain's torso flopped onto the roof. "We know all about it," Michael said as he walked over to the sniper's body. He grabbed the sniper's wrists and pulled the body closer to where the chopper was hovering. "You did this to a four-year-old boy, too. Don't think you're not going to pay for that."

The helicopter was now floating just feet above the roof. Its rotors were almost deafening, its downdraft ripping through their bodies. Michael picked up the sniper's body, carried it over to the chopper, and threw it into the cargo hold. He strode back to John Alpha.

Almost done now. Almost home.

"You're over and done, and you know it," Michael said, yanking Alpha to his feet. He pushed Alpha toward the open cargo door.

"It's never over. Have you even considered—"

Michael grabbed Alpha's handcuffed body and heaved him into the helicopter's cargo hold. Alpha slammed onto the metal floor, next to the sniper's body.

Michael climbed into the chopper. As he reached for the door, he glanced around the cramped space. It reeked of burned flesh and blood. He was surrounded by the bodies of the Vaporwear shades, the 7th Son soldiers. Durbin, Andrade, Travieso, Fleming, Tomasello . . . *Don't think about it, not now, not yet.* The helicopter swayed in midair, the pilot waiting for Michael to close the cargo door.

"I was saying something to you, Michael," Alpha shouted.

"Shut up." Michael grabbed the door handle.

"Amazing, that boy's suicide pill," Alpha said conversationally. "Shaped like a tooth, implanted into his gum. Just one good crunch is all it takes. You can put all kinds of things inside a fake tooth, Michael. Like I told you, a man needs his choppers—"

Michael whirled around. The helicopter swayed again.

"What are you talking about?" Michael roared, dashing toward Alpha. Alpha turned his head toward the dead sniper beside him and laughed.

It was the high-pitched laughter of the damned.

"WHAT HAVE YOU DONE?" Michael screamed. *"TELL ME!"*

John Alpha raised his eyebrows as if to say, *You poor thing.* "You can put all kinds of things inside a fake tooth. Like a radio transmitter. A transmitter to detonate a bomb."

Michael reached outward, trying to grab Alpha's face.

You're too slow. You'll never make it. He's done you in, hoss.

Alpha winked.

"Never over," he said.

John Alpha clenched his jaw, and Michael closed his eyes.

The outer walls of Folie à Deux trembled for a nanosecond, then blew outward, flinging flaming splinters of steel, plaster, and brick onto Sunset Boulevard, into neighboring buildings, into the night sky. Liquid fire soared across Sunset Boulevard like napalm, exploding streetlights, incinerating bystanders. Another explosion from deep within the club launched the charred, warped remains of Folie à Deux's thirty-foot-tall, centerpiece statue through the roof like a cannonball.

John, Dr. Mike, Dania Sheridan, and the 7th Son soldiers watched this through the portholes of their helicopter. They gazed, horrified, as the explosions consumed the helicopter hovering over the club. Michael's helicopter.

Michael's chopper was pushed upward from the blast. It tipped wildly on its right axis . . . struggled to regain its altitude and control . . . then plummeted nose-first toward the street. Its top rotor blades sawed across the fiery asphalt, crumpling, breaking away from the engine. The rotors sliced through the sky like mad boomerangs. One skewered a police car straight through its engine block. Another whizzed down the street, slicing a flaming palm tree in half.

The helicopter smashed onto Sunset Boulevard and exploded.

Flying away from the growing blaze in West Hollywood, the surviving Black Hawk soared back toward the San Gabriel Mountains, toward Edwards Air Force Base.

The mission was over.

THIRTY-TWO

F ather Thomas wandered the halls of the 7th Son complex with Hugh Sheridan. The old man led them up and down dangerously steep, dusty stairwells (apparently reserved only for emergencies), past a small gymnasium, countless doors and floors. The place seemed an exercise in excess; since the apparent heyday of the experiment, not much of the facility was used anymore.

"I knew you'd ask me that. I knew you'd ask me about Dania," Hugh Sheridan said as he stopped, and cupped his hand to light his third cigarette of the hour. He blew the smoke up at the hallway's ceiling. "I'll make you a deal. You tell me what you know about my ex-wife and her disappearance—the information you got from Kleinman. Then I'll tell you the truth."

Father Thomas slouched against a wall and rubbed his eyes. *God, I'm tired.*

"What we learned was told to us in Ops, after you were thrown out," Thomas said. "After you tried to warn us about Bregner."

"I remember that all too well," Hugh Sheridan said, blowing a ring of smoke.

"Kleinman and that up-and-comer intel guy . . . Durbin . . .

explained how NEPTH-charge was accidentally created during the early stages of the memory-recording process. Told us all about it in that storage area, the Lock Box. They called it something like a bioelectric kickback. Michael said it was like a neutron bomb for the mind."

Sheridan nodded. "Accurate, if simplistic. Continue."

"They said Dania Sheridan was the first to identify the cause of the kickback. She also realized the NEPTH-charge effect could be duplicated and used again and again. She realized it could be used as a weapon. But Kleinman said the 7th Son team had no interest in pursuing that."

"Also true." Sheridan motioned Thomas to move again, and they continued down the hall to a stairwell door. Sheridan opened it, and up they climbed, their footfalls ringing in the stairwell. "The secret of NEPTH-charge was placed in our archives, presumably to be forgotten." Sheridan gave a cynical smile. "We were shooting for loftier goals in the annals of amorality."

"You sound sick about the whole thing."

The old man nodded, sucked down another lungful of smoke, kept climbing. "When Dania and I came here in '73, we were told the stakes, took our vow of secrecy. I was your age when Dr. Kleinman recruited me. He promised me the things young people want to hear: unlimited resources, an obscene salary, research in a cutting-edge field of study. How could I say no?"

Thomas shrugged. "By saying no."

Sheridan stopped at a landing and eyed the number designating this level. He opened the door. Thomas realized they were now on the Ops level. While the Ops center was located somewhere down the winding network of halls and T-junctions, the door to the facility's Lock Box warehouse was mere feet away.

Sheridan punched in a code, and the door opened. They stepped inside.

"I tried for so long to not think about what we were doing here. It wouldn't rest. I finally left. They were glad to see me go. After seeing Kleinman and me earlier today, that should be obvious."

"Got the T-shirt," Thomas affirmed.

Sheridan smiled slightly. He wandered farther into the cavernous room, and Thomas understood why his father was doing this. He understood it as much as he did their destination. "You have a wit about you, Thomas."

"It's my defense mechanism. Listen. I can't wrap my brain around how you rationalized any of this. But somewhere in the game, you tried to make it right. You left."

"Far too little, far too late," the old man whispered.

"Maybe. And maybe this—this here, this conversation—is part of your confession, your penance. That's not insignificant—at least not to me." Thomas shrugged. "So. Back to what Kleinman told us. He said that five years ago, Mom left the 7th Son project to pursue NEPTH-charge research for the Department of Defense. This was after you two had divorced because you were resentful of Bregner's talent and position. His brilliance."

Sheridan chuckled bitterly. "Kleinman told you *that*?"

"Uh-huh."

Sheridan stopped in midstride and spat on the floor. "The old man's a liar. I didn't divorce her because I was jealous of *Bregner*." He said the name as if it were a slur. "In fact, I left 7th Son a year after she did. If anything, I divorced Dania because she was *becoming* Bregner."

Thomas sat up. "I don't understand."

"You don't understand because you haven't been given any understandable information. After the 'car accident,' Dania and I continued to raise John Alpha here at 7th Son. We convinced him to participate in the project: to learn from us, to watch you Betas grow, to give his perspective into your actions."

Sheridan looked up at the ceiling and shook his head. "It's very easy to manipulate a fourteen-year-old boy. Fourteen-year-old boys can't fathom the ethics of something like 7th Son. They think they know so much, but they know nothing."

"The same could be said for 7th Son's scientists," Thomas said.

"Indeed." Sheridan shook his head, and they resumed their trek to the device the clones had seen earlier today: the little machine that recorded the mice memories. The thing that created the bioelectric "hiccup" that eventually inspired the assassin-making NEPTH-charge technology.

"Alpha took to the science and mission of 7th Son with relish. He delved into the technologies, the way of life, became a team member," Sheridan said. "He was also educated here. Imagine having the world's premier researchers as your personal tutors. Imagine learning information technology from the man who designed and maintained a hypercomputer the size of three football fields. Imagine taking biology lessons from men and women who'd perfected human cloning."

John Alpha took an immediate shine to the cloning and MemR/I technologies, Hugh Sheridan explained. When Alpha wasn't being tutored by 7th Son staffers, he was in the Womb or Ops or the MemR/I Array with Bregner, immersing himself in the culture and mission of 7th Son.

"Frankly, I was glad he had so many diversions," Sheridan said, staring down at the peculiar machine that sparked the research for recording human memories. "I loved John, I did. He was my son. But he was my son with a caveat. We had *groomed* him; groomed him not for his future, but yours. Having the truth out in the open, and with John so understanding of it, made those first few years back here in Virginia some of the best years I experienced during the project."

Thomas nodded. "The secret was out. The pressure was off."

"That's how I thought of it back then. Though now I think John Alpha was grooming *us*, pumping us for information about the project. Taking mental notes."

"Did you—" Thomas stopped and shook his head. "I keep saying *you*. What I mean is *7th Son*."

"I'm the ambassador. Completely understandable. Come, walk with me again."

The made their way to the entrance of the Lock Box.

"Okay. So did 7th Son ever examine Alpha? Do a psych test? Did anyone ever suspect him?"

"He underwent annual psychological tests, just like the rest of us. There were the occasional gripes about the establishment, and feelings of disconnection from the rest of the world . . . but what teenager *hasn't* gone through that? Alpha was allowed to go topside and join the rest of the world. We encouraged him to do that. But he never did. Of course, we thought it was because he was so enamored with the project and the people involved in it. He was fascinated with you clones. We fell for it, we really did. But the psych tests never revealed anything abnormal."

Thomas laughed at that. "But his whole *existence* was abnormal. He never had a chance to *live*. He spent a lifetime under a microscope . . . and above a microscope, scrutinizing us. *We* were the ones playing on the basketball team, joining the debate club, going to the prom, cutting class, getting stoned, getting laid, whatever. *We* were the ones living his life. How could you people miss that?"

"Such is the blessing and the curse of hindsight," Sheridan replied. The bright lights of the hallway made them squint now. Thomas was grateful to be away from that room of secrets and bad history.

Thomas leaned against the wall. "So John Alpha gets cozy

with the world of 7th Son, and history tells us that he secretly plots revenge. So what happened to you and Mom?"

"What do all divorced couples say when they're asked that question?" Sheridan sighed. "It's simple. I changed. She changed. Trite? Predictable? Certainly. But it's true. We worked together, spent nearly every waking hour together."

Sheridan absently waved his hand. "Things became uninspired between Dania and I, and neither one of us was willing to do anything about it. Why expend the effort? I became more and more distraught with 7th Son and and my role in it. I was alarmed by how much time John Alpha was spending with Bregner. I watched you seven grow older . . . began to see you as something more than test subjects . . . and realized that I had checked my morality and ethics at the door long ago. And then Dania began going back to the origins of the project. Digging into the archives. At first, I thought it was nostalgia. It wasn't."

"NEPTH-charge."

"Yes."

They abandoned the doorway, Sheridan taking the lead once more. Thomas was far too engrossed to care where they were going now.

"This was just before we divorced," his father explained. "She never forgot about her discovery, and her realization that it could be controlled. She became obsessed with the science of NEPTH and occasionally shared her thoughts with me. That's when I knew the woman I married was long gone. She was talking like that goddamned Nazi. She spoke of NEPTH-charge applications in espionage, assassination, impersonation. She saw how, if the technology could be tweaked, it could have even greater potential as a weapon. I left her. She left 7th Son not long after, taking her research with her—and the secrets of the MemR/I technology. She went to the DARPA and received funding to continue her research. I stayed here."

"So she started working for the Department of Defense," Thomas said. "I understand that. But let me get this straight: she wanted to *improve* the NEPTH-charge technology? How's that possible? It wipes a human memory clean and allows you to download another memory in its place. What's more powerful than hijacking a brain?"

Hugh Sheridan looked up at Thomas.

"*Psy*jacking a brain."

THIRTY-THREE

B ack in the Common Room, Kilroy2.0 downloaded the other nine Greers Ferry Dam reports from the CDC Web site. He transmitted a message of thanks to his flock, insisting he'd found the needed data. He logged out of the chat programs.

"Let's see if our excursion has made headlines," Kilroy said, grinning at Jack and Jay. The hacker double-clicked an icon on the computer's desktop. A Web browser opened and loaded its default Web page: a compilation of the most recent news stories from around the world.

The assault on the CDC's Web site hadn't made headlines. But something else had.

A still photograph glared at them. Sunset Boulevard—blocks and blocks of it—was an inferno.

"What happened?" Jack whispered.

No one could answer. They read the story.

NORTH HOLLYWOOD, Calif. (AP)—Nearly a mile of this city's historic Sunset Boulevard is in flames after a building exploded, causing a helicopter that was hovering overhead to crash onto the street. More

than 50 people have been hospitalized due to the incident. More than a
dozen are feared dead.

　　According to police and rescue workers on the scene, the abandoned
building . . .

　　"Are they dead? Are they all dead?" Jay asked.

　　Jack slumped onto the circular couch. "I don't know."

　　Kilroy2.0 was clicking to other news sites now. His eyes jittered back and forth as he read the copy. "Same story, over and over." His voice was flat, disconnected.

　　Jack slumped forward, his potbelly sagging between his thighs. He ran his fingers through his hair. "Why? Why did the team have to go there?"

　　"They didn't," Kilroy said, still clicking through his bookmarked news sites. "They chose to go. They knew the risks."

　　"Bullshit." Jay's voice was nearly squeaking now. "They didn't know *this* was going to happen." The orange-and-black photo of Sunset Boulevard glared back at them.

　　"Yes, they did," Kilroy said. "They were willing to die to save Mom."

　　"She's gone, too," Jay said.

　　"No, she isn't," a voice called to them. It was Dr. Kleinman, standing in the Common Room's doorway. General Hill loomed behind him in the hall. How long they had been standing there, the three clones didn't know.

　　Jay stood up. "What? Tell us!"

　　Kleinman shifted his feet and took off his glasses. He was polishing them furiously with his wrinkled necktie. "Ah . . ."

　　"What is it?" Jay screamed.

　　General Hill stepped past Kleinman into the Common Room. Kleinman shuffled behind him.

　　"Dania Sheridan has been rescued, Jay." Hill's baritone voice was unsettling here in the newfound silence. "Most of our men didn't make it. John and Dr. Mike . . ."

"Dead," Kilroy2.0 said.

"No. Alive," Hill said. "Both were wounded—Dr. Mike was shot—but they'll recover. Dania Sheridan was tortured by John Alpha, apparently, but she'll live."

"And Michael?"

Hill looked at Jack. "I'm sorry."

"Are you sure?" Jay whispered, his voice trembling.

Hill nodded. "He was in the chopper that crashed, son. He's gone."

Jay put his hands over his face.

Kleinman walked over to the circular couch and sat down across from Jack. Hill worked his way toward the computers.

"They're already on the plane, on their way back," Kleinman told them. "They videoed us just after liftoff. It was a mess. The story isn't very coherent. John made the report."

"What happened?" Jay asked softly, wiping away the tears.

"And Alpha?" Kilroy2.0 said. "Did they capture him?"

"They did," General Hill replied. "Michael did that. Alpha was also aboard the chopper that crashed."

"John Alpha is dead," Kleinman said, nodding.

They sat and stood in silence for a moment.

A hopeful look emerged on Jay's gaunt face. "Then it's over. We can go home."

Kleinman smiled nervously. He was about to say something when Kilroy2.0 turned to his clone.

"Query," Kilroy2.0 said. "What about the documents we've spent the past two hours downloading? What about the data from the CDC?"

Hill stiffened. "What data? What messages?"

Jay waved away the questions. He was smiling now. It was a desperate, manic smile. "No. Alpha's dead. That means it's over. Don't you see? Whatever he planned, whatever he *wanted* to do—"

"What's this about the CDC?" Hill demanded.

"No, Jay," Jack said, ignoring the general. "Kilroy's right. We still don't know what Alpha wanted. There are dozens of people who've been brainrotted by NEPTH-charge. They died becau—"

"But it's *over*," Jay insisted.

Another voice, from the far end of the room: "No, it isn't."

The five men—Jay, Hill, and Kilroy2.0 by the computers, and Kleinman and Jack, on the couch—turned to see who'd spoken. Their eyes leveled on the two forms now standing in the doorway of the Common Room: Father Thomas and Hugh Sheridan.

"Tell them, Hugh," Thomas said. He glanced at Sheridan, then back to the group. "Tell them about Psyjack."

Kleinman stood up slowly. He glared at Sheridan.

"What are you talking about?" Kilroy2.0 asked. His eyes glimmered, curious.

"We're in it for the long haul, Mad Hacker," Thomas said. "You may be *everywhere*, but Alpha can be *anywhere*, or any*one*. It's worse than we thought."

The priest gazed upward, to the room's circular skylight. His eyes were lost in the darkness.

"He's still out there."

THIRTY-FOUR

ohn Alpha placed a pearl-handled comb on the executive-washroom sink and smiled. In the mirror, the face of Vice President Charles Caine smiled back. Now this was a sensation that was going to take some getting used to. Seeing someone in the mirror other than yourself, it was positively bizarre. The stuff of fun-house mirrors.

Alpha told Caine's brain to smile. To frown. To look surprised. The Charles Caine in the mirror did all those things. The elderly mime mimicked his every expression.

He could easily live with most of the strange machinations of Caine's body—the constant dull throb of arthritis in the arms and hands, the sagging flesh, the slower reflexes. All things considered, it was a fair trade-off: this mime was the secondmost powerful man on the planet.

John Alpha glanced away from his wrinkled face. He washed his hands, dried them on a plush hand towel, and stepped out of the restroom, into Charles Caine's private office in the Eisenhower Executive Office Building. It was 11:00 p.m. The White House glowed spectacularly through the windows just behind his desk.

He slid into the leather chair, switched on the PC before him. He closed his eyes for a moment, searching for Charles Caine's security-clearance password. It came quickly. *USERNAME: talon15, PASSWORD: willingandabel.*

Ha.

The fingers of Charles Caine moved across the keyboard, punching in the information. The CPU powered up. At the bottom of the screen, headlines crawled by in ticker-tape style. Another Iraqi oil pipeline was spewing fire into the sky. Good news.

Alpha clicked an icon and scanned the other stories. There it was. *Helicopter Crashes in West Hollywood, Dozens Killed, Fire Rages on Sunset Boulevard.*

Aha. So that was that. Time to prepare the main course.

Alpha pulled a small silver key out of Caine's pants pocket and gazed at the two telephones on his desk. One was a sleek, corporate thing. The other was white, positively plain-Jane in comparison. Aside from the key slot embedded just above the number buttons, it resembled a chunky office phone from the 1980s.

Alpha inserted the silver key into the slot, twisted it clockwise. The STE-VII, Secure Terminal Equipment, model VII, activated. Beauty. Outbound calls could not be traced or tapped. These conversations could be made in a bubble of anonymity.

Alpha dialed the first number. The phone on the other end rang once.

"Is the line secure?" a female voice answered.

"I'm calling from my office."

"Nice." Her British accent was nearly a purr. "How was your first day?"

"It's peculiar, getting used to another voice coming from my mouth."

"It gets easier, but not much," replied the nurse once named Mira Sanjah. A car horn blasted in the background. "We're on the

Strip, looking for him now. I'm enlisting a few Devlins to cover more ground."

"But you'll find him," Alpha said. "The timing on this is—"

"Of course we will," Sanjah snapped. "We won't keep Rookman waiting too long. Remember who you're talking to."

Alpha said he did. "I'll get in touch with the rest of the group now. And then it's off to home, to the wife I've never met."

Sanjah laughed. "No rest for the wicked. Take care, John."

John Alpha smiled. "You, too, John," he said, and hung up.

Caine-Alpha dialed the number in Moscow. It was a little after 7:00 a.m. there.

"Wake up. This is the vice president of the United States calling," Alpha said, sneering at the groggy staccato of Russian in his ear. "And for Christ's sake, speak English. Not all of us inherited a new language in this caper."

The male voice on the other end hesitated. When the man once named Defense Minister Boris Savin spoke again, his accent was pure *Amerikanski*. "So you're in. One of us."

"And like you, I have quite a bit of power at my fingertips." Alpha frowned at Caine's fingernails, buffed them on his suit coat. "You'd be amazed. The administration doesn't tell Caine everything, but they've informed him of quite a bit. Nuclear capabilities, NORAD, the works. The old man was sweating bullets at the time. You should've been there."

"Said the man who wasn't," Savin-Alpha replied.

"Ha. Let's talk about our little army of Devlins."

"They'll be in position in hours, and then it'll happen quickly. They set up, the rocket flies, they get the codes and launch. Twenty minutes later—"

"—the house of cards begins to fall," John Alpha said, nodding. He killed the line, then dialed one last number.

He spoke with the mole for three minutes. Ah. The Betas had been resourceful during their hack on the CDC. They'd found the NEPTH-charge files, and undoubtedly the messages scrawled on the Greers Ferry Dam wall. More dots for them to connect. That was all that mattered.

John Alpha pulled the key out of the STE-VII phone and placed it back into his pocket. He yawned. It was past this old man's bedtime.

He strode to the door to leave and stole a look back to the desk. To the White House through the window.

Not a bad first day at the office, he thought, and turned off the lights.

His laughter echoed through the halls beyond.

WITHDRAWN